A HISTORY
OF
MONTEZUMA
COUNTY

by

IRA S. FREEMAN

TRAFFORD

HISTORY OF MONTEZUMA COUNTY

Note for Librarians: a cataloguing record for this book that includes Dewey Decimal Classification and US Library of Congress numbers is available from the Library and Archives of Canada. The complete cataloguing record can be obtained from their online database at:
www.collectionscanada.ca/amicus/index-e.html
ISBN 1-4120-4338-7
Printed in Victoria, BC, Canada

Original Copyright 1958 by Ira S. Freeman.
This Reprinting Copyrighted 2005 by Books
124 Pinon Dr.Cortez, CO 81321 970-565-2503

TRAFFORD

Offices in Canada, USA, Ireland, UK and Spain
This book was published *on-demand* in cooperation with Trafford Publishing. On-demand publishing is a unique process and service of making a book available for retail sale to the public taking advantage of on-demand manufacturing and Internet marketing. On-demand publishing includes promotions, retail sales, manufacturing, order fulfilment, accounting and collecting royalties on behalf of the author.
Book sales for North America and international:
Trafford Publishing, 6E–2333 Government St.,
Victoria, BC v8t 4p4 CANADA
phone 250 383 6864 (toll-free 1 888 232 4444)
fax 250 383 6804; email to orders@trafford.com
Book sales in Europe:
Trafford Publishing (uk) Ltd., Enterprise House, Wistaston Road Business Centre,
Wistaston Road, Crewe, Cheshire cw2 7rp UNITED KINGDOM
phone 01270 251 396 (local rate 0845 230 9601)
facsimile 01270 254 983; orders.uk@trafford.com
Order online at:
www.trafford.com/robots/04-2145.html

10 9 8 7 6 5 4 3 2

A HISTORY OF

MONTEZUMA COUNTY

COLORADO

Land of Promise and Fulfillment

Being a Review of Prehistoric Races and an Account of the Earliest
Settlement by the White Man and Subsequent events and development
to the Present Day.

A Book for Every Montezuma
County Home

INTRODUCTORY STATEMENTS

This history of Montezuma County, Colorado, was at first conceived as a means of expressing some degree of appreciation of what the county has meant to the writer as a home for more than a half a century and the opportunities that have been ours to earn and to serve and to possess. It grew out of a feeling of obligation to the past and our duty to the future. It also sprang from a realization that if the history of the county was ever to become a heritage of the future, the work must be done now while it is called today. All original sources of historic information are rapidly passing and will soon be gone forever. The writer was fascinated with his subject from the beginning, and was determined that work should be complete enough in detail, and should be of such a nature, that the people would want to possess it in some enduring form.

Two circumstances impelled immediate action. First, the generation of the original pioneer in Montezuma County has been, and is at present, rapidly passing from their scene of action; second, the writer is the last, and the only living representative of the early newspaper men of the county who knew most of these original pioneers and who, in these early days, worked earnestly and faithfully with them in the interest of the general welfare of all. If any writer was to take advantage of this very important and vital source of information, something must be done at once to gather in all the information that remains and put it in written form. Subsequent events have proven the timeliness of the undertaking. No less than four of these original sources of information have passed to their eternal reward in the brief time since our interview with them.

As this work was undertaken on the part of the writer without selfish intent or hope of gain, perhaps the research part of the work was not as well nor as thoroughly done as it deserved to be done. Notwithstanding, a rather complete job of investigation was done, and a thorough exploration of our past was made as attested by the finished text itself. The work, under the circumstances, must be regarded as reasonably well done. Nevertheless, in spite of loyalty to the cause, and an earnest and patient effort, the writer feels that many important events and circumstances may have escaped our notice or were lost in the obscurity of the past. An earnest effort was made to preserve all that remained and to give a personal touch to the things that made county history.

The work itself, whatever it may lack, is our contribution in perpetuating the memory of our pioneers in some enduring form, and to record the work they did so faithfully and well. We commend this written record to those who have come after them; to build on the foundation they laid; and to gather in the riches to which they opened the way, and which, in a large measure, was denied to them. Too often they labored and waited in vain. To these pioneers, men and women, this history is respectfully dedicated.

TABLE OF CONTENTS

TABLE OF ILLUSTRATIONS

ACKNOWLEDGMENTS

On doing the research work for this writing, the author owes much to a number of pioneers yet among us, or but recently deceased. Our debt of appreciation to the following is hereby acknowledged:

At Mancos: To George W. Menefee, George Exon, Morris Decker, Miss Bessie Morefield, who is a sister to Mabyn Morefield Armstrong, the first white baby girl to be born in the Mancos Valley, Frank Sponsel of Thompson Park, "A Brief History of Mancos Pioneers" by Mrs. Lillian (Honaker) Rickner, short papers by Mrs. Laura Dillon, Mrs. George Morton and the files of the Mancos Times and the Mancos Times Tribune.

At Dolores, we are indebted to William J. Exon, Mr. and Mrs. William Brumley, Harry Pyle, Robert Dunham, Mrs. Lester King, Mrs. James Hammond, files of the Dolores Star.

Cortez and the Montezuma Valley: Mrs. Walter Longenbaugh, Lee Kelly, Bert Saylor, Mrs. Rose Dunham, Miss Grace Gordon, Mrs. Etta Middaugh, Mrs. George Omo, Myron Kruse, Mrs. James (Matilda) Treece, Mrs. Jessie (Billingsley) Bailey, Mrs. James Galloway, Mr. and Mrs. Walter Hall.

At Yellow Jacket: T. Gai, Gus Stevenson, Jr., of Mancos.

At Lewis: C. E. Grater, Homer Hughes, Ralph Dillon, Mrs. Charles Porter.

At Dove Creek: Dan Hunter.

In the brief time since our interviews with them, the following have become deceased: Robert Dunham, Harry Pyke, C. E. Krater and Mrs. Rose Dunham.

While the writer was collecting data, he made repeated efforts to contact Mr. Carter Clay, recommended as a source of much information on early times in the county. He passed away before we were able to contact him and whatever valuable knowledge he had perished with him.

We are indebted to Frank Pyle for most of the information on the Ute Tribe of Indians, to Whetzel Allen for data on Summit Reservoir, to Mrs. Claire (Winship) Watson for schools in the county, and to Lee Abel for historic information and data on the Cliff Dwellers. Access to Montezuma County records was through the courtesy of John Leavett. Montezuma Irrigation District was the source for valuable information on irrigation history. Cortez Library, with Mrs. Marie Fredericks as Librarian, gave use of books and papers.

For any name or person or matter we have unwittingly left out, we can only express our regrets.

IRA S. FREEMAN

Mancos, Colorado

CHAPTER I

THE STORY OF THE "CLIFF DWELLERS"

The history of mankind in Montezuma County, Colorado, began at a period so remote in the annals of time that even an approximate date is a matter of conjecture. It seems useless to speculate on who the first people were and what they were like, but it is reasonable to assume that the progenators of the North American Indian of historic times were much like them in character and habits of life, but simpler and cruder and more primitive, and that these, in turn, were preceded by a people simpler, cruder and more primitive still. The past is an eternity and the span of human existence reaches far back into this unknown time. Sometimes a thousand years in the history of a people has registered no change in their way of life. In connection with man's earliest existence in this local area we might just say that he has been here for a long, long time and nobody knows how long; that in some way he survived through the ages and has come down to our own times, and we know not how.

At about the beginning of the Christian era a people in this area came out of the past and appeared in the crudest form of civilized life. We don't know whether their primitive culture originated here, or was brought in from a similar civilization further south, but they had their being here whether or not they had their beginning, and we accept them for what they were when first they lifted the curtain on their existence here. We don't know the extent of their existence here, but we do know they lived within the confines of Montezuma County and in the immediate vicinity of Mesa Verde.

In common parlance these earliest people are called the Basketmakers, or Post Basketmakers, as the original Basketmakers never existed in this immediate vicinity. Their way of life differed from the savage life about them in that they had a home that was more or less permanent and they tilled the soil and grew a part of their food. Because all the people in the subsequent history of this immediate vicinity were an agricultural people as long as they occupied here, and followed the same pattern of life, it seems pretty certain that all these later generations of people were the offspring of this original foundation stock which gradually arose to a higher and better way of life and living through the passing centuries.

9

The first evidence that the Modified Basketmakers once inhabited this locality was found some years after Mesa Verde Park was created. In exploring and excavating the prehistoric ruins in the West side of the Park this evidence was found in shallow caves completely covered by the dust of time. Further evidence was also found in the deeper recesses where the habitations of later generations had been built, in many instances, directly on top of the earlier habitations of the Modified Basketmakers. These facts were established by the explorers in the course of their work here and, later, in the remnants of ruins found on the mesas and valley floors. These early top-of-the mesa dwellings, however, were hardly dwellings at all and were so completely erased by passing time that little is left to evidence their former existence.

The original Basketmaker, found in other localities in this southwest, had no pottery, no bows and arrows or spears. His only weapon for defense, or hunting, was a kind of dart, called by the Indians an atlatl, which was thrown by a stock with great accuracy and with deadly effect. The Modified Basketmakers, found in the Park, if he did not have the bow and arrow, the spear and pottery at the start, soon acquired them, and soon after acquired all the other characteristics of Modified Basketmakers early in his career here. His beginning was very primitive. He lived in part by hunting, snaring or trapping game such as rabbits, rock squirrels, porcupines, turkeys and deer, and other wild life, but he was a farmer and made progress in this art. He raised on his farm different colored corn, squash, perhaps some vegetables, and, a little later, beans which he was soon raising in different colors and kinds; and he gathered pinon nuts, and berries in season, which he no doubt dried for future use.

We might pause here to take a more critical view of the Modified Basketmaker and some other aspects of his way of life and living. The Modified Basketmaker, though his standard of life was low in the human scale of civilization, was not a savage, as were most of the North American Indians; nor was he a barbarian, like the early Mongols and the Huns. He was an agriculturalist and tilled the soil to get a part of his living, stored his products for future use, and hunted and trapped for whatever he could catch or kill. He had to be industrious in order to survive and he had to have a home and a family to perpetuate his kind. The remains of his home was the first evidence discovered that he existed here.

Then he was a man of peace, as were the generations that came after him; all he asked of his roving neighbors was that he be left alone. He would work out his own future. This might have been his fatal weakness in the end. He had a religion, as do all primitive people, savage or civilized. As with most human life, he worshiped because he feared. He knew that there was a great omnipresence around him, but he did not understand. He knew that light and heat from the sun brought life and growth to plants, but he didn't know how. Their own con-

10

cept of the matter may be expressed by the words of the old Indian, back in our own historic times, when he said "The Sun is my father, the earth is my mother." He had a sense of right and wrong, and he feared to do wrong.

His family was the unit of his organized society, just as it is with us in our own time, and, as with many other primitive people, some old mother or grandmother was the head of the family. The governing power was probably the tribal council, and it is probable also that there was no Chief, since the lack of strong leadership may have been one of the factors in the final failure of the race in these environs.

From his beginning here the Modified Basketmaker seems to have had a long period of peace in which to work out his destiny. At first they were few in numbers and they produced crops for food. For this reason the roving tribes in the larger area about him regarded him as no menace to their way of living and no threat to their game supply. They were seldom molested, if at all, and were apparently left free to work out any destiny that lay ahead.

He made some progress and during this early period he appears to have moved out from the caves and the canons to the top mesa country and we find his later habitations in the valleys and on the low mesas. His new home was the pit house. These appeared in small clusters here and there and were constructed by digging a pit two to three feet deep which they walled with large flat sandrock, set on edge, to the ground level, and building a top structure and roof of posts, poles and adobe mud reinforced with grass, cedar bark or like material. These homes were always near their farms and their remains (the pits) are still found in many places in the county.

Before he acquired the art of making pottery he cooked his food directly on the fire or over the fire; on hot stones, or, he might, as some tribes did, cooked it by putting it under ground and building a fire over it. Pottery came into use early in the time of the Modified Basketmakers. It was at first a plain solid gray earthenware without decorations or color of any kind and was used for cooking and serving; also for carrying water and for water containers.

This brings us up to about the year 750 A.D. and a new transition period as fixed by the scientists and investigators. This period has been designated as the Developmental Pueblo Period and there is supposed to be a new period—a new era—dawning. It is in reality a continuation of the old period and carried forward by the same people with new ideas and better ways of doing things. No doubt some of these new ideas, some of the new arts and skills, were brought in from the higher cultured people to the south. Notable progress was made, yet it was very slow, and accomplishments were modest when we consider that the period stretched out over a duration of several hundred years. The pit house, the dwelling structure of the old period, and characteristic of it for nearly the full time of its duration, was now re-

11

placed by the top ground rock walled structure. There is every evidence of an increase in population both in the old period and the new. There were, early in the new period, scores of Pueblo settlements in the valleys and on the low mesas to take the place of the cluster of Pit Houses found here and there. There were a great many small walled structures, large enough for only two or three families, in the farming areas, but here and there were many larger Pueblo settlements in the valleys and on the low mesas, with one or more large Kivas, and some of these must have housed from fifteen to thirty families. This same type of structure also came into use on Mesa Verde, at first in the open and on top of the mesa, and many ruins evidence their former existence.

Hitherto the people had lived in solitary houses, or groups of houses built separately, but during this period Pueblo, or village, life began to develop and houses were built adjoining each other suggesting the modern apartment house, and the idea later, developed a long way along this line, and finally, into the great palace like buildings in the cliffs of the great canons. The first Pueblo villages were built on high mesas, on low mesas and on the valley floors, and always near good farm land and a water supply, but apparently they began to have trouble with other Indian tribes in the area and they began to build more houses on the higher mesas and, later, in every conceivable place in the canon walls, evidently as a means of defense, unaware that a fortress in the cliffs for protection might also become a prison where they might starve. We find the new Pueblo period widespread throughout this southwest section and the same type of ruin found locally is found on the mesas and in the canon walls throughout the entire area.

Getting back to developments in Montezuma County, the new era was characterized by vast improvements in buildings, over the long period. It is called the Developmental Period because it was a period of development, a time of change from the old to the new. The experiences and accomplishments of the period paved the way for the great Classic Pueblo Period to follow.

Many building materials and ways of building were tried, with steady improvement. In successive steps they came from the early Modified Basketmaker period, when making baskets was the only art in which they excelled, and out of their homes in the caves; from adobe and pole to pit house structures, and from Pit Houses to crude rock walled structures above ground. From these crude irregular walled structures they came finally to buildings of true masonry, with straight, even walls and coursed layers, with stones cut to fit and laid in adobe mud as mortar. Where they were in the open, as many of them were, although well constructed for the time, none of these buildings are now standing, and most of them are only a large mound of dirt and rock and rubbish. Where these mounds have been excavated parts of the walls are found still standing and the style and nature of the

12

original building is revealed. Toward the close of this period some of the fine stone work in the caves was started.

Notable progress in the arts and crafts was also made during this period. Making pottery was being developed into a fine art. They began to make feather blankets; comforts and bedding and clothing were made from hides and pelts, and many articles for household use and for use in their arts, were made from stone and bone and toward the end of the period they were making a good grade of cotton cloth. Stone axes, hammers and cudgels, and grinding stones were in common use.

This period was also characterized by a large increase in population and the number of new villages that came into existence. This growth in population, of course, necessitated an increase in food supply. More land had to be cleared and cultivated. We can see that this condition had to result in considerable barter and the making (manufacturing we would say today) of many things the people needed or wanted. Artists and those skilled in the crafts, in the larger population centers, made many things for trade or barter, and that they could exchange for food and raw products like hides and raw furs. No doubt better living conditions had come about. More sanitation and better food and living conditions resulted in more babies and children surviving the danger period and growing into adult manhood and womanhood.

The end of the Developmental Period ushered in the great Classic Period of the Pueblo people in this area. Indian culture on Mesa Verde, and the environs, reached its zenith and their arts and crafts reached their highest point of development. This last period lasted approximately two centuries, from about the end of the eleventh century to the close of the thirteenth century, and with the close of the period the existence of this interesting people in this area came to an end. The entire population left the land that had been their home for centuries never to return.

But they left evidence of some notable achievements, and a strange civilization that had made slow but certain progress through the centuries, but never had the character and the qualities necessary for its final survival. During this period most of the great buildings along the canon walls, on Mesa Verde, and hundreds of smaller ones that, with vacant, eye-like windows peep out from the high cliffs and canon walls, were built and occupied. The buildings themselves were the measure of their architectural achievement and from within them has come the evidence of their skills in the arts and crafts and the manner of the life they lived. The buildings reveal little engineering skill, were built after no well defined plan, but only for a purpose. Apparently they started with one room, or a group of rooms; then built onto these with another group, and built in a kiva or a tower wherever they decided one was needed. Rooms for storing food were built in at the rear, in the deeper recesses of the cave, as that was the driest part

13

of the cave and there was no particular need for light, while living quarters were toward the front for light and to make is easier for the smoke from their fires to find an exit. The fires were necessary both for cooking and for heating their dwelling places. Yet the fact that these buildings, constructed with stone shaped only with stone tools and laid only in mud mortar, have stood for centuries is evidence of considerable building skill. Skilled masons of today, with modern tools, could have done little better under their conditions.

The same is true of their arts and crafts. In this late period their pottery products showed high skill and excellent taste. Apparently they never learned the art of glazing, yet some of their finer finished products have been polished and embellished with color designs so as to closely resemble hand painted china with their baked in designs. There are many articles and useful trinkets such as sewing needles, awles, knives, spoons, ladles, buttons and other fasteners for garments, and many others, all made from bone or flint, which seems to indicate that their way of living called for about the same utility articles as are common to our own life and times.

On the other hand, and in common with almost all other people, apart from the European and his descendants, the dwellers under the cliffs had no furniture, and nothing resembling furniture. They sat on the floor, or ground; ate out of pots and bowls as a common container of foods and, of course, ate with their fingers. But they had bone spoons and sharpened bone to answer the purpose of forks, and bone and flint knives to cut their food and skin the animals they killed. They sharpened their knives with an abrasive stone, just as you do.

And how did they sleep? On the floor or ground, but not directly on the floor or ground. They probably made a mat of straw or grass, for grass was plentiful, and they had no kind of stock to eat it; or of willows or other soft brush. For bedding, in the early periods, they had only the skins and hides and pelts of animals they killed for food, or of other wild animals such as coyotes, bobcats, etc. These they sewed together to make a large coverlet, for a top cover fur side down; for sleeping on, fur side up. At first their thread was made from yucca fiber or other fiber, or from the sinews of animals. In the late periods they made blankets with cotton thread and with turkey feathers, and other feathers, woven in with the warp and the woof. They learned the art of tanning very early and did an excellent job in later times. Tanned leather went into bags and many other articles of household use, and into clothing. Leather from the heavier skins, like deer skins, went into moccasins, mittens or similar articles.

These large collective buildings in the caves were constructed with a prodigious amount of labor and with many difficulties to be overcome. Every stone had to be brought from some place, near or far, and they had not even a wheel. Also the water and the adobe dirt for the mortar, and the poles that went into the structures, had to be

14

carried to the building sites. As much of the stone must have come from quite a distance an enormous amount of work was required. Instead of carrying all this stone they might have contrived some kind of sled which they could load with stone and draw over the ground with manpower, and save some labor. For most of the large buildings the stone could have been brought and thrown over the cliffs, but how they got the stone and other materials on the ground for the more inaccessable structures is still a problem to the modern mind. There was no slave labor, as in the days of Egyptians and Babylonian glory, but the work was done with a free will. There were many workers interested directly and the buildings were erected over a long period of time. Evidently time didn't mean much to these people. They had all the time there was.

Now let us study their manner of living and their means of getting it, for this interesting people are not just an object of idle curiosity and passing interest. They are a study, and the people themselves were a marvel of efficiency. They had to be efficient, and industrious, to produce food for so many people under the most adverse conditions, and perpetuate their own existence for so many centuries.

During the last three or four centuries of the existence of these people here there was a considerable population build-up. With more than two hundred buildings on Mesa Verde alone, and with Cliff Palace the home of more than four hundred people, and with a number of other collective houses that sheltered 150 or more each, there must have been at least two thousand people living on Mesa Verde at one time. Also there were scores of farming villages and small collective houses in the valleys and on the low mesas all of which made many hundreds of additional people that must be fed. Besides the low land farms there must have been hundreds of acres on Mesa Verde producing food, and we wonder how they ever produced enough. One thing to think about is that there was no "high standard" of living. as we know it. Practically the whole population ate the same food and all the products of the farms were consumed as food. No grain was fed to live stock to produce meat, milk, butter or lard. It was the plain, simple life for them.

And they produced food under the greatest handicaps and many difficulties. Corn of many colors; squash, whereby they could get a little sugar; several kinds of beans and some vegetables were grown. They gathered pinon nuts, when there were any, and wild berries in season. Before anything could be produced from the soil, however, the land must be cleared of brush and trees, and they had no metal implements or tools—no metal of any kind. For this work they had only stone axes to bruise off or break off the brush. Trees were deadened with fire and soon fell down, and were burned or removed. They had nothing with which to till the soil and plant crops but a sharp stick of hard wood of convenient length, or a similar stick with a nar-

15

row flat stone fastened on one end with rawhide thongs. Apparently they didn't even make use of the "forked stick," plow, as other tribes did, since no such "implement" has ever been found in their ruined habitations. Having no metal tools they must fight the weeds without a hoe, combat plant disease and insect pests without chemicals, and keep up the fertility of the soil without manure or other fertilizers, and no doubt some of this land had been producing crops for hundreds of years and was badly depleted in fertility. They had no knowledge of crop rotation but, like most primitive people, they had an intuitive knowledge of doing things in their own way that produced the desired results. Instead of planting corn and beans and squash in separate plots, these things were planted all mixed in together. This eliminated the necessity, or possibility, of cultivation or weeding, as the dense growth tended to control the weeds, and the combination of corn, beans and squash growing together tended to keep up the fertility of the soil. Their way of farming may have not conformed to the latest modern methods, but they harvested a crop, as we may know, or their population would have starved.

They had no beasts of burden. He was his own beast of burden. There were no domestic animals save, perhaps, a few turkeys and the inevitable dog. Their dog probably came from the wolf "tribe" and was domesticated early in the history of the people. There was not even a wheel. Everything moved from one place to another had to be carried, or dragged. After the crop was planted and grown it had to be harvested by hand and carried to a place of safe storage. If any of it had to be moved any distance it could only be carried there.

Under these conditions and with these methods it must have been very difficult to produce enough food for so many people, and any dry year, or other misfortune, could have resulted in a distressing shortage of food. This eventuality, however, was probably guarded against by storing food from the good years, since there was no market for these things. Food could only be eaten. It must have taken at least 90 per cent of the people to produce food for themselves and the other 10 per cent. The smaller number were artisans skilled in certain work and others in the arts and crafts. In their society, however, it seems that even the skilled workers took a hand, part time, producing food, and the people, generally, made pottery and other articles they needed.

Business, if there was any business, was carried on by barter, as there was no money in use, or anything to serve as money, that has ever come to our knowledge. Under these conditions there could have been no classes among the people. If they had any property, owned or claimed, we have no knowledge of it. The whole tribe had a governing council and it is probable that each local community had a board, or council, and these designated tracts of land for each family unit to be cultivated by them as long as they were faithful to the task. Strange as it may

16

"Cliff Palace" largest and most famous of the cliff ruins on Mesa Verde National Park. There were four hundred rooms before time wrecked a number of them.

Group of Montezuma County pioneers at semi-centennial celebration, Mesa Verde Park, June 29, 1956. Back Row: Erskine Mallett, Mel Springer, Ira Kelly, a Mr. Clark, (party unkown) Walter Logenbaugh, Charles Menefee, a Mr. Scott, George Menefee. George Exon, Lee Kelly, next unknown, Harley Longenbaugh. Front Row: Nellie Coston, Clara Swenk, Mrs. Walter Longen-baugh, Mrs. George Omo, Mrs. Grance Exon, Mrs. Bessie Longenbaugh, Mrs. Clayton Wetherill (nee Eugenia Faunce).

John Miller and Squaw. John Miller was Chief of the Utes one generation ago, and he probably lived in a hogan. Jack House, present chief, lives in a fine new frame residence gleaming with white paint, and drives a good car.

The Ute Indians of today are just one generation removed from the Ute Indians shown above. The hogan and the brush arbor went with these Indians. Their descendants ride in good cars and trucks, live in good houses and send their children to school.

Outfitting for trip to Cliff Ruins, before Park was created. C. B. Kelly, outfitter, Mancos, Colorado.

Ranger cabin, Mesa Verde, pre-park days. Built and used by Charles B. Kelly in taking care of tourists visiting the Cliff Ruins. At this time all visitors were taken in on horseback, with pack outfits.

Taylor Norton, pioneer prospector and desert scout, standing. His white mule—the mule that brought the body of Parley Jensen down from the scene of the great snow slide.

John and Clayton Wetherill—Mancos Valley cattlemen and pioneers—famous guides and scouts. Wetherill brothers were first to discover and explore Cliff Ruins.

Elegant new Dove Creek high school building. Splendid new Court House building stands just out of sight in background, and a new and thoroughly modern grade school building stands a few blocks to the north, on the right. This grade building has just been enlarged by the addition of seven new classrooms.

Daniel Hunter, Sage of Dove Creek, educator, editor and publisher of the Dove Creek Press for eight years. General benefactor, and public-minded citizen. See story of Dove Creek.

Walters Bros. outfitting for the Cliff Ruins. Cortez, Colorado.

Building Cortez, early day.

seem there were probably no rich or very poor people, excepting those who were indigent by their natures.

We have reviewed briefly the great Classic Period of these Pueblo people in this area wherein their every achievement reached its climax. Toward the close of the period the culture of this people was at its best. It was still a time when practically every one did some useful work. The period was characterized by the best built buildings and the finest buildings, and the best interior finish the civilization produced; the best things in utility articles of every kind; the best clothing and the finest articles for personal adornment; the finest and best pottery for every use and purpose. They had probably reached the zenith of their social organization. Then it was all over, all abandoned, all left behind, the whole population departed never to return. Where did they go and why?

It is practically certain that these people went southward into New Mexico or Arizona, or both, and joined themselves with and to a people very similar to them in manners and customs and in their way of living—the Zuni, the Hopi and other Pueblo groups with a thousand years of civilized life behind them. The final dramatic act of this interesting people, in this locality, didn't come to pass in a single day. As conditions that forced their departure from the land began to tighten about them infiltration to the south began to relieve a pressing situation, but toward the end of the movement there is evidence of an abrupt departure. It was natural that such an exit should end that way—fear grew into panic, and everything—home, art treasures, all that was dear to them, was left behind.

The Indians of other tribes seemed to have had a superstitious fear of these ruins, as the buildings, when first entered by the white man, were found very much as they were left by the former occupants.

They knew the way. There had been trade intercourse with these people to the south, and exchange of visits. The bringing in of cotton, and other articles, to Mesa Verde was proof of this, but why did they leave their all and go?

The men of learning who have investigated this matter, say it was a prolonged drouth that drove them from the land. That about the year 1276 a widespread drouth began to plague the land. Storms bringing moisture seldom came and the earth refused to yield her increase. This condition, they say, continued for almost 24 years. With the large population they had built up drouth could have easily brought disaster, but history does not support the theory of a long, unbroken drouth such as this; a blighting dryness and continuous crop failure. There is nothing like that in the history of the Southwest for a period of nearly three hundred years. Such a drouth would have prevailed over the entire Southwest if it prevailed at all.

Furthermore they left a land where natural moisture and climatic conditions were more favorable for the production of crops than in any land to the south, with the exception of the Rio Grande valley and two or three other valleys where irrigation was practiced. We grant that a series of dry years may have been a part of their trouble, but there were certainly other contributing causes, if not main causes. Here are a few other reasons, or probable reasons, for the departure of this people from the land of their birth and heritage, and some reasoning on the matter:

If it was a drouth not all of the people would have gone. If drouth was the cause of the land's being depopulated the people would have come back when the drouth was over; or some would have remained to stand guard over the homes and treasures of art that were left behind, and possibly to possess these treasures for themselves. Evidently fear possessed the minds of all of them. They never came back when the drouth was over, if there was a drouth. The same circumstances that caused them to move out of the land kept them out.

Briefly, we will mention some other causes that might have contributed to the failure of this people in this area.

One was the lack of a written language. Without the printed or written word to preserve what they learned and record their experiences they could not hold the line on their gains. The learning and accomplishments of one generation was largely lost to the next. Another reason was with the people themselves. They were peacefully inclined; too timid to fight for their homes and their rights, and they lost their all.

Another cause of failure may have been that the tribe had failed to produce strong leadership. One strong, aggressive leader, with a few hundred men well trained in their arts of war, could have saved the whole situation. As it was a few marauding savage bands probably drove the farm population out of the small outlying villages, which cut off the food supply from the dwellers in the cliffs as effectually as a prolonged drouth and finally brought starvation to the great strongholds in the canon walls. With one or two strong leaders the situation could have been saved and the "Cliff Dwellers" might still be in possession of this land instead of we who are here.

It is best as it is, for such are the ways of fate—the fittest survive. The Pueblos here were civilized, but it was not the kind of civilization to survive the time. The cause of his final failure was within himself. He did not have what it takes to meet a crisis when it came. Yet he was surely not without his merits. He survived for thirteen centuries when the wonder is that he should survive at all.

CHAPTER II

THE UTE INDIAN IN MONTEZUMA COUNTY

In the previous chapter we have given the dwellers in the cliffs precedence, in time and place, over the Ute Indian Tribe because the Cliff Dweller tribe is a long departed race and many people think of him as having come into these environs before the other Indians came. As a matter of fact the two were contemporary tribes, leading parallel lives for a long, long time, and each living his own life in his own way. We do not know what, if any, relations existed between the two tribes, but there appears to have been hostile relations toward the end of the "Cliff Dwellers" sojourn in this area.

The Ute Indian reservation is an integral part of Montezuma County with an area of 412,067 acres. The Ute Indian is a resident of Montezuma County, is still a ward of the government, in a way, but has just about attained the status of full citizenship. He has the right to vote and a voting precinct has been established on the reservation, at Towaoc, and in the general election of 1956 quite a number of the Indians cast their ballot, and more will vote as time goes by. The Ute Indian pays no taxes on any property he owns on the reservation, but must pay a tax on property they have acquired off the reservation. Other citizens must pay taxes on any property they own on the reservation.

The tribe is completely self-governing. The Tribal Council is the ruling body with the tribal chief at its head, and they act in all matters, of law and order, both civil and criminal. There is a well organized police force, they have complete authority, and they take action at once in case of law violation. The police are proving to be pretty efficient peace officers. Be it said that there is very little real trouble among the Indians. Our civil and criminal laws apply, but the enforcement of the law is in the hands of the Indians. Thus we have a government within our government and independent of it. It will no doubt be modified gradually as time goes by.

The Ute Indian, in this county, has been designated the Ute Mountain Indian Tribe. There is at present 680 Indians in the Ute Mountain tribe, on the registry. About 150 of these live in Allen Canon, in Utah, near the Blue Mountains, and the remaining number on the

19

reservation in this County. For many years before, and for some years after the Ute Indian became subject to the white man's law, the tribe barely held its own in numbers, disease arising from lack of sanitary methods of living being the main cause of the high death rate. Since about 1940 there has been a rapid increase in numbers. Education in matters of health, medical care and training in matters of sanitation reduced the death rate at once and in recent years there has been a rapid build-up in tribal numbers.

Also in recent years there has been much interest, and some real effort, on the part of the Indians to better their own welfare and condition. Just now, and for some time past, men of the Ute tribe have been putting their own money into a few head of cattle and sheep; they take a genuine interest in their stock and take as good care of them as conditions will permit. For feed for their stock they must depend on their range summer and winter, but bulls and bucks are fed during the severe part of winter since they understand the importance of keeping these animals in good thrifty condition. Some of the younger men show real ability in handling their flocks and herds and nearly all who have stock are making their own living, or enough for their own living. As an example Juan Bancraft built his herd of cattle up to 400 head, but had to be cut back some to allow grazing room for other growing herds. Many of the men have enough stock to make their own living, but they are having to make room on the range right along for others who want to build up a flock or herd.

Poor as we are apt to think the reservation lands are, there is feed for many small herds and flocks. The entire Ute mountain area provides many thousand acres of good summer grazing, and the lower Mesa Verde, the Mancos Canon and the mesas to the south provide vast amounts of good grazing. Even the lower flat lands, so like a desert under the summer sun, produces some good pasture in the average spring and early summer.

The old scrub cattle and sheep, once so characteristic of the flocks and herds on the reservation, are all gone. To take their place the government has shipped in, and bought locally, many car loads of well bred and registered cattle and sheep, as foundation stock, and the Ute Indians have some of the best bred cattle and sheep in the county. The Indians, especially the younger Indians, take an active interest in their own affairs, are alert and eager to learn and, what is more important, are happy and contented.

The tribe is also developing some real leadership among their numbers. Jack House, their present Chief, is a real and an able leader, and takes an active interest in the welfare of the tribe. Jack is, at this writing, about 63 years of age and has been Chief about twenty years, and was a Tribal Council member ten years before becoming Chief. House is regarded as the greatest chief of the tribe since Chief Ouray and more able in every way than Chief Ignacio, Mariana or John Miller who preceded him as Chief. House has done more for his own people than any tribal member of recent times. The Chief is chosen for character and his ability as a leader, and he has more influence and directing power than any member of the tribe or council. House has used his influence to induce his people to live better, to do something for themselves, to own property and have a good home and urges them to take care of their families and send their children to school. For a long time the tribe would not consent to have their land explored for gas or oil, and it took Jack House two years, aided by his council advisor, Frank Pyle, to persuade them to sign a lease. The leases signed since then have brought several million dollars into the tribal fund. House speaks little English, but he is an eloquent and forceful speaker in his own language. The tribe members appreciate his interest and leadership and only recently took a vote to thank him and Mr. Pyle for the good work they have done for the tribe.

There are others who show a public spirit and take an interest in the tribal welfare.

Nathan Wing is the grim old patriarch of the entire Ute Mountain Tribe. Crowding the century mark (some say he is now over a hundred years old) he is still alert and active and lives in contentment in his home on the Mancos River about twelve miles above the Cortez-Shiprock road. He has a small herd of good cattle to help keep up his interest in life. In his younger years he was strong in the Tribal Council of Chief Ouray.

In recent years the way of life of the Ute Indian has been greatly improved and family life and living standards are being made better right along. They take a special interest in health and education. At the beginning of the school year 1956-1957 almost every child of school age is in school. The Kindergarten and first, second and third grades attend school at Towaoc while the grades above the third attend school at Cortez. Two large buses take the children to school every day and bring them home. The schools at Cortez are completely integrated. The pupils learn their lessons in school and their new way of life from their associates.

The Utes are slowly advancing in other ways. No longer than fifteen to twenty years ago there were but few English speaking men among the tribesmen. Now nearly all the young men, and most of the young women, have a command of English sufficient for practical use; some speak English fluently, and many of the older people are learning some English. The children are all being educated in the English language and in the white man's way of life. There is a college fund for Indians who finish high school and in a few years there will be among the tribesmen and tribe women trained nurses, skilled artisans, professional men and good business men.

Towaoc (the first and simplest meaning of the word is good) is an Indian village, but not of the old type of skin and canvas covered tepees, but of modern houses and, except for a few white people in offices and stores, the population is all Indian. Most of the new homes are being equipped with hot and cold running water, toilet, bath, modern kitchen, electric lights and modern furniture, and telephones will later be installed. A million gallon concrete reservoir, supplemented by water hauled from Cortez, has been furnishing the water supply, but a well has been drilled and in February, 1957, a strong flow of water was encountered at a depth of 1270 feet. The well was drilled on down to the 1769 foot level with water rising to the 300 foot level. The well was put into production at once and the water haul from Cortez was discontinued. As a result of a forty-eight hour test by a U. S. Geological Survey crew it was determined that the well has a sustained production of 41 gallons per minute with the pump set at a depth of 800 feet. They were aiming for a well to produce 80 gallons per minute, to supply the needs of the village, but a second well will be drilled to reach this production. The water is a little heavy in fluorine content, but it will be tempered with a flow of pure water from a Ute Mountain source. Supplemented by the small flow of water they already had the well will furnish enough water for all present needs.

Out of their own funds the Indians have built a small hospital, nurses are employed to be in attendance at all hours and all minor cases of accident and sickness are treated there.

During the years when the Towaoc agency was not in use the building fell into neglect and depreciated badly. In the past few years the whole town has been rehabilitated, life and business have been reactivated and all the buildings are gleaming with new paint. The Tribal Council contributed $30,000 for this work, out of their own funds, the government putting in many thousands more. The village is growing, the Utes have money—money from the government due them on treaty agreements; money from oil leases; money from the sale of their own livestock, and their better future is assured.

One man who has been a factor in all this progress is Frank Pyle. Mr. Pyle has been among these Indians for forty years, first as a rider after livestock; then as trading post operator and owner for a number of years; then as interpreter and advisor at the agency. Now he is Chairman of the Approval Committee and Advisor on the Tribal Council Committee. It might be said that the Indian Agent represents the government, but Pyle represents the Indians. He speaks their language as perfectly as any one can ever learn it, the Ute language being a most difficult language to master if, indeed, any one ever does master it. Mr. Pyle's years with the Indians, both as business dealer and friend has won their entire trust and confidence. They trust his honesty and judgment and, for this reason, he is a power of influence with the tribe. His interest in the Indians is genuine and his desire to help is real.

The Ute Indian, as a tribe, has little historic background that we know about. Comparatively speaking we just haven't known him very long. For as long as anything has been known about him the Ute Mountain Utes and the Southern Utes have lived on the western slope of the Rocky Mountains in Colorado and in eastern Utah. Bands of Utes may have strayed into the intermountain region at times, and even over onto the edge of the western plains, but he invariably came back to the place that was home to him. They made frequent raids into the territory of neighboring tribes, stealing horses and food; then retreated to their own territory again.

Like nearly all North American tribes the Ute Indian lived in villages along the streams, getting his living by hunting, trapping and snaring game. They gathered pinon nuts and wild berries, such as choke cherries, squaw berries, etc., and might have dried some berries for future use. Also there was a wild plant with an edible root that he used for food. In times when game was plentiful he might have sliced some meat thin and dried it, much as many pioneer white men dried their "perky" and stored it in skin containers. If they ever did this thing, it was the squaws that did it.

In historic times the Indians raised a few sheep, and sometime after the Mormons came into Utah they had a few cattle, and an animal could be butchered in case of pinching times. Sheep probably came into the Ute tribe by way of the Navajo Indians since they have had sheep since early Spanish times in New Mexico. Horses came into the possession of the Ute Indians at an earlier date than sheep or cattle, about 1700.

As for raising a crop, this was completely beneath his dignity; he sowed not; neither did he reap. If a patch of corn did appear here and there it was the squaws that did the work. If he was like most Indian tribes hunger was a common experience, especially in winters of much snow.

Since we have known the Ute Indian his house was a tepee of a type probably borrowed from the plains Indians, and before his use of the tepee we know little about the type of shelter he might have contrived to protect him from the elements. He lived in one room where he cooked, ate and slept, and he lived with vermin and under conditions that were far from clean or sanitary. The death rate was high, especially among the children. Filth diseases, such as smallpox and diphtheria, were of common occurrence. They made little or no progress in their manner of living and in numbers barely held their own. Their way of living required much territory for each individual, subsisting as he did on only what nature provided for him. It was a wasteful use of the land, producing as it did, perhaps, less than a hundredth part of the good things of life it was capable of producing under modern tillage. He might have enjoyed living that way, but he could not expect forever to possess the land and make no better use of it than he did. Nature just didn't intend it that way.

The new life the Ute Indian has today is already infinitely better than the old way. Yet he resisted the change. It could not have been expected that he would understand.

The Ute Indian is still a primitive person in a way, and many of them are an easy prey to modern vices. In many individual instances it is impossible to protect him from himself in the exercise of his new-found privileges. Only wait. This menace, too will pass.

When the Ute Indian was finally compelled to submit to the White man's will he was given the choice of having a homestead, each for his own, and at a place of his own choosing, or going as a tribe onto a reservation there to continue his life much as he had always lived it. He chose the reservation, and in 1881, just after Fort Lewis had been built and occupied, both the Ute and the Navajo Indians were put on their respective reservations. They did not always stay there and made some trouble.

In tribal life there was marriage and family life, as with other peoples everywhere, and the family was the unit of his simply organized society. Marriage relations were respected, family ties held the family together in spite of the simplicity of it all, and the lack of the knowledge and understanding that could produce a fuller measure of happiness and a better family life. According to Ute customs, the groom in the case was not compelled to pay the father for his bride, as with many primitive people. In assuming marriage relations, there were no formalities, no ceremonies of any kind. Marriage was but a mutual understanding and an acceptance of each by the other, the practice being much the same as common law marriages recognized under our own laws. Most marriages among the Utes are now civil affairs, but quite a number still cling to the old tribal custom. In most cases there is real affection between man and wife and Chief Ouray and Princess Chipeta were a noble example in this respect. As in all family life, there was joy and sorrow, love and trials, distress and disappointment, not in a passionate way perhaps, but they were there and they were real.

All the schooling the children had was in the school of life. The boys learned to hunt and to capture and trap game, and to ride on horseback after horses came into use, and most of them became skilled riders. Getting a living was probably the most important concern of their lives. The girls did the more menial things the home and the village life required of them. Skilled men made bows and arrows for hunting, and other weapons of defense or offense. They had earthen vessels, or pottery, of the useful kind, but the making of these always fell to the squaws. Women did some weaving and made garments and bed covers from skins and did every other kind of work. It seems useless to speculate how the aboriginal Indian lived and got along. We just don't know. Food and clothing and bedding and shelter must have been a constant problem, and we must be content to know he managed it some way, without knowing how.

The Ute Indian has no knowledge of the time when he didn't have horses to ride and a few sheep. They didn't have cattle until a later period. They have had horses, the historians record, since about the year 1700, as noted elsewhere, and sheep probably came to the Ute Indian through the Navajo tribe since the Navajo has had sheep for a long time, probably since the early Spanish settlement in New Mexico. The Indians are nearly all good riders, but they didn't break their horses by getting on them and riding them outright as the western cowboy does. But first they harassed and worried a horse until he is hardly able to move; then he mounted the horse and rode him. He rode without a saddle, until recent times, and, if he was like the Comanche Indian, down in Texas, most of his horses had sore backs from being so ridden. The Indians now on the reservation are cowboys and sheep herders much like other cowboys and sheepherders, but too often the squaw is the sheepherder. Get acquainted with this modern Ute Indian. When you know him better you will think better of him.

QUEEN OF THE UTE TRIBE

Chipeta, "Queen of the Utes," and a famous Indian squaw, made one of her last appearances in the White man's public at Ouray the week of July 11, 1911, the first visit to the land of her childhood and early womanhood in 30 or 31 years. She was petted and fawned upon as though she were in reality a famous queen. Her husband, the famous Chief Ouray, had been dead some years, but Chipeta was still strong, upright of carriage, and still bore a trace of her youthful beauty. Her age, at this time, was fixed by those who knew her in early womanhood, at 66 or 67 years. She greatly enjoyed the honors that were showered upon her.

Chief Ouray, reburied in May, 1925, was a great Indian and a remarkable man. Gifted by nature with a rare wisdom and a wonderful understanding, he was unlettered and untaught save in the school of life. He was a great leader, a wise counselor and a firm friend of both the Indians and the white man. Chief Ouray, without education as we know it, was a leader of men; was statesman, prophet and seer surpassed by none and equaled by few. Every tribe and people, at intervals, produces such men. Some have the printed word to perpetuate their memory; others have not, and their memory fades and is soon forgotten.

CHAPTER III

SETTLEMENT OF THE MANCOS VALLEY

The first authentic history of the white man in Montezuma County, Colorado, is found in the record of the expedition of Don Juan Maria de Rivera who was sent out by the governor of New Mexico to find silver in the La Plata Mountains, where he had heard it might be found in great quantities, and, of course, to lay claim to the country in the name of the King of Spain. This expedition, headed by Rivera, consisted of a few soldiers and Indian guides, did little exploratory work, but charted the route thoroughly, wrote a description of the country here in the San Juan Basin, and named all the rivers and mountain ranges. All were given Spanish names some of which are: San Juan River, meaning in English St. John; the Piedra, the Stone; the Rio Pinos, the Pine River; Rio de los Animas, the River of the Lost Soul; the La Plata, the Silver, or Silver River; the Mancos, the Crippled One; and the Dolores, the River of Sorrow. It is related that the expedition, in attempting to cross the Dolores River at flood stage, had two of their number drowned in the swift moving stream—hence the name. It is not definitely known whether the La Plata Mountains were so named because there was supposed to be much silver there, or from the gray granite peaks, or silver peaks as they are called. It is recorded that the expedition camped for a few days on the West Mancos near its confluence with the combined flow of Middle and East Cancos, that one of their number had gotten badly crippled in one leg, at the knee, hence the name Mancos, the Crippled One. This expedition continued on Northward.

In 1776 a follow-up expedition, led by Father Escalante, was sent by the New Mexico Governor to further explore the country, following the same route laid out and charted by Rivera. It did more exploring and added considerable to this source of information on the early history of the country. Thus Montezuma County has definitely been under three flags; first the flag of Spain; then the flag of Mexico, after winning her independence from Spain in 1822; and the American flag since the treaty of Guadalupe Hidalgo, in 1848. From descriptions in his diary it is practically certain that Escalante visited the ruins on Hovenweep Canon, now a national monument.

After these expeditions almost a hundred years elapsed before white men came to make the first permanent settlements in the county. It is recorded that J. S. Newberry climbed to the top of Mesa Verde in 1859; that land surveys were made by the government in 1872-73 and that a Geological Survey party explored Mancos Canon and discovered two cliff ruins, W. H. Jackson, a well known early western photographer being one of the party.

The first permanent settlers came into the Mancos Valley in 1874. To make the story complete we will begin with four mining prospectors who discovered the Comstock mine, in the La Plata Mountains, in 1873. These four miners were Almarion Root, Alex K. Fleming, Robert Jones, and Henry Lightner. Having no funds to operate on, they went over to Del Norte to find some one they could interest in their new discovery. By good fortune they encountered Captain John Moss who was out scouting the mining camps for Parrott Bros., wealthy bankers and realtors of San Francisco. He came at once to look over their prospect. His cupidity was excited at once, and getting a few samples of rich ore, he set out by the nearest route for San Francisco. Parrott Bros. were so well pleased that they at once advanced all the money needed and in July, 1873, Capt. Moss got together a small group of men and started on the long journey to southwest Colorado. In this party were James Ratliff, A. L. Root, Dick Giles, Harry Lee, Ed Merrick, John Brewer and Fred Franks. They traveled on horseback with pack animals to carry bedding, food and equipment. They headed southeastward from San Francisco, crossed the Colorado River at Fort Mohave, journeyed across northern Arizona going from one Indian village or trading post to another to replenish their supplies of food. Finally the long journey brought them to the San Juan River, which they crossed near the four corners. Following the Mancos River and then the Navajo Draw they came into the Montezuma Valley from the south over Aztec Divide. From the crest of the divide a beautiful broad valley spread out before them. Captain Moss promptly named it Montezuma Valley. A few hours more brought the weary party over the low divide, probably at Point Lookout Lodge, and into the Mancos Valley, July, 1874, verdant with grass and trees and watered by a wonderful stream of pure mountain water. Here they paused to rest for a few days from their long journey, and the men in the party liked the place so well that they at once decided to make the valley their home. Ratliff located what is now the Louis Paquin place; Root took the Clark place, now occupied by Everett Humiston; Giles and Lee located on the Menefee ranch; Merrick took the place now owned by B. F. Davis, and John Brewer located on the river just east of the John White place, now owned by Harmon Mathews. H. M. Smith and Pete Lindstrom came the same year from Denver, Smith taking what is now the Dean Bradshaw place and Lindstrom taking the Manse Reid place now the property of George Mauler.

After resting a few days the California party went on up into the

27

mountain by way of La Plata River cañon, and put in the balance of the summer prospecting for Parrott Bros. Many mining claims were located, a great many ore samples were collected, the town of Parrott City was laid out and charted. In the late fall the party started to return to the Mancos Valley for the winter. They were short on food, so the party camped on a little stream where the TXT ranch now stands and Captain Moss and two other men set out for Tierra Amarillo, New Mexico, to get supplies. They were gone six weeks and the men left behind ran out of food and all but starved. In camp Giles accidently shot and wounded himself in the neck pretty badly so they couldn't move camp. They remained there subsisting on such game as they could kill or capture, and anything they could find to eat. They named the little creek Starvation Creek, and it bears the name to this day.

Moss returned in 1875 and established Parrott City. Many mining men came and Parrott City soon grew into a town with some business. This information is from article by Josiah M. Ward, and was taken from Moss's report to Parrott Bros.

Giles got well and in the spring of 1875 the men came on down into the Mancos Valley, began at once clearing land and improving their homesteads. Giles and Lee built a log cabin on what was later to be the Menefee place. It stood in the southwest corner of the orchard, near the old Menefee twelve roomed house. This was the first habitation built by the white man in the present confines of Montezuma County, Colorado. This was in the spring of 1875. The new settlers began at once to plant and raise a little grain, some potatoes, and a little garden produce. Getting a little seed to start with was a problem. Soon a few chickens and pigs appeared on the scene, and cattle and horses were soon everywhere.

In the spring of 1876 a few more settlers came. Manse Reid and Charley Frink came to the valley looking for cattle range and were so pleased they returned to their homes near Pueblo and came back in the fall bringing herds of cattle. Nick Bergstrand came and located the Ben Reid place, John McIntyre took the Webster Ahrens place and Bill Bullock a part of what is now the B. F. Davis ranch. In September of this year Major Sheets, John Gregor, Pat O'Donnell, Charles Frink, Wylie Graybeall and Lou Paquin brought in over a thousand head of cattle and turned them lose in the Mancos Valley. This was the beginning of a flourishing and prosperous cattle industry in Montezuma County. George West, later to serve as state senator for two or three terms, came with several hundred head of cattle the same year.

The Indians resented this encroachment on their domain and time after time ordered the settlers to get out. But the settlers stayed on their homeseads and used diplomacy with the Indians. To gain their favor they were given food or the settlers divided with them the little they had. H. M. Smith divided his last bit of flour with Chief Red-jacket, who had a sick squaw, and gained his lasting favor, and some protection. The Indians killed some cattle and now and then stole a horse, but there was never any serious trouble in the Mancos area.

During the winter of 1876-77 came Reese Richards and wife, the latter being the daughter of Peter Shirts. She was the first and only white woman, at this time, in the county of Montezuma. The family stayed a while on the Ratliff ranch, and a baby boy was born to them there, the first white child to be born in the county. Indian squaws helped take care of the mother and child and after a few weeks the family moved from the community. Because they remained only a short time this birth is not counted by the old timers as the first in Mancos Valley, but they reserve this honor for two babies, a boy and a girl, born a little later and who lived in the valley all their lives.

In the spring and summer of 1877 the men who made real history in the new country began to arrive, and many new settlers came into the valley to make their homes. Among these were Andy Menefee and wife Sarah, and three children, John, George and Edward; Will Menefee, Joe Morefield and young bride, John White, who had been here the previous summer and located the the Harmon Matthew place and built a good "dug out" home. He returned this year by oxteam from Walsenburg and brought his wife and only son, and household effects.

Also came Cal House, David Willis, wife and three boys, Joe Sheek and family, George Clay, Bill Spaulding and the Stanley Mitchell family; also the B. K. Witherills came at this time, the Mitchells and the Witherills coming together. Morefield took what is now the Wilburn place, Willis took the Ira Cox place, Joe Sheek took the Ernest Cox place and land south of the road, and the Mitchell family located on a place in the south part of the valley, where there is now a small producing oil well. Andy Menefee stopped at the White place for a while but when Dick Giles took ill of pneumonia, they moved to his place in the upper valley and took care of him until he died. Mr. Giles' death was the first to take place in the valley and he was buried on the west side of the Menefee ranch. Mr. Menefee later bought the place from the Administrator of the Giles estate. Some others who came at this time did not stay.

Late in 1877 and early in 1878 came T. W. Wattles, Manse and Dock Reid, Ed and Alex Ptolemy, James Frink, Jasper Butts, Robert McGrew, H. M. Barber, Frank Morgan, Chris Wisecarver, Nick Arney, Jim Downey, Lige Peterson and some others. Some of these men didn't stay long, but most of them were prominent in the country as long as they lived.

Manse and Dock Reid bought the places now owned by the Mauler boys. Wattles and Morgan went on over to the Dolores and located, but came back soon and took land in the Mancos Valley. Ed Ptolemy bought and sold land here the rest of his life, also running cattle; Alex Ptolemy was largely an investor; Jim Frink was a cowman; likewise

Jasper Butts who established his summer range at the T-down corrals and ran his cattle in the winter out in Yellow Jacket country. It was here, one evening, he had been helping his men with the cattle at the branding corral and near night, mounted his horse and rode off for camp. The men found him later dead. It was thought that his horse must have fallen with him as it was found, upon examination, that his neck was broken. Butts had the reputation of being a very fine man and was well liked by almost everyone who knew him well. R. T. McGrew located on land on Chicken Creek two miles north of Mancos. The original log house, much enlarged, still stands.

A Mr. Webber and wife located a homestead in the community that bears his name, taking the land later owned by George Halls. Here Webber met his death under mysterious circumstances, which were never well understood, and was buried on a wooded hill just east of his place. Peter Holmes homesteaded the place now owned by Harolson Weaver and Fred Franks took the land just southwest of town, later owned by Fayette Sheek, Soren Jensen and others. John Green and Tim Jenkins came about this time. They followed mining.

In September, 1877, William Menefee was born the fourth son of Mr. and Mrs. Andy Menefee, down on the John White Place. He is accredited the first white boy to be born in the Mancos Valley, and is still living on his ranch at this writing. Also Mabyn Morefield, first daughter, and child, of Mr. and Mrs. Joseph Morefield, was born at the ranch home in the lower valley in early 1878, and was accredited the first girl to be born in the Mancos Valley. She married Fred Armstrong, raised a large family and lived here all her life.

The first social event in the new land was a dance given at the Brewer cabin on the lower Mancos sometime in 1878. Manse Reid brought a fiddler (not a violinist) over from Dolores and Mrs. Morefield cooked the supper. The ladies present were Mrs. Andy Menefee, Mrs. Bradford, Mrs. Brewer, Mrs. Morefield and the Misses Clara and Callie Mitchell and Ida Sheek, and all the young men in the country. In the fall of 1878, Charley Mitchell died and was buried on the hillside, near Mitchell Springs, just south of the town of Cortez.

This year, 1878, the Mancos post office was established on the McIntyre place, now owned by Webster Ahrens, with Mr. McIntyre as postmaster and Mrs. Willis, assistant. Previous to this time all mail was brought from Parrott City where a small center of population and business had developed as a result of the mining boom, and mail was brought over, in bulk, by any one who happened to be going to that place and returning. Now a mail carrier was employed, but getting the mail through was still a difficult task as it was carried on horseback in summer and on snow shoes in winter. In 1880 or 1881 the mail carrier was stranded in Thompson Park by a heavy storm and frozen to death only a few hundred yards from the John Sponsel residence.

30

Before 1880 no lumber was available locally and any boards needed were sawed with a whip saw or hewn out with an ax.

Food was not easy to get in those first years. A little grain was grown and sometimes it was ground with a coffee mill to make their bread. At first the nearest railroad was at Pueblo, from which point all needed supplies were brought by way of Del Norte. The railroad reached Alamosa in 1878 and supplies were freighted from that place by horse drawn and ox drawn vehicles over almost impassable roads, some of them toll roads. The railroad was built into Durango in 1881, a good town sprung up at once and it became much easier to get supplies. Also stockmen began driving their cattle to Durango for shipment to the market which brought in considerable money and a great relief as, prior to this time, money had almost gone out of circulation in every part of the county. Before this the only money in circulation was the little brought in by new settlers and the little that could be gotten in by selling dressed beef, or live animals, in the mining camps and, with no roads, it was a long way to the mining camps. The only roads into and out of what was later to be Montezuma County was over Mancos Hill and over Bear Creek Hill and for the first few years both roads were all but impassable. The first wagons over Mancos Hill were rough locked with chains, to come down, and held back by ropes wrapped around a convenient tree. Wagons that were not strong were often broken down or damaged in the process. This road was improved little by little as the years went by.

Soon after White, Morefield and Brewer had settled in the lower valley other settlers came. Frank Morgan, later to become a leading citizen in upper Montezuma Valley, took the land just east of the Morefield place, John McGregor came in with cattle and took what is known as the Roger Gibbs place, on the river, started improvements and later sold to Charley Frink. Mr. Glasgo took the land just below and he and Mr. Brewer built the Brewer-Glasgo Ditch. Following closely on these settlements T. W. Wattles and Pete Holmes took the land now the Roger Gibbs homeplace and the land just to the west. Logan Whitlock homesteaded the land where Mr. Roberts now lives. He was soon killed by the accidental discharge of a gun in the hands of a negro who was working for him. Along with these events Adam Kramer settled on the place just south of the old Ormiston place, now owned by Mr. Fowler, and a little later Judge Morris, Mrs. Ormiston's father, took the Ormiston place. Nick Arnie, a brother-in-law to John White, settled on the Al Prater place, now the home of Bessie Morefield. Gus Stevenson, father of Gus Stevenson, Jr., who is still a resident here, took the old Bill Prater place, and George Comfort came over from Ft. Lewis and settled on the Fred Armstrong place, in the extreme lower end of the valley.

In the upper valley Clark Brittain came in and homesteaded the old Paquin place now owned by Harry Mace; William Brittain took the land just south of this place and Freed Brittain settled on the Redd and Summers Place. The Devenports came in about this time and filed a homestead on the place now owned by Clyde Sheek. Dr. Field located first on the old Joe Moore place six miles north of town and, later, acquired the Vern Robbins place, which later became the property of Wylie Graybeal. A. T. Samson located on land at the confluence of the East and Middle Mancos rivers and Wilson Daly took the place where the big sawmill stands. Grandpa Rush took land just north of town on Chicken Creek, Roy Weston homesteaded the Willis Smith place and in 1881, Sol Exon, Sr., acquired the old Exon ranch in the lower valley, now owned by Roger Gibbs.

W. J. Blatchford homesteaded the Ernest Adams place and operated a sawmill for a number of years. He called the place Forest Park. D. H. Lemmon took land on upper Lemmon Draw and also operated a sawmill. George Soulen located on the old Fox Farm and built the house there. Joe Moore homesteaded the Joe Moore place, later owned by Dr. Field. Frank Hallford took the Ira Kelly place and organized the Crystal Creek Ditch Company.

In about 1881 Benjamin Knight Wetherill came in and acquired the Albert Gilliland place, bought other land, and the Alamo Ranch became widely known and famous, in a way. There were five of the Wetherill Boys and by name they were Richard, Alfred, Winslow, John and Clayton, and one daughter, Mrs. Chas. Masons. They were first ranchers, and ran a herd of range cattle on Mesa Verde and other local ranges. Then they were exploiters and explorers, and passed from the local scene.

At first the Indians laid special claim to Mesa Verde and tried to keep the white man off, but local ranchers persisted and John White, Bill Prater, Bill Hayes, John Hammond and Jim Frink ran cattle on the Mesa for several years. To gain access to the top of the Mesa the White Trail, the John Hammond Trail, the Frink Trail and the Wetherill Trail, later to become the Prater Trail, were built. It was while riding after their cattle in the fall of 1888 that Richard and Clayton Wethterill discovered the great Cliff Palace ruin on the Mesa, details of which will be narrated more fully in a subsequent chapter.

Dave Willis and Bill Hayes took the land now owned by Ira Cox and part of that owned by B. F. Davie. John Brewer, on the lower river course, established and operated the first dairy in Montezuma County. He made butter and sold it at Parrott City. The valley was full of range cattle, and the cattlemen, after a while, put him out of business.

Some Firsts: Dick Giles was the first death in Montezuma County, present confines, followed soon after by the first Mrs. Manse Reid. Burial was on the west side of the Menefee place, the first burial ground. Some other burials were later made there. The first wedding was the marriage of Mr. Ratliff and Mrs. McGeoch. Rev. Howard was the first ordained minister, holding services at the Joe Sheek place now and then in early 1880's.

H. M. Smith had a thresher operated by hand and Ed Caldwell and Clark Brittain brought in the first threshing machine. In the fall of 1881 they were threshing for Joe Sheek, a big snow storm came on in October depositing a foot of snow. All was dismay. Everyone thought surely winter was here. But the snow soon disappeared and the entire threshing season was finished in fine shape.

In 1879 the postoffice was moved from the McIntyre place to the Menefee ranch and in 1881, a town having been laid out, the postoffice found a permanent location in Mancos. J. M. Rush, J. J. Wade, Dick Reid and Jim Ratliff started the town by establishing the first residences. A. C. Honaker came from Missouri about this time and built the first bridge across the Mancos River and used the Money ($100) to send for his family. Mrs. Tom Rickner, Mrs. Lou Jarrett and Mrs. Cord Bowen were of this family. D. H. Lemmon came about this time and built the first hotel—a long log structure on South Main Street.

In 1881 George Bauer came into the new town riding a mule and leading three burros heavily laden with grocery stock for a store—a ten-gallon cask of whiskey, flour, tobacco, coffee, bacon, sugar, etc. He fenced off a little space in the front corner of a log house that stood on the spot now occupied by the old Lou Soens blacksmith shop building, on South Main St., and started the first store business in Mancos, which was also the first in Montezuma County. He sold his stock out in no time and went back for more. We will trace his business career in Mancos in a later chapter.

In 1881 Jim Frink and John Duncan located the Reg Allum place and William Stevenson took land just above and on the river. About this time J. M. Rush established a sawmill and a grist mill and made "flour" for every part of the county. It was not flour; only a grist, but it was a big improvement over the hand ground meal. Rush also did custom grinding. He made grist for sale and many people used it for a time.

In 1878 there were already a number of children of school age in the new community. There were children in the Andy Menefee family, the William Hayes family, the David Willis family and some others had one or two children. Hayes and Menefee took it upon themselves to start a movement for a school. A small log building on the Root place, just south of town, was secured for temporary use and Miss Lizzie Allen was engaged at teacher. She was very young (only 16) and inexperienced, and it took some earnest persuasion to get her to take the job. She did take it, however, and taught four months.

At this time a movement was started to erect a building for school use, and as a public meeting place. Accordingly logs were cut and hauled and a building erected on a lonely spot (there was no town then) just across the alley north of the present Mancos Theater, and

33

the next term of school was held there with Miss Anna Bradford as teacher. She secured a teachers' certificate, School District No. 6 was organized, then in La Plata County, and the school became a permanent institution. It seems that the new school building was finished early enough for Miss Allen to teach the last weeks of her school there. Miss Anna Field came down from the Joe Moore place on horseback and taught the winter term of school. In 1889 the new school house got a board floor, the lumber being brought down from Parrott City, and on July 3, 1879, the new school house was dedicated with a dance, a feast and a general good time. Hereafter the new school was used for dances and every kind of public meeting. It served for school purposes until 1887, when a new school building was erected where the new grade school building now stands. This new building served for several years, was finally moved to the west end of the school ground and is now being used as a public library building.

The first election was held in a log cabin on the Root place, in 1880, and William Hayes was elected Justice of the Peace. His first official act was to marry William Brittain and Lou Devenport who lived in the County all their married life and raised a large family. Late in their married life Mr. Brittain became unable to work and Mrs. Brittain bravely took up the task of making the family living. For some years she hauled freight from Mancos and Dolores, sometimes from Durango, to Cortez, driving a two- or four-horse team. In season and out of season, through summers heat and the storms and cold of winter, at times, over muddy roads that were all but impassable, she never failed or faltered when it was at all possible to get the job done. She deserves a monument for her faithfulness and heroism.

In 1880 Frank Morgan ran a sawmill at the TXT ranch site. O. E. Noland hauled logs for him and the Mitchells ran the boarding house, and in September, Callie Mitchell and Mr. Noland were married.

Dr. Field, about this time, sought to build a ditch to bring water from the Dolores river into the Montezuma Valley, but the undertaking was too great, there was not enough funds, so he moved back to Mancos, and to the Joe Moore place to practice medicine.

There was a mail route now from Parrott City to Mancos and on to the Dolores, at Big Bend, and mail to Bluff City once a week.

Church work was not to be entirely neglected and soon after the new school building was completed a Sunday School was organized with R. T. McGrew, Superintendent, and Mrs. B. K. Wetherill assistant. It was popular, for it was the only public gathering for quite some time.

A lyceum, or "literary society," was next organized, an "Institution" in every pioneer community in the west. The people had to provide their own entertainment. The older men did most of the debating and many a heated argument was threshed out, pro and con. Among the speakers were many well known names—Mrs. Ratliff, D. H. Lem-

34

mon, Dr. Field, Judge M. T. Morris, C. M. Veits, A. T. Samson, O. C. Roberts and wife, Manse Reid and others.

The town of Mancos was laid out in part in 1881, and the postoffice was moved down from Menefee.

After the new school house was built the Indians became troublesome and made a number of raids into the white settlements and on the stockmen further west, and fear of an attack caused a stockade to be built about the buildings as a place of refuge should the Indians raid in this far. But no trouble came and, save once or twice when a few women and children went there when there was an Indian scare, the stockade was never used.

In 1885 the Town of Mancos had the following business establishments: C. J. Scharnhorst, shoemaker; Mr. Snyder, blacksmith, C. M. Veits, groceries on North Main St., the George Bauer establishment where the laundry now occupies, consisting of a large stock of general merchandise; a bank (after 1884) and the postoffice. There was a log hotel and two saloons.

At this time six of the early settlers had died. They were Dick Giles, John McIntyre, David Willis (killed by Indians), Mrs. Ratliff, George Frink and Minnie Weston Reid.

From 1885 to 1891, when the railroad was built through the valley, there was slow, but steady progress. New settlers came into the valley and all the choice land was taken; and some that was not so good. During this time, the Webber Community, south of Mancos, was settled; also the beautiful mountain cove known as Thompson Park. This narrative will be resumed under the title "Mancos Chronology," and the settlement of Webber and Thompson Park taken up forthwith.

SETTLEMENT OF THE WEBBER COMMUNITY

By 1881 all the good land along the Mancos river in the valley proper had been taken, but just to the south of the Town of Mancos was an area of very fine land still open to settlement. This area is known as the Webber Community and was named for the first and only settler in the locality prior to 1880.

The Webber Community was unique in that it was first settled wholly and exclusively by the Mormons. Briefly, they are called Mormons because of their belief in the Book of Mormon, a late revelation, they claim, of religious and spiritual teaching, given to them by special revelation to Joseph Smith, founder of the faith. They accept this new revelation as spiritual guidance along with and in addition to the Bible, embracing both the New and the Old Testament. They accept the Bible in its entirety, but claim they have new and additional revelation and commandments in the Book of Mormon.

The Mormons believe, and teach, that it is a religious duty to go out and settle and reclaim by irrigation or otherwise, any good land

they can find anywhere. The expedition to the San Juan, as herein-
after related, was prompted by this belief and, as a further adjunct
to their faith, they believe it is a duty to their forefathers to take up
and carry on any work their fathers were unable to finish. In this connection, each family is supposed to keep a family geneology in recorded
form.

To get a full picture of the Webber settlement it is necessary to go
back to 1879, and to Cedar City, Utah, for the beginning of this story.
In the late summer of this year, in response to a command by Brigham
Young, President of the Mormon Church, families from every part of
Utah, gathered at Cedar City and formed an immigration caravan to
move into and colonize the San Juan river country. Their first des-
tination point was Bluff City as it was later called. A train of eighty
wagons, piled high with supplies and household effects, left Cedar City
and journeyed first to Escalante. This part of the journey was made
over established roads without loss of time and without mishap. From
this point on the route was through a country without road or trail,
wild, unsettled and almost unknown. The country, and route, had
been scouted and a road blazed. A route or road is blazed by a scouting party that goes over the ground in advance of the wagon train,
selects the best route for the road and marks the trees along the route
by cutting trees with an ax exposing the white wood so it can be easily
seen; also by cutting off limbs, leaving them hang, or by chopping
down trees, or setting up some object to go by where there are no trees.
The wagon train makes the road as it proceeds along the route.

From Escalante the wagon train followed down the high plateau
south of the Escalante River and in the late fall reached the north rim
of the Grand Canon. Here they camped for the winter and, after for-
tifying the camp against cold and storm, all the men set to work to
build a road down the canon wall, almost a mile high, to the Colorado
River below. This was the famous "Hole-in-the-Rock" descent. There
were many very great difficulties tot be overcome and they labored in-
cessantly all winter. The "Hole-in-the-Rock" was not in reality a hole.
At one place in the route down the precipitous incline the road had
to pass between two immense rock formations through a crevice 3 to
10 feet wide and almost a mile long, opening to the sky above. They
set to work to widen this crevice so the wagons could pass through
without the wagons being unloaded or taken apart. By drilling and
blasting, and by dint of weeks of hard work, the job was done. The
"Hole-in-the-Rock" was a reality. At another place on the route the
road had to pass over a very sloping rock formation for several hundred
yards. They overcame this difficulty by drilling holes every few feet
along the lower side of the proposed road, drove hard wood stakes in
the holes, placed poles above them to serve as retaining walls and
filling in above the poles with rock and dirt. This reduced the side

grade so that the wagons could be safely brought over. These were only two of a great many other difficulties that had to be overcome.

When suitable weather came in the spring of 1880 the road was finished, they broke camp and started moving the wagons down the precipitous incline. So well was the work done that not a wagon was lost, or even damaged, and only one team was lost. It became unmanageable, fell over a bluff and was killed.

For crossing the great river they improvised a large raft by lashing and nailing together large, dry cottonwood logs and flooring it somehow so that the teams and wagons could be ferried across one at a time. The whole caravan was in this way moved across and again without loss. At the place of crossing there was a broad, still place in the current with sandy shores on either side, so that oars could be used to propel the raft as they had no suitable rope. Also the cattle were forced to swim across which was done without difficulty or loss.

The wagon train was now moved upon a low mesa, but still in the bottom of the canon. Here it halted for a rest as there was good water, plenty of it and plenty of green grass. Everything was turned loose to graze and rest up while the women did all the washing that had accumulated. The men set out to find a way out and make a road. They found the way and without any further very great difficulty, but with much hard labor, after a few days, came out on top of the canon rim. Thereafter progress was much more rapid and after a few weeks they came to the present site of Bluff City.

Here they found, to their great dismay, that there was not nearly enough good land for all the people to have farms large enough for a home and make them a living. Some moved on up the San Juan river, about 20 miles, to the mouth of Montezuma Creek where there was a little more good land, that could be irrigated, but still not enough. In this party was Joseph Stanford Smith, married and with three children. After getting his family settled with a friend, Smith journeyed on horseback in 1880 up McElmo Canon, going in search of work, but he knew not where. Coming on up Montezuma valley he finally reached Mancos, then a small village, and here he was able to get employment for a few weeks. He worked on a flume on East Mancos for Sandy and Billy Rush; also he worked for a while for the East Mancos Placer Mining Co. In the early fall he started on his return journey home, and seeing James Ratliff cradling and binding some very good grain on his farm just south of Mancos, he stopped to inquire about work. Ratliff had no work for him, but told Smith he knew little about irrigation and that if he would come back in the spring he would give him some work. Smith did return in the spring with his family, living for a time in Ratliff's granary and renting part of his land. Smith found that there was an area of very good land further south that could be irrigated and was still open for homesteading, and was so pleased with the country that he at once located the homestead just

37

south of Ratliff's place, beginning just at the foot of the hill and just east of the road. His land embraced the cemetery location and adjacent land. He built a small log house on the land and just at the foot of the hill east of the road. Smith was, by this act, the first Mormon to locate in the Webber Community; also the first to locate in the county and his was the first Mormon home. He lost no time in getting word to his Mormon friends, down on the San Juan, about the opportunities here.

This information started a new immigration movement, from the Bluff City country. In 1882 Amos Hyram Fielding came up from Bluff and located what is now the Lewis Halls place. Here he raised a large family and Mrs. Vosco Burnham and Mrs. George Spencer, mother of the Spencer boys, still residents here, were of this family. Also came a Mr. Smith and sister, Emma Smith Willden and her husband, Charles Willden. These Willdens are of the same family of Willdens that are still residents here, but these people moved on, to Red Mesa, after a few years here. Other families coming stopped at the Joseph Smith home, camping in tents and covered wagons until they could locate land and build a cabin for a home.

Among these were LaFayette Guymon, father of Enoch Guymon and Mrs. John Willden, and some others. Also J. Harvey Dunton came at this time and one branch of the family settled well upon the West Dolores river, founding the settlement that bears the name. Also came at about this time the Barkers, Will Robinson, Sidney Hadden, Willard Butts and Adam and John Robb. Adam Robb was the father of Frank Robb who was the father of the Robb boys who are still residents of Webber. These settlements developed in Webber a considerable community, much land was cleared and improved and the Mormon people began to think about a church organization. At first there was not a kindly feeling between the Mormons and their "Gentile" neighbors, and relations were distant, but, after a while, with better understanding and closer social relations, the feeling wore off and all were citizens together. They worked together in school matters, in community and county affairs, and in social functions they mixed and mingled to the great pleasure of all.

The first Mormon Church was organized in 1884. At this time Apostle Joseph T. Smith, Erastus Snow and Elder Morgan visited the small settlement and affected an organization, at the Roberts home, September 9, Elder James Harvey Dunton was appointed Presiding Elder, Joseph Smith, First Counselor, and a Sunday School was organized a few days later with seven teachers and forty-one pupils. Some leaving the settlement, and there being no place to hold meetings, disunion arose and the organization broke up.

Hitherto nearly all the new settlers had come up from the settlements on the San Juan, but about this time a road was opened up from Salt Lake City through to Monticello, by way of Moab and new settlers for the Webber community began to come this route. In 1885, among those coming were Samuel S. Hammond and family, William and Hannah Halls and two children, Joseph and Harriett Wheeler, and others.

On July 5, 1885, Stake President Francis A. Hammond came up from Bluff City and reorganized the church, set apart Albert S. Farnsworth as Presiding Elder and the branch was started going again. All auxiliaries of the church were soon organized and doing active work.

At this time it was decided that the branch must have a church as the membership was increasing and there was no place to hold meetings. The new families arriving about this time were Ellis and John Perkins and families, James Smith, and in 1886, Mr. and Mrs. George Halls, came and took the old Webber place, Lucy Ann Wheeler and children, who was James Wheeler's first wife, also came. At this time Congress was legislating against plural marriages and some such marriages were breaking up; others continued plural relations on the sly. It might be noted here that there were two mothers and 27 children in the Joseph Wheeler family.

Immigration continued. Into the valley in 1886, came Soren Jensen, his son, Jens Jensen, came in 1888. Joseph Smith, father of Joseph Stanford Smith, and Mr. and Mrs. John Hammond and family came. John Willden and family and Hi and Jim McEwen came from Cedar City, and in 1887 came Watson Bell, the Peter Browns, who were the parents of Rudolph Brown and Mrs. Roy Dean, and the Charles Lambs with a large family, Ammon Lamb being one of the family. A little later came George Burnham, Richard Shilton, Clark Brinkerhoff, Hyrum Taylor, the Zufelts and the Slades.

Arriving a little late on the scene, but early enough to get in on the hard work of clearing the land and building a new home, came the N. A. Decker family from Bluff City in 1889. Mr. and Mrs. Decker were of the original emigrant party that came through the "Hole-in-the-Rock" in the winter of 1879-1880. They arrived in the Webber Community in 1889, took land and began at once the work of improving a new farm and making a new home on the new land. They have been at it through the years. In time the younger members of the family took over the task; then the second generation, and the work goes on. Good farmers, good citizenship, useful lives has characterized the Decker family, one generation after another, to this day.

To digress just a little, in 1883, the whole Mancos valley, Mormons, Gentiles and all, met at the old Log School house in Mancos for a big Thanksgiving feast—dinner, supper and an all night dance. Clark Brittain, LaFayette Guymon, and Will Willden furnished the violin music.

Sentiments for a church building grew and Elder Farnsworth called a meeting and suggested that a meeting house be built. The call was responded to with a will. Joseph S. Smith donated the land and work was started at once, although it was the busy season of summer. The location was just at the foot of the hill west of the John Freeman brick residence about one mile south and a little west of Mancos and the building was 26x35 feet. An effort was made to get the building finished by July 24, 1886, so the annual Pioneer Day celebration could be held there, and so great was the interest and enthusiasm that the building was finished, all but windows and doors, although the time allowed was but a few short days. Nevertheless they held their celebration in the new building. The house was completed before winter so that thereafter they had a comfortable building and plenty of room for any and all meetings.

This was the first church building erected by and for the Mormons in Montezuma County. Here all church affairs, dances and social meetings were held. The old building resounded to the noise and music of many a good time as the people made life in the new land merry and decidedly worth while. Some time after the first building was completed an addition of lumber was built on making the structure a T shape. This building also served as a school house for a time. The first teacher was Mary Ann Barker Dunton. The first regular school house, built at the districts expense, was out in Webber, proper, 1896. For a time two teachers were employed. A second school was later established further down the canon in 1900, but it lasted only a short time.

On March 21, 1887, the Mancos Branch was made a Ward and George Halls was set apart as the first Bishop. On February 4, 1894, a meeting was called to decide on building a new church. Bishop Halls donated the northeast corner of his place for the building. Later the building site was changed to a location northeast of the first site, on the suggestion of Brigham Young, Jr. A stone structure was first planned and some excavation made and some rock hauled, but this seemed such a large undertaking at this time it was decided to change to a frame building, two stories high. The old Webber Hall was the result. It was finished in 1901, and although erected only as a temporary building, it served 28 years, until 1930. It was church, dance hall ,a place for all public meetings, and it was the scene of many a dance, play, program, basketball and was popular with the people of Mancos as well as with Webber people. A phonograph and a new organ were installed in 1918.

In 1929 work was started on a new and elegant chapel in the south side of Mancos and it was finished in 1930 at a cost of $22,000 exclusive of several thousand dollars in donated labor, the local church men being very liberal in giving their work. The work moved rapidly and on September 14, 1930, an elegant and imposing new church building, finished in white brick, was dedicated by Apostle Melvin J. Ballard.

There are fewer Mormons now, but the spirit to do things is still there and the Mormons are a part of all local and civic life.

George Halls, as Bishop, proved to be a tower of strength among his people and a true leader. He was Bishop twenty-four years, two months and one day, and during this time the Mancos Ward was the strongest Ward in the San Juan Stake and for some time there was a membership of almost 600. In later years the membership dropped to near 200. The Ward became over populated for the amount of land and many families removed to Red Mesa and built new homes. Bishop Halls was an able and useful man in many other ways. He served on the local school board, was elected County Superintendent of Schools and served two terms as County Commissioner from the Mancos district.

This is the early history of the Webber settlement. It was pioneering in its true sense, and attended by all the hardships and privations of pioneer life. As in all frontier settlements, there was practically no money in circulation and no way to make money. For a time there was nothing of consequence to sell; no place to sell what little there was to sell. But these Mormon people were born to that kind of life and they knew how to meet and overcome difficult situations. Any kind of building that would furnish protection from the elements and a degree of comfort, was home to them. Lumber was plentiful and cheap, and when the sale of livestock and crops began to bring in some money, good ranch homes took the place of the cabins on nearly every farm. This kind of life is more fully discussed in another chapter. Suffice it to say they lived in crude homes at first, almost all the log cabin type.

At first there was no water in the dry season and water for all domestic purposes was hauled from the river. They melted snow in winter. But there was an abundance of good wood for fuel. After a home of some kind was provided, came the work of clearing the land and producing food grains, vegetables and fruits for a means of livelihood. They had to grow practically all their living at first. Needless to say no one suffered for food. There were cows for milk, hens to lay eggs, hogs and yearlings to make meat. The land was rich and productive and the crudest methods produced abundant yields.

Clearing this land was heavy, slow work and an endless task for several years. In fact it is, to some extent, still going on as more land for dry land crops and pastures is cleared above the ditches and up to the very foot of the mesas. With only a grubbing hoe, an ax and a team progress was slow, but their toil was rewarded by the bringing of many rich acres into abundant production. Vegetables came first, and potatoes, as they produced much food from a small area of land. Then the grains, hay in a profusion of growth, and fruits. Fruit trees and berry plants were set out and the locality soon became well known for its fine fruit and berries.

As the community was settled irrigation was developed and extended in 1882, out beyond the present Joe Eppich place and later was again enlarged and extended and was then called the Webber Ditch

41

No. 2. For supplemental water they built a small reservoir in the west side of Webber and a much larger one northeast of Mancos which were of great value in furnishing water for late irrigation. About 1883 and 1884 the high line Webber Ditch was built to furnish water for an additional large acreage. When the Halls came it was extended to cover the Fielding, the Halls ranch, and many others. It was, of course, enlarged from time to time to carry more water as it was needed.

Webber people, as a rule, were, and are, thrifty and enterprising, and their leaders encourage industry and sobriety, and lead the way. Every bit of usable land has been taken and most of it improved. General farming, livestock farming and dairying and poultry, with some fruit, about covers their farming activities, and any lack of abundance is made up for by frugal living. Soil conservation practices are taking hold and the time is approaching when, regardless of how much the farming operations take from the soil, there will always be more left in the soil than was there before. From now on any increase in production must come from better and more intensive farming and a better use of all the land. Grass farming is a late development and more grass and more and better livestock is coming into the farm picture. Future problems will be worked out as they come to them.

THOMPSON PARK

Because of its close proximity to Montezuma County and the very close social and business relations with Mancos and Montezuma County people, we will include in this writing the story of Thompson Park that is both important and intensely interesting.

The beautiful little mountain park known as Thompson Park, lies just over the low divide, eastward from the Mancos Valley, and in La Plata County. It is a gem in nature's setting. Surrounded by high mountains and high mesas, intensely fertile and wonderful in its production of wealth, no agricultural area in the southwest has produced more wealth per square mile than this favored spot.

Attracted by its fine stand of ponderosa pine the lumberman came first. Frank Stubbs and Frank Morgan both operated sawmills there about 1881. Attracted also by the luxuriant growth of grass and a fine stream of water in Cherry Creek came the cattleman close upon the heels of the lumberman. George Thompson, for whom the cove was named, came first, in 1879, with a large herd of cattle and occupied the territory; then Jim Caviness, with a large herd for those times. After two or three years Thompson moved on, but Caviness stayed, improved a fine ranch and made a small fortune in the cattle business.

Then came the men who wanted land for a home—the homesteader. First came Gus Olbert, then George Olbert, the father of Philip, John, Fred, Tom and George Olbert, Jr., and Margaret and Lena Olbert, and about the same time came George Sponsel, about 1881, and then came George Dick, who was postmaster and had a little stock of groceries and whiskey, on the main road. The postoffice was either Dix or Dicks, no one seems to know. It didn't last long. Caviness had the place later acquired by John Sponsel and further improved by him.

Other very early settlers were Mr. McCalep—second and third generation still there; Joe S. Chatz, H. R. Shar, John Singer, Fred Myers, Matt Davis, Henry Davis' father; Jim Me Lugin. Matt Davis was a worker in the timber and an expert with the broad ax which he delighted to wield. The story is told that he built log houses, insured them; then burned them down for the insurance money, until the insurance companies got wise and refused to insure his houses. Mr. Riffey, father of John and Elmer Riffey, came early. John Sponsel, brother to George Sponsel, already on the ground, in 1885, and a little later came Andrew Hauert; George Geisler came later and some others still later.

All the homesteaders that came to make their homes in the Park engaged at once in farming, as they could get the land cleared, acquiring a few cattle and raising many others. The park was surrounded by an abundance of summer range, especially in the higher mountains, and there was soon feed on the farms for winter. Oats was the main grain crop. Phenomenal yields were produced and scores of car loads were shipped to the sawmills and mining camps, and the straw made excellent feed, along with hay, for the cattle in winter. Enormous yields of hay were obtained. Soon many fine herds were on the farms, and they are there to this day, more and better than ever, as it has long been the rule to produce only the best.

Life was exceedingly hard for the early homesteaders who came without livestock or funds. The land was covered with sage brush, rabbit brush, oak brush and pine timber, large and small; or if not pine trees, pine stumps, left by the lumber man. Only an ax or a grubbing hoe was available for doing the work. Only by reason of the very fertile land and its high productivity were they able to survive. They had only to get the seed in the ground. It would bring a harvest. As soon as possible, after occupying the land, the settlers organized and built a ditch to bring water from the La Plata River which was used to a very beneficial purpose. Everybody in every family worked to win, and they won abundantly. Many fine homes and many fine farms attest to their success.

The old grain market is about gone with the coming of the car, the truck and the tractor, so it was necessary to turn a little more fully to raising cattle. More grass farming is being done and the pastoral scenes are an inspiration. Some grain is still grown.

For a long time only short summer schools were held, on account of the long, cold winters and the deep snows. Now road equipment keeps the roads clean of snow and full nine month terms are being held.

In early settlement days the Indians frequently visited the park; they loved biscuits, and if they were fed, made no trouble. The women knew what to do when the Indians came, but sometimes, when they came in numbers, it was quite some job to fill their rapacious stomachs.

The period from 1880 to 1885 was one of hardships for all. As an example of this pioneering we call to your attention one remarkable career, similar to many others, as an outstanding example. John Sponsel and his wife were both born and reared in Germany. John's brother, George Sponsel, was already in America, and after three or four years working in the mines, had settled in Thompson Park. No doubt he had written his brother of the rich lands in the Park free for the taking. Influenced partly by this story of a new land, and partly by a burning desire to get away from the German Army draft, and to escape from his prison country, he managed some way to get through the guarded lines with enough money to take passage for America. This he did. Likewise Mrs. Sponsel, then a young woman and his betrothed, made her escape from the country and the two came to America at the same time, coming direct to Durango. Mr. Sponsel at once located and homesteaded the place now owned and occupied by George Sponsel, Jr., and after improvising a shelter that would pass for a home, the two were married in Durango, and then occupied the pioneer cabin, just built, as a home and settled down to work out their future in a strange new land and among people strange to their way of life. Most of their neighbors were of German descent, however, like themselves.

George Sponsel, the brother, had been here long enough to make a little start and no doubt helped some as he could, but nevertheless the first years were a struggle. Without an animal of any kind, and with only his two hands, an ax and a grubbing hoe he began the herculean task of conquering a portion of this wilderness and reducing it to the dominion of man, and to raise a family, which became a large family. To protect his planted acres he cut and carried poles on his shoulder to fence the ground. He dug and cut and trimmed and burned—burning out the old stumps the lumber men had left and, at first worked up a sled bed with a shovel. His first team was a horse and an ox worked together to a borrowed plow or wagon. Sufficient water for irrigation had not yet come, but the land got enough water to yield a good increase. To produce a garden, however, it was necessary to carry water in a pail to water the cabbage plants one at a time, and also other plants. Thus, with labor incessant, they worked to win their success. Husband and wife, with meager subsistence, toiled through days without end, but blissful sleep brought rest to their tired limbs at night.

At length water for irrigation came to the newly cleared land, and bountiful yields resulted. He sold some of his labor to those of his neighbors who were a little better fixed, soon had some feed and grain to sell, a milk cow, a better team and some other cattle. They added to what they had in every way they could and took good care of it all. After a few years the meager beginning grew into bountiful crops and the few cows into a fine range herd. Shelter for the stock; then a better home came into existence. The family grew in numbers and life was much easier and much better.

After a while there was help from the children that had been born into the home, more land was acquired and all production rapidly expanded. Oats found a ready market at sawmills, in the mining camps and at the growing town of Durango. At first a thousand or two bushels were produced; then up to 10,000 bushels were produced in a single year and, finally 15,000 bushels were produced in a single crop year. There was oat straw and hay for a large herd of cattle, and all prospered. Thirteen children were born into the family and all grew into a valuable citizenship in a land where opportunity beckoned and life was free.

Here is a picture of Thompson Park and its industries in the year 1900. Hay and grain and livestock are the main products. There was 800 acres of grain, principally oats in this year. Harvested this year: Olbert Brothers 125 acres, Sponsel Brothers 300 acres, Joe Schatz 90 acres, H. R. Schar 60 acres, John Single 50 acres, Fred Myers 40 acres, and several smaller growers. Three years previous there was 47,000 bushels produced in the Park. In 1900 the total yield was near 80,000 bushels. Mancos is the nearest trading point—only 8 miles over the divide, road at this time on an 18 per cent grade. In this year they raised their school tax from 5 to 15 mills, built a new school house 24 by 40 feet dimension with an annex 10x20 and increased the school term to nine months. There is an abundance of summer range near and livestock is the most important industry. No less than 2,000 head of cattle are kept on the ranches. Winter feed was hay and oat straw. Jim Caviness has the most cattle and raises feed for 350 head. Olbert Bros. have 150 head, Schatz 150 head, Sponsel 135 head. Singer, Schar, Myers and others have from 35 to 50 head each.

Today the population has changed. All the old pioneers have passed from the scene of action, but other conditions are little changed. Not so much grain is grown, but there is more grass and livestock. Rail transportation is gone, but good roads, cars and trucks are making a better life than ever before and prosperity and contentment characterize the entire scene.

MANCOS PUBLIC SCHOOLS

The Mancos public school system had its beginning in the late summer and fall of 1878, Miss Lizzie Allen, a young girl of only 16 years, taught the first school, and the first few weeks of the school were taught in a small log building on the Root place, now the Clark place, just

45

south of the town of Mancos. A movement for a building for school purposes was started, a building was under way and before Miss Allen's term was out the building was completed and she taught the last few weeks of her term in the new building. This was a very good log structure and served for school purposes and for all public meetings and social events for nine years or until 1897. This was the first school to be taught in Montezuma Co., or the territory that was to become Montezuma Co. The log structure stood just across the alley north of the present Mancos Theater, but it was a lonely spot then. Not even the first house had been built in the town.

The next year Miss Anna Bradford was the teacher. The third school was a winter term and Miss Anna Field, daughter of Dr. Field, came down from the family home on the Joe Moore place and taught the school. A board floor had been put in the building by this time to take the place of the bare ground.

In 1887, the first frame building for school purposes was built on the east side of the present school grounds, the land just having been acquired by the school district. This building served as the only school building until 1897, and for a grade school building and a sloyd shop for some years after that. In 1951 it was moved to the west side of the school grounds and is presently in use as a public library building.

In 1897 the large frame building, recently torn down, embracing five large class rooms, was built, and about 1907 two additional class rooms were added to this building. In 1893 the school district had 247 children of school age and two country schools—the Webber school and the Wattles school—were going institutions. The Menefee district was formed July 2, 1897, and became School District No. 17.

In 1901 the school spirit was getting a little stronger and at the annual school meeting the people voted a school tax of 15 mills and an eight months term of school. In May, 1906, by a vote of the people one more teacher was added to the teaching force and an additional high school year was added bringing the high school up to and including the eleventh grade.

Another high school year was added in 1907 and on May 12, 1908, the school turned out its first graduating class—the first for the school and the first in the county. The personnel of the first class was Jeanie Weston, Belle Roberts, Ruth Wattles, Eva Rutherford, Sadie Todd and James Rickner. Misses Emilie Longenbaugh, class of 1909, and Todd were from Cortez and all the girls in this class became teachers in the county and Miss Wattles, later, finished her education at Fort Collins A. & M. College and was then employed as a professor in the English department of the College until she retired in 1952. The Mancos High School was fully accredited in this year. In addition to the high school work a course was offered in stenography, typewriting, bookkeeping, penmanship, music and domestic science.

In 1909, $2,500 in bonds was voted to build a concrete school building in the Wattles community. In 1910 sports were organized in the Mancos schools—basketball, baseball, track work and field sports. Mancos was the first to organize athletics in the school, but Cortez and Dolores soon followed and interesting and spirited competition in sports sprang up between the three towns in a few years.

In 1909 the people voted bonds in the sum of $10,000 to erect a high school building. The bonds sold at once, contracts were let and in early fall a new high school building was completed and occupied. The new building was of stone and 36 by 82 feet dimensions, with full basement and two stories above ground. An additional $5,000 in bonds was voted to finish the building, install a heating plant and buy furnishings.

In 1912, fire broke out in the roof of the high school building and burned off the roof down to the second floor. The Baptist Church was rented for school use, school went right on and in a few weeks the upper story and roof on the building had been rebuilt and no school time was lost.

At the opening of the term in 1915 the Wattles and the Webber schools were closed and all the pupils transported by bus to the town schools. These were the first school buses to come into use in the county. In three or four years all the country schools in the district were closed and the pupils brought to the town school. In recent years most of the rural school districts have been disorganized and the pupils transported to the town schools of the county.

In May, 1916, the Mancos High School classed near the top of the accredited list in high standards, merit and high standing.

In April, 1919, the Mancos school was designated to have the Smith-Hughes agricultural course in the county. H. M. Griffith of Fort Collins was employed to teach the course.

In 1922 the growth in school population required more school room, so bonds were voted and an addition, 42x82 feet, was built onto the high school providing a large auditorium, also used for basketball, entertainments, public events and school dances, and five more class rooms.

The school population continued to increase and by 1951 the need for more class rooms for grade pupils became so great that a new grade school building was erected at a cost of $120,000. It provides 8 class rooms, a principal's room, a music room and a large modern cafeteria to serve school lunches around two hundred at a time.

Then the high school building became overcrowded and facilities inadequate, and in 1956 the high school building was remodeled to provide several additional class rooms and a large auditorium and basketball court was built and connected with a corridor arrangement, at a total cost of above $140,000.

An oil surfaced tennis court was built by private donations, and a large area of ground at the rear of the buildings was leveled off and

47

seeded to grass for baseball, football and field sports, and the whole lit brilliantly by electric lights so the field can be used night or day. It seems now that all school requirements have been taken care of for a while.

The Menefee school disorganized in 1947 and the pupils are being transported to the Mancos Schools. Three medium sized buses and two 50 passenger buses are now required to bring in all the rural pupils.

George Bauer, pioneer merchant and banker. Established the first merchandise business in Mancos, 1881, and therefore the first in Montezuma County. See text for life story.

Mrs. John Sponsel.

John Sponsel. See story of Thompson Park.

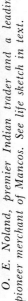

Callie (Mitchell) Noland (Mrs. O. E. Noland)

O. E. Noland, premier Indian trader and a leading pioneer merchant of Mancos. See life sketch in text.

Andy Menefee and "Aunt Sarah," pioneers of the first rank. Mancos Valley, 1877. See text for details.

*Bishop George Halls, first bishop of the Webber Ward,
L.D.S. Church. He served continuously for twenty-four
years. See Chapter on Webber Community.*

Thomas Rickner, Mancos Valley pioneer.

Mrs. Thomas Rickner, Mancos Valley pioneer.

*"Bill" Menefee, 80 years old, and fourth son of Andrew and Sarah Mene-
fee, and the first white boy to be born in the Mancos Valley and, therefore,
the first born in Montezuma County. Still rides almost every day after cattle.
Standing in door of Menefee cabin.*

The original Menefee homestead built in 1879 or 1880, and still being used. Charles and Louis Menefee were born in this building. It stands right near the place where the old Dick Giles cabin stood—the first habitation built by the white man in the Mancos Valley and in Montezuma Co. It was built sometime in 1875.

CHAPTER IV

EARLY SETTLEMENT OF THE DOLORES RIVER VALLEY

Almost simultaneous with the early settlement of the Mancos Valley came the settlement of the Dolores River valley. It was not possible that a land so inviting, so filled with promise, could remain unclaimed for long. Here was wealth for the taking. Nature had been lavish in bestowing her bounties, and advanced scouting parties were not slow in recognizing these facts and conditions; glowing reports were made and the homeseeker and the stockman came in to possess the land and its riches.

Beginning about 1877 the homeseeker took, in a few years, all the land along the Dolores river. He came with a small herd of cattle or began at once to build one. Also came the men with the big herds, one to five thousand in a herd. Cattle, and later sheep, rapidly became the leading industry of the new country and the main property asset. They were the foundation and life of business, but overgrazing and unwise use of the grass and browsing resources, soon created problems. But overgrazing went on. There was still profit in it. They were, for several years, still able to turn these natural resources into great personal wealth until grazing and browsing, as an asset, were, in a large measure, destroyed.

About 1910, and the few years following, it began to look to the herd and flock owners that the day of the cattle and sheep industry was coming to an end, and cattlemen and sheepmen, both at Mancos and Dolores, began to ask: After cattle and sheep, what? It was evident that a change had come, and was coming, but the cattlemen and the sheepmen didn't have the answer. First, grazing in the Montezuma valley was gone. Grazing on the Indian reservation was being held for the Indians who were building up flocks and herds of their own. The settlers were coming in and homesteading all that area in the northwest part of the county, known as the dry farming country, that had, until now, been a source of such abundant feed, and Utah people were stocking the area beyond the state line and using it the year around. It did look for a time that it was the end of cattle and sheep on the open range, and, in a measure, it was.

49

But it was only the end, or partial end, of winter grazing. There is still, even now, some winter grazing available—more for sheep than for cattle—as they are able to utilize more browsing, but the answer to winter feed for the herds is feeding on the ranches in winter. Winter feeding produces better results in many ways than the old way of starving through the winter, as they frequently did, on the winter range. There are more small herds and more people are being bene-fitted; better quality cattle and sheep are being produced; larger calf and lamb crops are being saved and grown out, and the natural ferti-lizers produced are helping to keep up or restore the depleted fertility of the soil. Farming is rapidly becoming livestock farming, which is the only real farming. The tax roll shows there are more and better range sheep and cattle, and more dairy cattle, in the county than ever before, and the land is producing more new wealth.

The first settlers in the Dolores River Valley came in 1877. There were William Quick and George, William and Richard May. They took the land that had just been taken and abandoned by F. H. Mor-gan, W. T. Wattles and Ben Ford of the Mancos valley. Quick and the Mays were cattlemen. In 1878 came Denby, Hess, Crumley, Georgetta Brothers and a Mr. Burch in 1880. There were others along the river by 1880 and the need of a postoffice began to be felt, so a postoffice, called Dolores, was established at the Crumley ranch in this year, some two miles above the present town of Dolores. One record says that Mr. Crumley was the first postmaster; another says it was Billy May. The first election in the valley was held at the Crumley place in 1880 and O. D. Pyle was elected Justice of the Peace, an office he held for 25 years, or until he died. All these years, though not a man of wealth, Mr. Pyle was a leader and a prominent influence in community affairs, first at Big Bend, then at the town of Dolores.

About this time the local population began to center around Big Bend. A store was opened here and apparently the William Darrow business was the first. George Burnett was the first minister. It is re-ported that he traded horses during the week and preached on Sunday. Several families had settled lower down on the Dolores river at a place called Lone Dome, about 1882, and among them were J. T. Tremble, George P. Moore, A. W. Dillon and Matt Dickerson. Moore was famous for his quick trips to Durango by mule team to get supplies. Jim Tremble was a famous shot and killed enough coyotes and hawks to buy a wagon, the state paying a bounty on these. A. W. Dillon moved from Lone Dome to Big Bend. Tremble became a well known and successful cattleman. Kuhlman Brothers and Cal House located on land in 1879 and Grandpa Charles Johnson, better known as "Race Horse" Johnson came over from Pine River in 1881 bringing two thou-sand head of cattle and a bunch of race horses, some of them quite famous. The famous horse, Jim Douglas, was one of these. This horse was one of the fastest in the entire west and won many great races.

50

Johnson took land in the open valley, where the McPhee sawmill stood. He wintered in a small cabin, but the following year he built a house. This house was built large and strong, of adobe brick, according to the report of a contemporary, and out in the wide valley so that the approach of Indians could be seen. The building became a kind of strong hold and once, when rumors of Indian raids were current, the people gathered at the building for protection. No Indians appeared so they all went back home.

Old Charley Johnson had a long list of lineal descendants, the fourth generation reaching down into our own times, and his cattle operation spread far and wide. In later years the race horse business was allowed to become of much less importance as there seemed to be no one with interest, or ability, enough to keep it going. The cattle dwindled later to a much smaller herd, with the passing of the winter range. Finally the old adobe house went down to ruin, and Sam Johnson built a large, two story, frame building across west of the road, near the school house.

The Johnson land holdings, large at first, has been divided into parts and several small ranches are now comprised in the original holdings.

In the Johnson family were two boys—Charley and Sam. Charley Johnson shot and killed himself accidentally while practicing shooting with a revolver, and only Sam Johnson was left to carry on the family tradition and name. There were five daughters in the family, Mrs. Al Nunn being one of them.

W. H. Brumley came in 1882 and John Brumley a year later. They first settled on Brumley Drow, in Montezuma Valley and then acquired land just below Big Bend, on the river. These are the elder Brumleys that came in to manage the large L. C. herd of cattle belonging to their sister, Mrs. Lacy. A Mr. McQuaig came to Big Bend and started a blacksmith shop.

There is a report to the effect that, in the fall of 1882, Ben Quick was thrown from his horse and his hand was badly injured. Blood poison set in, and Dr. Field was summoned from Mancos, but it was too late. Quick was the first person to be buried in the old Dolores Cemetery.

It seem that tragic things must come to pass in every pioneer community and they came many times in the history of Montezuma County. One of the first was the killing of Isaac Denby, a settler on the Dolores, by Jasper Bean, another settler. Denby was the father of Emma Denby, the first white child born in the Dolores river valley.

About this time, in 1881 or 1882, a road was laid out, and partly built, from Big Bend to Rico. It was hardly a road, according to reports on it. It followed the river and some work was done. It is said to have crossed the Dolores fifty-six times in a distance of less than fifty miles. In 1889 some rich strikes of gold and silver were made at

51

Rico and some sensational discoveries were reported, there was great excitement and many people came to the new mining camp. It is recorded that potatoes and vegetables were worth five cents a pound in the new mining camp, grain was five to seven cents a pound, hay was $50 a ton and there was a good market for beef. This gave impetus to the road building movement, for the people in the new community sure did need a little of that mining camp money in circulation in their settlements.

There were many people along the Dolores by 1883 and the record snows of 1883 and 1884 struck with compelling force in all the new settlements, as well as in the entire San Juan Basin, and it struck with particular severity along the Dolores. The passes were closed for three months and train service into Durango was halted for weeks. Travel was confined to going on snow shoes. Bacon, flour, sugar, tea, coffee, and most other staples gave out. Even salt was scarce. A little flour could be had at Rush grist mill at Mancos, but the quality was poor. Beef was poor and scarce; venison likewise poor and hardly fit to eat. A. W. Dillon made a heroic effort to get a few supplies by going all the way to Durango and back on skis. He returned with only a little flour and a small amount of tobacco. The tobacco was a balm to many of the old fellows. Their being out of food was not an important matter, but when they got out of tobacco anything might happen.

At this time two interesting episodes took place. The Lewis Simons were celebrating their Silver wedding anniversary, a band of Indians came as self-invited guests and devoured all the good food that had been prepared for the feast. Another incident of the silver wedding celebration was that it was attended by Mr. and Mrs. D. H. Saylor, well known in the county's history, and while they were away from home the Indians ransacked their house and took everything they wanted, including all their food. They, of course, spent the night with the Simons. This was the first silver wedding anniversary to be celebrated in Montezuma Valley.

Some time prior to this incident, on July 11, 1881, to be exact, Mr. and Mrs. Matt Hammond were married at Parrott City and came to the Dolores valley at once, and were escorted on the trip by a detachment of the State Guard, as a safety precaution against Indian attacks. Mrs. Hammond was one of the five Simon girls. She relates in an article, that at this time, there were a great many men in the Dolores River Valley and eleven women. It might be stated here that the marriage of Mr. and Mrs. Fred Taylor was the first wedding to take place in Montezuma County after it was formed in 1889, and that Mrs. Taylor was also a daughter of Mr. and Mrs. Simon.

The first land taken in Montezuma Valley was homesteaded just prior to this time by John Brewer, who came over from the Mancos valley; William Wooley and Lewis Simon, Wooley Draw derived its name from Mr. Wooley and Simon Draw from Mr. Simon. Brewer

52

tried to find artesian water by digging for it and when he failed he gave up his homestead and moved away. Lewis Simon and Wm. Wooley, and his son, Douglas Wooley, remained and continued to live on their homesteads as long as they lived.

In the winter of 1883-84, the winter of deep snows, J. P. Akin was en route to the Dolores valley, and was stranded by the storms for 21 days on Cumbres Pass. He reached the Dolores country in the spring and afterward became a well known and leading citizen, in business for years.

The first settlement on the Dolores river that began to assume the importance of a town was at Big Bend. It was so named because of its location on the broad turn in the course of the Dolores river about three miles west of the present town of Dolores and less than a mile west and a little north of the new steel bridge. As one ascends the hill on the Cortez road, just after crossing the big canal, a good view can be had of the big bend and the exact location of the community which was located on the hillside west of the river.

Probably William Darrow had the first store and business. Wm. Ordway must have come down from Parrott City about the same time and started a business, and Mr. and Mrs. George W. Morton came from Huerfano County about this time with household goods and a small stock of merchandise in their wagon. They bought 40 acres of land from Billy May and put up a building for a store and a home, put in their little stock of merchandise and opened for business. Soon thereafter the postoffice was moved from the Crumley ranch and located in the Morton store with Mr. Morton as postmaster. A Mr. Craig had a blacksmith shop and a small building served as a hotel and the start of a livery business was made. The town was Big Bend and was known by that name far and near, but the name of the post-office was always Dolores.

After the town had made a start, and promised to have a future, Harris Brothers, Andrew and John, in 1886, put up a building and moved their stock of merchandise over from Mitchell Springs. They had quite a stock and added considerably to the business importance of the town. The Harrises came first to Mancos, Andy Menefee freighting their stock of goods over from Durango, and set up a business on North Main Street, opposite the Bauer store; but the Bauer competition proved too strong so they moved to Mitchell Springs, a mile or so south of the present town of Cortez, about 1884, Sol and Bill Exon hauled their stock of merchandise from Mancos to the new location. This was the first store at Mitchell Springs, but soon there was a saloon and some time later the Mitchells put in a store and a post-office was established they called Toltec. Porter Mitchell seems to have been in charge of the store and must have had the postoffice. We have been unable to get authentic information on this point.

There were many hundred of cattle being grazed in this territory

53

and two strong springs furnished a supply of good water for man and beast, and made Mitchell Springs, or Toltec, a natural focal point for the cattlemen. Harrises were here only two years or so when they moved to Big Bend. The future looked bright for Big Bend just at this time. No one could of course invisage the coming of the railroad and the future town of Dolores. The Harrises increased their stock of merchandise and started a private bank in 1886. About this time George Bauer and C. J. Scharnhorst came over from Mancos and bought the store of Mr. Darrow and Scharnhorst took charge of the business. Big Bend now began to take on the aspects of a town.

Many settlers came to the Dolores River Valley in 1882, and shortly after, and all the land along the river was taken. Among those coming in 1882 was W. H. Brumley, J. T. Tremble, J. P. Moore, A. W. Dillon from Lone Dome, and O. D. Pyle came about this time and worked first at the carpenters' trade.

By 1883 there were a number of children of school age and plans were made for a school. When it was decided definitely the people went to work with a will and built a log school house. A school district was organized in 1883 and William Brumley was elected president of the board, John Brumley, treasurer and O. D. Pyle, secretary. As the school house was not quite finished school was started in the Bill Brumley dugout. The log school building was soon finished and, aside from being a school building, it became a community asset from the start and served for all public meetings and social affairs—feasts, dances and local events. Shortly after the building was finished Anton Georgetta was married, the first wedding in the Dolores River Valley, and the occasion was celebrated with a big feast, a dance and a general good time.

Miss Lula Swenk taught the first school and both the seats and the desks for this school were dry goods boxes. About this time Emma Denby was born. She was the first white child to be born in the Dolores River Valley.

Some other new citizens coming at this time were Luna Morrison's parents, Bob Dunham, down at Lone Dome; Matt Hammond and bride from Parrott City; also Jim Tremble and two sons, John and Tobie. Tobie was soon after killed in a gun battle. Mike O'Donnel, a brother to Pat O'Donnel also came at this time or a little later, and he was also killed in a shooting affray. Also coming were A. Waldron, a Mr. Formby, an Englishman; Cal House, Mr. Coleman and Dr. Landon, the first doctor in the settlement, and William Roessler, who came over from Mancos for a while and carried the mail from Mancos to Dolores postoffice. It appears that J. J. Wade of Mancos was the first mail carrier on this route. Jerald Neal and Zene Robinson had come in 1879 and Tom Thornell came over from Mancos in 1882.

It was a new people in a new land and the people were all poor in purse to start with and during the first winters trapping became a local industry and added considerably to the community income. Beaver, mink and muskrats were plentiful, some other fur-bearers were shot or trapped, and the furs brought good prices.

Among the best known and most influential citizens of Big Bend were Mr. and Mrs. George W. Morton. Mrs. Morton wrote interestingly of their trip from Huerfano County over the mountains in 1882. They came by team and wagon bringing household goods and a small amount of merchandise with which to start a store. The road was long and rough and very difficult, but they had heard that, beyond the mountains was a goodly land—a good cattle country well watered; good agricultural land, lots of timber and an abundance of good grass. It was all this, they found, so they settled down to make their home. Mr. Morton was a prominent and a public spirited citizen, the old "Morton Flume," on Canal No. 2, which was near by, was named for him and he was the first county judge for Montezuma County.

Many others, no doubt, had heard that the Dolores Country was good cattle country for, in 1879 and thereafter, many large herds of cattle came into the country. We have mentioned the elder Charley Johnson coming with 2,000 head of cattle and a herd of horses, most of them highly bred racing stock. A little previous, about 1878 apparently, Rudy Hudson came with a large herd of cattle and went on west to the Dove Creek and the Blue Mountain country. This movement was designed, in part, to protect the settlement on the west from Indian raids while those in the Dolores vicinity protected from the east.

In 1879 came the large LC herd of 5,000 cattle in charge of Henry Goodman, the cattle belonging to a Mrs. Lacy of New Mexico. This herd was located, first, in Montezuma Valley and spread out westward over a large territory. Mr. Lacy was killed at Fort Lewis in the fall of 1881 and in 1882 Jim Brumley came to take charge of the L.C. herd and John Brumley came in 1883, to help with the herd, Mrs. Lacy, the owner of the cattle, being their sister.

Hunt Quick came in with a large herd about 1880; then the King Brothers with another large herd. Also came, about this time the large G.P. herd in charge of George Phelps. The Kings and Quick located on the Dolores river and ranged north and eastward, and George Phelps, with the GP herd located on Lost Canon and ranged eastward on Hay Camp Mesa.

In 1886 a late comer was Irving McGrew with a large herd of cattle from Texas and Chireau, Mexico, bearing the brand "Flying Diamond," a diamond shaped figure with a slightly curved bar extending from each end of the diamond. He located on Disappointment and in the Lone Cone area. Parties familiar with these herds and the times, say the numbers in these herds, as given above, were considerably exaggerated and that none of the herds were so large as the numbers given. We have taken the figures from the written statements of other parties whom we did not know.

There were some other herds brought in upon which the writer has failed to get a record, but these were the foundation herds of a vast and prosperous cattle industry. The larger herds were soon broken down into smaller herds or were dispersed altogether. Many smaller herds, locally owned, soon appeared on the scene. Several men, who at first were only riders, were later successful and prominent stockmen. Bob Dunham, Jim Tremble, Luna Morrison, W. W. Dunlap, and several others, were among these. Nearly every ranch along the river had either a herd of cattle or a flock of sheep, and still has. New wealth by livestock production goes on.

Now for a general picture of the early situation. Cattle were everywhere, thousands of head worth hundreds of thousands of dollars. There was no law that could protect life or property. Livestock owners must combine for strength and protection. In the absence of punishment by law they must take the law into their own hands to meet out justice that was swift and sure. Ruthlessness and brigandage must be met by merciless retribution. This was the only way to make rights to property respected and life secure. This state of affairs led to many tragic incidents and it was a long time before law and order came in to take the place of violence.

The method was effective. The criminal that had no fear of the law had a deathly fear of the mob. Swinging bodies were often left hanging for a while as a warning to the evil minded that crime was never a safe practice and it didn't pay.

Every rider carried a gun, usually a revolver or a "six shooter" as it was most often called. It was never a five shooter or a pistol, and almost always it was a Colt, and nearly everyone wanted a .45. In addition to a revolver many carried a repeating rifle of the Winchester type, which was carried in a scabbard under the left stirrup leather. The revolver was also carried in a holster attached to a belt filled with loaded cartridges. This made quite a lot of weight, but it didn't matter, the horse had to carry it. The average rider never walked.

Nearly every rider was skilled in the use of these fire arms. They practiced shooting all their purse would allow, and the aim was to be quick on the draw. Often just how quick a man was, was the difference between life and death.

The old Colt revolver is reputed to be the gun that brought law and order to the West. It also brought many a tragic and unnecessary death, and bitter sorrow to many, many homes.

Riders in the region of the Colorado-Utah border had reason to go armed and be constantly on their guard. This area seemed to have been the hot trail of outlaws and lawless gangs fleeing from some hot spot in the north to some place of safety or refuge further south, or the other way around. When ever an individual or gang of this char-

56

acter was encountered, they were usually shunned or were let severely alone. When an outlaw person or gang was met it was always safest not to recognize them as such, and invite them to camp, to eat if it was near meal time. These fellows, even when eating, never got out of reach of their gun. Those were truly troublesome times, and the outlaw or outlaws had more trouble than any one.

During 1880 and 1881 all the homestead land along the Dolores River Valley was taken by the settlers and almost every settler had a herd of cattle or soon had a small herd. Into the valley above the present town of Dolores came Jack Lynton and son, John Lynton, and located two miles above town. They were cattlemen from the start. Ross Thompson and E. L. Wilbur took land further up stream and a Mr. Boose had a homestead and a few cattle. Dave Georgetta owned the land that is now the site of the Dolores Fish Rearing Unit, and Steve Tom had a place on the river above. Other homesteaders were Jim Longwell, "Dad" Birch, a Mr. Hammond and Mr. Robinson and his well known son, Jesse Robinson, who had land at the mouth of Bear Creek. Gib Coon and the Morarities had land in the upper valley; also a Mr. Goules. The Sullivan ranch was at the mouth of Taylor Creek. There are doubtless many others lost to the memory of the old timer, there are so few left to know or tell the tale, and the thin thread of memory that reaches back into the distant past gives only a dim view of he picture that "hangs on memory's wall."

The cattle that were brought in early were not the best—long legs and long horns prevailed—but considerable good cattle, for the time, were brought in. Although they were many in number, they did not represent great fortune. An average good cow with a calf by her side, was worth from $7 to $8 and, at first, it was difficult to find sale for cattle, ready for the market, at any price. After the railroad came to Durango in 1881, all cattle going to the general market were driven to Durango and shipped from that point. This gave a big impetus to the cattle and sheep industry of the entire county. Cattle and sheep began to bring in lots of money which gave stimulus to progress and growth to business.

But the country was ideal for cattle and sheep raising and it cost little to produce them. Small herds were kept on the ranches in winter and given some shelter and feed, but the larger herds were fed nothing. They ranged on a thousand hills and in many small valleys on the upper Dolores and tributaries, during summer and were driven, or drifted, to the lower range on the Colorado-Utah border and beyond for winter grazing, and it was all without cost or price. Grass was everywhere. It grew up to the saddle stirrup and waved and billowed in the passing breeze. Water was somewhat of a problem on the winter range, but they made the best use of the available watering places, and when the snow came the cattle were spread out to ungrazed areas and made to depend on snow for their water, and thus all available range was used. They usually wintered well, until dry years and overgrazing came, and were ready to grow and put on flesh when new grass came in the spring. All the native grasses were wonderful feed and produced a beef animal that brought top prices on all the markets.

And the cattlemen made money. The town of Dolores was their home town and the many fine homes attest to the wealth that was poured into them. And the J. J. Harris & Co. bank was bulging with money. At one time, and for quite some time, it carried the highest per capita deposits of any bank in the United States, and that is some distinction. Other banks of the county made extra good showings during these halcyon days of the cattle and sheep industry.

In the early settlement days the Indians were a constant menace. Although their raids were not many and their atrocities few, there was constant fear, especially on the part of the women and children. To forestall this menace, in 1885, a rather strong fortress was built at the head of Narraguinep Canon. Many of the logs were as large as two feet through and were rolled into place in the walls on skids with the help of a good team. The builders of the fort were Jud Pierce, George Robinson, Ben Robinson, Bert Robinson, John and Sant Bowen, R. B. Dunham, James Moore, John Tremble and Sam Todd all names familiar to the early settlers in the county. A small stream of water was diverted through the fort for use in case of siege. John Spalding and family were installed as caretakers. There is no record that the fort was ever used. Scant remnants of some of the big logs is the only evidence that the fort ever stood there.

Most of the settlers in the Dolores country came in by way of Mancos, over the Mancos Hill. Some came over the Bear Creek road by way of the Animas Valley and a few came down from the Rico mining camp. All the big herds of cattle came in from Texas and New Mexico by way of the southern gateway of Montezuma Valley but some small herds were brought in from Pueblo and Rio Grande Co., in San Luis Valley, by way of Durango and Mancos. On the farms, or ranches as they were called, some grain was produced, but the farming effort was directed mostly tot raising hay for the small herds and flocks. The many big barns along the Dolores river is evidence that the ranchers thought that both the feed and the livestock needed some protection during the long stormy winters with their cold and their snow.

Bob Dunham is one of the settlers that came in by way of Rico, in 1881. He located first on Disappointment Creek. A little later he acquired by purchase a small ranch on the Dolores river, ten miles below Rico, and started to raise horses. Then he sold his horses and traded for a ranch on the river at Lone Dome and started in the cattle business with two milk cows. With this modest start Mr. Dunham built up one of the best herds in the Dolores area and was a leading cattleman for many years. In later years he moved to the town of

Dolores, got into politics and was elected to serve two terms as representative in the State Assembly from this district.

At Lone Dome he had for neighbors George Moore who had a very good herd of cattle well bred; Don Williams, who raised grain, and one year had 40 acres of fine wheat and when it was just ready to harvest the Indians set fire to it and burned the entire field. Then there was Jim Tremble, who first worked for Jud Purse, on Plateau Creek, but later became a successful cattleman at Lone Dome. Then there was William, George and Richard May, of 1877, all successful with cattle and horses. William Ormiston was an early settler in these parts. He was the father of W. C. Ormiston long a resident of the Mancos Valley. "Uncle Bob" Dunham is still among his old friends at Dolores, his active career long since ended. Uncle Bob is 93 years old.

Luna Morrison was another well known and successful cattleman that got into politics and served two terms as state senator, and Jim Belmear was also well and favorably known, and successful in the cattle business.

William Brumley came in 1882 to take charge of Mrs. Lacy's cattle, she being his sister, and John Brumley came in 1883. They established headquarters first in Brumley Draw, in Montezuma Valley, just northwest of Lewis, this being a convenient point from which to manage the large herd. They also acquired land below Big Bend on the river, and this, later, became headquarters for their cattle operations.

This sketch about covers the early settlement of the area about Dolores up to the coming of the railroad and the start of Dolores town. The narrative is resumed at this point under the heading "Dolores Chronology."

SETTLEMENT OF DOLORES

We have traced some of the early settlement in the Dolores river valley and the establishing of the small community at Big Bend. Big Bend continued to be the business and population center in the area until the building of the Denver & Rio Grande Southern railroad in 1891.

The Town of Dolores had its beginning with the coming of the railroad. As soon as it was apparent that the road would be built John and Andrew Harris, associated with Judge Adair Wilson, acquired the Sherman Phelps homestead and laid out the Dolores townsite. Since Adair Wilson was attorney for the railroad and had shares of stock in the company, there was no opposition to the location of the townsite and no other site was proposed. As soon as the townsite was laid out Harris Brothers began the erection of a large brick building preparatory to moving their mercantile business up from Big Bend. This building is the building on the corner now occupied by the Taylor Hardware Co. The building next to it on the west was erected later and the Harrises occupied both buildings with a large stock of general merchandise for a number of years.

With the start of the new town William Ordway erected a building and moved his stock of merchandise up from Big Bend and brought the postoffice along with it. The Morton business at Big Bend was apparently discontinued and the Mortons moved over into Montezuma Valley as we hear of them later in the vicinity of Totten Lake. They later moved to California. All other business at Big Bend was discontinued or moved to the new town and Big Bend, as a town, was no more.

Dolores grew slowly at first all the early settlers were living on their homesteads and the ranchmen had established headquarters at convenient places so there was no one to move into the new town except the businessmen themselves. Harris brothers put in a large stock of merchandise for so small a place and handled nearly all the business and conducted a small private banking business along with their other business. It was kind of a "one man's town."

But it was not quite that. Sil and Fred Kramer had a blacksmith shop, Wm. Brumley had put in a saloon, a livery barn was built on the ground where Koenig Brothers filling station now stands with Reece Ray in charge. William Exon opened a meat market south of the railroad track and Henry Cadwell bought hides and pelts. Exon soon moved to a new site where Hollywood Bar now occupies, and bid for more business by adding a line of groceries. Martin Rush joined the enterprise and the business became Exon and Rush. They bought lots and later erected the stone block which was, for years, occupied by the Exon Mercantile Co., and the grocery line is still going under Mr. Exon's management after 60 years, in 1956. The Southern Hotel was erected on the corner of 5th and Main Street.

In 1896 Fred Holt started a little paper he called the Dolores Herald, a weekly paper. It suspended, after a few months, and in 1897 R. B. Hawkins established the Silver Star. For nine years the railroad had only an old flat car boxed in and fixed up for use as a railway station and the telegraph office was in the Harris store with John Harris as telegraph operator.

The first school in the town of Dolores was opened in 1895 in a rather large two-room frame building that stood on the ground where the new Harris Bank building now occupies. The teachers were Miss Rosa Sleeth, in charge of the lower grades, and W. C. Armiston, later a well known teacher in the county, in charge of the higher grades. One of the pupils of this school was William Exon, then 22 years of age. Pupils came in to the school from a distance of several miles, and it was quite a large school for the first in the community. This building was used for school purposes and all public meetings and social occasions for several years, or until the first high school was built in

1917. It was enlarged by building on an upper story and adding two or three rooms to the ground floor.

O. D. Pyle moved up from Big Bend, worked as a builder and contractor, and later built and owned the opera house and conducted an undertaking business, and served for 25 years as justice of the peace. Mrs. Pyle was talented in instrumental music, had a piano class for years and trained many accomplished musicians.

William James Exon came to Dolores in 1895 and went into business in 1896, and rounded out his 60th year in business in 1956. He was born in Wabaunsee County, Kansas, May 17, 1873. He was named for the noted outlaw, Jesse James, and he relates that his mother cooked many a meal for Jesse James over the open fire, in the fireplace, during his banditry years. He came to Mancos with his parents and family in 1882, arriving June 30. There were four girls and four boys in the family and of these only Bill, and George Exon of Mancos, survive.

John and Andrew Harris made for themselves a highly successful business career and were for many years strong factors for progress in the development of the community. John Harris served ably for two terms in the State Senate and filled many public functions in a private way. Andy Harris was more of a retiring disposition and was not well known apart from his business dealings.

As we have noted above the first frame school building served school and general purposes until the old high school building was erected in 1917. This new building was a very good building for the time and the standard of requirements was fixed to meet all specifications of the State Board and in 1919 the high school, as established, was made a fully accredited high school. The first graduation exercises were held at the close of school, 1919, Miss Alice Lynton, youngest daughter of Mr. and Mrs. Jack Lynton, was the first graduate and the only member of the first class.

Some other well known graduate of subsequent years were Ronald Mair, Ward C. Robinson, Newell Musgrave, Erwen Webb, Lois Rash, Mrs. Millard Lynton, George Reed of California; Mrs. Mildred Denby, local resident.

The Lynton homestead was two miles up the river from Dolores, at the mouth of Bean Canon. There was no town of Dolores then and the nearest school was at the town of Big Bend, five miles distant. Here the elder Lynton children went to school going on horseback. The Lynton's were a typical case of the many other families along the river and indicates the lengths to which many parents had to go in order to educate their children.

Up Bean Canon, from the Lynton ranch, was the ranch of Jasper Bean. We met Mr. Bean before on Pine River when he set a broken collar bone for Andy Menefee. Also up Bean Canon was the sawmill of Al Rust. This was a considerable enterprise and for a long time a large lumber producer. Mr. Rust also had a lumber yard in the town of Dolores, and other business.

Jim Belmear and Minnie Belmear, his wife, were prominent residents and successful in the cattle business. Luna Morrison and his brother were at first just riders, but later became successful with herds of their own.

To make a clear statement about the Brumleys, Bill Brumley came in 1881 to take charge of the LC herd of cattle belonging to his sister, Mrs. Lacy, and in 1883 came John Brumley and Jim Brumley, and Milt McConnell, Mrs. McConnell being another sister of the Brumley boys. They all homesteaded land on Brumley Draw, near Lewis, in Montezuma Valley. Later they bought land on the Dolores river, below Big Bend. The second generation of Brumleys was Bill Brumley, Jr., and Irving Brumley. Bill Brumley married Miss Lula Coombs and they still have a home in Dolores, among their old friends. There is a third generation of Brumleys well known to local residents. The big LC herd of cattle was finally dispersed, Mrs. Lacy went to Oregon to make her home and the Brumley boys became cattlemen in their own right.

Jim Hammond was an 1884 resident of Rico, came to Dolores in 1903 and bought a ranch just below town, and he and Mrs. Hammond were married in 1906, Mrs. Hammond being previous to their marriage a teacher in the primary department in the Cortez schools. Mrs. Hammond was a skilled car driver and they made long trips in the interest of Mr. Hammonds health. They were in Washington, D.C., on his 80th birthday, and visited at his old home in New York state. Mr. Hammond died at the age of 98, but Mrs. Hammond still lives on a small tract of the old ranch just in the west edge of Dolores and is enjoying good health and the companionship of friends at the age of eighty-three.

The oldtimers gave the Dolores section a long and colorful early history, but, in recent years the town and community have gradually merged into a more peaceful state of affairs and a more orderly progress in development. New wealth and population came and the measure of growth is indicated by the growth in the school population. The first high school had its beginning in the original school building that housed the first school, and before the first high school building was erected in 1917 two years of high school was given in this building. As noted in the foregoing chapter the high school became fully accredited in the new building, in 1919.

The press for more class room was answered in 1948 by the erection of a new grade school building on the spacious school grounds on east Main Street. This building is of the latest design and splendidly built at a cost of $70,000 and it provides nine new class rooms.

In 1956, the old high school building having become completely inadequate to meet the needs of the school, a new high school building and gym was constructed at a cost of $150,000. These buildings are the very last word in high school construction and are designed to answer every school need. The high school building provides nine large class rooms, a library and study room, an office room and a dispensary room for the general use of the teachers, and there is a fully equipped cafeteria for serving hot lunches to scores of children at one time. In 1956, 18 teachers are employed in the schools, including the superintendent and principal.

In connection with the high school a large gymnasium was built in the latest design and pattern. It is equipped for basketball, theatrical performances, public meetings, and all school exercises, programs and dances. The school population is still growing, but the school authorities hope their school needs are taken care of for a while.

On the school grounds room for games of every kind has been provided and a battery of strong lights flood the athletic field so that night games may be played, thus gaining the children the use of the ground in both the daytime and the evening. The new tennis court was dedicated to and named in honor of the high school's first graduate, Miss Alice Lynton, who later became Mrs. Sam Ethridge.

Previous steps having been taken, in 1956, the Town of Dolores erected a new and imposing town hall that is the pride of the town. The new hall is centrally located on the south side of Flanders Park and was built at a cost of $70,000. It houses the office of the town clerk and all necessary office equipment and a meeting place for the town board; a public library and reading room; office of water superintendent, the town's police force and a special room for the Town's Volunteer Fire Department. The structure is of pressed brick and is built for permanency.

J. J. HARRIS & CO. BANKERS

The banking firm of J. J. Harris & Co., Bankers, apparently had its beginning in 1886 at old Big Bend. It was conducted at first in connection with the Harris Brother's mercantile business and for some time, was a private bank and was conducted as a matter of convenience to local people who, by this time, had begun to make a little money in their livestock operations.

When it became pretty certain that a railroad would be built into the Dolores river valley, by way of Lost Canon, the Harrises made preparation to move their business to a new location on the railroad soon to be built. They bought the Sherman Phelps place, took in Judge Adair Wilson as an interested partner in the town site and, after erecting a substantial brick building, moved their entire business up from Big Bend and located the banking business in especially prepared quarters in the rear of the mercantile building, about 1891.

The banking enterprise soon began to be a business of considerable importance and the bank was, a few months later, incorporated with a capital stock of $50,000. There was no record of the surplus or reserves at this time, but the banking business grew rapidly and the bank was soon a little giant among the banking firms of the southwest. On July 14, 1948, the capital stock was increased to $75,000, and on July 30, 1952 the capital stock was again increased, this time to $100,000. At this time—late 1956— there is a surplus fund of $100,000 and a combined cash reserve and undivided profits of $160,000. There are about 1,900 checking accounts, 900 savings accounts, and an average of about 450 loan accounts serviced continuously. The number of full time employees, when the business was first organized, was three and at the present time there are eight.

About 1910 a new building, 30 by 60, and designed especially for the bank was built and occupied. These quarters were gradually outgrown and in 1953, to relieve a pressing need, new and spacious quarters, 44x56 feet, was erected of pressed brick at a cost of $90,000. The bank business occupies the ground floor and the full basement floor is given over entirely to a public library, reading room, and other public uses. The new building commemorates the 70th anniversary of the founding of the business.

In July, 1925, George and Gilbert T. Cline of Mancos sold their interest in the First National Bank of Dolores to the Harris bank, and, a few months later, the Harris bank took over the remaining assets, and certain liabilities of the First National Bank of Dolores. As of November 15, 1956, the total deposits of the Harris bank aggregated $4,047,000. The bank has always been very strong in cash assets and for some years the Town of Dolores bore the distinction of having the largest per capita bank deposits of any town in the United States. This was determined by a special investigation made by the bank management. The bank rode out the long depression, 1929 to 1935, in safety and was closed only during the maritorium proclaimed by the government. The stockholders were all strong, financially, when the crises came, and they came to the rescue of the bank with all the cash needed to tide the business over to better times.

In February, 1931, the Harrises retired from ownership in the bank selling their entire interest to George Taylor, John Ritter and Dr. Le Furgy, and Mr. Taylor became the president of the new organization. Mr. Taylor served in this capacity until Nov. 1, 1956, when he retired from the business.

The Harris Bank has always been a community asset and a factor for progress in the community and the county. It had its beginning before the county was organized and has grown with the county— grown in assets, in service and in the public confidence. It draws its business from a wide territory far beyond its local confines, but the main stay is, and always has been, the local wealth, the many local

Street Scene, Town of Dolores. "Off for the San Juan Gold Rush, 1893."

Group of Dolores Pioneers. Rear, standing: Will Exon, Gred Kramer, John Harris, Carrol Pyle, Irvin Brumley. Middle Row: Ida Broadhead, Dora Barker, Myrtle Brumley, Ollie Wilbur, Louise Scharnhorst, Augusta Scharnhorst. Seated: Harry Pyle, Louise Pyle, Lena Sennenger, Hanna McConnell, Billy Brumley.

Dolores High School in right foreground. Grade school building in background at left. Large auditorium at rear of the high school building just visible over top of building. See story of "Town of Dolores."

Site of old Big Bend (Dolores Post Office). Originally the George Morton Place. Dolores River Valley.

Bill Brumley, Sr., in 1881. Early pioneer cattleman in Montezuma Valley.

Jim Douglas, famous race horse owned by Grandpa Charley Johnson. Won most famous race at Chicago June 29, 1886. Was never beaten in a race Born and raised in Montezuma County.

Robert Dunham, pioneer cattleman, Dolores Valley.

A. W. Dillon, pioneer settler, Dolores Valley and Montezuma Valley.

Early street scene, Town of Dolores. City Park at left.

Typical pioneer cabin; home of Lex Blumis on Beaver Creek, Dolores area. Forlorn and forsaken it stands telling a mute story of the past.

Band of Sheep on Summer range. Harry Morgan, on horse. Sheep are a basic industry in Montezuma County.

citizens that have built up small fortunes from the cattle and sheep industry, and kept the money working at home.

THE MOUNTAIN PACKING CO.

The Mountain Packing Co. is the name of a prosperous and growing business by the Dolores River one mile up stream from the town of Dolores. The business was founded in 1948 by E. G. McRae and Harry Evarts and it has been serving the public in a satisfactory way for eight years. In 1949 the entire business was taken over by Mr. McRae who associated his son with him in the business. They do both custom work in slaughtering, curing and freezing; slaughter and dress meats for the butcher trade, and cure meats, mostly pork, for storage and, later, for sale to the trade. Since this service has been available very little slaughtering and curing has been done on the farm, as formerly. Slaughtering, dressing and curing, or freezing, is now an important part of their business.

In the beginning facilities for handling the work were not the best, the work was poorly organized, and it required the work of seven or eight men to keep the business going. Now four employees do all the work and a vastly increased amount of business is handled. The work has been fully reorganized, electric power runs everything, power grinders, power saws, and every kind of modern machine is in use—even an automatic smokehouse and a 20x20 freezer to handle meats in quantities. On the average 15 hogs and 20 beeves are slaughtered each week.

Their aim is to turn out a standard, high grade product for the trade. To this end feed pens have been built, with feed bunks, and every animal is put on full feed rations to put them in prime condition before slaughter, and the old sales barn has been acquired and is used for processing, mixing and storing feeds for putting on a good finish on the animals. In the winter truck loads of cattle are taken to near Phoenix, Arizona, for fattening; then returned to the pens here for slaughter. From 150 to 200 cattle are also kept in the pens at the plant for finishing on feed bought locally, the needed concentrates being shipped in. In the curing compartment are five separate rooms each one used for a different curing process. No less than 80 head of cattle are always on feed and a dozen to twenty carcasses are always in the curing room.

The firm furnishes the meat trade in Mancos, Rico, Dolores, Dove Creek and a part of Cortez. Their trade territory is gradually expanding and the business is growing. In a few months they expect to be going into the larger Basin towns for a part of their trade.

CHAPTER V

CORTEZ, IT'S BEGINNING

Cortez had its beginning along with the beginning and building of the Montezuma Valley irrigating system, and since that time the two have had a parallel existence. The town was laid out in 1886 by M. J. Mack, engineer for the Montezuma Valley Water Supply Co., and on the land owned by James W. Hanna, manager and part owner of the water supply company. The Water Company soon took over the townsite and named the town Cortez. Mat Hammond and one other party brought the first loads of lumber to the townsite in the fall of 1886. The town had just been laid out, no streets were named or marked and there was not a single building. No one was around and they couldn't find the place where they were supposed to unload the lumber. It is not known whether this lumber was for the Goodykoontz restaurant or the Major E. H. Cooper residence.

F. M. Goodykoontz started the first restaurant, and the first business, in the new town, in January, 1887. The irrigating system was just getting under way, there was much traffic, much coming and going, but there was no place to stop or stay. Probably the only habitable place anywhere was a tent, or covered wagon. The E. H. Cooper residence was the first permanent building since the building for the restaurant, which was on the Safeway corner, was only temporary. After Goodykoontz, Charles Johnson and wife ran a restaurant on the same corner. Mr. and Mrs. Wm. Wooley ran a restaurant on the corner occupied by the Dr. Quinn building, in a very small building.

There were, by the spring of 1887, hundreds of teams and men at work on the new ditch system and there was lots of business for restaurants and livery barns. A livery barn was built on the Mexirado site, on north Market street, by Pearley Wasson, the first county sheriff, who had the stage and mail line and ran a livery barn in connection with that business. There was a livery stable where the Owl Tavern stands, built and conducted by a Mr. Brittain. There was a livery barn across from the County Court House and owned by Dick Kermode and run by George Clucas. Then there was a big barn on the corner where the Toggery now occupies, later converted by the Bozman's into a garage.

The first blacksmith shop was owned and conducted by Charles Minter and Dan Schirp. So many people working on the ditch, there was bound to be much breakage making lots of blacksmith work.

At first there was no water in Cortez except what was hauled. Water was brought from Mitchell Springs by wagon and teams in barrels. One report says it cost 25c a barrel; another says 50c. The writer was told by one party that he and another fellow paid 5c a glass for water to drink. A large well was dug 40 feet deep in the street between the bank building and the Toggery. No water. On July 4, 1890, the town of Cortez got its first flowing water. The big flume, bringing water to the town and 40 feet high in the highest place, had just been completed, which ended the water haul. The town still consisted of only a few houses.

John Curry, recently of Telluride, started the Montezuma Journal in 1888 in the rear end of a grocery store on the present site of the Wheeler Market. It had a hectic career for about 18 years and suspended publication five or six times. Some of the early editors were S. P. Thomas, Frank Hartman, Charley Day (in and out, try again) Will and Melvin Springer, Dave Longenbaugh, Harry and Will Beall. In August, 1906, C. A. Frederick took over the paper and put it on a firm business basis.

Dr. Bernard Byrns came over from Ft. Lewis and established a residence and put in a drug store, the first drug store. The Cortez post-office was established, probably early in 1888, before the paper was started, and Dr. Byrns was the first postmaster. Dr. Byrns states in his book that his drug store and the postoffice were in a room on the ground floor of the old courthouse building. Others are positive that the postoffice was first located in a small building on Main Street, just west of the Safeway building. You can take your own choice.

In 1887 Al and Frank Thompson started the first store in Cortez when they brought in three wagon loads of groceries, dry goods and clothing and began business in a building that stood on the Safeway corner. In 1890, Guillet Brothers bought the business and moved it soon after to the Farmer's Drug Store site; then from there to the stone block. There they occupied two sections of the ground floor, built up a large business that continued for about 40 years.

The old Court House building was finished in 1888, and the large stone block was finished soon after as to walls and roof; then stood for over a year without doors or windows or interior finish. It was finally finished some time in 1890, and was occupied at once.

Some time after Guillets vacated the Safeway corner Charles Duff put in a small stock of staple merchandise.

Mr. and Mrs. E. R. Lamb came to Cortez in 1887 and started a small drug store and sundries on the corner one block south of the Safeway corner. About 1889 he moved to the stone block and added general merchandise and millinery.

In 1896 R. R. Smith moved in from the ranch and started a general merchandise business, first in the stone block; then in the McMillan building, with two stories and a basement. The business was expanded into quite a large store for so small a town.

The old Clifton Hotel was the first hotel of any consequence to be built in Cortez. It stood just west of the stone block, on Main St., and was owned and conducted by Mr. and Mrs. J. O. Brown (Johnny Brown), Dr. Harrington's drug store stood just next to it, and small buildings further west. About 1908 the hotel and all the buildings westward, were burned. Brown then built the "Brown Palace" hotel. This hotel was later much enlarged and was then called the Hotel Cortez. It still stands, is popular and has a large patronage.

Sam Walker finally put in a large, modern building on the corner of Main and Market Streets and it was later occupied by the Safeway store. This building was later much enlarged and rebuilt by the Safeway Company.

Cortez hits its first period of real growth in 1927.

The following are the census figures:

1910	1920	1930	1940	1950
565	541	921	1778	2651

Meantime, while the town of Cortez was trying to get started, the big ditch and canal system was being built, details of which may be found in a separate chapter. A little water came through the tunnel in late 1888, but it was 1889 before a real head was run and water came to most parts of the valley. It was several years before the Mesa Verde lateral was finished, and later still when Canal No. 2 and the U lateral were finished.

The first school in Cortez was started in August 1887, with Dave Longenbaugh as teacher, in a small frame building located on the present site of Mrs. Hatfield's house on South Linden St. By 1890 a two story stone building had been built on Montezuma Avenue on the site of Mrs. Maude Bryce's home. Mrs. Chase was a resident at this time. Her husband owned the toll road to Durango and she taught. She was the first woman teacher in the Cortez school. School facilities were simple and crude the first few years. There was little taxable property and only meager school funds.

The stone building was soon overcrowded and the old Dr. Quinn building in its early, crude form and another building equally simple and crude, where the Havran dry cleaners stands, were used for the lower grades for some time. After using every kind of makeshift quarters and enduring over-crowded conditions for years, the district built a stone structure on 1st and 6th streets to serve as high school and grade school. This was the first real school building the town had; it was a very good building, well planned, and cost $14,000. This was in 1909 and I. E. Levey was the first school superintendent.

In 1889 quite a large and imposing Congregational Church was erected on the corner of Market Street and Montezuma Avenue, the first church in the town, and it was a land mark for 40 years. It burned about 1930, and the Catholic Church now occupies the old Congregational site. Other churches are Methodist, Baptist, Presbyterian, Four Square, Church of Christ, Christian Science, and the Church of Jesus Christ of Latter Day Saints (Mormon), a large and very fine structure which they are planning to further enlarge. A Sunday school was organized early and for a time the children of all denominations attended and received religious and Bible teaching.

Now for a general view of the town from its earliest to its latest developments. The Town of Cortez was incorporated November 10, 1902. The first ordinance, Ordinance No. 1, was passed December 3, 1902, and was signed by H. M. Guillet as Mayor and H. E. Black as Town Clerk and Recorder. There is no record available as to the personnel of the first town board or other town officers. According to the general census of 1900 the population of the town at that time was 125 so the town must have started on a pretty low taxation basis on which o support a town government. There was a newspaper, the Montezuma Journal, being published intermittantly in the town, but the files of the paper have been misplaced or destroyed. The records of town meeting give little in the way of history. Growth was comparatively rapid in the decade after 1900 the population had risen to 565. After 1910 troubles came thick and fast for all the people of the big valley details of which are discussed at length in other chapters.

The original townsite was laid out on a modest scale, but when growth finally came, additions became necessary. Year after year the town covered a little more ground. In recent years growth has been much more rapid so that to the original townsite we find the following additions: First, the Thompson Annex, in 1890, which was made a part of the original townsite and the town was replotted. Then came the Coffin addition, Rice addition, Phelan's addition, Koehler addition, Hiltzville addition, Slaven's addition, Western addition, C.R.S.P. addition, Park Ridge addition, Smith addition, Barrett addition, Hopper addition, Park addition, and the McBride addition.

With these steps in expansion the population has grown, in 1956, to an estimated 4,300 people and there are several hundred people in the fringe area just outside the city limit. Other large areas are soon to be annexed to the town and the increase in population is filling every available building and hundreds of trailer houses are parked in every available space.

In recent years many improvements have come to the town. Main street was first graveled to take this part of the town out of the mud, about 1922. Later more gravel was put out, and in 1951, Main Street was oil paved in the center. Later the town put on oil paving to the curb on each side and extended the pavement a half block on each side of Main Street at every Avenue crossing. Later still, in 1954, Pinon

Drive was oil paved and 12 additional blocks in different parts of town. In 1953 all the other streets and avenues of the town were gravel surfaced. This was effectual in taking the balance of the town out of the mud for the first time. It is planned to begin oil surfacing the graveled streets and alleys in the near future thus largely settling the dust nuisance.

Cortez became a city of the second class in January, 1952. The town owns its own water system and water rights from the Dolores River. The water tests almost free from objectionable impurities, but it is chlorinated in the interest of absolute safety. The town also has a municipal sewer system to take care of all sewage originating within the town, and both the sewer system and the water system are being expanded to meet the growing demands. The water system is a gravity system and two reservoirs are maintained. This greatly lessens the current expense of the system.

The town has three parks: one small park called Town Park; lawn and trees chiefly, recreational and ornamental, and City Park consisting of 10 acres, which serves as a ball park and other municipal purposes; lastly the Denny Park, which came into the town's possession in 1954 by gift from A. W. Denny. There is a fine lake on the park covering approximately five acres and the entire park area embraces about 20 acres. It is being improved as an amusement, recreation and fishing area and, in winter for skating and other ice sports.

Within the main business area parking meters were installed in 1952 which yield some revenue above expenses and are a definite aid in enforcing parking regulations. Improved street lighting on Main Street and Pinon Drive was installed in 1952. The town is paying for these and they will eventually be the property of the town.

There is an up-to-date and very efficient Fire Department with two late model fire trucks and a rescue truck fully equipped with life saving apparatus.

The Police Department consists of eight full-time salaried employees.

To crown all their recent achievements the town erected, in 1956, a new town hall which is fully adequate for all municipal purposes, is a very fine building and a model of excellence in every way. The cost was $83,000 and at present it houses all the city business, a two room library space and reading room, a spacious museum in the basement, and office and meeting quarters for the Chamber of Commerce. The town has a "Boot Strap" Club and a 20-30 Club that are more or less active.

And last, but not least, there is the Southwest Memorial Hospital which stands as a monument to the enterprise and public spirit of the town. The local Lions Club was the prime mover in the undertaking, and through their efforts enough support was rallied to the cause to finance the undertaking to its completion, the government contributing about one-third of the cost.

As noted previously the Cortez postoffice was established in 1887 with Dr. Bernard Byrnes as the first postmaster. After being moved from place to place since it was first established the postoffice was moved to its present quarters in 1954 and it was thought that the matter of a permanent home for the postoffice was settled, but so rapid has been the growth in the town's population that the business of the postoffice has already outgrown its quarters.

In 1939 there were 365 lock postoffice boxes and in 1956 there are 1,220, and still not enough. There are nine full time employees and they are busy every hour of the day. The postoffice services only one rural route 45.55 miles in length. It brings mail service to most of the north end of the valley, a part of the valley being serviced from Dolores. In addition there are seven Star Routes, one of which is Air Star Route No. 1, to White Canon, Utah, and intervening points.

The Cortez postoffice became an office of the second class July 1, 1937, then doing an annual business of $8,000. On July 1, 1953, it became a postoffice of the first class and, in 1956, the business transacted is expected to run between $60,000 and $65,000.

Through the years many postoffices have been established in the county and discontinued. The coming of the rural mail service displaced some. Changes in population centers have caused others to be closed. In 1956 the postoffices still doing business in the county were Cortez, Dolores, Mancos, Mesa Verde, Towaoc, Lewis, Yellow Jacket, and Pleasant View. Some of the offices discontinued are Arriola, Arloa, Lebanon, Stoner, Ackmen, Moqui, Toltec, McPhee, Golconda and some others.

PERIOD OF GROWTH

Cortez, in 1950, had a population of 2,680. To this date, it might be said, Cortez had been primarily an agricultural town with general farming, fruit growing and livestock its resource foundation. The town had grown slowly, but steadily, as these resources were developed. As new lines of business were developed they came to take a place in the business pattern—garages, filling stations, creameries, sales barns, packing plants, etc. As the trade center increased in importance came the chain store to compete with local concerns—J. C. Penney, Safeway, Ben Franklin, and later, a City Market, each with its line of business, and adding to the importance of the town as a trade center.

It was about 1950 when uranium began to give a little fresh impetus to growth and development. First, homes were in demand by those working or managing the mines; then the ore trucking industry sprang into being along with the item of trucking acid to the various smelters and reducing plants. Then, in 1954, oil in the Aneth field, in nearby

71

Utah, began to have an influence on local business and local growth. There being no water for a town, ruling out the possibility of building desirable homes, the population of the new oil field came to Cortez as the nearest and most convenient place to live and commute to their field of labor and operation. This gave new life and growth. From one rig operating two years ago, and one producing well with a capacity of 1,200 barrels daily there are now six companies operating in the field and an estimated 25 rigs are on the ground and nearly all doing actual work.

Workers, operators, promoters, all must have a place to live and a tent city could never answer the need. In Cortez, the nearest town, are many modern homes; more homes coming into being to meet the increasing demand. There is a water supply system, sewage system, a power and light system, paved and graveled surfaced streets, a large volume of modern businesses in every line. There are schools, churches, lodges, a hospital, local radio broadcasting, and television coming in with the years end. Local and long distance telephone—you can't have all these things out in the desert, hence the business in coming to Montezuma County and to Cortez. Both Dolores and Mancos, being ideal places for homes, are profiting to some extent as a result of the new industries.

Along with housing, school facilities are feeling the pressure of new growth. A new $88,000 vocational agricultural building is to be ready by Christmas, 1956, and six new class rooms are being added to the Manaugh elementary school. Plans are complete for nine elementary class rooms and school officials are working on plans for another ten room elementary school. More high school room must come soon.

In 1956 the number of oil, gas and mining instruments filed are three times the 1950 level, and the county licenses 6,705 motor vehicles in 1956.

Note: The development history of Cortez, Dolores and Mancos may be found in the Chronology of each town.

A. W. DILLON AND FRANK MORGAN

Two well-known and influential citizens that came into the valley early were A. W. Dillon and Frank Morgan.

A. W. Dillon and wife, Laura M. Dillon, first came to Telluride, from Chicago, in 1878, and from Telluride to Rico in 1879, and thence to the Dolores river valley in 1884, and Mrs. Dillon was appointed postmistress at Lone Dome. In 1885 the Dillons moved up to the little community at Big Bend and shortly after, over into Montezuma Valley. They stopped for a time near Lebanon. Work on the big irrigating system was getting under way, so Mr. Dillon took a contract to build a large stretch of No. 1 lateral, one of the main canals in the new ditch system. At the same time he took a homestead near Arriola,

72

which he began improving at once and where he made his home for the rest of his days. He planted the first orchard in this part of the county, now becoming quite noted as a fruit producing area, and improved his homestead. Aside from this he was always a community benefactor. He helped to get the second school in the valley going at Arriola and took an active interest in all community and county affairs. Friendship and hospitality was a strong characteristic of his life and Laura Dillon was the beloved friend of all who knew her.

Frank Morgan also homesteaded at Arriola, right near the Dillon home, and improved a fine farm; also put out an orchard which, along with the Dillon orchard, suggested the possibility of the locality as a fruit growing country. Mr. Morgan first appeared on the local scene with a sawmill in Thompson Park, but about the same time took a homestead in the lower Mancos Valley, about 1881. We next find him with his sawmill in Lost Canon, and then in the big valley. Here, his public service began and he put in several years as a member of the board of directors of the newly organized irrigating district, which took over the entire irrigating system of the old water company. This was the most difficult job and most important work of his career, and required much thought and planning and earnest effort, along with the work of other members of the board, to finally bring these troublesome matters to a successful conclusion. Meantime he improved his homestead, making it one of the best in the valley, and became an outstanding success in the cattle and sheep industries. He spent his last days on the farm he loved.

GEORGE M. LONGENBAUGH

George M. Longenbaugh was born February 22, 1853, died June 1, 1923. Married to Mary B. Yantis, March 29, 1879. Five children: Walter, Harley, Edward, George and Bertha. La Plata County, 1884. Homesteaded 1885, one mile south of the James Sucla place, near Beulah school. Twenty years on homestead; then to new home in Hartman Draw. Always public minded, he was generous with his time, and with his means, even to a fault. He helped organize and get the Beulah school started, the first school after the county was organized, district No. 1. He helped organize the Montezuma Valley Irrigation District and served on the first Board, with John Duncan and Tom Coppinger. He was a member of the Western Slope Congress, served on the committee for revising Colorado irrigation laws and was clerk in the House of Representatives, 21st. General Assembly, the end of his public service in a long and useful career.

JIMMIE BARRETT

One settler that helped to make history in Montezuma County, though not an Oldtimer, is Jimmie Barrett, still with us and still working. He arrived at Dolores March 23, 1911, by immigrant car six days on the road out of Pueblo, getting a foretaste, first hand, of our transportation service. He acquired by purchase the old Hayhurst place just across Alkali Draw from the Beulah school house, 80 acres of solid, dense sage. He first cleared a site so he could build a house; then built a new house on the new land. It was not an elegant building, but it was home. Once settled with his family he began work on the sagebrush and smote it with might and main (main strength). With rich, new land and plenty of water, but with poor markets, poor roads, poor transportation, and poor people all around, it was a struggle for survival. Finally, after seventeen years, he decided to try business in Cortez, bought property on North Market Street, put in a stock of furniture. Then the long depression struck, and hard times such as the farm never knew. With the support of friends, who stood by, he somehow survived the long depression. With finances finally relieved, in the spring of 1944 he took over the Cortez Sales Barn, and the useful part of his life began. He began to furnish a useful and valuable service, built up a good business and prospered. After seven years in the business, health conditions in the family compelled him to give up the sales barn. The furniture business having attained to a fair measure of success, and some prosperity, the people of Cortez decided, in 1950, that he ought to begin working for the town for nothing, so they made him mayor of the town, and have kept him on the job ever since. He made a good mayor, and also made good. The town grew and prospered as never before in its eventful history, but the Mayor doesn't take all the credit. Since he has been mayor they have graveled all the streets, paved Main Street, in part, improved and extended the water and sewer systems, put in parking meters, built a new town hall, and did many other things too numerous to mention, and now he is beginning to think he has done his share of the work. The chances are, however, he will just keep on working.

CHAPTER VI

SOIL CONSERVATION

The Federal Soil Conservation Service was created by an act of Congress in 1935, under Public Law 46, of the 74th Congress. The basic purpose of the soil conservation law is to assist farmers and land owners in bringing about physical adjustment in land use and management to better the welfare of all, conserve the natural soil and water resources, establish a permanent and balanced agriculture, reduce the frequency of floods and to prevent soil erosion. This purpose is attained by developing a thorough-going program of soil and water conservation and applying it to the individual farm by adopting the best know and most successful methods of maintaining soil fertility, saving water and using the best soil management practices in accordance with the needs and capabilities of the land.

The work of soil conservation is directed at the top by the Federal Soil Conservation Service, with the National Association of Soil Conservation Districts assisting in every way it can in carrying out the plans and aims of the Service. It is directed at the state level by the Colorado State Conservationist and Staff, and on the district level by the District Conservationist working in conjunction with the local District Board of Supervisors.

One of the 18 district conservationists of Colorado is located in Montezuma County with office at Cortez, and the place is now filled by Harold W. Bradford. He has general supervision over the Mancos, Dolores and Dove Creek Soil Conservation districts.

The Dolores Soil Conservation District was the first to organize, on May 1, 1942, with an area of 1,208,678 acres and embracing all the central and southwest part of Montezuma Co. The second to organize was Dove Creek with 300,000 acres and embracing a part of Montezuma Co., west Dolores County and a part of San Miguel County. And, last, the Mancos district, September 3, 1948, 155,000 acres and embracing roughly the Mancos river drainage and a part of the Lost Canon drainage. Conservation work was started in the Mancos area, under the Case-Wheeler Act, about 1946, giving place to Soil Conservation Service in 1948. The districts are created under state law, passed in 1937, by vote of the land owners much as a school district is created.

75

They are self-governing in every respect, the local Board directing and carrying out the plans and purposes of the District on every farm. The Dolores District is the largest in the state.

The aim of Soil Conservation in Montezuma County is to save soil and water and restore to the land what has been lost in soil fertility and soil erosion, and restore to the land desirable vegetable coverage and growth. Since their organization the three districts have accomplished a great deal in carrying out their purposes, but they still have a long way to go. The work has been ably directed by the technicians, assisted by competent engineers, and many farmers have become soil conscious in relation to their land. One great hinderance to the success of the program is indifference on the part of too many people, and a second is the failure of many to realize that soil conservation doesn't cost; it pays; that we live by the land, and that caring for the land is an obligation that is almost sacred.

The work must go on. Erosion must be stopped; the fertility of the soil must be restored. The pioneers of Montezuma County moved into one of the richest treasurehouses of natural resources ever opened to man: soil fertility of the highest measure; grass lands that extended far and wide—grass that grew in luxurious abundance on a thousand hills; stately forest that had been in the making for untold centuries; all were his. He over-grazed and weakened the grass that held the soil in place and prevented erosion, and replaced it with worthless brush; he destroyed noble forests for greed of grain, and he mined out the fertility of the soil and exchanged it for the money it would bring. The way back is a long, hard pull. But we need not blame too much our own pioneers. Our pioneers did what pioneers have always done. The march of destruction started on the eastern seaboard 300 years ago. It is ours to build back the fertility of the soil; to destroy the brush and restore the grass lands; to grow again, in so far as we may, the great commercial forests on mesas and mountains, and protect them from destruction by fire; to reclaim the thousands of acres of seep land and alkali swamps that has come about from misuse of the water and the land.

Soil Conservation must go on. The safety of our future demands it. We must correct the mistakes of the past. We must plant and grow and harvest, and yet leave more in the soil than we have taken away. This is soil conservation at its very best. The future of all humanity depends on the care that is taken of those few inches of precious top soil. In this county, agriculture is our basic industry. Oil fields and rich mines come and go, but agriculture and livestock will always be in our county's future. To save the soil and the water is our work. Let us all say, with one accord: Montezuma County, we will not fail thee.

In the summer of 1937 plans were made and put into effect to map the entire farming area of Montezuma County by photography from the air. The work was done for the Soil Conservation Service to obtain permanent and accurate records of all individual farms in the county. Pictures were taken from a height of 16,000 to 18,000 feet. The territory was flown in two mile strips north and south. Enlargement of the prints were made and the fields are scaled on the map with a planimeter and measurements made to no more than one per cent variation from perfect. The records are permanent and will last and be useful through the years and will be a great aid to the work of the Soil Conservation Service. As the Service proceeds with its work the maps are in constant use and are a continual source of information and reference.

In applying soil conservation practices on the farm leveling operations and a revamped ditch system is usually the first to receive attention on irrigated farms. Leveling, for the most part, means leveling one way, cutting down the high places and filling in the low. A new ditch system means realigning all ditches on grade, that need it, and putting in new drops and headgates where needed. On non-irrigated farms leveling, broad based terraces on the steeper slopes; contour lines for gentler slopes, grassed in water ways to carry water from terraces and natural drains. These and many other practices are recommended, and are in use, to the end that the soil may produce without depletion and the land be used without loss of precious topsoil and its fertility elements. To restore fertility in depleted soils the fertility elements in commercial forms are applied, crops are rotated, soil building crops are grown and, to replenish humus, animal fertilizers, green manure crops, and every form of organic matter from every possible source are applied to the land to make humus, for soil without humus is dead soil. This, in brief, is the work of the Soil Conservation Service. No other work done by man at any time, at any place, is more important to human welfare and human happiness.

CHAPTER VII

INDIAN ATROCITIES

When the very first settlements were being made in Montezuma County, the Indians made no serious trouble. They came among the white people frequently, made threats sometimes, or ordered the white people to leave the country, but they gave no real trouble. They were always hungry and, if fed, were content for the time being. When the white man came in bringing large herds of cattle the Indians began to see that they were going to lose their "happy hunting ground" and they began to resent the encroachment of the white man with some violence.

The first serious trouble came in the spring of 1881. It was roundup time out on the range and a number of men were out on the Colorado-Utah border country rounding up cattle and branding calves, and John Thurman was looking after a herd of fine horses that belonged to himself and J. H. Alderson. At this time Richard May and Byron Smith came out to the camp as Smith wished to buy some horses. It was while this parley was going on that the Indians attacked the men and Thurman, May and Smith were killed. This was near the Thurman and Willis ranch and word of the killing reached camp the next day. A rider was dispatched to Fort Lewis for soldiers. The third day after the atrocity a number of men from Dolores and Mancos went out to the scene of the tragic event, but found no Indians. In this party were H. C. Goodman, C. A. Frink, A. M. Puett, M. W. Reid, George and William May, brothers of the slain man, George Phelps, Mike O'Donnel, Benjamin Quick, and some others. They buried Thurman and May, but the body of Smith was never found. Thurman had some money on his person. This was gone and only a few of the horses could be found.

On May 14, the same spring, David Willis of Mancos, and some other men, were fired upon, while riding after cattle, by the same band of Indians. They came to Mancos and organized a force of about fifteen men, and being joined by others, went back the first of June to try to find the stolen cattle. On June 15, they came upon the Indians near the Blue Mountains where a battle ensued and ten men were killed, among them Mr. Willis and Mr. McLaine. Whether any Indians were killed, or not, the white men never knew.

In October Mrs. Willis, attended by H. M. Barber, Orsey Renyeld, Dalty Renyeld, and others from Mancos, and Cal House of Dolores went out and took up the bodies of Willis and May and brought them back. The body of Willis was buried in the cemetery at Mancos, and Cal House took the body of May and buried it on his ranch in the Dolores valley.

The next spring, 1882, Dan William's Cabin was burned and he was fired upon. In 1884 two cowboys were killed out on White Canon, near where all the other Indian troubles had taken place. This time the soldiers went out from Ft. Lewis only to have one of their scouts, named Warrington, killed and a cowboy, named Willson, killed.

These matters settled down and there was no more Indian trouble for a while. But the Indians continued to kill cattle and steal horses. They would kill a cow or steer, take out a little of the choice meat and leave the rest to rot on the ground. This took place so frequently that the cattlemen became angered and determined to do something to stop the practice. One day, in the summer of 1885, they discovered a band of Indians camped in the canon of Beaver Creek. They approached the camp from the side and fired on the Indians from the nearby rimrock killing seven bucks and wounding a squaw. The squaw made her escape by creeping along under the rimrock until she was out of sight of the white men, then made her way across Montezuma Valley to the reservation and made the news of the tragic incident known. Public opinion was divided on this incident. Many people strongly condemned the white men for the atrocious act. It surely did make more trouble. Two or three days after the above mentioned incident some Indians came to the home of a Mr. Genther, just south of Lakeview and attempted to set fire to his home. Mr. and Mrs. Genther were up late reading their mail, just received that day, Mr. Genther smelled smoke and went out to see what was taking place, and was putting out the fire; they shot and killed him; then shot Mrs. Genther in the shoulder. She got her children, in some way, to a nearby arroyo and made her escape with the children, one a baby under one year of age. (This baby was the first white child born in Montezuma Valley.) One account says she spent the night in the arroyo, then went to the Wooley home for help. Another says she went to the Wooley home the same night and, finding no one at home, went on to the home of Lewis Simon. On her way she ran across Doug Wooley who she took for an Indian, and was badly frightened again. Doug had taken some bedding and gone out into the sage brush to sleep to lessen the danger of the Indians finding him. The next morning, upon going back to the Genther home, they found everything about as they had left it in the night, and the Indians were gone. It was soon after this that the Indians visited the Simon home, during their Silver Wedding Anniversary celebration, and devoured all the good food prepared for the feast.

In 1886 William Ball was killed near Paiute Springs where he is buried. This was the last white man to be killed by the Indians in Montezuma County.

The death of William Ball brought to an end the Indian warfare in Montezuma County, but there were some near brushes with trouble later on. As an example, shortly after the Indian troubles out on the Utah line Lee Sheek, Mike O'Donnel, Mat Hosea and George Menefee were out there looking after cattle. They camped for the night in a woody draw, concealed their camp fire and put out the fire as soon as they were through with it. When they spread their beds they decided it would be safer to conceal them in some way. So Sheek and Hosea made their bed out among some big rocks and O'Donnel and Menefee made theirs under a large, low spreading cedar tree. There was no disturbance during the night and the next morning Menefee got up early and went in search of the horses. A little way out from camp he stopped and struck a match to see if there were horse tracks in the path. Instead of horse tracks he found moccasin tracks. When it became light they found moccasin tracks all around in their camp and all around the big cedar tree.

The next day, on their way to the horse pasture, up beyond Dove Creek, they observed a large cloud of dust to the southwest. After watching it a while they saw it was moving and rapidly approaching in their direction. They immediately put spurs to their horses, but still the dust cloud gained on them. Their only thought was that they were being pursued by a band of Indians. Pat O'Donnel, being the elder man, was directing the retreat. He planned that if the dust cloud was close upon them when they reached the crest of the next rise, they would take to the rocks under the Dolores Canon rim. But when they reached the next crest and looked back, they saw it was only a band of horses running madly. They had, no doubt, been chased or frightened by the Indians.

The last Indian scare came the last week in February, 1915, when there was something like an uprising of a small band of Paiute Indians out in the edge of Utah. The Indians, about 25 in number, were resisting arrest for killing a Mexican—some days previous. It was only a detached band of the Paiute tribe, led by Old Polk, their chief and Posey, his son, both of a renegade nature. They were encamped in Cow Canon, near Bluff, when the posse from Montezuma County came upon them just before daylight. The Indians saw them, however, and opened fire at once, and a general skirmish ensued. One of the posse, Joe Akin of Dolores, was hit in the head by a glancing bullet and was killed, and a Mexican was shot through the shoulder. The fire of the posse was directed on the Indian tepees, one papoose was killed, one wounded and one squaw was drowned trying to cross the San Juan river. After firing ceased, three Indians were dead, two wounded and five Indians and one Mexican captured. Four of the posse were missing, but came to camp later. Sunday night one of the Indians captured tried to escape and was shot and badly wounded. No further effort was made to get the Indians. The Indians and the posse barricaded themselves among and behind rocks. Akin was apparently killed by a bullet that struck a rock, ricocheted and struck him in the forehead. Marshal Nebeker and the posse remained on the scene of action, but the Indians moved to and barricaded themselves in the hills to the west. General Scott was coming so nothing was to be done until he should arrive. The posse was composed entirely of boys from Mancos, Cortez and Dolores and all had volunteered their service.

CHAPTER VIII

LIFE OF THE EARLY SETTLERS

The life of the early settlers in Montezuma County was not one of constant privation, of unending hardships, nor of fear and constant dread. While these were present here, as in every community in a newly settled country, they never made life a burden, and there was always happiness and friendship and love. There was neighborly kindness, sincere sympathy, and always a helping hand. There was always a shoulder to lean upon and sob out one's grief; always those who cared.

And what is life but these? Everywhere in lands of plenty, in homes of luxurious appointment, in lofty dwellings where luxury takes its ease, if these attributes of life are not present, there is unhappiness. And what is life without happiness? It was to the credit of the pioneer that these things were present, and present in great abundance. This ever kindly feeling, this ever-present spirit of helpfulness—this was their social security. There was all too often little money in their pockets, there was no monthly gratuity from an all generous government, but there was never any want. There was never a luxury, but of the necessities there was a great plenty; and if there wasn't plenty it would be supplied. There was no gleaming hospitals to open their doors to the sick and the afflicted, no learned physicians or skilled surgeons, but there were helpful hands, kindly hearts and loving dispositions that did all they could to bring relief in sorrow or pain. There were the home remedies, often mercifully effective; there was kindly ministration and often some kind of professional care. There was sorrow in sorrow and joy in joy. If bad times came to the worst; if death came to reap his harvest, there was not a burial to cost a thousand or five thousand dollars, but one that didn't cost the bereaved ones a cent. Friends dug the grave in an appointed place. Some one, with crude skill perhaps, made—not a casket—but a coffin, covered with black cloth, perhaps, and lined inside in white with, perhaps, a meager lace trimming, and a box to enclose all. People attended funerals because there was a genuine sorrow and loved ones grieved deeply because of their loss.

But life also had its brighter side. As with mankind everywhere the

82

social instinct asserted itself. Feasting, frolic and fun inspired every get-together in the rural scene. There was the festal board, the pioneer version of the pot-luck. There was the social dance, the old fashioned romp-around square dance, and music and song. There was always those who could teach the inexperienced and unpracticed the rhythmical movement and the measured tread, and somehow from somewhere there was fiddle music available, perhaps enlarged by a guitar or an accordion into a rudimentary orchestra. On feast days, like the Fourth of July, Thanksgiving or Christmas, there were outdoor sports, wrestling, racing; Contests—logging, sawing and drilling, in season; and indoor entertainment on winter time occasions.

Although there were hardships, hindrances and impossibilities, love found a way. Romance rode the range from towering pines to distant purple planes; it lingered by murmuring brooks and strolled through sunny dells. Such relations could but result in marriage, and marry they did. New homes and new families had to be, and out of the old blossomed the new.

Home life, as you would expect, was a makeshift life; crude with every inconvenience. As the first settler, begining about 1875, came first to the Mancos Valley, and a year or so later, to the Dolores River Valley, it was here that the first crude habitations appeared. As there was not a sawmill in the country, the first dwelling places were either "dug outs" excavated in a hillside or a log structure with door and windows without shutters or closures. A blanket or a canvas served in most cases for a door and window openings, always small, were covered by heavy oiled paper to let in a little light, or a plain white cloth. Until lumber became available the earth was the floor. In most cases one room served for cooking, eating and sleeping, especially where there were only men; but for a family there were mostly two rooms and sometimes three. The furnishings were simple and few—just such as the immigrants were able to bring along in a wagon with the many other things they had to have. Sometimes a few boards were hewn out with an ax or cut with a whipsaw and these boards made into a cupboard, stools, a bench, or other simple requirements. There might have been one bedstead, but most likely the bed was made on the floor with a mat of grass to lend something to comfort.

Of course there was the big fireplace, built of stone, for the most part, and occupying a place in the rear wall of the building, if but one room, and at one side, or in the inner partition, if two or more rooms. Sometimes there was a cook stove, but more often the cooking was done on, or over, the open fire pot fashion, and the baking done in a dutch oven. The roof could be only of poles and dirt, and during any considerable rain leaked some and often continued to leak for a while after the storm was over. The dugouts could be heaped up with enough dirt to make a pretty effective roof and leaked only after a prolonged storm. These living quarters were crude, but clean, and there was nothing of the filth and squalor some might expect. There was dirt, but it was clean dirt.

The coming in of many people, and the sawmill, soon brought better things, and frame houses, well finished and painted a gleaming white, could be seen on many local homesteads. Fences, good crops and good vegetable gardens soon contributed to a better life and better living.

In the Mancos Valley and in the Dolores River Valley all habitations were built along near the streams in order that fuel wood and water might be handy. Domestic water was simply carried in a pail from the creek or river and the water was always cool, clean and pure, a real luxury in many places in the west. The weekly wash was taken down to the flowing stream and done there. Some of the old bachelor boys were wont to anchor their garments out in the swift part of the stream with a rope or a piece of wire and let the swift moving water do the cleaning. There is no record as to how effective this was.

Montezuma Valley had no such streams. In fact there were only weak springs here and there to furnish water for every purpose and the first habitations were naturally built near these springs. Mitchell Springs, just south of Cortez, were two good springs. Navajo Springs, down on the Ute reservation, Willow Springs, Stafford Springs, and in the upper valley there were weak springs here and there in most of the main draws. Goodman Lake, a natural basin, rock enclosed, was strong enough to furnish much stock water and many cattle drank there. There were widely scattered springs all over the range territory westward. Many settlers resorted to the use of a wagon and team and the old water barrel to provide themselves with domestic water. This condition continued until water was brought in through the tunnel in 1889 and distributed to every part of the valley.

In every part of the county home life was largely an outdoor life. The mild climate, the many fair days and long stretches of fine weather was conducive to life in the open. The young folks especially reveled in it. Every boy and girl, early in life, learned to ride; every boy had is own pony and many of the girls, and all could ride like Indians. In this school of life the three R's still applied—Riding, Roping and Racing, and these arts stood them well in hand when the later responsibilities of life came to rest upon their shoulders. At first the entire country was primarily a cow country, and the man on horseback was about the most common sight on the local landscape.

Pioneer life was not all smooth sailing; not all joy and song. The winters were often long and cold, and snow fell deep over all the landscape. Some winters the snow laid on the ground for many weeks and there was nearly always five or six weeks of good sledding. In the first years one could get around only on snow shoes or on horseback where trails were not broken, but when roads were laid out many bob sleds came into use and now and then a cutter might be seen. Winter sports were indulged in but little. Coasting, skating and bob sled parties were the outdoor pastimes.

The earliest settlers brought with them but few supplies and getting food soon became a problem, especially in winter. A few supplies became available at old Parrot City, on the upper La Plata River, but the supply, even there, was very meager. Lack of any kind of road was the great handicap in winter and trips to Parrott City and points east could be made only on snowshoes. Meat was abundant. There were cattle everywhere, and nearly everyone had a few. Then wild game— deer, bear, wild turkey and grouse—was plentiful. As an example of the difficulty of getting supplies, Andy Menefee took a wagon and team and a herd of horses all the way to Salt Lake City for supplies and, after three months, came back with some flour and other groceries, two pigs and eight chickens, and 200 head of cattle he had traded horses for. A. W. Dillon made the trip from Big Bend, on the Dolores River, all the way to Animas City 55 miles one way, and was able to get a little bag of flour and some tobacco.

Such was pioneer life on the Mancos and on the Dolores. By the time Montezuma Valley was being settled, conditions had changed some for the better. The railroad was built into Durango in 1881, and a road, only slightly improved, made it easier to get necessities, if one had the money, and privations of this kind were relieved. But money was another difficulty, as in every pioneer settlement. Such a thing as a local market was unknown. Some beef and a little grain was sold at the mining camp, but, under road conditions, the mining camps were a long way off. For a time money almost quit circulating. After a time, however, roads were built, very poor roads at the start, but vastly better than no roads at all.

In the early times law and order was sometimes broken into by lawlessness and violence, but, for the most part, the first settlers were a very good class of people, and good citizenship was the rule, and men and women with high ideals and sturdy characters were common. As time went on all the amenities of social life began to appear. Churches were organized and buildings erected. The Methodist and Baptist were the first followed by the Catholic and the Episcopal. They have been active through the years and have been a constant influence for the higher and better life. Lodges were very popular and early in the history of the county all the leading lodges were organized; some weakened and faded out of the picture. Others, the Masons and the Odd Fellows, are still well organized and going strong. Also the Eastern Star and the Rebeccas have strong working organizations. The P. E. O., Study Clubs and other cultural organizations are active and doing some splendid work. School work has been reviewed and brought down to present times in other chapters. So much for our early pioneers. They wrought well in their time, and their work has long since ended, except here and there one who has lived beyond his

85

time. We have tried to relive with the "old-timers" his life and times, and record them faithfully for future generations.

LIFE ON THE RANGE

Right here we would like to leave a picture of the early cattle industry and the life of the riders whose endurance and fortitude; whose efforts and skill, first brought success to a vast wealth producing industry which, in a modified form, has come down to our own times.

The life of the riders was life in the open. He rode in the wind and the sun day after day, and slept beneath the stars at night. His bedding he kept in the form of a bed roll, and it consisted of two or three blankets and a "suggin" which was a very heavy bed comfort, and the whole was wrapped in a water proofed canvas called a tarp. Usually there was a coat for a pillow, or the saddle blanket, when it was not needed in the bedding, was used, and often the saddle itself. The bed roll was kept in the chuck wagon. When riding the range it was the riders bedding in all weather. When it rained or snowed the tarp kept him dry and helped to keep him warm. He was usually too tired to worry about anything else. When not working the cattle and not riding herd, as in mid-winter, a shelter was often provided as a kind of headquarters and from these points the cowboys would ride out to look after the cattle to "keep track" of their whereabouts, to change them to new grazing locations and see that they did not stray too far afield. Shelters were also provided at convenient places on the summer range as the frequent summer rains made it disagreeable to be out in the open at night, and they often came in handy on rainy days.

The clothes and equipment of the rider belonged characteristically to his calling, and it grew out of the necessities of his case. He wore a broad brimmed hat to protect him from the sun's rays as he rode in it day after day. The style, as you may see, grew out of his need. He wore close fitting trousers of strong denim or jeans as a matter of convenience so they would not be catching or hanging onto things, thus impeding freedom of action. He wore the conventional cowboy boots, pointed toes, high heels set well forward under the arch of the foot and, in the old days, high tops. This boot, too, was not just a style. It grew out of his necessity. The pointed toes were so made that the booted foot could find and enter the stirrup with quick precision, and be as easily and quickly withdrawn; and those high heels—they need no defense. The booted foot, going through the stirrup in times of swift and unconscious action, is something that must never happen. To guard against this the heels are made high. The front of the heel is made to come well forward toward the center of the arch. This is to keep the foot from slipping too deep into the stirrup, thus bringing the shin bone with some pressure, against the top of the stirrup causing pain and irritation on the bone. The heel, set well forward, prevents this. These heels look awkward and clumsy, but we must remember the cowboy boot is made to ride in—not to walk in.

Then those spurs: they are not the wicked and cruel things they look to be. They are necessary because of their convenience. When a rider is working he needs both hands all the time. He can't be hampered with a quirt, or any other persuader held in the hand, and the spur is the only answer. A horse that is well trained never has to be "dug" with the spurs. Almost always just a touch with the spurs will get quick and instant action whenever it is needed. A belt, always, for keeping up the trousers. A pair of suspenders would be the height of the ridiculous; they wouldn't last one race after a cow brute through the thick brush. Heavy leather cuffs are worn by most riders, especially when working in the brush. When riding at full tilt through brush or low trees, the cuff, reaching from the hand to the elbow, is always needed so the rider can protect his face from the limbs or brush in his path. He does this by throwing up his cuffed arm to catch the force of the branches or brush as he rushes by. The hands need protection, too; riders need gloves and nearly all wear them when working. They are especially needed when roping or handling struggling animals with a rope. One could get his hands badly burned if he did not have gloves. Then the shaps, or leggins, as they are called in many places. Shaps are about the most necessary article in the rider's equipment. One must have them to protect the legs from the tearing, whipping action of the brush or low trees; he must have chaps to protect his clothing, or have them torn off by the brush, and lastly, chaps are a great comfort when riding out in the cold or a wet storm. The average rider would prefer being without any other article of his riding equipment than his shaps.

The rider, in the old days, always had six or eight horses in his mounts, when working the range. Many people ask: Why so many horses for one person to ride? The answer is, because he needed them. When working cattle on the range, when the rider rides, he rides, and there is no "fooling around." He is paid to work, and when he works his horse works, and works hard. There must be a change every half day, and, on the plains, the riders often change mounts four times a day. When rounding up cattle to cut or brand, one would get nothing done if he rode his horse only in a walk. A fast trot or gallop is the usual pace. Then cow horses are never fed, even when in hardest use. For this reason horses must have time between rides to rest and graze. One can see that a rider had to have more than one or two horses.

Here in the west cow ponies were not the rule. The average rider wanted a cow horse—a real horse with weight and strength to carry a big man up hill and down hill, through the rocks and brush and over any kind of terrain, and he wanted a mount big enough and strong enough that he could rope any kind of animal and tie it to his saddle horn with safety. A flat footed horse was out. The rider wanted a horse with straight hoofs well gathered in and strong, and when in regular use, the horse must always be shod, to guard against lameness when riding in the rocks and, in the hills and mountains, there were rocks everywhere. The horse with a good strong hoof was usually a sure-footed animal not given to stumbling or falling.

The average rider was strong, inclined to be lean, and tough, and able to endure hardships and hard work. Long hours in the saddle, riding hard, every day; often on guard two or three hours every night, or every other night, required strength and endurance. Bringing in wild animals often required much very hard riding. On long rides from one distant point to another, horses were trained to go in an even "jog trot" and keep it up hours on end.

Typical of all range work was the round-up. Roundup grounds are selected for their convenient location to a certain range territory and the same place is used year after year, when there is nothing to change the basic situation. On the morning of the roundup the chuckwagon is driven to a point near the roundup ground and the cook prepared to get dinner for fifteen or twenty men. The riders are sent out in every direction, five to ten miles distant, to find the cattle and bring them in. For example the town of Cortez is located on an old roundup ground. The riders went out to every distant part of the valley to bring in the cattle and the whole valley would be worked thoroughly to get every animal.

By ten o'clock enough cattle are usually in so they can start branding. Two or three persons are assigned to hold the herd, a hot fire is built and the branding irons are soon hot. Three or four persons are assigned to do the branding and one rider that is very good with a rope takes the job of bringing out the calves, as this is a typical spring roundup and there are many calves. He rides into the herd, selects a calf that is following close by its mother. He takes a note of the brand that is on the cow, throws his rope on the calf, catching him by the neck; then he drags the calf from the herd, often bleating and, with all four feet set forward, pulling back with all is might. The mother cow follows a way smelling and mooing; then goes back into the herd. The calf is dragged to a point near the fire, a man catches the rope and follows it down to the calf, maneuvers it into place, then catches it in the flank and under the neck and lays, or "busts" him down, takes the rope off the calf's neck and the roper goes back to the herd for another calf. The roper has called out the brand that was on the mother cow, the calf has been thrown down with the side upward that takes the brand. The man assigned to do the branding is a fellow that is handy at the work. He knows where the brand goes and how it is made. A man with a sharp knife puts in the ear mark that goes with the brand and, if it is a male calf, the castrating job is done. Meantime two men, one at the head and the other at the hind feet, are holding the calf. In the old days this was all. Now, in addition to the above work, the calf is often dehorned by cutting out his nubbs and burning them thoroughly with a hot iron to prevent regrowth and stop bleeding, and he is vaccinated for blackleg, septicemia, and, if it is a heifer calf between the ages of four and eight months, it is vaccinated for abortion disease. This makes a long and somewhat cruel ordeal, and the vaccinating job requires an extra man. The work done, the calf is turned loose and it goes back to the herd, the mother cow meeting him at the edge of the herd smelling and mooing, as before. By this time another calf is there and the work goes on, in the heat of the sun, in the heat of the fire, and in the dust and grime and sweat, all day long. This is real work.

Two kinds of irons are used. Some owners have their branding iron made into shape and the brand is just stamped on. Most owners prefer to have their brands run on. A beaver tail or a round rod of iron about a half inch in diameter with a loop in one end is used. The brand is marked out with the hot iron and then burned until it is a solid golden brown; then it will stay there as long as the animal lives. The brand grows with the animal, but if it is well burned in it will always be a good plain brand. Poor brands often grow out until one can't tell what brand it is.

Often one man is especially skilled in putting on the brands. It takes a good steady hand to put on a good clean brand when an animal is twisting and struggling with all his strength.

While the branding is going on other riders are out rounding in more cattle and every little while a new bunch of cattle is brought in and thrown into the herd. As a rule one long day does the job. The outfit then moves to another roundup ground and the operation is repeated. Sometimes a calf is overlooked or not found. Before another roundup time he may be a yearling and weaned, and has no brand. He is then called a maverick. In times past anyone finding such an animal could put his brand on it and it was his. In recent years such animals are turned in and sold and the money used to help defray roundup expenses, or other operating expenses.

In roundup time every person having cattle on the range had men in the roundup crew to help with the work. The main food in the diet, of course, was beef. When meat was needed a fat animal was butchered, and there was no seasoning or cooling the meat before using. It was used right now. If the weather was warm, since there was no ice or other ways of cooling, the meat must be used before very long. The beef animal would be taken from one man's herd one time, from another the next, and so on around to all owners. Then start over again.

There are two roundup seasons and in the fall, at the proper time, the cattle are rounded up as before, this time on the summer range. All late calves are branded, but there are not nearly so many as in the spring. After branding the herd is "cut" to get out the beef animals each owner wishes to ship to the market. The herd may be cut again to give each man his own cattle to take to his ranch. Usually this work is done as the cattle are brought down from the summer range. All cattle going back to the winter range are usually taken down all in one herd.

The herd of horses used in this work is in charge of one man called the horse wrangler, or simply the wrangler. The horses assigned to each man for his use is called his mount, and all the horses together are called the remuda or, often, the army term, the cavayard, is used. Every mount has one or two horses especially trained for cutting a herd and he is called a cutting horse. Similarly horses are trained for roping, and for holding animals after they have been roped. They are trained also to "But 'em down" until the rider, or some one else, can get to the animal and hold him or tie him. Cutting horses are often so well trained that when the rider goes to take an animal out of the herd, all he has to do is to let the horse know which animal is wanted and the horse will do the rest. All the rider has to do is ride.

Ways of rearing cattle have changed radically in recent years, but the ways of working cattle are much the same. The old time cowboy who went out on the range and, for weeks or months, saw no one but his working companions, is a personage of the past. Working cattle is easier and better now. It is still hard work when you are really working, but one can often be home every night, or sleep in a comfortable cabin where it is warm and dry. This chapter is written to preserve for the future a picture of the work and the old life out on the range.

AT HOME WITH THE SHEEP

The sheep industry has nothing of the glamour and the alluring appeal of the cattle industry, but the profits are fully as appealing and many people had rather run sheep than cattle. Several people of the county have been very successful with sheep, and made small fortunes. Among these we might mention W. I. Myler, the Ritter Brothers, Frank Morgan and sons, Tom Fowler, Redd and Summers, and others.

The sheep industry in the county had a meager beginning. Not long after the first cattle herds came in a few sheep began to appear. Efforts were made to bring sheep in from Utah, early, but they were effectively discouraged. The writer has failed to learn where the first sheep came from or when they came. There were some sheep on the range in the county sixty or more years ago. The sheep industry has never reached nearly the importance of the cattle industry but have a distinct place in our economy and are important in that they fill a place in the livestock industry better than it can be filled by any other livestock. As an example sheep are adapted to grazing in the high ranges, up near timberline, and this high range is assigned to the sheepmen by the Forest Service. They are also better adapted to grazing very rough

90

range areas. Steep, rough hills and rocky terrain have no terrors for the sheep. They go anywhere they can find feed they like. One drawback is that they can't go to these high ranges until late, even to early summer, and they must come down out of the high areas early in the fall to avoid a possibility of being trapped in by an early storm. However the sheepmen are usually given some lower grazing to lengthen somewhat their grazing season.

In winter they fit in in another way. The winter range for cattle is almost no more, but there is still quite a lot of winter range that can be utilized by sheep, by reason of the fact that they browse more and do well on some feeds that cattle will hardly eat at all unless starved to it. White sage and salt sage they eat readily and vast amounts of the common sage if other feed becomes scarce. Various weeds are eaten in season and the sheep won't scorn good grass if it is available.

Running sheep is radically different from running cattle, and the sheep is a different animal—different in makeup and different in temperament. In fact the sheep is very temperamental, and about the first thing one must learn is how to get along with him. Sheep require much more attention than cattle. They must be herded and kept rather close together all the time when out on the range, and this is about all the time with the range herds. One thing necessary to be successful with sheep is a good herder—one that understands the sheep's nature and knows how to deal with him. A good herder has much less difficulty with the sheep than a poor herder and the sheep do much better under a good herder. Another thing that reflects on profit is lambing time. Various methods are used in lambing, but the main object of every method is to save every lamb one can. This always takes a lot of attention and care—often night and day for a while, and it is especially difficult in stormy weather. Many successful sheep men have shelter quarters for lambing, especially if they lamb early. Some sheepmen prefer to lamb late and out in the open. The right method for every person is the one he can be most successful in using.

As every one knows, in the sheep industry there are two crops a year for the market. One owner will stress wool as the most important, another the lamb crop. Both are important because it usually takes all one can make out of both crops to show a good profit. There is no rule to go by. One can but use his own judgment and do the best he can.

In earlier times cattle and sheep men didn't get along too well, and there was sometimes trouble, but now the Forest Service designates the range for each permittee on the Forest, and off the Forest each have range rights by established use which are generally respected, and the troubles of the old days are no more. A few cattlemen have quit cattle and gone into sheep. It is a matter of personal choice, although a person may think his setup is better for sheep than for cattle and decides to change over. In the old days all sheep shearing was done with hand shears. A big flock took several shearers and several days of work. Machine shearing is a better job, produces a better fleece and is three or four times faster.

Every band of sheep has a camp for one or more herders. The Forest Service regulations require that sheep must be changed from one range to another every few days, so the camp must be as often moved. Sheep damage range if kept on one range too long hence the necessity for a change. The same practice is followed on range off the Forest.

Life with the sheep is a very prosaic life, and very lonely, especially if there is but one herder to the band. But sheep men like sheep. They are so innocent and helpless, and so willing to give up when the going gets tough. But, ordinarily, they will respond to good care and return to the owner a profit, often when other livestock are losing money to their owners, or making a very slim profit.

THE MENEFEES

Of the settlers of the Mancos Valley prior to 1880 only the Menefees are still with us. In 1877 the family arrived in the valley, not the first, but close to the first. The following account from the life history of Mrs. Menefee covers the family career as completely as we are able to give it. The sketch was written before Mrs. Menefee's death and is her own account of the family career: Sarah A. Menefee (Mrs. William Andrew Menefee) was born in Iowa as Sarah A. Demais, February 19, 1850, one of a family of 21 children. In 1863 the family moved to Walla Walla, Washington, then a village of only 13 houses. They crossed the plains in a caravan of 60 wagons, the Indians were on the war path and they saw along the way where many small companies had been wiped out. In Walla Walla she grew to womanhood, married William Andrew Menefee. Enticing stories from friends in Denver induced them to come to Colorado. They traded their farm and land for a herd of highly bred horses, most of them of a racing strain, left Walla Walla in September, 1876, with three children and a herd of horses and came to Denver late in the fall. There they found there was no sale for horses, as they had been told, and there was no feed and no grass, so they came on down to Huerfano County, in the south part of the state, to winter. There being no road, progress was very slow. There they met John White, who had homesteaded land in the Mancos Valley, and Mr. White persuaded them to come on to Mancos. On their way they camped on the Florida, near the Pine river, to scout out the country. While camped there Mr. Menefee was breaking a young stallion, which fell with him, or threw him, and broke his collar bone. They were delayed two weeks. Finally another traveler came along, a Mr. Jasper Bean; he set the bone and bound up the arm so the bone would stay in place, and they came on. Mrs. Menefee, being a good teamster, drove the four horse team with Mr. Menefee in

92

the seat beside her. They still had the horses. They were three days coming from Durango to the Mancos Valley, having to build the road as they came, and arrived here July 28, 1877. They got down the Mancos Hill by rough locking and a rope around a tree to help hold back on the steepest places, Mrs. Menefee managing the team. They found abundant grass and water—grass that completely hid the cattle when they were lying down. From the upper valley they moved by the old road along the hill on the north side, met a group of Indians at the river crossing, on the Vern Robbins place, and went on down to the Mitchell place, the old Weston place, who had arrived a few days previous, then on down to the White place in the lower valley. At this place now were Mr. and Mrs. White and young son, J. J. Morefield and young bride and the Menefees. Here they had more experiences with the Indians, but no trouble.

Early next spring the Menefees moved to the Dick Giles place to care for Mr. Giles who was very ill of pneumonia. Giles died and they later bought the place from the Giles estate, and it became their home as long as they needed a home. This home being on the main road, if road it may be called, became the stopping place for many people coming and going. They fed people in numbers and bedded them down in a small cabin, on the floor, when it was storming, as it often was. It was first planned to build the town of the valley on the Menefee ranch, the post office was moved up from the McIntyre place but the town on the Mancos site came into existence first. However the ranch was cowboy headquarters for a while and the cowboys were always friendly and helpful. The large 13 room Menefee residence was erected in 1886, Mrs. Menefee helping to haul in lumber. Mr. Menefee died in 1902. In the fall of 1877 Mr. Menefee took all the stock horses to Salt Lake City, as related in another chapter, sold some and traded the rest for cattle, returning in the late fall.

There were six boys in the Menefee family. The oldest, John Menefee, died in Missouri, where he had been sent to attend school. George, the next oldest, is still a resident on the old Menefee ranch, as this is being written; Ed, the next, lives in Indiana, William Menefee, the next in age and the first white male child to be born in the Mancos valley, and likewise, in Montezuma County, still makes his home on a part of the old home place, Charles and Lewis still reside in Mancos. There were no girls.

It has been a remarkable family in more ways than one. Of the five boys still living, four are still here in the Mancos valley, all but two are above eighty years of age, and all have led useful, active lives.

THE DAIRY INDUSTRY

The first attempt at dairying in the County dates from about 1880 when John Brewer milked a few cows in the lower Mancos Valley, made butter and sold it at old Parrott City. After that various efforts at producing milk in a small way and finding a market in the local demand, were made. About 1903 C. E. Rentz, an experienced dairyman, attempted to produce milk, cream and butter for the local demand at Mancos, the business changed hands and soon ceased to be. Through the years, at every town in the County, there was usually some person trying to fill the local demand for milk with indifferent success.

On March 17, 1905, a meeting was held in Mancos and plans made to build a creamery, $5,000.00 was soon subscribed for stock and 200 cows were signed up, a company was organized and incorporated, and by the end of March the building of the creamery was under way and by early June the plant was ready for operation. It turned out a quality product from the start and it found a ready market, but the enterprise was never a complete success. Efforts to operate the creamery continued for twelve or fifteen years, first as a locally owned corporation; then under private management. Finally all effort to operate was given up and the machinery sold.

The cream separator came into use as a result of building the Mancos Creamery and many farmers continued to produce cream and the dairy industry went on and grew slowly. Outside competition for the cream was the main factor in closing the creamery.

After the closing of the Mancos Creamery, and before it was closed, outside interests established cream receiving stations in every part of the county, cream found a ready market and the dairy industry continued to develop. There was not much in producing cream, the price being low, but it was cash. During the depression, along with all other farm produce, cream was low, selling for many months at eleven cents a pound. In 1932, the cream price went up from 11 to 13 cents a pound.

In March, 1931, the movement for a cooperative creamery for Cortez was put over and the money for the stock subscribed. Work was started at once on a building and a building 40x56 feet was built and a full equipment of up-to-date machinery was installed. P. T. Kuhre is chosen manager and Walter Carpenter employed to operate the plant, which was opened for business, Sept. 7, 1931.

As in the case of the Mancos Creamery, there was initial success. The output grew rapidly, a good product was put on the market and a ready demand took the full output. Again outside creameries offered a little more for butter fat than the Coop could pay, and they got the business. The cream producers went back on their own enterprise. The creamery struggled along for a few years, made little headway and was finally closed down for keeps.

Toward the end of the life of the creamery milk producers of the county organized to produce milk for the market. They found that producing milk for the market was more profitable and less work. At first the market for milk was quite limited and much cream continued to be produced. New markets for milk opened up at Salt Lake and Albuquerque and a much larger volume of milk was produced, and the dairy industry grew rapidly. Many small producers are marketing cream and the larger producers are marketing milk and many grade A barns have come into existence. They are of the latest pattern and design and comply with all sanitation requirements. Just now the tank system is coming into use and a number of the larger producers are installing this system.

In the summer of 1956 an effort was made to put the industry on a better basis and statistics were collected that indicated that the county had an overall dairy production of about $400,000 annually. The milk industry, like the creameries, is meeting strong outside competition. Outside firms have the local market all over the county and milk producers are compelled to go to Gallup, Albuquerque and Salt Lake City for their market, and are marketing their product at a big expense. The need, as everyone knows, is for a local processing plant, but establishing a plant and a business presents more difficulties than most people realize. There is a confident feeling that the matter will work itself out. The local producers, assuredly, are entitled to the local market. Local production and the local market are growing, and it seems as if a local processing plant must be the ultimate end.

Dairying, or milk production, has grown to be one of the major industries in the county, and it is still growing. Producing milk is one of the things the farmers of the county can do, and do very well. Natural conditions are right and local demand is growing. Many dairymen in the county are producing from 1,000 pounds up to 2,000 pounds of milk per day, and the overall production would be greatly increased with proper market incentive. A processing plant in the county would solve many problems.

A few of the Mancos producers are Foster Halls, Willis Smith, G. E. Humiston, Harry Halls, Robert Jones, Harmon Matthews, Kent Schmitt, J. W. Wright and Son, Vern Eschelman, John Decker and Charles and Al Gilliland.

Some Montezuma Valley producers are Tom Cox, Tony Sucla, Jerald Neil, Earl Hart, John Carver, Francis McCabe, Jerry Pryor, Pete Katzendorn, Gordon Maness and many others.

Many farmers over the county are producing cream on a small scale, as a sideline and the aggregate income would run into many thousand dollars during the course of a year.

CHAPTER IX

MONTEZUMA VALLEY IRRIGATION

After some years of patient waiting lifegiving water came to the Montezuma Valley in 1889. James W. Hanna was the man that finally made the dream of years come true. In 1885 he interested men of wealth in the future of the big valley, organized a company and built the ditch system that brought the water to the waiting land. The Montezuma Valley Water Supply Co. was the name of the first company and it was perfected in November, 1885. The main personnel of the company were B. L. Arbecan of Boston, President; James W. Hanna of Cortez, Vice President, and General Manager; E. S. Turner of New York, Secretary, and A. B. Chamberlain of Denver, Treasurer. M. J. Mark was first employed as head engineer to lay out the irrigating system and the town of Cortez. He was replaced later by George Stanford and James Gawith.

It was the purpose of this company to bring the water of the Dolores River through and under the divide that separates the river from the big valley by means of a tunnel and distribute the water by means of canals and ditches to every part of the valley and the country west of the main valley. The money having been made available, the first matter in hand was to lay out the purposed irrigating system and plan the work.

It was slow going at first as everything for doing the work had to be brought in or induced to come in. Teams by the score, plows, scrapers and shovels and hundreds of men would be needed for such a large undertaking. By 1887 the work was going in a big way. Getting the tunnel through the divide, a distance of 5,400 feet, was the largest single task, but contractors of experience were put on this work and a little water was gotten through the tunnel in late 1888, but it was 1889 before it was completed to carry a full head of water.

When the construction of the tunnel and canal system was assured many men and families came into the valley and many of them, perhaps most of them, took up land under the homestead law and planned to make a home. Almost all had teams and most of them planned to work on the construction of the ditches and canals as a means of getting a living and making some money with which to improve their

Early Cortez Scene: Lee Kelly and his freighting outfit. About 1893.

Montezuma County Officers, 1912. Left to right: Sam Burke, Judge Morefield, Clark Brittain, Harry Sprague, S. W. Carpenter, Harry Kelly, James Gawith, Evarts, Bill Myler, Lalla Durwood, Charley Ried, Frank Miller.

Southwest Memorial Hospital, Cortez, Colorado. Less than half of building shown. Forty rooms for patients, special rooms of every kind. Every kind of modern service and equipment.

Partial view, Montezuma County High School at Cortez. In addition there are four excellen grade school buildings.

Jake and Cora Dobbins, early settlers, McElmo Canon.

One of the first houses built in McElmo Canon. Home of Elsworth Porter. Mary Wallace was born here.

Old Morton Flume, Canal No. 2. Replaced by canal; carries 350 second feet of water. Montezuma Valley irrigating system.

River portal of tunnel, conveying water to Montezuma Valley. Built 1887-1889. Lester Frailey, Supt.

Peter T. Guillet, pioneer Indian trader and Cortez merchant for 40 years.

Herman Guillet

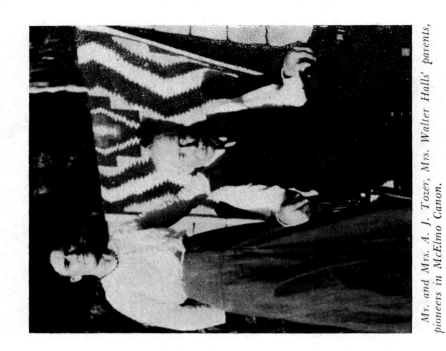

Mr. and Mrs. A. J. Tozer, Mrs. Walter Halls' parents, pioneers in McElmo Canon.

James K. P. Gollaway early in McElmo Canon. He won prizes and blue ribbons by the score on his fine fruit.

homesteads. They usually joined forces in small groups and took as large a contract as they figured they could handle. This made scores of contracts, but they got the work done. Regular contracting companies took larger contracts and the more difficult work. Teams, plows, slip scrapers, wheel scrapers, and black powder was about the best, and only, building equipment available at that time. Later dirt elevators and dump wagons were put on the job. Power machinery for moving dirt had not yet come into use here in the west, so a great many men and teams were put on the work. The work moved rapidly for the most part and by the time the water was coming through the tunnel in volume most of the canals were ready to carry the water, locks and valves and headgates being in place.

There were handicaps, in a way. Water was scarce in the valley before the water was brought in, or was obtainable only at widely scattered springs, some of the springs weer very weak and some of the water was not usable, being strong with alkali. Much water had to be hauled from the better springs and even from the Dolores river.

All the feed for the work animals, save and excepting that provided by the native grasses, had to be hauled from the Mancos Valley, 15 to 25 miles away. Hay and grain had already become fairly abundant in the valley so that this necessity could be taken care of and the work proceeded.

About the time work on the system bringing water through the tunnel got well under way, a second company, to be known as the Dolores Number Two Land and Canal Co. was organized and, in April, 1887, commenced the construction of the big canal that takes off from the tunnel intake and goes down the river and was known as the Dolores No. 2 Canal. On this canal was the big Morton Flume and the great cut through the divide between the Dolores river and the valley. This cut was over 4,000 feet long and 40 feet deep in the deepest place. Also the flume was a little over a mile long and a notation states that it was 18 feet wide and 7 feet deep. This flume has just been replaced entirely by a canal 18 feet wide at the bottom and with a carrying capacity of about 350 second-feet. These two parts of the big canal made the construction of the canal very expensive. The work was finally finished about 1907 and the canal, in itself will carry a small river of water. It was designed to carry water to an elaborate ditch and canal system and irrigate many square miles of territory out on the Yellow Jacket, the Hovenweep, Trail, Alkali and a part of the McElmo Canon. The Narraguinep reservoir is filled each year from this canal.

With so many small groups working on the system and almost all inexperienced in such work progress was necessarily slow, but the work was done at last and the lifegiving water came to the thirsty land. The valley was unfortunate in a way in the kind of new citizens it attracted. They came in three classes: First were the men who came with an earnest and determined purpose to create a farm and make a home. They worked on the ditch some; perhaps a good deal; but they worked on their land, built a place to live and got some land ready for the water when it should come. These were the most desirable ones. Then there was another class of settler who intended well, but worked right through the ditch construction period and when the water came to his land he had no land ready and there was no way to use the water. Then a third class filed homesteads for no other purpose than holding them until they could sell their claim for whatever money he could induce some one to pay. This created a bad situation, especially for the company who had put their money into the ditch system. When they brought the water to the land most of the landholders were not ready to buy and use it, and the remote location, lack of markets, poor transportation, and other hindrances, made it difficult for even the best farmers to make ends meet. The result was that the company that built the canal system went broke before they got started. They sold comparatively little water and found it difficult to collect for most they did sell.

Very soon after the Montezuma Valley Water Supply Co. got to operating it was taken over by the Colorado Water Supply Co. This new company met the same difficulties and continued to operate only until 1890 when it was merged with the Dolores No. 2 Canal Co., that built the big canal down the river, and the new company thus formed was called the Colorado Consolidated Land & Water Co.

Sometime after 1894, the Colorado Consolidated Land & Water Co. transferred its holdings to the Montezuma Water and Land Co. At a later date this company became insolvent and a receiver was appointed and the affairs of the company was handled by the receiver until 1907.

In the year 1892 there was perfected out of the water appropriation from the Dolores river to the Colorado Land and Water Co., a decree for 64.6 second feet of water. At this same time a conditional decree for 1,234.4 second feet of water was obtained from the same source, making a total of 1,300 second feet of water.

After the Montezuma Water and Land Co. took over the water system, or the service, the revenues from the operation of the system, and the delivery of water, after expenses, paid but little on the investment and did not justify further expenses for improving the system. Operation of the company under the receivership was anything but satisfactory, and there was constant conflict and dissatisfaction, and Mr. Freeman, the receiver, became thoroughly disliked and soundly abused by the water-users. The dissatisfaction on the part of the water users became so great that it led to the formation of the Montezuma Valley Irrigation District, by the landowners under the water system, and on January 7, 1902, the first meeting of the board of Directors was held. The plan of the district was to buy out and take over the water system and operate it wholly in the interest of the water users. The Board was inexperienced, every one was inexperienced, and had no definite idea what to do or how to do it. Everyone knew they must bond the district to raise the money, and many were in favor of building a new water system and let the old system go. This was, of course, absurd, since the ditch company owned the water rights and the rights-of-way for the present ditches and canals. Various sums were proposed for the purchase of the old company, the sums varying from $80,000 to $325,000.

The strife continued and conditions grew worse, if any change, and it was the year 1907, five years after the formation of the irrigation district, before a workable plan was finally proposed, and one that both sides would consider. At this time a bond issue of $795,000 was voted and a contract with the Empire Construction Co. was entered into by the terms of which the Construction Company was to take the bonds, acquire all the property and water rights of the old company, rebuild the irrigating system and construct two new storage reservoirs. In the purchase arrangements $325,000 was to go for the purchase of the water rights and the old ditch system; $45,000 for the first years interest on the bonds, and $425,000 for construction and reconstruction purposes.

After months of negotiation a contract was finally signed, in late 1906, between the new Montezuma Valley Irrigation District and the Empire Construction Co., D. A. Canfield, Pres., by the terms of which contract the construction company takes over $795,000 in District bonds, already voted, for which they agree to acquire the old water system and water rights, complete the proposed system, including two large reservoirs, on specifications that will assure an abundant water supply for 50,000 irrigatable acres of land in the District and to turn the same over to the District fully completed by May 1, 1908, and pay the first years interest on the bonds. The contract was submitted to the voters of the District April 13, 1907, and was ratified by the voters by a vote of 160 for and 20 against, and settled, for a time, the largest and most important matter ever to come before the voters of the big valley. The deal was closed in Denver April 30, 1907. The Empire Construction Co. already had option price and terms on the old system, so there was no delay. "The ditch is ours" is the message that came over the wires from Denver to the Mancos Times Tribune May 3, 1907. Also came the order to the two board members at Cortez to take possession of the irrigating system and begin signing water contracts for the current year.

The Empire Construction Co. takes steps at once to get some of their heavy equipment on the ground to start the work. Busy times for everyone are just ahead.

W. H. Crawford takes a big contract and sets 80 teams and 200 men to work on ditches and laterals. Groundhog work was to start as soon as the snow was out of the way. In May two dirt elevators and 20 dump wagons go up to the Groundhog site, much other equipment and many men. Loftus and Skidmore have a contract to furnish 80 or 90 thousand dollars worth of lumber for fluming and piping on the new construction in the valley.

This was the hour of triumph, but days of tribulations lay ahead. The large bond issue created a tremendous burden for the landowners, since the valley was very much undeveloped and there were so few people to bear the burden. It was now a race between getting in new people and capital, and increasing the wealth producing capacity of the country so it can meet the increased burden of interest payments and operating expenses, before the increased burden of interest payments and operating expenses should bring on a crisis and the whole arrangement collapse under the burden. More money was needed and an additional bond issue of $125,000 was voted.

There was not enough money for carrying out the terms of the contract with regard to construction and reconstruction, and the assessment levy for paying interest and operating expenses was so great that many landowners could not or would not pay. This began rapidly to create a bad condition. To add to all this trouble many expensive errors were made by the management, and a decision of the federal court in Denver held that the bonds were all inclusive and that the payment of assessments by any one person did not relieve him from having to pay as long as there were claims against the district. This caused many who could pay to refuse to pay, and there were few buyers at the tax sales.

It can now be seen that the situation was nearing the impossible. A great many taxes remained unpaid and the unsatisfactory condition led to a movement for a division of the county, creating a new county out of the east end of Montezuma County. The movement met with opposition, but it aroused the Montezuma Valley people to a new realization of their responsibility; that the movement for a new county was, in a measure, justified, and a feeling of pride asserted itself. A determination was born anew to get more of the taxes paid and to meet every responsibility regardless of the burden it imposed.

The taking over of the water system by the Irrigation District had given new life and confidence for a few years, the spending of the district money on construction had built up local finances, many new people came into the valley and much new capital, but not enough. This new confidence, for a while, caused new growth. The town of Cortez, and the farming area, grew in population and wealth. A new town was laid out at Lebanon, roads were improved, telephone systems and lines were built, much new land was cleared and put into cultivation and hundreds of acres of orchards were planted, but the old handicap still remained. Our remote situation—far out from wealth and population centers; poor transportation and high freight rates, poor markets and lack of local capital and local industries, and

100

not enough people, all combined to create a difficult situation that it was well nigh impossible to overcome. The period from about 1913 to 1919, was especially trying, more and more taxes remained unpaid and the Irrigation District was in a state of bankruptcy all through the period. The population seems to have declined and the census figures for the town of Cortez showed a decline in population from 565 in 1910 to 541 in 1920. That the District survived at all may be attributed to the extraordinary natural resources of the big valley and the power of the land to produce. Notwithstanding water shortages, year after year good crops were produced and dairying, fruit and other industries were developed, and the people did everything they could to make a dollar. When they decided they could do better they did do better, by themselves and by the other people of the county. And, notwithstanding all the unfavorable conditions, the Irrigation District won through somehow and survived for eighteen years, or until 1920, when the District was reorganized and a new plan evolved.

For some time the District Board, realizing that something must be done, had been working on a plan to put all the indebtedness of the District on an individual liability basis and Ex-governor Carlson was employed to work out a plan. By 1920 the plan had been worked out and means of putting the plan into effect was adopted. Some time previous the Farm Land Securities Co. had been prevailed upon to undertake the matter of refinancing the debt of the District on the new basis, and by 1920 they were ready to take the affairs of the District in hand to liquidate all the district indebtedness, dissolve the old district and form a new irrigation district and a mutual ditch company under the name "The Montezuma Valley Irrigation Co.," incorporated under the laws of Colorado. Under the new plan individual mortgages were executed for all water users and the aggregate value of all these mortgages was given as security for the payment of the outstanding indebtedness. By this plan the new irrigation district began business out of debt and its only function was administrative. The new plan was put up to a vote of the people and was adopted by them by a vote of 209 for and 20 against. The near unanimous vote was a big asset to the new order of things. All the bonds of the old district were then called in and paid off and the new financial plan put into effect. With the action of Judge W. N. Searcy rendering a decision dissolving the old irrigation district, and all its liabilities being taken care of by the individual liability method, the old district became a thing of the past.

The decision dissolving the old district took effect September 20, 1920. The new association organized and started to operate about Nov. 1, 1920, the following men having been elected to serve on the first board: E. H. Kittell, Pres., W. I. Myler, Vice President, John Wesch, Sec'y-Treas., E. W. Henry was retained as Superintendent with John Wesch as assistant.

101

The individual liability plan gave new value to all property, new life to business, new hope for the future. Land could now be bought and sold, clear titles could be given and every person was responsible only for his own debts. Land now had a real value and if taxes were not paid the land could be sold with no risk to the buyer.

This new plan has continued to this day. Taxes and assessments have been lowered, much more land has been put under cultivation and county and town populations have grown. Good prices for farm products and livestock from about 1942 to 1954, put every farmer on a sound financial basis that made any real effort to help himself and the financial troubles of the district, and the people, after so many years of failure and disappointment, that plagued them so long, are all over, or as nearly all over as such matters ever get to be.

Since the reorganization of the district, affairs have gone much smoother and better, and there has been a steady development of the resources of the district. Wealth and population have increased, thus dividing the tax burden between many more people and reducing the amount each person must pay.

The number of water users in the District on December 1, 1955 was 694, including many small users in and near the town. The District now has an absolute decreed water right, out of the Dolores river, for 538.5 second feet of water and a conditional decree for 761.5 acre feet making a total of 1300 second feet of water right. In addition it has rights to flood water to fill Groundhog reservoir and the Narraguinep reservoir, and any other reservoir that may be built. There are now about 25 canals, laterals and ditches comprised in the system with a total length of about 175 miles, the longest, Mesa Verde or East lateral, being 30 miles in length. In addition there are hundreds of miles of small ditches individually built and owned or built and owned by associations.

There are two main distributing systems. One distributes the water that comes through the tunnel to all the main part of the valley, proper; the other is the No. 2 Canal that goes down the river from the diversion point, through the newly constructed portion of the canal that takes the place of the old Morton Flume, and on out through the big cut through the divide. This canal fills the Narraguinep reservoir and irrigates the west side of the valley and a part of McElmo Canon, by the Trail Canon ditch. The whole system is in good state of repair and will carry all the water needed on all the farms when the water is available. In 1956 about 35,000 acres in the district are under irrigation and several thousand acres more could be irrigated if there was sufficient water. The great need is for more storage water for late season use.

As this is being written so much new land has been cleared and put under cultivation that the valley is again suffering a shortage of water, especially in dry seasons and bonds have been voted and sold in the amount of one-half million dollars and work is under way to more than double the storage capacity of the Narraguinep reservoir. This will not provide nearly enough water for all the land, and the additional water will be expensive—too expensive to be wasted.

One good answer to the water shortage problem is more water and soil conservation. The entire county need water saving practices and soil saving practices put into effect. The present production of the soil, on the average, is far short of the production of the old days. The soil has been eroded by irrigation and robbed of its fertility elements, by use and abuse, and the only remedy is restorative methods and practices that will build back the old fertility; practices that will always add more to the soil than is being taken out.

Two principal things are needed. One is land leveling, leveling, leveling, and the other is new and better ditches, or a new ditch system, needed on nearly every farm. When this is done the farmer can save water, save labor, save the soil from washing and leeching, and, with better control of water, the work of reclaiming hundreds of acres of swamp land can be carried out. Hundreds of acres of our best land is producing only sedge grasses, swamp grasses, cattails and other growth equally undesirable and equally worthless.

Then, instead of spending money for more water, it would be infinitely better to make a better use of the water we have—better for the land, better for the crops, better for everyone. Your water may not cost very much, but we repeat, it costs too much to be wasted. The northeast part of the state is getting fully twice as much production out of an acre foot of water as we get, and they are figuring all the time on how to get more. We haven't even come to the first stage yet in saving water.

Then we have robbed the land so long, and mined out its fertility, that it is badly in need of restorative measures. You have the information about how to build back the fertility of your soil, or, if you haven't it, you can get it. The man that is getting the most out of his soil is the man that is putting the most into it. Building the soil is not an expense; it's an investment, and one that pays dividends. Instead of buying more land to increase your harvest, you get the same results, or better results, by building back the fertility of the land. If you buy more land you must buy more water and pay more taxes, but better land will get the same result without these additional costs.

This discussion is not out of place. Soil and water conservation is in our present history, and it is in our future history.

You have two agencies in this county that are here to help you solve almost any problem that confronts you as an agriculturalist. They are the Agricultural Extension Agent and his assistant and the Soil Conservation Service. If properly used their services could be worth a million dollars a year to the producers of this county. We challenge you to put this statement to the test.

103

CHAPTER X

MONTEZUMA COUNTY SCHOOLS

Following close on the heels of the earliest settlements in Montezuma County came that All-American institution—the public school. Education for the children was never neglected anywhere in the county and the first generation following the pioneers was as well trained mentally, and as competent in every way, as in the average rural community of the older states. In fact among the "old timers" themselves it was remarkable the extent of the learning and special talent that could be found. So schools came to all the settlements very early in their history.

A few school districts were formed before La Plata County was divided and these retained the numbers they had in the parent county. For example the Mancos district was No. 6 in La Plata County and it became No. 6 in Montezuma County. Likewise the Dolores district, No. 4, became No. 4 in the new county. After the formation of the new county, new school districts continued to be established as new settlements were made until about 1931 when there were 31 organized districts in the county. After this the school districts began to consolidate and many of the smaller and weaker districts were discontinued.

The Beulah district, northwest of Cortez, was the first to be formed after the formation of the new county and became District No. 1. Later Cortez took the District No. 1 place and Beulah was given place No. 2. The records of the original districts that were formed before the new county was created, and of some of the other early districts in the county, are incomplete, so we will not endeavor to trace these. It might be stated that every settlement in the county, that was of any consequence at all, had a school. Some single districts had from one to as many as seven separate schools.

The movement to consolidate districts in the interest of better schools for all the children got under way in 1947 when the people of Sunnyside, also known as the Georgetta school (No. 10), Stoner, No. 14; Bear Creek, No. 16; Oak Hill, also known as the Thomas school, No. 20; and Granath Mesa, No. 24, all voted to dissolve and consolidate with Dolores, District No. 4, and in 1952 the Independence School District was contained in the Dolores district.

District No. 6, Mancos, was always a large district and, at one time, had 6 country schools in addition to the town schools. All these country schools, one after another, were discontinued and the children transported to the town schools, and in 1947, the Menefee school district No. 17, in the upper Mancos Valley, dissolved and consolidated with the Mancos School.

The schools next to follow suit were those about Cortez. In 1953 the people of Blue Door, No. 7; Aztec, No. 12; Arbor, No. 13; voted to dissolve and consolidate with Cortez. In 1954 Beulah, District No. 2, was dissolved and consolidated with Cortez, and in 1955 Mesa Verde school dissolved and consolidated with Cortez.

Consolidation next came to No. 10, known as Pleasant View. In 1954 Dripping Springs, No. 18; Sylvan, No. 21; (Also known as Hovenweep), Rhyman, No. 23; Ackmen, No. 28; Prospect, No. 30, and Fair View all consolidated to form the new district No. 10, known as Pleasant View.

The County districts that have retained their organization and continued to function are as follows:

District No. 3, Lakeview. They have just recently erected a fine, modern grade school building.

District No. 5, Lebanon. Good building, old style.

District No. 8, Arriola. Arriola has always maintained a good building and a good school.

District No. 9, Lewis. Building adequate for present needs.

District No. 11, McElmo, also known as Battle Rock school, has a good stone building.

District No. 15, Mildred. A very good country school.

District No. 19, Goodman Point (Also known as Shilo). Good country school.

District No. 26, Four Corners. Good country school.

District No. 27, Towaoc. Students above third grade transported by bus to Cortez schools.

District No. 29, McPhee. All pupils transported to the Cortez schools.

The Cortez Union High School was organized May 20, 1940, and was transferred to the Montezuma County High School in 1947. The Montezuma County High School now includes all the districts in the county excepting Dolores (No. 4) and Mancos (No. 6). The county high school offers high school privileges to every high school student in the county, outside districts No. 4 and No. 6, and where it is at all possible the high school boys and girls of the county, aside from the two districts noted above, are taking advantage of these privileges.

Very good high schools fully accredited, and excellent grade schools are being maintained in both Dolores and Mancos. Their buildings are modern and high educational standards are maintained.

CHAPTER XI

THE FRUIT INDUSTRY IN MONTEZUMA COUNTY

Two fruit growing areas may be designated for Montezuma County. The first locality to be tested out and to become widely known for its excellent friut is McElmo Canon. The second is an area two to three miles wide and extending from the Burrell orchard on the west to the West Lake View community on the east. It has been a fully established fact that this altitude, soil and climatic conditions are effective in producing the finest quality fruit in flavor and texture, and in color and food value, that comes onto the general market anywhere from far or near. Fruit experts from famous fruit growing areas in other states are ready to admit that Montezuma apples tops them all in every quality that determines an excellent product.

This goes for peaches too. Early in the history of the industry, when fruit growing was only getting started, peaches from McElmo Canon won the highest national award at the World Fair at St. Louis in 1904, and many other high awards, which brought widespread notoriety to McElmo Canon and caused one orchard, the present Vincel orchard to be named the "Gold Medal Orchard" because, in its time, it has won so many gold medals.

Strange as it may seem there is no organization among the county fruit growers. The quality, so far, has been maintained by the individual growers and the market, in the case of apples, is at the orchard. They use sorters and polishers, and every apple with a flaw or blemish is thrown out and the best pack is used. The quality is high and the fruit is firm, crisp and highly flavored, and the apple market appears to be firmly established. There seems to be an unlimited demand at the orchard. Trucks load out directly from the orchard, or from farm storage. Apple varieties are red and yellow Delicious, Rome Beauty and the large improved Winesap and some Jonathans.

In the years from 1909 to 1912 many orchards were set out in the vicinity of Lebanon, but the growers were unfortunate in getting varieties unsuited to the locality. Some of these trees were top-grafted with the more desirable varieties; others were pulled out or are being pulled out. Thousands of new trees are being set out.

Large, top ground cold storage units have been built on two fruit farms, the only ones in the San Juan Basin, and they are proving to be highly successful. When the door is opened one gets no ripened fruit odor, an indication that the fruit is keeping perfectly. Trucks back into these cellars and load out a full load of fruit at one time. The best proof of successful fruit growing is the fact that the growers have a firmly established market and are making money. This applies, of course, to growers who are growing the best varieties and are using strictly modern methods.

In the fall of 1956 the writer visited some of these orchards and wrote the following paragraphs:

The fruit harvest is on. In these last days of September the orchards are marvels of beauty and productivity. Many trees there are that will yield twenty-five dollars in fruit to the single tree, and the fruit is large, well formed and is taking on gleaming colors. The trees are not overloaded, though the branches hang low with the weight, and such perfect fruit. The Delicious have the correct form—slightly elongated, tapering to the blossom end with the characteristic five points distinctly in evidence. The golden delicious slightly more spherical, blossom end points less pronounced, golden in color and in pure worth. The Stamared, a larger and redder edition of the Stamen Winesap, and the glorious Rome Beauty, alike excellent for cooking and eating are also being harvested. The harvest season is yet early, but, even now, the big trucks are trailing in for their part of the bountiful harvest. To the far off places it is moving; away down into thirsty Texas; New Mexico and Arizona want a part and now, of all states, comes California. For two years now they have been hauling the big red apples all the way across the desert, and are coming back for more—the finest, best flavored fruit the season produces anywhere. We say, without fear of successful contradiction, that northern Montezuma Valley produces as fine an apple in texture, color and flavor, and in food value, as can be found anywhere else in the world, and vastly superior to most fruit that comes on the market even from favored locations. The consuming public is proving it. Where else, and to what other place is a far away population making a beaten path to a producing area attracted solely by quality of product? This market seems firmly established. Nothing but gross neglect, mismanagement, or downright carelessness could ever lose it to the growers.

Every apple producing area of any consequence has selling agents pushing its fruit on the market. Here no one tells the story of Montezuma County apples but the person who eats it. It sells on its merits. The producing area is not large, but it has distinct possibilities, if the industry is properly developed. It is only one of the many things the people here do, and are beginning to do well. We will give a brief summary of a few growers who have made history, or are making history, in the fruit industry in Montezuma County.

THE BURRELL ORCHARD

D. V. Burrell is one of a number of people who has made history in fruit growing in Montezuma County. Mr. Burrell's first notable work was the establishing of the D. V. Burrell Seed Co. at Rocky Ford, Colo., where he built up a successful and very profitable business in growing and distributing flower and vegetable garden seed. Having realized fully on his plans at Rocky Ford, he began scouting around for a suitable location for another enterprise—that of growing fruit on a large scale. After having looked over several locations he selected Montezuma Valley as the most desirable place, and the place where his proposed enterprise would most likely succeed.

Mr. Burrell's first interest was in growing flower and garden seed, about 1932. With a gradually changing purpose seed production was discontinued and, in 1937, he started a small nursery to produce fruit tree stock for his own planting and in 1939, 1940 and 1941, he set out orchard after orchard until he had 240 acres set to all the common kinds of fruit, with apples far in the lead and peaches next. Adopted varieties had already been proven by local growers so, guided by local experience, he planted entirely to Red Delicious and Golden Delicious as the leaders; then Rome Beauty, Jonathan and Improved Winesap. In eight years the trees reached profitable production and in the past three years the orchard has been fulfilling the hopes the owner had entertained for it. Production came and found good highways in place, truck transportation in abundance, and a waiting market. Besides a good crop of peaches, and some smaller fruit, apple production in 1955 was 35,000 bushels, and in 1956 production will run about 25,000 bushels. Peach production hasn't proven so satisfactory as apple growing owing mostly to irregularities in the market, so the peach crop will gradually be eliminated and apples grown in their place. Frost drainage is good in this area, frost damage is light, taken through the years, and it is not regarded as a damaging factor in the industry.

D. V. Burrell, the prime mover in this enterprise, and the master mind that steered its certain course to a successful conclusion, died in 1953. But he lived to see the fruits of his endeavors reaching assurance of success. He was well pleased with the results he had accomplished and could look into the future and see the time when his investments and his labors would be a great blessing to the land he loved. When he was developing the enterprise he confided to a neighbor fruit grower that he would never live to reap the full reward of his undertaking, but those who should come after him would be the happier, and experience more contentment by reason of his work.

Jerre Burrell, a grandson, is now in full charge of the orchard and responsible for results. Though a young man he seems to be making good. Everything that is necessary to be done to make a high producing orchard and for the production of a high class marketable product, is being done and results are counting in his favor. Grandma Burrell, still hale and active at 81, takes a vivid interest in the orchard and comes over from Rocky Ford frequently to visit her grandson and keep in touch with the enterprise. Plans are under way to put out 7,000 additional Delicious apple trees in 1957.

PHILIP RUNCK

Among the growers producing fruit on a larger scale we find Philip Runck who has the fine tract of land originally homesteaded by Pat O'Donnel. Mr. Runck's residence dates from 1909, and he has been growing fruit for several years. He now has some 25 acres in full producing orchard and it is yielding a very fine quality of commercial fruit, almost all apples. Leading varieties are Red and Golden Delicious, Improved Winesaps and Rome Beauties. Like others, he depends on demand to move his fruit. Large trucks come direct to the orchard during harvest and take the fruit. Machines sort and polish the fruit and the fruit is hand sorted as it goes through the machine. To handle any fruit that might not be taken at harvest time he has an up-to-date top ground cellar that stores 3,500 50 pound boxes. The temperature in this storage space is kept at 32 degrees and the fruit keeps perfectly until it is moved to market—even until the next spring.

Mr. Runck came early enough to have all the distressing experiences of the old days—unsuited varieties, poor rail transportation, high freight rates and poor markets. Year after year the producer worked for practically nothing. The experience was a nightmare compared to the smooth going, profitable business of these present times. Mr. Runck likes the fruit business and he likes to talk fruit.

Just across the road south of the Runck orchard is the orchard of John Doyle—only 10 acres. It is one of those early plantings that had to be top worked and changes over to the new and better varieties. This orchard is a part of the original Bill Myler place and is choice fruit land. Like all the better orchards, this orchard gets good care: careful pruning, thinning and spraying—seven or eight times to insure clean fruit. He uses cover crops to hold and build up the soil and liberal applications of commercial fertilizers. An established market means nearly all the fruit sold and moved at harvest time.

Two up and coming young orchardists are Richard and Everett Tibbitts, near Lebanon. They have the well-known Oscar Prichard orchard, which the boys acquired by purchase two years ago, and, in 1956 ,are taking off their second crop. They have a full crop of beautiful, well formed fruit of the highest quality in texture and flavor. Delicious almost all—Red and Golden Delicious. There are 17 acres in the present orchard—five in peaches and 12 in apples. Plans are under way to put out 35 additional acres in the next two years. The Prichard orchard is a very fine orchard, well kept and cared for under the expert management of Mr. Prichard himself. The boys paid a good price for it, but were so confident of their success that they planned to pay for it out of the earnings in three years. As the harvest starts in 1956 it looks as if they will very near make the grade in two years.

They have adopted all the latest requirements in fine fruit production—careful pruning, thinning, spraying, fertilizing, sorting, polishing and fancy packs. They are also doing some early picking of high colors, leaving the less mature fruit to ripen further. With many new producers coming in they can see clearly that organization will soon be necessary in the interest of uniform grading and packing and a uniform price for standard grades.

The Lebanon locality seems to experience less damage from hail and frost than some adjacent areas. About one year in 25, they claim, they suffer loss from hail damage and about one in eight they have loss from frost. The lowest yield recorded from the Prichard orchard is 2,000 boxes.

There is Eli Neal, Bill Wedel and a number of other successful producers in the Lebanon locality.

THE TOM COX ORCHARD

This orchard of thirty-five acres in down near Arriola, close to where the first orchards in this area were put out. It is on slightly higher ground with better frost drainage. This is a very fine, well-kept orchard and the crop of 1956 was a wonderful showing of fine fruit. Mr. Cox probably has the finest sorting, polishing and packing outfit in the area and employs from 25 to 35 people in the harvest season. Most of the fruit moves to market at picking time, but there is an immense top-ground storage cellar to take care of all fruit that must be stored. The fruit that comes out of this orchard shows expert knowledge and care in its production. It is as nearly perfect as fruit can be grown.

We have picked one orchard in each locality to show what is being done in fruit production. There are many other fine orchards and good producers. Fruit growing in this area is bound to expand. Good profits will bring many more growers in. These will be good, poor and indifferent, poor quality fruit will be produced which will be offered for sale for whatever it is worth. This will necessitate organization. There is little danger of over-production if quality is maintained. There is always a market for the best.

CHAPTER XII

THE ERA OF CHANGE

From the beginning cattle has been a basic industry in Montezuma County. At first, and for years, cattle were wintered on the range and without feed. Even as high as Mancos beef was often taken off the range in early to mid-winter, and for a long time there was no thought of feeding cattle in winter. It was the same on the Dolores river. As the number of cattle increased it became necessary to forage a little further afield to find enough feed and, finally, after the coming of the large herds, it was necessary to use range far to the west and southwest. It seems a little strange to think of this whole country as being covered with tall waving grass, but it was. There was always a little sage brush in the grass, but the grass was the dominant growth and held the sage brush in check.

Then came the cattle, thousands of head, to eat the grass, and then, or later, came dry years. There was less grass, but more cattle, and the grass was overgrazed—grazed to the ground and kept that way, but the cattle would not eat the sage brush unless they were starved to it, so the sage grew and took over from the grass. Then the sage soon became the dominant growth, and when it did, the grass never had a chance again. We do not know how long grass had been dominant, nor how long it would have continued to be the dominant growth if it had not been grazed, but we can see how the change came, and why. Too heavy grazing changed the whole nature of things.

Blue stem grass could never take heavy grazing, in the first place, and the stand weakened quickly and easily; then all but disappeared. As long as there was a good sod of grass the run off from heavy rains and melting snows was held back by the grass stand and the water was taken up by the root-filled soil. This kept the soil from washing and gave the grass the benefit of all the moisture that came in any form. The soil being held in place by the grass and there being little or no run-off, no gullies or deep arroyos were formed. Man and his agents, the cattle, changed all this.

The grasses in the mountains furnished abundant summer feed, and it was good feed. Cattle got fat and young animals grew fast. But there were so many, when they came down to the winter range, they

111

must range far and wide to find enough feed. The older cattle never waited to be brought down from the mountains. When the cold and the snow began to make it uncomfortable in the high country they came down of their own accord and headed for the winter range. Grass and browse had been growing all summer on the low range and they knew feed awaited them. The same was true in the spring when it began to get dry and hot in the low country; they headed for the hills.

There were plain, well worn trails leading back and forth. In the immediate vicinity of Yellow Jacket there were four distinct well worn trails, and there were many others further out and some this way. One much used trail lead down Trail Canon into McElmo Canon. There weer always riders on hand to look after the cattle summer and winter, and this was about the only expense attached to raising cattle in those early days.

The cattle ranged far out to the Blue Mountains and southward to the San Juan escarpment and the deep canons that cut into the upland. Down into these canons some cattle would stray and would never come back. There were considerable numbers in places. Calves would be born and grow to full maturity without a brand . Ever so often the riders would go into these canons and make a drive to get the cattle out. They were wild as deer and it was a good deal like trying to drive a herd of deer, but once they got them started in the right direction and kept them going they could be picked up with a bunch of gentler cattle and taken to any place desired.

George Menefee was one of these riders. Not being needed on the ranch in the Mancos Valley, when he was sixteen years old he went over on the Dolores river to train race horses for Charley Johnson, the elder. Race Horse Johnson as he was generally called. There was a race track and many horses, and all day every day he would exercise and work out the horse on this track, one after another, there being a man there to catch and saddle horses so that there was no waiting between rides. There was a big ranch on the river in the wide valley below where the McPhee sawmill stood, and, besides the horses, there were one or two thousand head of cattle, so, after the race horse training was over, George began to make a regular hand riding the range. This took him to the mountains in summer and to every part of the winter range country in winter. George says he knew every road and trail, every spring and water hole, and where all the best feed was to be found. At first the grass grew in billowing waves above the stinted sage. Then, as noted previously in this narrative, the sage took over and there was much less grass. The short grass, in the white sage, held its own better than the blue stem, so that there was always considerable winter feed, and there was still a profit for the cattleman for a long time, but the high rolling land, where the soil was rich and deep, became a sea of purple sage.

112

But the devastation of dry years and overgrazing was not to be the end of things. The gray expanse of sage yet had a master. Came the homesteader, after the cattleman, and the ax and the grubbing hoe was brought into use. Teams and tractor tore at the brittle growth and made bare the earth by the acre, many acres in a place. Then the crawling monsters of iron and steel snorted over the landscape, and grunted and groaned under pressure of great power, and the gray expanses of sage and the black splotches of pinon and cedar gave place to bald, naked plain. It looked like another debacle of nature was in the making; that water erosion was to give place to both water and wind erosion. But it was not to be. Man had learned how to curry and comb the top soil and hold it in place against the destructive forces of wind, and make it drink up the water that fell from the skies. He learned to mulch the top soil and store the moisture from year to year for the use of his plant life in seasons of growth. Instead of the grass that grew and billowed in the wind; died and perished, then grew again; instead of the sage that cumbered the ground, but did not check the erosive power of water, there came waving fields of golden grain that ripened under the mellow glow of the summer sun; acres and acres of beans, straight rowed, making green the gently rolling ridges mile after mile and providing the comforts of life to many, many homes, and food for the hungry nations.

The cattleman had his day in this area, but that day has forever departed. Nature has its moods, and extremes in climate and seasons come and go, but man has his way. Grasses that were hitherto strangers to this land, now grow as if indigenous to it. Brome and crested wheat and intermediate wheat grasses are being grown to heal the scars. The deep gullies, where the erosive power of water gashed the earth, have been filled in again, and new grasses, defying drouth and summer sun, are lacing down the soil so securely that it will never move again. Here and there a carpet of green is coming to the undulating plain, and well-bred cattle, once a factor so destructive to the native range, dot the landscape and lend beauty and harmony to the rural scene. Livestock in numbers are coming to the land again and the careful work of the husbandman is holding securely all that has been gained. In Montezuma, Dolores and San Miguel Counties no less than four hundred thousand acres of this reddish-brown land has come into this new life. It looks like a condition that will never change, except for the better. It could last for all time.

POLITICAL ALIGNMENT

In politics there was also an era of change. In the early history of the county party lines were drawn sharply along the lines of old party issues. The pioneer was too free and busy to take politics seriously; but they were also in too close a proximity to the ravages of the Civil War and the evils of reconstruction days for the old issues to be completely ignored; so most of the older people brought their politics with them into the west. A majority of these first settlers in Montezuma County were from Missouri and Texas. Democracy was strong in the county and the Democratic party claimed a majority of the county's voting strength. At the very first issues were drawn almost entirely along old party lines, but when the old veterans in both parties began to fade from the picture, the individuality of the candidates began to count for more in the campaigns. The election of Cleveland in 1884 gave rise to a surge of party loyalty and the old Democratic feeling, but he disappointment of the people, especially here in the west, with Cleveland's second term, the demonetization of silver in 1893, a severe depression, or panic, as they called it then, combined with a wide spread drouth all over the west, almost completely broke down old party lines, and the Populist party was born and grew strong at the expense of both the old parties. Populist candidates were elected to office in both the county and the state, during the early nineties, and the nomination of Bryan in 1896, and "Free Silver" as a dominant issue, and Bryan's "Crown of Thorns and Cross of Gold' speeches just about swept everything in the county into the Populist party.

But it was not to last. The Populist leaders, for the most part, were a blatant, unreasoning group, and appealed mostly to the people's prejudice and discontent. When the drouth and the panic were over and times became better, they lost ground rapidly.

The voters, generally, went back to the old party to which they were born, but politics were never to be quite the same again. Party lines were less closely drawn and, in later years, almost disappeared in local politics. Both Republicans and Democrats were elected to office in the county and men with outstanding ability and a likeable disposition were often elected to office term after term, regardless of party affiliations.

Democracy, in its broader sense, grew out of our environment, just as it did in our nation's history, and all along the frontier line since this early time. The people in Montezuma County were at first completely free; almost free to do as they pleased. They soon saw they had to surrender some of their rights in order to be protected in others. They realized that if people were not protected in their property rights, property would not be worth anything; that it was law that gave value to property. Also that law must protect every one's life in order to make life safe for anyone. So the people surrendered one after another of their free rights in order to be protected in all their just rights. That's the kind of freedom Americans were born to. While Americans were born free and surrendered some of their rights in the interest of law and order and good government, in the old world, men were born subjects and serfs, and had to fight to gain the right to live

114

happy and free. This has been a struggle of the centuries, and it is still going on.

The voters of Montezuma County are now divided, for the most part, only on local issues. Every one wants good government justly and economically administered. Mistakes are mostly business mistakes; mistakes of judgment. Nearly every office holder is given credit for being honest. Being able and equal to the task is a responsibility every office holder must take for himself. When political issues are drawn along such broad lines we can expect good local government administered in the common interest of all.

PUBLIC ROADS

No function of government in Montezuma County is more vitally important to the general welfare than the building of the county highways and roads. Because of our soil and our climatic conditions something better than dirt roads were absolutely necessary to the county's development and the people's well being. Roads are the arteries of our business life and carry the life-blood of business and industry. Having no railroad service, roads and highways must carry our commerce and, aside from air transportation, it is the only transportation we have. Hence the importance of good and adequate roads.

The county began its history with practically no road and few bridges. It is safe to say that the people of the county paid for roads that they never did get, so the county began life in the mud.

The first effort at building roads consisted in building up the center road bed a little higher than the ground on either side, construct a drain ditch on either side of the roadbed and put in a culvert where necessary to carry the water under the road. Larger draws and creeks had a wooden bridge. This much done one was supposed to have a good road. For a long time in the county's history such a road rated as a good road. When long storm periods came, or spring thaws, such roads often became no roads at all.

The first effort at making a good road came in July, 1913, when the Durango-Mancos road was designated as a highway and $18,000 was appropriated by the state, work was started at the east county line and built westward as far as the money would build it. This was to be a first class road, yet it was only dirt, and cars and trucks were here.

Nothing more was done until 1919. The same plan to rebuild the Durango-Mancos road was resumed. Reduce the grades, broaden the sharp curves and build better bridges were in the plan. Gravel surfacing was mentioned for the first time and $40,000 was made available. This was to be the first gravel surface work in the San Juan Basin.

There were no cars on the road in winter as late as 1921.

The first gravel surfaced road in the county was built in 1923 on

South Main St., in Mancos and on out to the foot of Cemetery Hill. This was a very bad stretch of road in muddy times, and it was graveled as an experiment. The county had bought a small crusher, the people donated all the work and a good job was done under the direction of a state highway employee. The gravel stood up and made a good all-weather road. After that the county knew it could safely build gravel surfaced roads.

As another experiment, the county, in the winter of 1923-24, tried pushing the snow off the Mancos-Cortez road. That was a success. Cars used the road all winter and when the frost went out in the spring the road was much better, and dried up much quicker, than on roads where the snow was left on.

Road improvement came slow at the start. It was June 12, 1925, before the first seven mile stretch of road from Mancos eastward, on the Mancos-Durango road, was finished. This gravel surfacing job was continued from Mancos westward for five miles, at once. Also a stretch of road was gravel surfaced from Hesperus to Thompson Park.

It was not until 1936 that the first oil surface road was built. In September the work of rebuilding and oil surfacing Highway 160 was started east of Mancos. The First National Bank building was torn down and the road was built on its present route through town.

The road from Durango to Mancos and on to Cortez and to the Utah state line was declared a national highway in fall of 1925, and numbered 160.

We have traced the beginning of good roads and highways in the county. The gravel surfacing of roads was continued in every part of the county, mail routes and school bus lines were the first to receive attention after the highways were surfaced. In 1927 to 1929 many miles of gravel surfacing was done on all the County highways.

In 1937, heavy road machinery began to come into use and the county purchased a heavy truck with snow plow and drag line at a cost of $10,395.

In 1937 was opened a new era for new and better roads, and miles and miles of roads were rebuilt, where rebuilding was needed, and oil surfaced. Twenty-seven miles of Highway 666, south from Cortez, was regraveled and oiled. Then the outfit was moved to Mancos and three miles of the Mancos-Cortez road was oil surfaced. Oil surface work on the highway out of Cortez toward Dove Creek was gotten under way. Twenty miles of the highway in the vicinity of Dove Creek was improved at an expense of $200,000.

Dolores was connected with Cortez by oil surfaced road by way of Lewis, and some oil was put on the Cortez-Dolores road by way of the Y. A long stretch of road between Cortez and Mancos was oiled toward the end of the season. Much of this work was rather light surfacing and in a few years had to be resurfaced to carry the heavier traffic that the roads were called upon to carry. Some of the roads carrying the heaviest traffic, have been oil surfaced for the third time, and the work of resurfacing and widening the oil mat, putting in three lane and four lane highways in places, goes on and now comes the freeways to facilitate handling the heaviest traffic.

While these things were going on in Montezuma County, some very important things were taking place in other parts of the San Juan Country that were almost as important to the county's welfare as the work that was being done on Montezuma County roads.

In 1937, twenty-two miles of highway between Durango and Pagosa Springs was oil surfaced and five and one-half miles between Pagosa and Wolf Creek Pass.

It was on August 16, 1916, that the state highway over Wolf Creek Pass was completed. This was the gateway into the San Juan Basin from the east and opened our main artery of overland commerce.

In 1916 the road across the Navajo reservation received $15,000 to make surveys and start construction work, and, a little later, received another $15,000. This road was then designated the Indian Highway.

On Feb. 18, 1924, Congress appropriated $800,000 to build the Durango-Gallup road, and the work was to be done in the spring and summer of 1924. This road is the southern gateway into the San Juan Basin and our second main artery carrying our overland commerce.

A new bridge, adequate to handle any and all traffic, was built across the San Juan River at Shiprock in 1936.

Getting back to county roads, the first effort to get a real road from Dolores to Rico was made in 1893, when $9,753 was made available for the work. They were still working on the old route on the valley floor, an almost impossible proposition. It was several years before they decided to lay out a road on the north hillside and above the river.

In 1913, the county began dragging the roads just as they began drying up in the spring and after storm periods. Steel drags were bought and certain men in given localities were hired to do the work just at the time it would do the most good. It did help, but we were still a long way from good roads.

The gravel surface work on the Durango-Mancos road was finally completed in 1925. The road was now gravel surfaced all the way.

In Jan., 1922, the county road fund had paid up the last of its warrant indebtedness and showed a cash balance of $15,000. Income from car and truck licenses and from the gas tax was beginning to produce revenue. Gravel surfacing was soon to get under way in earnest.

The first crawler tractor for road work was purchased in 1922. It was put to work at once on the Cortez-Dolores road.

In 1924, two Fordson wheeled tractors were purchased and put into the road work. It was an improvement over team work.

In 1924, gravel surfacing was started on the Cortez-Dolores road when two miles were so improved out of Cortez.

At this time the Work Progress Administration lent a hand and five and one-half miles of road was gravel surfaced on the Dolores-Summit Ridge road, beginning at the Cemetery, and five miles was gravel surfaced on the school bus route in the lower Mancos Valley.

In the fall of 1925, 40 miles of road in the county was designated as state highway, in addition to that already made a state highway. This meant that the state takes over the building and maintaining of these roads.

In 1927, the county bought a small gravel crusher that could easily be moved from place to place and several small stretches of roads were graveled in the next few years.

The Cortez-Dove Creek road, laid out as a state highway in 1925, later designated as U. S. Highway 160, was constructed, gravel surfaced and, in 1937, was oil surfaced all the way through to the Utah State line.

We leave the subject of public roads here. The work will never be finished, but must go on and on. We may eventually find that even now only a beginning has been made. We know that greater things are ahead in every line of the counties industries and as these develop the volume of traffic will grow and grow. More and better roads will be constantly in demand.

CHAPTER XIII

THE NEW COUNTY IS FORMED

About the time the construction work on the big irrigation project in Montezuma Valley got under way the people began to think of a new county to be created out of the west end of La Plata County. This was about 1885. Matters rocked along slowly for a while; then the proposition was taken up in earnest, the proper preliminary steps were taken and an act creating the County of Montezuma was introduced into the General Assembly and was approved April 16, 1889. The Act creating the new county designated the boundaries in the following words:

Beginning at the southwest corner of La Plata County, thence east along the southern line of La Plata County to a point on the Apex of the ridge dividing the waters of the Rio Mancos from the waters of the Rio La Plata; thence northerly along said apex to the south boundary line of Dolores County, in Colorado; thence west along said boundary line to the east line of the Territory of Utah; thence south along said eastern boundary line to the place of beginning, all that portion of La Plata County drained by the Rio Mancos, Bear Creek and the Dolores River. These are the words used. It may be added that the county also embraces territory drained by McElmo Creek.

The total area of the county in acres is 1,342,080 acres and in square miles it is 2,095 square miles. The width north to south is about 45 miles, and east to west, the south line is about 40 miles and the north line about 68 miles. The population in 1950 was 4.8 persons per square mile. The altitude at Cortez is 6,198 feet; at Dolores 6,936 feet, and at Mancos 7,035 feet. The country northwest of Cortez rises again to about 7,000 feet. The highest point in the county is Mount Hesperus 13,223 feet, wholly within the county, and the lowest point is in lower McElmo Creek, somewhat over 4,000 feet. That part near the four corners is also around 4,000 feet in elevation.

The Ute Indian Reservation takes 412,067 acres in the south part of the county; a part of the San Juan National Forest takes 260,672 acres in the higher elevations in the east end of the county; Mesa Verde Park takes 51,167 acres on Mesa Verde and there is a total of 354,748 acres of privately owned land. The resources and industries of the county are fully discussed in other chapters.

The act creating the county makes the following provisions: All the county and precinct officers of La Plata County, serving in territory of Montezuma County are declared to be legal officers of Montezuma County and are to hold office until the next general election or until their successors are elected and qualified according to law. The Governor shall appoint other officers necessary to carry on the county government, all county officers to be elected at the next general election. The County Seat of said county shall be at Cortez until changed by law.

There shall be four terms of the County Court each term starting on the first Monday in December, March, June and September. The District Court term shall begin on the fourth Tuesday of October of each year.

All records in La Plata County, properly belonging to Montezuma County, shall be furnished by the County Clerk of said county to the County Clerk of Montezuma County. Montezuma County must furnish the books and pay for the work.

Montezuma County must assume her share of La Plata County indebtedness in proportion to the valuation of property in each county, assessment of 1888. The County Commissioners from each county shall meet and settle all matters of differences on matters of revenue; also apportion indebtedness. They shall meet at Durango after due notice is given.

The county shall come in as a county of the second class, thus establishing salaries and fees. The county shall come in as a part of the 21st Senatorial District and La Plata and Montezuma County representative district, and shall be attached to the 6th Judicial District, all to be effective immediately.

It was found that Montezuma County had no representation, officially, in La Plata County and that all the officers for the new county had to be appointed by Governor Thomas who appointed the following: County Commissioners, Wm. F. Ordway, Dolores; Frank W. Thomas of Cortez; George Bauer, Mancos. The County Treasurer had to be appointed first and J. J. Harris was selected. Harris refusing to serve, F. W. Kroeger was appointed. Wm. M. Smith was appointed County Clerk and Recorder; Perley Wasson, Sheriff; Dr. Geo. Williams, Coroner; George W. Morton, County Judge; T. W. Wattles, Assessor; D. M. Longenbaugh, was appointed County Superintendent of Schools, but not accepting, I. O. Miller was appointed. Also Kroeger refused to serve as Treasurer and Thomas L. Payson was appointed.

The first meeting of the Board of County Commissioners was held May 3, 1889, and Wm. F. Ordway was elected Chairman and Frank W. Thomas was elected Clerk. After approving the bonds of all the county officers, the first business transacted by the commissioners was to rent the upper story of the old County Court House to serve as a Courthouse. The price to be paid was $600 a year the owners of the building to accept warrants drawn on an empty treasury in payment. Snyder, now Clerk of the Board, was to get $50 a month. Books, blanks and stationery was ordered and the board ordered the clerk to contract with some carpenter to make tables, desks and filing cabinets, etc., for the use of all the county officers.

George W. Spencer was appointed first road commissioner, Chauncy W. Blackman was appointed County Attorney, at a salary of $500, and five ballot boxes were ordered.

Transcripts of all the land of the county were ordered to be made from the La Plata County records for the use of the County Assessor, and the County is divided into three commissioners districts as follows: No. 1, Dolores; No. 2, Cortez, and No. 3, Mancos.

Payson has trouble making acceptable bond as County Treasurer.

The new county begins business without a dollar in the treasury, and must pay all current bills and salaries in warrants on the treasury, which may be discounted for cash at the banks. Besides this, the county's share of the La Plata County debt was figured to be about $23,000 and, in addition to this, the new county must pay several thousand dollars for necessary records, books, and the work of transcribing the records of La Plata County that pertains to Montezuma County. To finance these items it was necessary to bond the county at once and in 1890 the people voted a bonded debt of $30,000. About thirty-five years elapsed before this debt was fully paid. The people, generally, were almost as poor as the county was.

The debt to La Plata County was unjust in a way. Nearly all the La Plata debt was for money spent in La Plata County. In addition Montezuma County people had been paying tax money into the La Plata County treasury for years and nearly all this money was spent in La Plata County. When the new county was formed it had nothing to show for all this money but a few roads that were little better than trails, and a few very poor wooden bridges. The record shows that J. J. Morefield served one term as County Commissioner and the writer has been told that Wm. F. Ordway served one term in some office, perhaps commissioner. These are the only persons we can find any account of to have served in any official capacity in La Plata County. When the new county was formed not a single county officer was from the west end of La Plata County.

The Board of County Commissioners began at once to make small tax levies to pay the various expenses of the county, but a year must pass before any revenue is derived.

Payson has trouble as County Treasurer. His books are not right, his bond was rejected as insufficient and his bondsmen try to withdraw from his bond. He is dismissed by the Board and John White is appointed County Treasurer, and makes a satisfactory bond in the sum of $50,000.

Roads were a problem from the start. What roads there were, were all in the wrong place or on some one's land. Road petitions, road viewing and road surveying was going on most of the time, and there was no money to build the roads.

The Board decided they didn't need a county attorney and Blackman was accordingly dismissed.

As a result of the first election in 1891 the following officers were installed in January, 1892:

County Commissioners, Mancos, A. T. Samson, who was elected chairman; J. T. Giles, Cortez and Charles Matson, Dolores.

County Assessor, M. W. Reid; Clerk, Frank Humble; County Sheriff, Adam Lewy; Treasurer, John White; Supt. of Schools, D. M. Longenbaugh; Judge M. T. Morris.

The county installs jail cells at a cost of $3,000.

We will not pursue the county records further. We give the foregoing account to indicate the trouble the new county had in getting started and the many difficulties that had to be overcome. The new county finally made it through to better times. It was fortunate, from the start, in having able and resourceful men to direct and control, and pass judgment on the many problems that confronted them. Progress was necessarily slow. Too few people, too little wealth, poor local markets, long distances to the general markets, and high freight rates in and out, all combined to make the road rough and very difficult. But the people had a pioneering spirit. They lived on what they could make and paid their taxes when they could.

As a matter for the record, and for reference, we give the following lists of county officers which is about as nearly complete as we were able to get them.

First Set of Officers appointed in 1889.

Board of County Commissioners: William F. Ordway, Chairman, from Dolores; Frank W. Thomas, Cortez; George Bauer, Mancos. First Frank W. Thomas was Clerk; then Wm. M. Snyder.

Clerk & Recorder—Wm. M. Smith   Co. Supt. of Schools—I. O. Miller
Sheriff—Pearley Wasson   Treasurer—F. L. Payson
Coroner—Dr. G. W. Williams   F. L. Payson succeeded by John
Co. Judge—Geo. W. Morton   White, as County Treasurer
Assessor—T. W. Wattles

Installed in January, 1892

County Commissioners: A. T. Samson, Mancos, Chairman; J. T. Giles, Cortez; Charles Matson, Dolores.

County Assessor—M. W. Reid   Supt. of Schools—D. M.
County Sheriff—Adam Lewy   Longenbaugh
County Treas.—John White   County Clerk—Frank Humble
                                    Co. Judge—M. T. Morris

Election Nov. 1893, Installed Jan. 1894

Co. Clerk—Frank Humble
Treasurer—J. J. Morefield
Sheriff—S. P. Thomas
Assessor—M. W. Reid
Supt. of Schools—Geo. W.
Burnett
Coroner—D. B. Shutt
Surveyor—A. L. Fellows
County Commissioner 1st. Dist.—W. M. May
County Commissioner 3rd. Dist.—W. J. Blatchford

Election, 1895
(Not Available)

Election Nov. 5, 1897

Clerk—John Wesch
Treasurer—J. J. Morefield
Sheriff—Jno. T. Duncan
Assessor—T. C. Brittain
Supt. of Schools—Wm. Halls
Co. Judge—A. P. Edmonson
County Commissioner, 3d Dist.—John White

Elected in 1899

Sheriff—John T. Duncan
Clerk & Recorder—John Wesch
Treasurer—J. T. Giles
Assessor—Henry Kroeger
Supt. of Schools—A. T. Samson
Surveyor—Geo. Mills
Coroner—E. R. Lamb
Com. Dist. 1—W. F. Ordway

County Officials Elected Nov. 8, 1901

Clerk—S. J. Smith
Treasurer—J. T. Giles
Sheriff—R. C. Kermode
Assessor—T. C. Brittain
Commissioner—Roscoe Thompson
Judge—C. J. Scharnhorst
Supt. of Schools—E. N. Lowe
Surveyor—W. M. May
Coroner—F. W. Wagner

Elected Nov. 12, 1903
County Officers—1904

State Senator—J. J. Harris
State Rep.—George Hutt
Judge—C. J. Scharnhorst
Clerk—H. N. Sprague
Sheriff—R. C. Kermode
Treasurer—H. Brigham, Jr.
Assessor—T. C. Brittain
Supt. of Schools—Anna Graybeall
Surveyor—Geo. Mills
Coroner—M. M. Blair
County Commissioner, 3rd Dist.—Louis Paquin
County Commissioner, 2nd Dist.—Charles Schalles

County Officers—1906

Representative—W. J. Blatchford
District Judge—C. A. Pike
Clerk—Henry N. Sprague
Sheriff—Jim Clark
Treasurer—John Wesch
Assessor—T. C. Brittain
Supt. of School—J. W. Denny
Surveyor—W. H. Blake
Coroner—M. W. Blair
County Commissioner, 1st District—W. W. Byers

123

Election, Nov. 3, 1908

Bryan carries county. John Shafroth, Governor

State Senator—George West
State Rep.—E. B. Clark
Dist. Att.—Geo. Lane
County Judge—J. J. Morefield
Clerk & Recorder—Harry Sprague
Sheriff—James Gawith

Treasurer—John Wesch
Assessor—H. J. Lynton
Supt. of Schools—Hanna Durward
Surveyor—Geo. Mills
Co. Com. 1st Dist.—W. I. Myler
Co. Com. 3d Dist.—Wm. Halls

Election, Nov. 10, 1910

Rep. to Assembly—W. B. Ebbert
Sheriff—James Gawith
Clerk—S. M. Burke
Treasurer—Chas. B. Reid
Assessor—Clark Brittain

Co. Commissioner—B. P. Porter
Surveyor—O. C. Stone
Supt. of Schools—Hanna Durward
Coroner—Dr. Cabel

Election, Nov. 1912

Dist. Judge—W. N. Searcy
Dist. Attorney—Geo. Lane
State Senator—Geo. West
State Rep.—P. B. Gates
Judge—J. J. Downey
Clerk—S. M. Burke
Sheriff—Sam Todd

Treasurer—Chas. B. Reid
Assessor—Clark Brittain
Supt. of Schools—Mrs. Frank Taylor
Surveyor—E. C. Cline
Coroner—Dr. Beall
Com. 2nd Dist.—Herman Guillet
Com. 3d Dist.—Ernest Broadhead

1914 (Not Available)

Offices—1916—County

Co. Judge—C. R. Hickman
Clerk & Recorder—S. M. Burke
Treasurer—C. R. Smith
Sheriff—Henry Crawford
Assessor—E. H. Kittell

Supt. of Schools—Mrs. Artie Lewis
Surveyor—C. C. Knight
Coroner—E. E. Johnson
Com. 1st. Dist.—W. I. Myler
Com. 3d Dist.—C. B. Kelly

Election Results, 1918

Representative—J. L. Morrison
Clerk—S. M. Burke
Sheriff—Frank Philley
Treasurer—Chas. R. Smith
Supt. of Schools—Lola Taylor

Commissioner—R. B. Dunham
Surveyor—Geo. Mills
Coroner—Dr. E. E. Johnson
Rep. in Congress—Edward T. Taylor

Election Returns, 1920

State Senate—J. L. Morrison
Rep. Assembly—Dr. Calkins
Clerk—S. M. Burke

Judge—J. M. Brunley
Supt.—Nora S. Hutchings
Coroner—F. C. Ames

Treasurer—C. R. Smith
Sheriff—F. A. Wheatland
  Non-Partisan League Strong Factor. Utter defeat.

Com. 2 Dist.—Henry Crawford
Com. 3 Dist.—F. C. Hallar

Election Results, 1922

Rep.—Dr. Calkins
Dist. Judge—W. N. Searcy
Dist. Attorney—Bruce Jacobson
Co. Judge—J. M. Brumley
Clerk—S. M. Burke
Treasurer—Byron D. Brown

Sheriff—Arthur Cowling
Supt.—Avis Miller
Coroner—E. E. Johnson
Surveyor—C. C. Knight
Com. 2 Dist.—Henry Crawford
Com. 3 Dist.—F. C. Hallar

Election Results, 1924

State Senator—Grant Sanders
State Rep.—R. W. Calkins
Dist. Judge—W. N. Searcy
Dist. Att.—Bruce Jacobson
Co. Judge—J. M. Brumley
Clerk—S. M. Burke
Treasurer—B. D. Brown

Sheriff—Arthur Cowling
Supt.—Avis Miller
Coroner—E. E. Johnson
Com. 2 Dist.—Henry Crawford
Com. 3 Dist.—F. C. Hallar
Surveyor—C. C. Knight

Election Results—1926

Com. 1 Dist.—Philip Runck
Treasurer—Byron D. Brown
Representative—R. W. Calkins
Sheriff—W. W. Dunlap
Assessor—J. G. Dunning

School Supt.—Avis E. Miller
Clerk & Recorder—Mabel
  Waldron
Governor—Wm. Adams
Congress—Ed. T. Taylor

Elected 1928

State Senator—J. L. Morrison
State Rep.—Royal W. Calkins
Clerk & Rec.—Mabel C. Waldron
Sheriff—W. W. Dunlap
Treasurer—John Wesch
Judge—J. M. Brumley

Assessor—J. G. Dunning
School Supt.—Myrtle E. Jordan
Surveyor—John Bauer
Coroner—E. E. Johnson
Com. 2 Dist.—O. S. Englehart
Com. 3 Dist.—George Menefee

Elected 1930

Dist. Judge—W. N. Searcy
State Rep.—Fred C. Hallar
Clerk & Rec.—Mabel C. Waldron
Sheriff—W. W. Dunlap
Treasurer—Claude Wilson

Assessor—J. G. Dunning
School Supt.—Myrtle Jordan
Surveyor—W. H. Blake
Coroner—E. E. Johnson
Com. 1 Dist.—E. S. Porter

November—1932

Dist. Judge—John B. O'Rourke
Representative—R. W. Calkins
Co. Judge—J. M. Brumley
Clerk—Mabel Waldron
Sheriff—W. W. Dunlap

Treasurer—Claude Wilson
Assessor—John Dunning
School Supt.—Myrtle Jordan
Surveyor—Owens
Coroner—E. E. Johnson

County Comm. 2nd. Dist.—Frank Philley
County Comm. 3rd. Dist.—George Menefee

November—1934

Legislature—T. C. Henry
Clerk—Mabel Waldron
Sheriff—W. W. Dunlap
Treasurer—Claude Wilson

Assessor—John Dunning
School Supt.—Myrtle Jordan
Surveyor—Owens
Coroner—E. E. Johnson

Election Results—1936

President—Franklin D. Roosevelt
U. S. Senator—Edwin C. Johnson
Governor—Teller Ammons
State Senator—Grant Sanders
Representative—Tom Akin
Dist. Judge—John B. O'Rourke
Co. Judge—J. M. Brumley

Clerk & Rec.—Chas. B. Reid
Sheriff—Jesse Robinson
Treasurer—Claude H. Wilson
Assessor—John Dunning
School Supt.—Myrtle Jordan

Election, Nov. 8, 1938

U. S. Senator—Alva B. Adams
Congress—Edw. T. Taylor
Governor—Ralph L. Carr
State Rep.—T. H. Akin

Sheriff—Jesse Robinson
Assessor—John Dunning
School Supt.—Lotta Manaugh
Com. 1 Dist.—Harry Rogers

Election Results, Nov., 1940

County Judge—C. R. Hickman
Clerk & Rec.—Henry Thorpe
Sheriff—Ray Smith
Treasurer—Claude H. Wilson
Assessor—J. C. Rumberg

School Supt.—Lotta Manaugh
Surveyor—David C. Hickman
Coroner—J. W. Ertel
Com. 2 Dist.—S. G. Walker
Com. 3 Dist.—Ira E. Kelly

Election, Nov. 3, 1942

Sheriff—Jim Baker
Coroner—J. W. Ertel
Com. 2 Dist.—W. R. McCabe
Clerk—Henry Thorpe

Rep. Legis.—Harry Rogers
Dist. Judge—John B. O'Rourke
Treasurer—Claude Wilson
Assessor—J. C. Rumberg
School Supt.—Lotta W. Manaugh

Election Results, Nov. 1, 1944

Sheriff—James R. Baker
School Supt.—Lotta Manaugh
Assessor—J. C. Rumberg
Clerk—Henry Thorpe
Co. Judge—Geo. Lofquist

Treasurer—Lee E. Tripp
Com. 2 Dist.—S. G. Walker
Com. 3 Dist.—Ira E. Kelly

Nov. 5, 1946

Rep.—Harry Rogers
Co. Judge—Hoyt Dow
Clerk—Gladys Hinton
Sheriff—Frank Weaver

Treasurer—A. F. Hopper
To fill vacancy—A. F. Hopper
Assessor—J. C. Rumberg
School Supt.—Lotta Manaugh

Sheriff to fill vacancy—Frank
  Weaver

Coroner—J. W. Ertel
Com. 1 Dist.—Chas. T. Porter

Nov. 2, 1948

Rep.—Eliz. E. Pellett
Dist. Judge—Jas. M. Noland
To fill vacancy—Jas. M. Noland
Co. Judge—Jas. F. Miller
Clerk & Rec.—John Leavitt

Sheriff—Frank Weaver
Treasurer—Lois Miller
Assessor—Chas. R. Bauer
School Supt.—Lotta Manaugh
Surveyor—Dave Hickman

Nov. 7, 1950

Rep.—Eliz. E. Pellett
Clerk—John Levitt
Sheriff—A. W. Anderson
Treasurer—Lois Miller

Assessor—Ray Wilson
School Supt.—Lotta Manaugh
Surveyor—Herb Owens

Nov. 4, 1952

Rep.—Eliz. E. Pellett
Dist. Att.—J. L. Mason
Co. Judge—Jas. F. Miller
Clerk—John Levitt
Coroner—J. W. Ertel
Com. 2 Dist.—C. R. Hickman

Sheriff—A. W. Anderson
Treasurer—Irwin Matlock
Assessor—J. C. Rumberg
School Supt.—Lotta Manaugh
Surveyor—Dave Hickman
Com. 3 Dist.—Grady Clampitt

Nov. 2, 1954

Rep.—Eliz. E. Pellett
Dist. Judge—James M. Noland
Clerk & Rec.—John Leavitt
Sheriff—A. W. Anderson
Assessor—Clyde Rumberg

Treasurer—Irwin Matlock
School Supt.—Claire J. Watson
Coroner—Walter Ertel
Com. 1 Dist.—Wayne Rogers

Nov. 6, 1956

Rep.—Eliz. Pellett
Co. Judge—Anna Patton
Com. 2 Dist.—Thomas J. Wark
Com. 3 Dist.—Claude Gawthrop

Senator—Chas. T. Porter
Dist. Att.—Wm. M. Caldwell

LOWER MONTEZUMA VALLEY

The early settlement of south Montezuma Valley starts with the
simultaneous coming of the cattlemen and the establishing of the Indian trading posts. The coming of the cattlemen is related in the
early history of Mancos and Dolores. They covered the whole country
with cattle in the early eighties, and a small business and a postoffice,
called Toltec, was established at Mitchell Springs, one mile south of
the town of Cortez on McElmo Creek. There were two fine springs
there and after the establishing of the first business there, the place
became a supply point and a kind of cowboy renedezvous for the

cattlemen. The springs took their name from the Mitchell family that came into the Mancos valley with the B. K. Wetherill family in 1881, and Porter Mitchell had something to do with a business established at the Springs later. About 1884 John and Andrew Harris moved quite a stock of goods over from Mancos and established a business at the Springs. There was a frame building and a cellar at this time, on the ground, and that was all. Bill Exon, of Dolores, and Sol Exon of Mancos (both of Mancos at the time) freighted the Harris stock of good from Mancos to the springs, there was several wagon loads and made quite a store. Apparently this was the first business at the Springs. We can get no information as to when the postoffice was established or who established it. There is a record that Porter Mitchell had a store there, but the exact time is not known. Lee Kelly is authority for the statement that by 1889 all the buildings and business that was at Mitchell Springs were gone. Harrises, we know, moved over to Big Bend, on the Dolores River and opened a mercantile business there about 1886, as that is the date they claim for the starting of the Harris Bank. It is reported that Geo. Bauer bought Harris' Mitchell Springs stock.

The Mitchells had a store at Mitchell Springs, and had the postoffice, called Toltec, and it is recorded that Charley Mitchell died there in 1884, and was buried on the hillside, north of the Creek.

Probably the first Indian trading post was established by O. E. Noland, of Mancos, down near the Four Corners, on the San Juan river, about 1884. It might have been 1885. A strong building made of cottonwood logs was put up for the store and a little later a stone structure was built for a warehouse and storeroom for wool, hides, pelts, etc. About this time Mr. Noland and Stanley Mitchell started a second trading post at Riverview, near where the McElmo Canon enters the San Juan River. Mitchell was in charge of this post, had trouble with the Indians, killed one Indian, and was forced to "clear out" of Riverview (later changed to Aneth). He goes to the trading post at Four Corners and took refuge there. The Indians, knowing Mitchell was there, laid siege to the trading post for a week trying to get Noland to turn Mitchell over to them, but Noland talked and argued and threatened the Indians with the coming of the soldiers, and the Indians finally gave it up. A Navajo Indian boy had been gotten out of the trading post by night and sent to Fort Lewis for help. Finally the soldiers did come from Fort Lewis and cleared up the situation.

About this time, about 1885, Pete Guillet came from Missouri and took charge of the trading post at Riverview for Mr. Noland and worked for him. The next year Herman Guillet arrived from Missouri and he and Pete Guillet bought the Riverview trading post from Noland, and in 1889, Walter Lee Kelly came from Missouri to take the job of driving a freight team for Guillet Brothers. With Kelly came Mrs. Guillet, mother of the boys, and Georgia Guillet, their sister, now Mrs. Omo, and then only 5 or 6 years old. After a few months they return to Missouri to remain until 1903.

Kelly hauled freight, first from Durango to Riverview, then from Mancos after the railroad came in 1891. The Guillet trading post, by a mutual arrangement, was turned over to Sterl Thomas, a half brother, and a little later, was sold to A. J. Ames and Jesse West.

After a few years in business at Four Corners Noland sells that trading post to Ames and West and erects a good frame building at Navajo Springs and puts in a large stock of goods, the government Indian Agency for the Ute Tribe having recently, or about this time, been established at the Springs. Noland now gave all his time to the trading post at Navajo Springs while Guillet Brothers, in the fall of 1890, came to the new town of Cortez and bought the merchandise business then being conducted by Al and Frank Thompson in a frame building that stood on the corner where the Safeway store now stands, thus establishing a business that was to make history in Cortez for many years. We will trace this business further at the proper time and place. Lee Kelly continued to haul freight, now with his own outfit, for the Indian traders until 1896 and helped to make a lot of history during this time.

When water came to the valley below Cortez in 1889, and a little before that time, permanent settlers came in to homestead and occupy the land. One of the earliest of these was George Stafford, who, about 1883, took the land where the old Aztec ruins occupy, and which have since been created the Yucca House National Monument, on 10 acres of acquired land, and now under the auspices of Mesa Verde National Park. The springs were known as Stafford springs and Stafford was in the cattle business. When the ditches and canals were being built, Stafford had a big barn and quite a number of good horse and mule teams and took and finished, a number of contracts on the ditch system. Stafford Springs, Mitchell Springs, Navajo Springs, weak springs at Towaoc, known then as Willow Springs, and Soda Springs, just in the head of McElmo Canon, and some other springs, perhaps, we have not learned about, made it possible to stock the whole country with cattle, and the fine grasses that grew everywhere in such abundance, were grazed heavily and weakened until it was an easy prey to sage and other brush that soon cumbered the land.

The coming of water, or the promise of water, brought in many other settlers. Some of these early settlers were Bob and Jim Honaker who came over from the Mancos Valley and settled on the Aztec Divide. Frank Belcher, who had a nice ranch and home near Cortez; John Belcher, and three other Belcher boys, all owned land and all were good farmers.

Also located near Cortez was John Duncan where he had a small ranch and a very nice house near the Mowry mill and was later elected Sheriff. Joe Tanner had a good farm and a very nice ranch residence.

Bob Smith located in the lower valley but moved to town early and went into business.

Ern Guillet came in from Missouri about 1895, age about 15, was a part time rancher and a resident of the county for the rest of his life.

Dick Kermode was the first farmer to locate near Cortez on the north. Later came Alph and Ridgway Kermode who also became farmers in this locality and Allen Kermode came and ran a bakery in town. All the Kermodes were born on the Island of Wight, in the English Channel, and made very acceptable American citizens.

The Coppingers were all good farmers and stockmen. Joe Coppinger had a good ranch and a nice home just across the road west from the Blue Door school house, and Hag Coppinger had a good livestock farm just west of this place. Tom Coppinger was over in the big grove of trees in the central valley, was a grain farmer and, later, owned sheep. Bill Coppinger had a good productive farm just at the south end of the airport runway and kept a good herd of range cattle, and Jim Casey, a son-in-law had a farm near by. Walt Coppinger, late of Mancos, was the cow man of the family and looked after the range herd, and Bob Coppinger was the younger boy of the family. He still resides near Mancos.

Fred and Allen Kroeger both had farms in this part of the valley. They were good farmers and valuable citizens in the early settlement of the county. And, more important still, they had four sisters. Also John Kroeger, engineer, owned land for a while.

Walters Brothers, Joe and Arch, and their parents, Mr. and Mrs. Henry Walters, came in early from Utah and all took land and were good farmers and very acceptable citizens. Henry Walters was one of the original Mormons who crossed the plains, pushing a hand cart, shortly after the first Mormon immigration into Utah in 1847. Charles Winship came somewhat before the Walters and stopped first in the Mancos valley, renting the Judge Morris ranch. He later moved to the lower valley. He married one of the Walters daughters, and Mrs. Clara Watson, present county Superintendent of Schools, was a daughter in the Winship family.

We first find C. J. Scharnhorst as a shoemaker in Mancos about 1882. He is next managing a business at Big Bend, owned by himself and George Bauer. Then on a Homestead just at the south side of Cortez when the town was very new. He improved a farm and was postmaster for a time when the town was just getting started. He was elected County Judge in 1901 and reelected in 1903. Carl Scharnhorst, a son, did some pioneering on the Dolores river, owning the land where the McPhee sawmill stood and was a successful livestock farmer. Of the two daughters, one became Mrs. Walter W. Wallace of Mancos and the other Mrs. Harry Pyle of Dolores who is still with us at the age of 80 years.

W. B. Wilson owned and improved a good ranch just south of the airport and Clark Brittain, who settled first in the Mancos valley, had land near the Wilson place. Wm. Brittain, also from Mancos valley, lived on the land occupied by the Blue Door school house.

F. M. Goodykoontz improved a homestead near the lower end of East, or Mesa Verde, lateral, near the reservation line. He was farmer, postmaster at Cortez, served a term as representative in the State Assembly, and was then farmer again.

Tom Fowler, the sheep man, and father of Ralph Fowler, present Marshall of Cortez, had a homestead down on Navajo Draw and Frank Philley, later working man, County Sheriff, County Commissioner for two terms owned land adjoining the Fowler land.

Alva and John Morgan, brothers of Mrs. Pete Guillet and Mrs. Ern Guillet, took land under East lateral, but when the canal was not completed for a time, they gave up their land and moved away.

Al Puett homesteaded early in the lower valley, southeast of Cortez, but moved to the Summit Ridge country later, built a small reservoir and improved land there. Hi McEwen homesteaded the land that is now the Gordon Maness dairy farm. D. H. Saylor, before moving to Cortez, had a homestead near Totten Lake. Gus Stevenson lived in the lower valley for a while, early, and later lived in the Mildred community. He was a good farmer and a fine horseman.

James Stinson was a sturdy old pioneer farmer and stockman who took and improved land on the Aztec Divide. He was riding after his cattle in the La Plata Mountains when he was 87 years of age. When remonstrated with it he replied, "The eyes of the master maketh his cattle fat."

A Mr. Berlin was an early and successful farmer southeast of Cortez, and Bill Graham now owns the land that was owned very early by George Stafford.

Lee and Dick Winborn came early to the lower valley and were leading farmers. Lee Winborn took for his wife Miss Kitty Dillon, an early school teacher in the valley and a scion of an early and well known pioneer family.

Sam Todd was very early in the county. He homesteaded the Wayne Denny place and built Todd Lake, now Denny Lake and Cortez City Park. He had a long career in the county and was County Sheriff for one term in the early history of the county.

In its virgin state the lower Montezuma Valley was high in fertility and wonderful in production. It was amazing the large yield of hay and grain the settlers took from the land. From 40 to 60 bushels of wheat per acre were common yields made by the better farmers—wheat that tested 62 to 64 pounds per bushel and high in gluten content to make it the best of milling wheat. Of oats, 60 to 100 bushels per acre were common yields and these oats weighed 40 to 42 pounds per bushel whereas the government standard is 32 pounds per bushel. Barley yields were equally good and the hay crop was simply amazing. Hay was harvested then by mowing, raking and curing the hay in shocks. This method made hay of very excellent quality barring damage by rain. Then it was loaded onto slips, with a sling in place, drawn by a team to the stack, picked up by a "Mormon" swinging stacker, swung around and dumped on top of the stack and the stacker placed it to make a large, smooth stack. Then it was worth, probably, $5 a ton, if there was any market. Hay was consumed as feed for range cattle and sheep and for draft animals, and that use created the only market.

MC ELMO CANON

McElmo Canon comprises the lowest part of Montezuma Valley and is, in reality, a valley extension rather than a part of the valley proper. It channels off the waste and flood water from the valley basin. It was explored further back in local history than we have any record of, and no one knows how the canon got its name or the origin or significance of the name. In the early days McElmo Creek was a dry creek except small flowing springs here and there along its course, and remained so until flowing water was brought to the valley proper. After that it caught all waste and seepage and became a flowing stream the year around. When the canon first became known to the white man there was only a shallow channel that could be crossed with team and wagon almost anywhere along its upper course. When water from the irrigating system above began to flow down the canon in the brisk stream that was common, erosion began, the weakened grass stand could not hold the soil, and the channel washed out deeper and wider until we have very near a second canon within and at the bottom of the canon proper. Flood waters also worked havoc, and during the very rainy seasons of 1909 and 1911 flood waters came down the canon in such volume and with such terrific force that it washed away houses and large parts of orchards and farms causing damage that ran into the thousands of dollars. One farmer lost 40 acres of grain and several acres of his farm went with it. Two and three acres were a common loss. It was at this time that the channel was widened and deepened to what it is today.

The first and only road to Bluff City and the various trading posts westward traversed the canon. There was never a road laid out for some years, and none built, except a little work here and there to make the way passable. The wagons and teams simply followed the way of least resistance, and, since all the arroyos were shallow, or didn't exist at all, the road could follow the best route almost anywhere.

The early settlers about Mancos and Dolores drove their cattle to this lower country for the winter. First after being taken down, they had to stay near the springs or water holes, which were rather few and far between, but after the snow came the cattle could be driven out to the best feed, depending on snow for water, and could be wintered in good shape and with very little loss. In early times it was necessary for a number of men to be on guard all the time, as the Indians killed the cattle for meat, if they had a chance, or drove them away. They also took any horses they could get hold of.

When water came to the big valley McElmo Canon was settled along with the rest of the country. Water was taken out of the channel or ditch extensions at the upper end of the canon floor for irrigating. A little further down a large ditch of water was brought down Trail Canon, so called because this was the main route or trail used to bring cattle from the summer range down into the canon in the fall and take them back again in the spring. This stream furnished water to several good farms and orchards where Trail Canon came in, and on down the canon floor for some miles. In the lower end of the canon water was taken by ditch from the channel again.

McElmo Canon land was very fertile and responded in a wonderful way to good methods of cultivation. And it attracted some of the finest farmers and fruit growers the county ever had. Men came in with real talent and "know how." They soon got developing processes to working and many fine grain, hay and livestock farms came into being, and several fine orchards were put out that were, in a short time, to become the wonder of the intermountain west.

The canon differs from other parts of the county in that corn is a main crop. It reaches full maturity, the climate and soil is adapted to it, and wonderful crops are produced.

The canon widens, in the upper floor, into several good farms and some very fine orchards; then narrows to a string of small farms along the channel; then down just above Battle Rock widens again to embrace many very good farms and fine orchards on down for some miles.

Permanent citizens came with the water, or just before. Among the first were Porter Mitchell and Stanley Mitchell, his son, and other Mitchells related to these. We have Stanley Mitchell in the Mancos Valley, Mitchells at Mitchell Springs and Mitchells in the canon. Then there was George Edmonson, Henry Bowdish, George Ashbaugh, Jim Giles and Rev. Antes. Antes was first a missionary to the Indians. He cared for and raised Indian children, and later, acquires land and becomes an influential and useful citizen, and a successful fruit grower. Elsworth Porter was farmer and stockman, down by Battle Rock, Jim Hawley, Billy Meadows with a large family, Galloway Brothers—Jim, George and John—well known fruit growers in the upper fruit belt; Stanley Mitchell, trading post operator and farmer, Jesse West, also farmer and trading post operator; and Andy Majors, widely and favorably known. And of the other Mitchells there was Hernand and Henry Mitchell, farmers.

Jasper Halls and Norman Halls, brothers, were very useful and influential citizens in that they came early and introduced fruit growing in the canon and might be said to have been the fathers of the fruit industry in Montezuma County. They brought in a wagon load of fruit trees of various varieties and kinds from Canon City, Colorado, planted them out and were soon producing some phenomenal fruit. Fruit growing "Caught on" and the canon, in a very few years, had many orchards, small and large, that were producing fruit that was simply amazing—large yields and quality unsurpassed. Jasper Halls was the fruit wizard of the canon and the others learned from him. Rev. Antes came second with some knowledge and strong convictions. He took over the Giles place and planted and grew the far famed "Gold Medal Orchard" now owned by Mr. Vincel.

Then there was Tom and Jim Lamb, orchardists and farmers. George Ashbaugh and Rick Ashbaugh, well and favorably known fruit growers and farmers, and, too, Norman Halls was always active with his brother, Jasper, in developing the fruit industry and leading the way.

Ellsworth Porter came in 1888 and settled near Battle Rock, raised a family and many range cattle. And Noah Barnes of the upper canon, became famous for his watermelons and was known as the "Watermelon King.' Grant Carpenter had a farm and a large family and one of the boys was killed in a shooting affray with Jesse Hallar and Hallar and the Carpenters later had other troubles in which Hallar, the aggressor, was badly wounded and lost a leg, from the knee down.

Jim Holly owned the last ranch down the canon, and Frank Ottoway was next to him. Fred Taylor owned these ranches later, and now John Ismay owns them. Mr. Gifiord and Mr. Jessup, Dick Jessup's father, were farmers, and O. W. Duncan, lived in the upper corner, and was a brother to Mrs. Jim Galloway who still lives on her little fruit farm in the upper canon, is quite well, and is close to the last of the original residents that still survive.

Mr. and Mrs. A. J. Tozer, well known residents, lived in the stone residence just below the dry ice plant and north of the road, owned the farm and lived there for many years. Mrs. Walter Halls, a daughter, was reared from childhood in this home.

John Wilson and Charles Schalles were very good early day farmers. Mr. Schalles had the farm on McElmo Creek just below the high wooden bridge that once spanned the Creek near the head of the canon. Wilson was lower down the canon. He was the father of Claude Wilson.

About five miles below Battle Rock, Walter Halls still carries on the work of his father, Jasper Halls. He produces fruits and grapes and berries, but, in addition, has quite a large farm, produces vast quantities of hay and other feeds, and together with his son-in-law, Eldon Zwicker, runs from 500 to 600 head of very fine range cattle which they summer on Bear Creek, on the National Forest, and keep them on or near the ranch in the winter.

At one time there were two postoffices in the canon. "Sandy" Tozer had the old Moqui postoffice, and Harrison Hill about 1891, had the McElmo postoffice.

The first school house in the canon was near Battle Rock and was first located on the corner of the present Vincel place.

Noah Barnes had the present Dobbins place. Ezra Hamilton owned a farm south of the Creek and just below the present Walter Halls place. He had a son—Joe Hamilton. Walter Halls has the original Tozer place.

Rev. Burnett was the first minister to locate in the canon, and Walter Brown homesteaded a farm some distance below Battle Rock. A Mr. Bowman, father of Allie Bowman, formerly of the Mancos valley, located near Mr. Brown.

Jim Holly had a trading post down near the Utah state line, and owned the last ranch down the canon.

Of the Andy Majors family only the daughter, Etta, survives. She was first Mrs. Jno. Dawson, then Mrs. Jordan; then, after being widowed, became Mrs. Middaugh. She is again a widow and makes her home in Cortez, still quite well and bright of mind.

Henry Bowdish came into the canon with Majors and Geo. Edmonson, from the old Indian Territory in 1891. Bowdish had two sisters. Lucindy Bowdish married Phil Krout, at Big Bend and Mollie married Sil Kramer, at Big Bend. Henry Bowdish had seven children—Jack, Frank, Bob, Maude, Elmer, Jesse and Wiles.

The old timers of McElmo Canon are gone, almost to the last man, but their work still goes on. Fruit is not stressed as it once was because of market conditions, but there are some new orchards, all the growers are caring for their trees and are still producing as fine a quality of peaches, pears, plums, and grapes as can be found anywhere in the world. Apples are not a crop just now, but one prominent grower made the remark that they could produce the finest apple in the world if they could only control and overcome the insect pests. Alfalfa hay and corn are standard products and all goes into livestock feed.

LAKE VIEW DISTRICT

The Lake View District, roughly speaking, occupies the northeast section of Montezuma Valley, excluding the higher land further north and east under the Summit Reservoir. The first white man to harvest a crop here was the cattleman, but he did not stay. He took a few crops of grass with his herd and moved on to make room for the per-

135

manent resident. The Lake View district occupies the drainage area of Wooley Draw and Simon Draw. The floor of these draws are broad and level, with very good soil and many fine farms. The balance is slightly upland and somewhat uneven, but the soil is good and some of the best farms are there. The industry, for the most part, is general farming, with dairying and fruit growing important, and growing. Sheep and range cattle have a place with Oscar Schlegal and Douglas Hindmarsh, the principal flock owners, running about 1500 head each. There is a slight trend from hay farming to cutting alfalfa and grass mixtures and feeding it green from the field. The good results obtained seem to indicate the practice will grow. Siloing is a common practice of preserving feeds and most grains produced are fed, although there is considerable wheat grown for the market. The milk income to the farmers of Montezuma County aggregated above $400,-000 last year and the Lake View community produced an estimated one-third of this.

The earliest settler in these parts was probably William Wooly, wife and son, Douglas Wooley, who date from about 1881. They settled on Wooly Draw and the Draw took their name. The elder Wooley died soon after the early settlement of the locality and Douglas about 1940. They were both well known characters, eccentric in their ways, and many amusing stories are told of them.

Another early settler was Lewis Simon who came, with his family about 1882 or a little later. He went first to the Big Bend country, but very soon after came out and settled a homestead on the draw that bears his name. Lewis Simon and wife were French by birth, having been born in the Swiss area of France, and came to America, and to Kansas, soon after marriage. After a few years in dry Kansas they came on west by way of Denver, next we hear of them at Parrott City and a little later at Big Bend, then on their homestead. These were Indian times and they built a good house, which became a kind of refuge for local people when danger threatened. There were five daughters. At Parrott City, Elizabeth Simon was married to Matt Hammond about 1881, and they were escorted down to Big Bend by a unit of the State Guard, the Indians making trouble at the time. The balance of the family soon came on to Big Bend and, later, to Simon Draw. The other four girls soon married; Mary Became Mrs. Fred Taylor, Lydia became Mrs. Millard, Sarah became Mrs. Al Rust, well known sawmill man and businessman of Dolores, and Rachel became Mrs. Dickenson. Mr. and Mrs. Fred Taylor became well and favorably known in the county. Theirs was the first marriage in Montezuma County after the county was formed in 1889.

Other early settlers in the locality were W. I. Myler, John, Bill and Earl Ritter. All were successful sheepman and ran some cattle; they prospered and were well known and highly esteemed in the county. The M. B. Stones were here for a while. Mabel Stone Puett married

Harry French, an enterprising young farmer, and Blaine Stone was a son.

Then there was Pat O'Donnel that had the homestead that Philip Runck has turned into a wonderful apple orchard and dairy farm.

Other early settlers were Mr. and Mrs. A. Paul Gordon, and their daughter, Miss Grace Gordon, is still a very well known resident of the community. Frank and Fred Taylor were early homesteaders, Bob Dunham based his cattle operations here for a while, William Ellermeyer was a well known early settler and raised a large family—all girls. Pete Taylor was an early settler down on the Dolores road. He was the father of George Taylor, well known businessman of Dolores, and of Bert and John Taylor, local farmers. A. G. Dunning was a well known early homesteader. He was the father of Frank and John Dunning, the latter well known as County Tax Assessor for a number of years. Jeff Tibbets lived down by Totten Lake for a while, but moved away.

James Totten homesteaded the land upon which Totten Lake is built and he and George W. Morton, first county judge, built the dam that created the lake about 1896.

Joel Estes was an early resident. There was a large family connection in the Estes family and they became akin to many local people. Mrs. W. I. Myler was a daughter in the Estes family.

Mr. S. Skinner, father of Bert Skinner, homesteaded here early and Royce Bishop also came in to help occupy and improve the new land. Mr. and Mrs. Myron Crews, while not pioneers, have been there quite some time and own a fine farm just west of the Lake View School. Mrs. Crews was formerly Miss Sada Rauh, a sister to Crayton Rauh. Theodore McDill was an early man in the community and helped to build it almost from the beginning.

Two early and prominent settlers of Lake View were George and Christopher Wilkerson, who came into the community in 1886 from the vicinity of Denver. They stopped a year in the Dolores Valley, then homesteaded land in Lake View in 1887. For two years they worked under every handicap one of which was having to haul water for man and beast eight miles from the Dolores river, using three barrels and a horse drawn wagon. This job lasted two years. These men had taken sub-contracts to help build the tunnel that brings water from the Dolores river to the valley. They finished their contract in 1889; also the water haulng job. They lived the rest of their lives in the Lake View community. Chris and Cora Wilkerson were the parents of Mrs. May Dunham, until recently of Mancos, and George Wilkerson was father of the late Taylor Wilkerson.

One of the best known residents of Lake View was D. H. Saylor, a Civil War Veteran. He was married to Alice M. Mulkey, Oct., 1880, came west and took a homestead near Totten Lake 1882. While attending the Simon wedding anniversary one night the Indians came and took about everything they had. They moved to Durango for four years, then returned to their homestead. Later they moved to Cortez, then a growing town, and Mr. Saylor became postmaster in 1900 and served twelve years. He continued to make his home in Cortez until he died in 1933.

Bert Saylor, the oldest son, was, by special arrangement, born in Illinois in 1881. In 1882 the family settled in Durango for 4 or 5 years, then returned to their homestead at Lake View. He lived the rest of his life in the county farming and raising livestock, first near Totten Lake then 2 miles west of Cortez. He is still a resident of Cortez, retired and taking life easy.

Other early settlers of Lake View were John Willis, Jack Pearson, Irving Ewing, "Stout" Atherton, and George Washington Taylor, a kind of renegade character, not well or favorably known. He seemed to have been a tough character and people of this kind often stopped at his place.

John Heffernan located the old Heffernan place in 1881, died and was buried there. Joe Heffernan took over the place, and later, became an Indian trader.

A Mr. Topping had the land just east of the Heffernan place and George and Rick Oshbaugh took land on each side of the road just on the hill to the east. They moved to McElmo later.

The Genther family lived up on the higher ground south of Lake View School house, and it was here that Mr. Genther was killed by the Indians.

Jerald Neal and Earl Harte are two present day residents who are doing excellent jobs at modern dairy farming, and raising some other livestock. Harte is out in front as a dairyman, has an up-to-date, Grade A milking establishment and one of the best dairy set-ups in the county. At the time this story is being written he is producing one ton of grade A milk every day for the market.

There are many other very good farmers in the Lake View community, several good dairymen, and as an indication of the population there is a Grange organization with a membership of some 125 members and they own a good hall. The Lake View school district still has its own grade school and a year ago built a very fine modern brick building for their grade school. All high school pupils are taken by bus to the county High School in Cortez.

THE MILDRED COMMUNITY

The Mildred Community lies to the west and northwest of Lake View. It is drained mainly by Hartman Draw and was at first known as the German Community, being settled largely by people of German birth or descent. Some of the early settlers were Fred Lupke and family, Henry Lupke and family. The Lupkes first hauled freight

138

from Durango to Parrott City in 1884 and in 1885 came to homestead in the German settlement. A daughter of Henry Lupke married Lester King and they still live on the old home place. Mr. King became a well known cattleman and was quite successful. Other early settlers were George Myers, George King, Pat O'Donnell, who owned the Philip Runck place and was widely known in this county and La Plata County; George Osterfeld, Frank Roelker, Henry Ablen, Frank Hartman Sr. and "Uncle Albey."

Henry Lupke was a skilled stone mason and helped with the stone work on buildings in Cortez and in his home community.

Ed Porter and Ben Porter were early settlers here, Ben Porter coming and homesteading land in 1884. He did some farming before water came to the valley. Then there was O. E. Stone and "Sandy" Garlinghouse, well known residents. A Mr. Sutherlin was very early in this settlement. He was the father of Mrs. Gus Stevenson and grandfather to Gus Stevenson of the Mancos Valley. He was notable as a maker of sorghum molasses growing the cane for its manufacture. Hartman Draw was named for Frank Hartman, senior, who, perhaps, was best known as the father of Frank Hartman, Jr., a noted newspaper man, and Lillian Hartman Johnson, a well known writer of her time.

The Mildred locality is a prosperous farming community and the hardy, industrious German pioneers soon carved many fine farms out of the native brush and timber and good sets of improvements are characteristic of almost every farm. The north part of the settlement is given over mostly to general farming, stock raising and some dairying while the south part has, in addition, several fine orchards. The community supports a very good country school for grade pupils and high school pupils go to the County High School at Cortez.

ARRIOLA COMMUNITY

The Arriola area was early recognized as one of the choice locations in Montezuma Valley and, as soon as it was apparent that water for irrigation was coming to the valley homesteaders began coming in to take up the land. Of course the choice lands were taken first. Among these earliest settlers was A. W. Dillon who came over from the Big Bend country, on the Dolores river, about 1885, and Frank Morgan, who, at the time, was operating a sawmill on Lost Canon. Morgan first took land in the Mancos Valley; then operated a sawmill in Thompson Park, removing it later to Lost Canon. The Dillons were first attracted to Rico as a lively mining town. They moved down to Lone Dome, well down on the Dolores river; then to Big Bend, then to the big valley and a homestead where they lived out their remaining days, and became well and favorably known and very useful, public spirited citizens. Morgan became very successful in the sheep business and accumulated some wealth. He also served long and faithfully on the board of managers of the Montezuma Valley Irrigation District. Dillon and Morgan each put out a small orchard on their homesteads shortly after moving onto them. These were the first fruit trees to be set out in this part of the county, an area that was to become widely known for the abundance and very high quality of the fruit it produces. The first trees were varieties that were not suited to the climate or the soil and didn't do well.

Other early settlers at Arriola were Henry Hechtman, and Carter Clay, a very early settler and an old time cowboy. A Mr. Morgarelle and three sons, Hugh, Bob and Reid Morgarelle, were residents in this community.

Two lands owners that became well known for the good job of farming they did were Mike and Frank Knight. They were born in England, but were very good and acceptable citizens, and they were very good and successful farmers.

Henry Hechtman and Ira Holston hauled lumber from Parrott City to build their homes. J. A. Bondurant, an uncle of Johnny McClure of Mancos, came in and soon had a home and a farm under way. Other early settlers were M. Wyman, Kate Lynch, a well known character of the time, Bill Lexton, Mother Johnson, I. O. Miller, W. J. Jackson, a carpenter who built many houses in Cortez and in the country, J. W. Skidmore, father of Tom Skidmore of Dolores—that recently made a small fortune in uranium. Also came a Mr. Newhouse, Emil Fisher, Ike Stephens, who mined vanadium ore containing uranium, years ago, stored it in a shed in Dolores until he had enough to make a shipment. Recently some one went into the old building with a geiger counter which immediately went wild with clicking. It was finally explained. Nick Krone and Emil Fisher homesteaded the land occupied partly by the Arriola Cemetery.

The post office was established at Arriola about 1892 and served until it was replaced by rural free delivery. Arriola has always been a leading rural community in Montezuma Valley. It has always had a splendid country school, a nice church building one or two good stores, and the postoffice made it a point of considerable rural importance for a while.

Arriola District was the 2nd school district to be organized, 1887. Mrs. I. O. Miller, teacher and the pupils were Mrs. Edna Dillon Longenbaugh, Evalena Hechtman Cebelles, Bertha Bondurant Morrison (Mrs. Luna Morrison), Verna Jackson Sheets and John T. Miller.

BEULAH

The little community of Beulah, down on Alkali Draw, was settled early but has never become prominent.

The first settler in the community was George Longenbaugh who came over from Durango in 1885 and took a homestead. In the same

140

year and about the same time came Frank Thomas from Gunnison and took a homestead. Thomas returned to Gunnison later and in 1887 returned with his family. There being a few children of school age a movement was started and in 1889 or 1890 a school district was organized and it was the first district to be organized in the new county and became School District No. 1. Mr. Thomas, being public minded, managed to contrive a small building for a school house, but the first school had to be held in one room of the Thomas home. Here the Thomas children and the Longenbaugh children went to school together and grew up together, Walter, Harley, Bertha Longenbaugh, and two or three others, well known in the valley, and Matilda Thomas, who, in 1898, became Mrs. James Treece. These families knew all the hardships of early life in the big valley and can tell many stories of the struggle to stay with their land and get along. Charles Allen, Mr. Thomas and Mr. Longenbaugh constituted the first school board. A little later Joe and Dave McClure and Frank Blackmer were residents, and several others whose names the writer was unable to get. Later Cortez took the No. 1 district from Beulah and Beulah became No. 2. It has recently dissolved and consolidated with Cortez. A Mr. Campbell, Pete Shetz, C. B. Stone, son Blaine, and daughter, Mabel, who married William Puett, were other local residents.

Another settler that came to Beulah along with the very first was Joe Billingsley, a mine contractor. Here he met and married Mrs. Lucy Ann Hardesty, a widow who had a little daughter, Jessie. He helped to establish the first school at Beulah and his little step-daughter, Jessie Billingsley was one of the pupils in the first term of school at that place. After growing to womanhood Jessie was married to a Mr. Bailey and is still a resident in the town of Cortez.

The family lived at Silverton in 1898, when Jessie was eleven years old. She tells a story of an old miner who stopped at their home, sat down on a rock near the house to rest and when she went out to investigate him, he asked her to bring him a glass of water and to put some pepper in the water. She went in the house and told her mother about the old man and his request for water. The mother and the young daughter went out taking the water and the pepper. After some talk the old miner, unnamed, told of once having a mining partner named McElmo who was ill of tuberculosis and that one fall, as the sick man was getting worse, they left the mountains and started west for the Colorado river for the winter. Upon reaching McElmo Canon they stopped at a nice spring of water to rest a while, McElmo got much worse and died. The old miner dug a grave and buried his partner where he died and named the canon McElmo Canon. This is the story of the naming of McElmo Canon according to Mrs. Bailey's story of the old miner.

LEBANON

The Lebanon locality was first called Hardscrabble by local resi-

141

dents, and it was not until about 1909 that it was named Lebanon by the Colorado Land and Improvement Co. The first school was in a small log building, which served for a number of years, and the first teacher was John Adams, and he had a son named Bernard Adams. Among the early settlers we find "Sandy" Garlinghouse, Serge Garlinghouse, Enoch Chapman, George Pierceall, Mr. Leavell, Elic Bishop, W. W. Byers, Mrs. Armstrong and Ben Porter.

In about 1909 the Colorado Land and Improvement Co. was organized by a group of Pueblo people, nearly all railroad men; they had 250 shareholders and bought 1,100 acres of land in this community, laid out a town, and established a postoffice they called Lebanon. A townsite was laid out, a small hotel was built; a building was erected and a stock of merchandise put in. Three or four residences and a small office building were built. They cleared land, put out several 10 acre tracts to orchard, planned new roads and built telephone lines, advertised, and "boosted" the country as a great fruit country, and brought in a number of new families. The company became insolvent and went into bankruptcy, and all the assets were sold to satisfy creditors. The company failed in its purpose, but it did a lot of good for the community and the country. They were right in one thing; the locality of Lebanon is regarded as about the best fruit area in the county and the safest from frost and hail damage. They have many fine orchards and they produce the best apples grown anywhere in the world.

The community has a fine church, not being used, and a very nice country grade school. The high school pupils go to Cortez to the County High School.

LEWIS

The Lewis area made a slow start, but it has made up for it by becoming one of the finest communities in the county. When the irrigating system for the valley was started a number of settlers came in and took up the land in the Lewis vicinity. Then they failed to get the big No. 2 Canal finished to this locality, so the first settlers abandoned their claims and moved away. The record says water came to Lewis in 1906, but local residents say it was 1908 or 1909 before they got a head of water. When the water at last did come all the land was soon taken and several of the first settlers came back to their claims.

Among the very first settlers we find Milt McConnell, John, Jim and Bill Brumley, Jim and Bill South, Del Raplee, Charles Hosea, a cattleman, and Bill and Matt Hosea, riders, Will (Pop) Peel, James and George Reid, Ed Porter, Ed Winborn and C. E. Krater, a dry farmer. The Brumleys came in 1882 and 1883 to take charge of the large L. C. herd of cattle belonging to their sister, Mrs. Lacy, formerly in charge of Henry Goodman, and the Souths came about the same time.

The L. C. herd was ranged westward to the Utah border and the Brumleys seem to have taken land here on Brumley Draw as a convenient place for operations headquarters.

After the water came, came also W. R. Lewis in 1910, bought the old Del Raplee place and, in 1911, established the postoffice which was named Lewis. Lewis put in a small store and, a little later, came C. F. McAfee and opened up a merchandise business which he conducted for a number of years. Ralph Dillon has a good farm a mile west of Lewis.

After the water came, and the people came in and took land they had to have a school, so a little rough building was put up and Miss Stevie Duncan taught the first school. This first building burned down and a second school building was erected on the site of the present building and the second term of school was taught by Miss Emily Longenbaugh. A fine modern county school building now serves all grade school purposes and a bus takes all high school pupils to the County High School in Cortez.

A new church building is being erected to be known as the Lewis Community Church under the present auspices of the Methodist Church at Dolores. There is a flourishing National Grange organization with approximately 150 members and they have a large modern building for their meetings, which they own.

When the water came into the ditch at Lewis it was not long before settlers began to go above and beyond the ditch and take nonirrigated farms. Some of the dry land farmers were Henry Todd, Steve Masten, Bill Coop, George Schaff, Griff Rutherford, who came very early; Sam Rutherford, Harry Rutherford, Homer Hughes, who accomplished heavy execution on the sage brush with a mammoth drag and four teams for power; Jim Uplon, Francis Uplon, Robert Larrier, who also cleared lots of land; Clara Bradfield of near Yellow Jacket; Bud Simmons, a large landholder, Glen Grace, Wread Jobes, Aregy Wynders, who also had a store at Ackmen; Shelly Reed, Charley Wilson, Mr. Ives, John Schaff, C. F. McAfee, Billie Campbell. These people nearly all pioneered in Dry Farming and are improving on their earlier successes. The old veteran that led the way to successful dry farming was C. E. Krater, who died in October, 1956, at the advanced age of 90 years after a long and active career. About 40 years ago Mr. Krater was growing potatoes and corn without irrigation. He was the first to demonstrate the growing of alfalfa and grass in rows for a seed crop or a hay crop, and, of course, he grew all the small grains. Mr. Krater used to exhibit his products regularly at the county fair, and often at the state fair, and his dry farming products were a revelation to a great many people.

The extreme west side high line ditch, that takes water from the large No. 2 Canal, and covers land within a mile of Gai's warehouse, was not finished until 1912 or 1913. It brought a large area of very fine land under irrigation. This ditch extension is called the U lateral.

YELLOW JACKET AREA

It was natural that the first effort to produce crops without irrigation should be made in the immediate proximity of irrigated areas, good and suitable land being available. And so it was that the dry farming practice started first, in this county, in the area adjoining the Montezuma Valley Irrigation district on the northwest, north of Lewis and in the Yellow Jacket country. About 1909 and 1910 the first experiments in dry farming began to be made in this area and for some time only a few families came to engage in the experiment. At first the practice of farming without irrigation in a semi-arid territory was not well understood and the settlers had to learn the practices that gave the best results. Some had read in their farm papers about methods of conserving the moisture content of the soil and growing crops on semidry land, but it took experience to show the way. Some of these first settlers came over from the nearby irrigated area where they had been farming convinced that the good sage brush land would produce valuable crops once the brush was removed and good tillage practices put into use.

So, in 1912 and 1913 a few families and individuals settled in and about Yellow Jacket where there were some springs that furnished some good water for domestic use, and among these were Grandpa Gilliland and family, Mrs. Gus Stevenson and family consisting of a number of growing girls and boys. Three of the boys were Had Stevenson, Ed Stevenson and Gus Stevenson. Charles Wilson, a local homesteader, married one of the Stephenson girls and Shelly Reed married another. They are all still there save Gus Stevenson of the Mancos Valley, and Mrs. Stevenson who passed away some years ago. Other settlers were Ed Gilliland, Mr. and Mrs. Rutherford, George Schaaf, John Schaaf, Bill Troup, Harry Jobes, Roy Schafer, William Smith, and others.

On March 1, 1913, came T. Gai and family preempting a homestead one mile north of Yellow Jacket and joined fortunes with the others, to help improve the country and wrest a living from the virgin soil. These founded the new community and began at once to create a home in the sage brush wastes.

Theirs was the hard way, as with all pioneer settlers who were the first. Little or no money to start on, nothing at the start to create a dollar in new wealth that was tangible. Some kind of a home to protect them from the elements had to be built, land mut be cleared and some kind of a farm started to produce food for man and feed for beasts. The nearby settlements under the Montezuma Valley irrigation system offered little advantage, but some got a little work to earn

144

a grubstake and enable them to carry on in their undertaking. The first thing was to get some land producing so that there would be food. There were no tractors in those days; frequently the settler didn't have a team; so they tackled the sage brush with ax and grubbing hoe. Those with teams made some kind of a heavy contrivance they could drag back and forth over the brittle sage dragging it down and breaking it off. If teams were available two or more teams would be hitched to a very heavy drag and commit fearful execution on the "Purple Sage." Some improvised a brush rake; other piled brush with a pitch fork, or with their hands. Father, mother and all the "kids" large enough to work frequently engaged in the task. It was a race between getting some production from the soil or starving out. Fortunately the land was rich in fertility and responded wonderfully to cultivation. In a few months there was some food for the table and feed for the livestock, but money, for a long time, was scarce as hens teeth. It was some years before any real wealth could be created but the settlers clearly envisaged financial success, and the work went on.

Corn was the first crop, and some potatoes. They had to grow a crop they could plant and harvest without machinery. At first neither beans nor wheat were a crop. When beans finally came they had to pull them up root and all and thresh them by hand. Small patches of wheat could only be cut with a scythe or reap hook and threshed by hand. Finally production was great enough that a thresher could be brought in from the irrigated area to do custom work. More settlers came, more land was cleared and more and larger crops were produced.

After the first settlers had come in and taken land in the vicinity of Yellow Jacket, others came and among them we find Lincoln Banter who had the first store at Yellow Jacket, also had the postoffice and a Mr. Merritt was the first postmaster. This first location was four miles west and one south of the present location. The mail was brought from Lewis and Gus Stevenson was the first mail carrier. George Schaaf homesteaded and bought the Yellow Jacket store. E. C. Ives was early on the scene and two of his grand children are still residents there. Mr. Goutzen, John Willis, Bill Lakey, Sid Benton, Morton Jackson, Charles Tanner, the Eggars boys, a Mr. Wyman, and many others, came into the new land.

Being near older settlements under irrigation the Yellow Jacket dry farmers had available nearby threshing outfits and for this reason this area was the first to begin growing wheat and beans for the market. By 1920 considerable wheat was being raised and some good sized fields of beans were planted and harvested. Larger fields of beans began to be planted. First they had to be gathered and threshed by hand, but the crop increased rapidly when machinery became available.

Among the names of the early settlers mentioned above is that of T. Gai and family. Mr. Gai has made an outstanding success and has been a real benefactor in the community. He started his grain and bean business in 1940 after making an unqualified success as a producer. His first storage was a building 40x100 feet, but there was already a big production of beans and wheat and the business soon outgrew this building. Year after year it was found necessary to enlarge again. Now, in the fall of 1956, the total storage capacity is a full one-half million bushels and every building is filled to its capacity, and this is one of the shortest crop years the locality has ever experienced. In the average crop year the buildings are filled, and kept full, with truck after truck loading out almost every day. A 700,000 bushel wheat crop is the largest handled to date. There is probably a 200,000 bushel bean crop this season, one of the lightest ever produced and a 300,000 bushel wheat crop.

Clearing land and plowing with power machinery got started first in the Yellow Jacket settlement also. P. K. Davis brought in a steam tractor for clearing land, and Dorsey Orr brought in from Mancos a large Reeves steam tractor and large, specially made plow for clearing land. Floyd Larrimore brought in a gas tractor and George Schaaf a Fordson. Floyd Cunningham brought in and used the first row crop tractor, International make, about 1928. More powerful machinery came into use, huge crawler type tractors, four row planters and cultivators, drills, chisels, gang plows; first the grain binder; then the combine, and the mechanical bean harvester and the pickup combine and other machinery.

Today the dry land section is a land of many hundred fine farms and many, many homes. It is marvelous the development that has taken place: miles and miles of cultivated land, hundreds of farms in solid phalanx, border to border, and there is no evidence that the land is even beginning to exhaust itself.

There are many stories of families who sacrificed everything to get started on the new land and have a home of their own. Some lived for a time on potatoes and beans. Some had oatmeal and coffee without sugar or milk, and so the stories go. And the jack rabbits—they seemed to think the new farmers were growing crops just for them. They were everywhere—thousands of them, and they plagued the whole land— all the dry land area. Finally they, too, ceased to be a menace.

With so many families, there had to be schools. Yellow Jacket had the first school about 1915. The first school was called by the beautiful, euphoneous name—Fair View. It was two and one-half miles west of the present site of Yellow Jacket. Guy Townsend was an early settler there and his wife, Ora Townsend, was the first teacher. The Lyman school and the Prospect school came soon after. Many other schools came as the country was filled with new families.

About 1920 the Eggars boys brought in a new horsepower threshing outfit and the community had a thresher of its own. This gave new and fresh impetus to wheat and bean growing.

146

PLEASANT VIEW

A few miles further out on the Dove Creek highway brings one to the beautiful and attractive little town of Pleasant View, new, and just showing signs of new life and growth. There is not more than 150 people in the place, but they envisage a bright future.

The first settlements in the Pleasant View vicinity was probably the Ackmen community, two or three miles southwest of Pleasant View, starting about 1913. A number of settlers came in about this time and a postoffice was established they called Ackmen and after a time there were two or three small business establishments. The early settlement was very much as it was at Yellow Jacket. The settlers came in and homesteaded the land and began the work of clearing the brush from the land in the same way and under the same handicaps. H. H. Beaber started a newspaper he called the "Pioneer Chieftain" which survived for a year or two.

Some of the early settlers about Ackmen were Emery Rutherford, 1916, who filed the first homestead under the 320 acre preemption law. After serving a term in the first World War he came back to his homestead. Other settlers were Roy G. Marr, Clyde Laird, "Old Man" Pigg, Ben Williford, Clint Woods, Bob Laurie, Clem Gray, Bob Lanier, Samson Rutherford, Francis Jones, and others. These came in to pioneer in the new community and get some development started. Many new settlers kept coming and in a few years had taken the whole country on each side of the highway for miles. Corn and potatoes were the very first crops. There being no machinery they had to raise something they could plant, tend and harvest with their hands or the simple tools they had, and something to make food for man and feed for beasts. A few people tried milking some cows, both here and at Cahone, to bring in a little money.

A road on out to Dove Creek had been laid out in a rather indifferent way, but in 1935 the state highway department declared the road from Cortez to Dove Creek and on out to the state line, a state highway. The road had been laid out on the route of the present highway and some work done. This action meant that a real road would be built. For some years it was only a dirt road, but in 1936 the work of gravel surfacing began and in 1937 almost all the road was gravel surfaced out to the Utah state line. This was pretty effective in taking the highway out of the mud. In 1941 some oil surfacing had been done and in 1942 a long stretch of the road was reoiled starting at Cortez, and in the next two or three years the highway was oiled all the way through to the Utah state line. When the highway was laid out and improved it was soon realized that the town of the locality had to be on the highway. Accordingly a new town was laid out on the highway which they called Pleasant View. The postoffice was discontinued at

147

Ackmen and the new town absorbed the business interests and the newspaper plant was moved to Dove Creek.

A school district was organized and a regular term of school was held. Telephone service and electric power and lights came to the new town right along with the oil surfaced highway, light and power about 1941. The telephone about the same time.

In 1955 the need of a good school building was felt, bonds were voted and an excellent and modern grade school building was erected, and all high school pupils go by bus to the County High School at Cortez.

The town has one nice church building, two lodge organizations and a strong National Grange is organized. A consolidated school district supports the town school and buses bring the grade children in from the outlying districts, giving them the advantage of the best educational facilities.

CAHONE

The village of Cahone is one the Cortez-Dove Creek highway, just north of the county line, in the southern part of west Dolores County. It is not known when the first settlers came into this locality, but by 1914 there were a number on the land, having filed homesteads. At this time there was no town and the nearest postoffice was at Lewis, distant some 12 or 13 miles. In the spring of 1916 many settlers came and filed homesteads. Early in 1917 a postoffice was granted and named Cahone after Cahone Canon. The name is a Spanish word signifying "box" because, a little further down, the creek is boxed in by high perpendicular walls on each side and is spoken of as box canon. The postoffice was first at the Bert Ballenger place, about a mile northeast of the present town, and Mr. Ballenger was the first postmaster. The present highway was laid out as a road early and Floyd Johnson established a store where Cahone now stands, in 1921, and started the town. The postoffice was moved from the Ballenger place to the Jeff Simmons place, a mile south of Cahone, but the Ballenger Bros., also put up a building and opened a store at the new town site and the postoffice was moved to the new location. A school district had been organized and a building erected near the original postoffice site and the first school was taught there in 1916 with Otis Selig as teacher. After a year or two the school was moved to the new townsite at Cahone.

The settlers had to have some income so they raised corn for feed and several of the farmers milked cows, and a cream receiving station was established. Corn and potatoes were their first crops, but by 1927 they had started producing beans and by 1928 winter wheat had become a crop. Bean raising and wheat raising spread rapidly and potatoes and dairy cows were soon discontinued and corn was grown

148

less extensively. Today, at Cahone, there is one church, two filling stations, a bean warehouse and bean packaging plant, the usual lines of other business and a population of about 150. Four local school districts have been consolidated, there is a $60,000 grade school building and buses bring the country children into school. There is also a bus to pick up the high school pupils and take them to the Dolores County High School at Dove Creek.

A few of the early settlers about Cahone, coming about 1914 and shortly after, were Statler Lovett, Bert Davis, still a local resident; Cal Fink, Charles Turner, Sam Fink, a Mr. Neeley, John Casper and his boys—Prentis, Clifford, and Dennis; J. L. Shira, Jim Wilson, a Mr. Calhoun, G. L. Crugan, Mr. Cox, Eugene Johnson, James Johnson, John Proffer, Jeff Simmons, Sr., Mr. Leslie, "Uncle Jim" Neeley, a Mr. Chenewerth, Mr. Morgan and Bert Ballenger, first Postmaster and, later, a veteran in the postal service at Denver.

Edgar E. Ballenger is probably the best known and best informed citizen about Cahone. He filed for his homestead in 1914 and, in 1915, after working for a year at Dolores, moved out to his land, one-half mile east of Cahone. At the time of his coming Mr. Ballenger states that there was not more than 500 acres in cultivation in the entire locality, but shortly after many people came in and located on and occupied the land. As in all frontier settlements for the first few years, he relates, life was pretty tough going. By the terms of the law homesteaders had to live on their claims to make final proof and get title to their land, and before he could make final proof they had to clear up and put into cultivation a certain amount of land, 20 acres on a 160 acre claim and 40 acres on a 320 acre claim. To meet the conditions the whole family worked, if there was a family. Many of the settlers had only a grubbing hoe and an ax. Some had good teams and could do more effective work by pulling a heavy "drag" back and forth over the brush, but quite a few had not even a team. Some who had teams put their teams together on a much heavier drag and made better progress at clearing land.

Mr. Ballenger likes the stories reminiscent of these old days; pioneering in the sage brush, the struggle to stay on the land and win a livelihood while getting the first production from the rich, new soil; the long journeys, at first, to Lewis to get the mail, and the one time he rode a mule, bareback, sixteen miles to Coal Bed to cast his vote, that being the closest and only polling place in this part of the county at this time. This was certainly doing one's duty as a citizen with a vengeance. He helped to get the first schools started and helped to improve them; he helped to get new roads laid out and built and finally, when duty called, he spent four years at County Commissioner; then four years as Tax Assessor, and in January, 1937, he starts another four year term as County Commissioner. His battle for success on a homestead is typical of many others who took land in the sage brush and carved out of it a farm and a home. But when he sees the good land selling at $100 and $125 an acre he is convinced it was worth all the effort and the sacrifice.

DOVE CREEK

Before the time of the homesteader the Dove Creek country was a vast area of waving grass. There was a stinted growth of sage in the grass, but the grass prevailed and held the sage in check. The grassy plain was interspersed with black splotches of pinon and cedar trees, but, for the most part, the timber was much thinner and lighter then than in recent years and grass grew everywhere and provided abundant feed for range cattle and sheep. In the higher elevations it was blue stem grass, called Western Wheat Grass by the College folks, and intermixed with it was a light growth of grama grass and some other short grasses. In the lower areas grama grass and other short grasses prevailed and the common sage brush gave place, mostly, to white sage and rabbit brush, thus making very good winter feed for stock. Stock water was scarce in the entire area, but the cattlemen and sheepmen found enough to supply their needs when supplemented by winter snows.

For these reasons all this dry farming area was first a cattle country. From about 1880 to 1890 the Dolores river valley was settled, mostly by cattlemen, who brought in many herds of cattle, as related elsewhere in this narrative, and some of the herds were quite large. These herds were summer grazed on the vast range to the east and northeast beyond the Dolores river. In the fall they were drifted or driven to that vast area west and sotuhwest of the Cortez-Dove Creek highway and extending westward to the Blue Mountains and southwest to the San Juan river. This operation continued for 25 to 30 years before the homesteader claimed the range land. It was natural that the grass should soon be overgrazed and that the overgrazed and weakened stand of grass should yield to the more aggressive sage. The cattle kept the grass eaten down but didn't eat the sage as long as there was anything else to eat, thus giving the sage brush a better chance. The operations of the cattlemen are more fully detailed in the chapters on the Dolores and the Dolores river valley.

In August, 1912, the trip by the then existing road from Dolores to Monticello passed only three homesteaders after leaving the irrigated country. These were Phillip Melott, a Mr. Vaughn and a Mr. Handcock. From information obtainable these men must be regarded as the vanguard of the settlement by homesteaders in the Dove Creek-Cahone area. About this time, or a year later, one R. A. Butt took land where the town of Dove Creek now stands and built the large house just across the street from the Hunter hotel, used for a number of years as the Dolores County Courthouse, having bought a small

150

store that was being run by Stokes Bros. Here he put in a large stock of dry goods and groceries. The postoffice, established in 1915 with R. R. Butt as postmaster was given the name Dove Creek, from the name of the nearby creek, which was named by the early cattlemen. At this time there was only one other house in the place, a log cabin down by the creek. This cabin was built some years previous, no doubt by the cattlemen, and was a sort of cowboy rendezvous for the stockmen for years.

On August 26, 1918, came Dan B. Hunter from Dallas, Texas, to Dove Creek, and these were the only houses he found on the area of the present townsie, but at this time, and a little later, homesteaders began to come in and take the land. It might be related that some of the earliest were Charles Morgan, two miles north of town; B. F. Handcock, one and one-half miles north. Phillip Mellot, one-half mile east; Loyd F. Davis, 3 miles southwest; Charles Harter, one mile west; Karl Butt, one-half mile west; A. L. Grabeel, four and one-half miles west; Arthur Baker, four miles west; Jim McCaleb, two miles west; Bob Livingstone, eight miles south; T. C. Hall, eight and one-half miles south; Norris Tucker, seven miles southwest; Charles Griffith, eleven miles southwest; Glen and Columbus Wright, twelve miles southwest; Oscar Crabb, four miles north; Dave Knuckles, eight miles north; Ed Baird, four and one-half miles east; John Griffin, 12 miles north. These are the first few that first tackled the sage brush and pinon and cedar groves and to try to win a livelihood from the new and untried land. After them and along with them many, many others came. Every one who is familiar with this dry farming country knows the extent of the area. From Dove Creek southwestward fifteen miles or more to Cedar Point, extends the homestead area; large blocks of solid farms lying border to border, and to the north and east to the Dolores Divide. This development came gradually through the years. Almost all the early settlers were people in limited circumstances. All the land had to be cleared before it could be planted. With the poor people there was no way of clearing the land but with hand tools and hard labor. As in other settlements, those who had teams drug down the brush and broke most of it off and piled the brush by hand, but this was slow and it took a long time to clear a farm as in other localities, sometimes several homesteaders would go in together with two or four teams and a very heavy drag and get along much faster. Often it was just pa and ma and all the kids large enough to do any work. Many of the homesteaders filed a claim, occupies it as a home, in whatever kind of building they were able to provide, and worked as long as money and food lasted. They would then go some place and find work, accumulate a little money and another food supply, then return to the homestead, and work as long as their new supply of food would last.

As at Ackmen, the first crop grown on this non-irrigated land was not wheat and beans, but corn and potatoes, crops they could grow

151

without the use of machinery. Then, too, they figured these were about the best crops they could grow and the surest to make a crop. They sold potatoes on the market when they could, but in order to get anything out of the corn, quite a few milked a few cows and sold cream. This yielded but a small income, but the homesteaders had to have a little cash. Salt and sugar and soda and coffee didn't grow on trees. The first beans were grown in this locality about 1927 and the first wheat about 1928. Sam James, of near Ackmen, raised and shipped the first car of beans to be produced in the dry land in 1926. Once started with beans and wheat, potatoes and milk cows were abandoned.

In 1921 and 1922 the tractor began coming into use and this was the start of real development. The old way was soon abandoned when it was found that the one-way disk plow was very effective in uprooting the sage, and this implement served to greatly speed up the job of clearing the land. Soon the land was being cleared of brush and timber by the square mile. The bulldozer came into use for clearing heavy timber; also for pushing off the sage brush, further speeding up the land clearing job.

With the coming of more people there had to be more roads and schools. As in the early history of the county every one wanted roads, and new roads were viewed and laid out in every new community, and a little done toward making a road, often by the settlers themselves; and another thing of prime importance was public schools. For a time after the Cortez-Dove Creek highway was laid out, it was difficult to provide school buildings fast enough as school district after school district was organized. The first school in the west end of Dolores county was on George Snyder's place, in 1916. Also at this time and place the first voting precinct was created, on Coal Bank Canon, 14 miles west and north of Cahone. The first school in the Dove Creek area was the High Hill school, a log building, five miles west of Dove Creek, in 1919. There were 65 pupils indicating the number of settlers, and Dan B. Hunter was the teacher. The first school in Dove Creek was taught in 1921. There were 85 pupils in a very nice frame building—of ample size with Dan Hunter as teacher, Freddie Comsvek was his assistant. This building continued to serve for school purposes until the new, modern grade school building was erected in the north side of town. Another school building, a rock structure, was built with W. P. A. work about 1932.

The highway was laid out in the early 20's and this was the occasion for the coming of many new settlers. This road was later surveyed by the State Highway Commission, a permanent route laid out and, in 1935, the work of gravel surfacing was started at the Utah state line, and the following year, 1936, the work of oil surfacing was begun, and the town of Dove Creek began to make long strides of progress in growth and development.

From two business houses in 1918 the town has grown to a population of about 1200 in 1956. As a measure of this growth the town now has five grain and bean storage units, including one elevator, The Fraser Elevator Co. owners, with a storage capacity of one and one-quarter million bushels; the Millbourn Grain and Elevator Co., capacity one-half million bushels or a little more; The Denver Elevator Co. with a million bushels storage capacity, and the Gai recleaning unit of 400,000 bushels. The Romer Mercantile Co. also handles beans and wheat. New public buildings are keeping pace with growth in business and population. There is a new court house that cost $125,000; a grade school building that cost $100,000; an additional grade school that cost $125,000; a County High School, built and used in connection with Memorial Hall, that cost $80,000.

Water for the town has been a problem. Various plans have been tried, and the town outgrew them all. A reservoir was built that proved inadequate and unsatisfactory; then deep wells were drilled, but still not enough water, and the water itself not the best for domestic use. Then a pumping station was installed over on the Dolores river and four-inch pipe line built to convey water to the town. In the summer of 1956, an extremely dry period in the weather, and on account of so much water being taken out above, the river quit running at the pump station and the town was again desperately short on water for a while. Then it was decided to drill for water down at the pumping station on the river. A well 80 feet deep was drilled which tapped the underflow of the river, which filled the well nearly to the top, and the pumping tests lifting 800 gallons a minute from the well failed to lower the water in the well perceptibly. They are sure now they have a sufficient and reliable water supply for a town of 6,000 people and that their water supply problem is at last finally and completely settled.

In late 1956 a movement is under way for a sewage system, and the plan is to have the system installed within a year adequate for present needs and substantial future growth. Power and light service was provided for the town by the Empire Electric Association and on May 5, 1941, power and light was turned on to 187 Dove Creek customers, and a modern telephone system furnishes local and long distance service. Both light and power, and telephone service have been enlarged several times over since the first installation.

At the general election in November 1944, a proposition was submitted to a vote of the people to move the county seat from Rico to Dove Creek. It was carried favorably by a substantial majority. The election was contested, but the decision of the majority was allowed to stand.

So much for the Town of Dove Creek. Now we must say a word for the town's leading citizen and public benefactor through the years, Dan B. Hunter, 82 years of age in this good year 1956. He came from Dallas, Texas, and arrived at Dove Creek August 26, 1918. Upon his arrival there were but two houses in the future town, which hadn't even been laid out. His first service to the community was as school teacher. He taught 16 years in the Dove Creek schools. He edited and published the Inland Empire, Dove Creek's local paper, for eight years from 1942 to 1950. He helped to get the Empire Electric Association organized and started in business and has been a member of its Board of Directors since the Association started operations; ran a drug store, had active management of two other stores, was for years representative for the Southwestern Water Conservancy District, served on the State Water Board for years and has just been succeeded by Ira E. Kelly of Mancos, 1956. He has been a life member of the National Reclamation Association since 1928, and is now Dean Emeritus of the State Water Board.

Mr. Hunter has been working for twenty years, both privately and in an official capacity, for the big Dolores River dam and reclamation project. This project now comes under the Upper Colorado River Basin project, passed by a recent session of Congress. Money is now available for the final survey, and Mr. Hunter is convinced that work on the big project will be under way within three years. The project involves a 230 foot dam in the Dolores River Canon and impounding 185,000 acre feet of water, all designated for irrigating 40,000 acres of land in the Dove Creek area. The lake so created will inundate several farms in the river valley and will extend almost to the bridge on the Dolores-Cortez highway.

As Mr. Hunter is passing from the active local scene, his place is being ably filled by Mr. William A. Lawrence, who is intensely interested in the present and future of the community and is a live wire all the time. He is prominent, public spirited and a leader of men, and nothing escapes his attention that promises to benefit the locality in any way.

The first bank came to Dove Creek in 1951 when F. A. Sitton incorporated and established the Dove Creek State Bank, with a capital stock of $150,000. The new bank furnished a valuable service to the community from the start and has been a complete success in every way. After the bank had been operating for some four years Charles Steen, the well known uranium operator, and Bill McCormick bought large shares of stock and added strength and prestige to the institution. The business of the bank grew rapidly and their published statement of March 14, 1957, showed total assets of $2,295,077.05. Loans and discounts total $1,059,064.94 which indicates the extent of the service the bank is rendering to the community.

The Stokes Brothers store, the first in the locality, was taken over by purchase, by R. S. Butt in 1915. There was a large family connection in the Butt family and fourteen members of the family were living in the community at one time. Butt was the first postmaster.

As in other settlements in the dry lands, jack rabbits plagued the land the first three or four years and, for two years, when there were only small fields here and there, they took just about everything.

The uranium industry has been an asset to the town since uranium mining became active a few years back and at present the uranium activity in nearby territory has a payroll of approximately $40,000 a month. But the main community asset is still, and probably will always be, agriculture. The past few years have been rather drier than the average season, but there has been fair crop right along, nothing approaching a complete failure, and during the summer of 1956, good bean and wheat land was exchanging right along at $100 to $125 an acre.

Television came to the town in 1956, relayed from Cortez. The town has seven organized churches, several of the leading lodges, and a strong National Grange organization. The story goes that Zane Gray wrote his story—Riders of the Purple Sage, while staying at the old log house that stood down by the creek in early days.

CHAPTER XIV

THE EMPIRE ELECTRIC ASSOCIATION

One great benefactor to the entire Montezuma County area, and parts of adjoining counties, is the Empire Electric Association. Consumer owned and consumer managed, the Association has been an unqualified success since it first started operations. In 1939 a few of those most interested began canvassing the territory for support, and making plans. After signing up a long list of prospective members and taking proper steps to get a government loan, as provided by law in such matters, active steps were taken to get an organization formed and in working order. Support was general and plans moved forward rapidly, and actual construction was soon under way. Poles were set, lines strung, and power installed, and by 1941 they were able to start delivering electricity to consumers on 84.4 miles of line and to 260 homes that received electricity for the first time. The first power station was located at Lewis and the power was generated with two 50 kilowatt diesel powered generators. Now, in the fall of 1956, there are over 3800 consumers—owners and a property valuation of over two million dollars, and electric units are operated in Cortez, Mancos, and Dolores.

The Association began its first operations about Lewis; then extended their lines to Yellow Jacket, Pleasant View, Cahone and Dove Creek. In 1944 the Highlands Utilities, which operated plants at Cortez, Dolores and Mancos, sold these plants in their entirety to the Empire Association and the Association began at once to consolidate all their holdings and operate them under one system. By acquiring these systems the Empire Association was able to buy their power from the Western Colorado Power Co. which opened up great possibilities for development and expansion. Expansion began in earnest and now power is furnished for almost every purpose and to every part of Montezuma County, West Dolores County, west San Miguel County, aed out into Utah, north and south of Monticello, wherever there are consumers enough to justify extending the lines.

The first power plant to operate in Cortez was in 1922 or '23, when W. J. Bozman, Ed Johnson, A. W. Cowling and John Coleman organized and built a small plant at the Mowry flour mill, on South Market St. The plant was powered by the engine that drove the mill and was designed to furnish light and limited power to homes and business houses. The Highland Utilities bought this plant and, later, sold it to the Empire Electric.

Growth has been general and rapid. Today the Association energizes 850 miles of transmission and distributing lines. In 1956, 236 kilowatt hours per month per domestic consumer was delivered, and the annual delivery to all consumers was 15,400,000 kilowatt hours. The business is staffed by 20 specially trained permanent employees.

The first meeting to organize was held at Dove Creek Nov. 15, 1939. Incorporation was perfected and, under provisions of the R. E. A. Act of 1936, the company proceeded to borrow the funds from the government special fund to purchase materials, machinery and equipment to build a power plant and distributing system and, in a few weeks, were able to begin operating. Since that time several additional loans have been made as they were necessary for expansion. Regular payments on the loans have been made and, at this time, payments are already some years in advance of the payments required by the contracts, and the Association is positively on a safe and firm financial basis. The association will soon be needing very much more power and, in common with all the other rural electric companies associated in the Colorado-Ute Electric Generation and Transmission Co., now building their large plant at Nucla, are looking to the mammoth plant for an abundance of cheap and reliable power, which is beginning to be so badly needed. As an evidence of the approaching need we find the Empire Electric Association now furnishing power for two big sawmills each with a capacity of 25,000 board feet of lumber per day, the Wark flour mill, the Potts sawmill in part, the match factory at Mancos, the dry ice plant in McElmo Canon, numerous dairy farms that are heavy consumers, a dozen or more wheat and bean elevator and cleaning plants, has contracted to furnish electric power for the Hansen & Son lumber processing plant, now being built on the highway between Cortez and Dolores, and 3,700 smaller consumers. Cheap and abundant power is needed.

The power that is being developed and used is a tremendous asset. It is bringing increased value to all property where the power is available. Electric power has replaced man power in a hundred places and ways, and doing the work cheaper and better. Every horsepower in use is making money for the user, which indicates the wealth creating possibilities present and future, for electric power. The secret of the success of electric power lies in the fact that it can be produced in any place where water power or fuel deposits make production possible at a low cost figure and distributed to any point where it is needed over a wide area and at a low cost for distribution to consumers. Electricity doesn't cost; it pays.

THE DRY ICE PLANT
COLORADO CARBONICS. INC.

A few years previous to this writing a company in search for oil, drilled two wells in the upper McElmo Canon. In one they struck a heavy flow of natural gas at a depth of 1500 feet. In the other they struck a strong flow of carbon dioxide gas at a depth of 7000 feet. This gas tested 99 per cent pure gas and when the well was capped and the gas confined it built up a pressure of 800 pounds to the square inch. In 1949 a company entitled Colorado Carbonics Incorporated was organized to put in some machinery and make a test run to determine if the product known as dry ice could be successfully and commercially produced. The gas was piped from the well to a point on the county road four and one-half miles down the canon to a convenient and suitable site where the plant was built. Another pipe paralleling this one was put in from the natural gas well, a distance of one and one-half miles to bring fuel gas to the plant for power and heating purposes.

The first run proved that making dry ice on a commercial scale was entirely feasible and very economical. The pressure from the gas wells delivered the gases to the plant without expense other than putting in the gas lines. The carbon dioxide being 99 per cent pure required no processing save a little to get rid of the 1 per cent impurity, and having fuel gas right in the plant for all processing work made production possible at a very low cost. This was a great advantage since dry ice is made in many localities and competition is keen.

Starting in with a production of two tons per day, the plant has been expanded twice and, at present, the plant is producing 20 tons daily on a 24 hour a day schedule. Four 60 pound blocks are made in one complete operation. There is every evidence of an inexhaustible supply of gas from the well as the great pressure it builds up is not lessening in the least. Their market is in Denver, Phoenix, Tucson and Albuquerque, in the main. There is only a small demand locally, but it is fully supplied. The product is used for many kinds of refrigeration, mainly for freezing meats, fish and making ice cream, this last use being the largest of any one use.

Making dry ice is quite a process in the last stages of which the gas is put under a pressure of 2500 pounds per square inch and reduced in temperature to 110 degrees below zero at which point it solidifies. The market is pretty constant and is using about all the present production. When the demand justifies it, the plant will be enlarged again.

BROADCASTING

Radio Station KVFC is the broadcastng unit that furnishes radio service and entertainment for Cortez and surrounding territory. It is owned and operated by Jack Hawkins and Barney Hubbs who report excellent support and fine business relations both in Cortez and surrounding territory, and they are well pleased with their location and prospects. Their opening day was February 27, 1955, and their first broadcast was on 250 watts. This was increased Jan. 1, 1956, to 1000 watts so that now their programs may be heard to Grand Junction and beyond, to Thompson and Price, Utah; and to well below Gallup and nearly to Flagstaff. Regular programs and advertising are broadcast daily and regular programs and correspondence from surrounding towns. Station KVFC is on the ground to furnish a valuable service, to work with and for the people of its territory and to help in promoting the growth and development of every desirable interest or enterprise, and, finally, to grow and expand with a growing and expanding community.

THE CORTEZ FLYING SERVICE

The Cortez Flying Service was established in 1941 by R. N. Usher, well known local citizen. The purpose was to furnish air transportation to local people and transients, to train new pilots in the art and science of flying and sell new planes. The management had the dealership on the Piper Cub, a two-place plane, and a few were sold.

An airport was laid out about 3 miles southwest of the town of Cortez, some buildings erected and a runway was constructed for plane take-off and landing. The runway being only dirt surfaced it could be used only in dry weather, or when the ground was not too wet, which was a handicap, in a way and made for an irregular service. However, there was a fair business from the start and, in spite of its being new and strange to most local people, the business survived on its own merits and soon gave promise that it had come to stay. Local people learned to fly and they rode the planes.

The business was sold to Vic Reynolds, of Albuquerque, who took over in August, 1949. The new management has the Cessna dealership, has given up most of the training work and is giving almost all his attention to the transportation end of the service. Planes are chartered to any place any time for from one to six passengers to the plane. There are just now six full time employees in the service, and only thoroughly trained pilots are used. The service has an almost 100 per cent safety record and every precaution is taken to maintain this record. The business is growing with the rapid growth of the community and the increasing travel to the new oil field is especially gratifying. The service is being expanded right along to handle the rapidly growing business.

THE MONARCH AIR LINES, FRONTIER AIR LINES, INC.

The Monarch Air Lines began service in April, 1946, with terminal

159

points at Salt Lake City, Albuquerque and Denver. They started giving air service to Cortez in August, 1949. The grounds had previously been laid out, a usable runway constructed and the necessary buildings erected, the Town of Cortez, Montezuma County and the government sharing the expense of this work. The port is named the Montezuma County Air Port. From the beginning the air line had a mail contract, but it had to build up passenger business and air freight and express.

In July, 1950 this business was merged with the Challenge Air Lines serving Wyoming and Montana and with Arizona Air Ways, serving Arizona, New Mexico and Old Mexico, and the combined business was called The Frontier Air Lines, Inc. The new company serves territory from near the Canadian border to the Mexican border. The service furnished has been popular from the beginning and there has been a rapid and steady growth in business. The first year they boarded 411 passengers at the Cortez Air Port, and in 1955, the last year a full report is available, they boarded 4,049 passengers. The mail service and air freight and express show a similar gain. In the beginning the business was pretty heavily subsidized by the government in order to furnish air service to this part of the Southwest. Now the earnings of the company are just about keeping even with the expense and the enterprise should very soon be showing a profit, there being a rapid growth in all lines of traffic just now. At present there are five full time employees in the service of the company at the local air port.

The runway has been somewhat of a handicap, but this weakness has been, in a large measure, corrected. At first there was only a thinly graveled runway which could not be used in wet times. In 1954 the runway and grounds were regraveled and in 1956 they were regraveled again and sealed with oil. It is planned to pave the whole with a standard Keystone Oil Mat similar to that used on all the main highways, and when this is done the Montezuma County Air Port will have one of the best runways in Colorado, and one that will stand up under the heaviest planes that are ever expected to land here. The runway is 6100 feet long and is considered long enough for all practical purposes.

Fred Klatt was manager at the local air port from August, 1949, to April, 1953. Dave Burr from April, 1953, to the present time. The company makes two flights each way every day and a full load for most planes is 25 passengers. The company, from first to last, has had a remarkable record for safety, not having had a single accident of any consequence during the years of their operation.

As this is being written both the government and the county have set aside funds for oil surfacing the Air Port runway and grounds and the work is scheduled to be done in the summer of 1957.

THE CORTEZ SALES BARN

The Cortez Sales Barn, since its organization in 1936, has been a strong factor in promoting the welfare of the livestock producers, and a great convenience as well. The first buildings were erected and the yards built in 1938 by W. D. Watson. There was necessarily a modest beginning and progress was slow since the business was new to the people and they had to be educated up to the use of it. After two or three years Jack Majors took over the business and conducted it until Jimmie Barrett & Son took over the business in 1944 and conducted it until 1951. The business prospered under the Barrett management and during their period the enterprise began to be a real help to the livestock industry and a factor for better conditions in the business community. The volume of business expanded rapidly. Owing to circumstances over which they had no control, the Barretts were compelled to give up the business in 1951, and Bill Lichliter acquired the business and conducted it with fair success until 1954. At this time James Sucla took over the business in its entirety and from the beginning has made an outstanding success of it and extended its field of operation far and wide.

In the first year the new management ran through the sale ring 18,000 head of cattle, 11,000 sheep, 6,500 hogs and 900 horses and did a gross business of one and one-half million dollars.

In 1955 the years run was 23,000 head of cattle, 14,000 sheep, 7,250 hogs and 1,150 horses and the total sales amounted to one and three-fourths million dollars.

In 1956 the business is expected to go over the two million mark in spite of the much lower prices on cattle. Up to October, 1956, the busines clearly indicated that this figure will be reached.

The largest run of cattle ever made in the San Juan Basin, in a single day, was made on Saturday, Oct. 13, 1955, at the Cortez Sales Barn, at a special feeders sale when 2,031 head of cattle were put through the ring.

The Cortez Sales Barn now, in 1956, gathers in business from every part of the San Juan basin in Colorado, New Mexico and Utah and there is every indication that, under good management, the business will continue to grow.

Buyers from Arizona and from California take 70 per cent of the sales and, with an increasing population in this market territory, there is little chance that the demand for cattle from the local area will ever be less than it is today. About 20 per cent of the sales is consumed locally, mostly by the local processing plants, and the remaining 10 per cent is dispersed in various other ways. Local dealers, packers, and processors pay prices that correspond to, and are equal to, the general market at Denver or Kansas City. It looks now as if this enterprise must always be a very important factor in local business and in the livestock industry.

THE CORTEZ PACKING CO.

The Cortez Packing Co., is another fast growing business that is filling a long-felt want in Montezuma County. J. E. Bertwell, Sr., first started the business in 1945, continuing to 1949. In the latter date J. E. Bertwell, Jr., took over the entire business and to this date in October, 1956, is still in charge. Like all enterprises of this kind, the business had to be established and built up on its merits. The first object was to furnish a valuable and reliable service at a price that would attract business. This policy was successful from the start and the business is growing in popularity.

Before the days of the processing plant farmers butchered their own beef and pork using their own crude methods and equipment. Their method was often both crude and poor and often produced poor results. And it involved a lot of trouble, and a lot of disagreeable work, and often required the hiring of help. After the packing plant was established a bid was made for this kind of processing. Customers brought in their live animals which, with modern facilities, were killed, dressed and cooled the proper length of time; then cured, in the case of pork, and trimmings and fragments worked into ground meat. In the case of beef, the meat is cut into suitable parts, wrapped by the most approved methods, marked and frozen in a quick freeze ready for the deep freezer in the home. By-products are all made into a finished product.

This service has been valuable both to the meat dealers and to their rural customers. As a result the business has grown. Two new additions have been made to the plant and the business is again crowding the capacity of the plant to handle it. It is evident that extensive enlargement must be made very soon.

Beginning with three helpers in the plant, the work now requires six, and they are very busy every minute of the time. In addition to this increased help, the use of modern machinery and appliances, power driven, enables each worked to turn off much more work than at the beginning. They buy animals and process them for the trade and do custom processing for any one bringing in their live animals. At this time their rate of slaughter is from 1200 to 1400 beef animals a year, and around 1,500 hogs. This, of course, is not a large showing, but it is a very good start. The new growth in local population is bound to bring about a rapid growth in this line of business. The field is also widening and the business will soon be reaching out into other consumer territory. There is increasing evidence that the little business may grow into a major local industry.

THE WARK MILLING CO., T. W. WARK AND W. C. WARK

The Wark Milling Co. is a manufacturing industry. Their business is making and distributing flour. In this behalf they have gained an enviable reputation in a broad field. The business was started by T. W. Wark and Son in 1926 and the first mill had a daily capacity of 50 barrels of flour. This was increased to a 125 barrel daily capacity where it remained until a fire destroyed the entire plant in 1950. The loss was a terrific blow to the owners, but the business had been firmly established in a wide field of satisfied customers and, with a large stock of milling wheat on hand, and all their storage capacity left, the management decided to rebuild at once. To this end they went into the market and bought improved machinery that was the last word in flour milling equipment. Experts from the machinery company drew and furnished the plans for the new building, and when the plant was completed the management knew they had the finest mill modern milling science could devise. The new mill was built for a daily capacity of 250 barrels, and it has been operating at full capacity almost constantly since it was completed. They have a grain storage capacity of 90,000 bushels and, in good crop years, grain is milled in an amount from two to three times the storage capacity.

This makes a market for a large per cent of the wheat grown in the county, creates employment for local people and a finished product for a large consuming trade locally and in the states of New Mexico, Arizona and Utah. Their leading brand is Valley Queen and its high standard makes it staple in many markets far and near.

Aside from their high classed milling machinery and their superior skill in milling, they have superior quality in grain for producing their product. All wheat in this county that is carefully grown, both irrigated and non-irrigated, has a test weight of 62 to 63 pounds per measured bushel which insures high gluten content and superior milling quality. This wheat processes into the very best flour.

The new mill is powered entirely by electricity and runs so smoothly and silently that one on the outside of the building can hardly notice it is operating.

The manufacture of mixed feeds, started as a side line, is rapidly growing into a second milling enterprise. Large quantities of prepared stock feed, mainly for dairy cattle and poultry, are turned out and the local demand is good. The formulas for preparing these feeds aer obtained from the Colorado A.&M. College, and other state colleges. All these formulas have been tested out at the colleges under strict supervision and are recommended by the colleges so testing them.

The Carpenter warehouse is processing and mixing feed under similar conditions for the local trade.

Author's Note: The foregoing writeups, and similar writing found elsewhere in this narrative, are complimentary to firms that are a real factor for progress and development. Their business and their work goes hand in hand with the best interest of the local community, and their service means that their success is the success of all and is a measure of the progress that the whole community, or a whole industry, is making. We have no apology for stressing their importance.

RAILROAD ABANDONED

On December 20, 1950, Federal Judge Lee Knous in the Circuit Court at Denver, signed the order for the Denver & Rio Grande Southern railroad to be abandoned. The first application to abandon the road was made in 1945, but the war being on, protests were filed, and the matter was deferred again and again until finally it became fully apparent that the railroad was doomed and could not be saved. Receiver J. Pierpont Fuller testified that he had done all that could be done to make the road self-supporting, and insisted that it be abandoned. Wrecking operations were started in a short time and in a few months all the rails had been taken up and moved away and all other tangible assets of the company disposed of, and the Denver & Rio Grande Southern was no more. A few relics of the rolling stock have been acquired and kept as souvenirs of what has been.

The Rio Grande Southern was built through the county in 1891, it operated for 60 years and a few months, when changing times ended its usefulness. The abandonment of the road ended the era of rail transportation in the county and ushered in the era of highway transportation. Cars and buses had already taken over the passenger traffic, public and private, and the body truck and the semi-trailer took over the freight and the express. Other changes are in the offing. Airplane transportation is already modifying the new conditions and cutting deeply into ground transportation. The only thing certain about the future is that it will bring new changes.

The county still has a number of citizens who saw the railroad built and saw it torn up and moved away.

THE CITIZENS' STATE BANK OF CORTEZ

Just as the trying times of the long depression were drawing to a close, and memories of recent bank failures and the stress of hard times were yet fresh in the minds of the people, a number of citizens about Cortez, under the leadership of N. R. Usher, late of Dolores, decided to supply the town's need for a bank. On June 1st, 1936, all necessary steps having been previously taken, the new Citizens' State Bank of Cortez was opened for business. The capital stock, to start with, was $25,000 and forty local citizens came in as stockholders, which gave the new institution a broad and substantial base to start on. The first set of directors was W. J. Bozman, P. P. Schifferer, N. E. Carpenter, C. S. Warren, W. C. Wark and R. N. Usher, cashier. The new bank occupied the building vacated by the Montezuma Valley National Bank and started business by insuring all deposits under the newly enacted federal insurance law.

The new bank started its career with a small business, but with a lot of confidence and hope, and in neither have they been disappointed. The first published statement in June, 1936, showed deposits totaling

$14,000. From this meager beginning the bank has gone through two increases in capital stock which now stands at $150,000. By the latest published statement, March 4, 1957, the total assets of the bank amounted to $6,462,046.67, with total deposits on the liability side of $5,462,104.67. There is $100,000 in the surplus fund, $250,941.36 in undivided profits and reserves. The first of January, 1957, the bank was moved into a new building on the corner of Pinon Drive and Montezuma Avenue, that cost $110,000 to build and with furniture and bookkeeping equipment in total worth amounting to $38,201.32. Everything in the latest and best bookkeeping equipment has been installed, and drive-in deposit facilities have been provided which is popular and much used.

The bank has around 3,000 depositors, 1,000 savings accounts and services continuously 900 to 1000 loan accounts.

The present officers are R. N. Usher, President; W. V. Dunlap, Executive Vice President and Cashier; C. C. McAfee, Vice President; A. W. Denny, Vice President; Jack Hawkins, Vice President; Paula Slavens, Assistant Cashier; Bert C. Ray, Assistant Cashier; R. N. Usher, Jr., Assistant Cashier.

Directors: A. W. Denny, W. V. Dunlap, Jack Hawkins, C. C. McAfee, Dan O'Laurie, Pauline Usher, R. N. Usher, and R. N. Usher, Jr.

CHAPTER XV

LEGENDS

THE STORY OF BATTLE ROCK

An old story comes to us out of the past that concerns the peculiar rock formation in McElmo Canon known as Battle Rock and how it came to be so named. While the story is legendary in character, it could have a basis of fact. The story is told, without any authoritative source, that some time in the long ago two Indian tribes were at war with each other and one tribe, by reason of superior strength defeated the other and that the defeated tribe, in flight, took refuge on this rock formation. Battle Rock, as is well known, rises out of the canon floor in an inclined plane from the west and ends abruptly in an almost perpendicular cliff on the east that is from 800 to 1000 feet high. The story goes that when the defeated tribe took refuge on this sloping plane, the victors followed close upon them in hot pursuit, drove them headlong to the brink of the great cliff and forced them over the precipice to their death on the canon floor hundreds of feet below. The story, traditional in character, could have a foundation of fact. It is known that the American Indian tribes were often at war with each other in prehistoric times, and the savage nature of Indian warfare could easily have led to an atrocious deed of this kind. At any rate, the rock is still there to perpetuate the legend and the name will cling to it as long as there is a living man to tell the story of its origin.

THE STORY OF THE SLEEPING UTE

Another Indian legend, that has more the character of a myth than a legend, comes to us also out of the past, is the story of the Ute Mountain and the "Sleeping Ute" as the image is called by local people. It is a story of the Ute Mountain and the image of a man lying prone on his back, as depicted by the mountain skyline as seen from any vantage point a few miles to the northeast. One need not draw very strongly on his imagination to discern clearly this outline. With head to the north and face upturned to the sky there is a mountain formation to indicate the head, the folded arms across the chest, the thighs, the knees, and lastly, the toes. In the old days the Utes maintained

166

that this natural formation was one of their gods, who, at some remote time, it doesn't matter when, became angered with his people, for some reason not given, gathered all the rain clouds together in his pockets and laid down on his back and went to sleep; that when the clouds are hanging about the peaks, as they often do in times of storm, those clouds are slipping out of the old rain God's pockets. It is rather a fanciful story, and even an Indian must be very credulous to believe it.

There is a further belief, equally fanciful, that the old god will arise some day and help the Ute Indians fight their enemies. But the old days of intertribal warfare are forever passed and the Ute Indians are firm friends of the white man, so there may never be any real need for the old rain god, or warrior god, which ever it may be, to come forth from his eternal sleep to fight in any cause. So, we will just let him sleep on until there shal cease to be any reality in the old, old story, even to the old Utes who cherish so many fond memories of the past.

CHAPTER XVI

MESA VERDE PARK

The Mesa Verde Park was created by an act of Congress passed June 29, 1906. It is the ninth National Park so created and there are three local National Monuments under Park supervision, being Aztec National Monument, Yucca House National Monument and Hovenweep National Monument.

There is considerable pre-park history connected with the Park which will be gone into only briefly. Mesa Verde was first under the flag of Spain. After Mexico won her freedom in 1822 this territory was under the flag of Mexico until the Treaty of Guadalupe Hidalgo, in 1848, when the country came under the American flag.

The first record of any white person visiting Mesa Verde was in 1859, when Prof. J. S. Newberry, with J. M. Macomb exploring expedition, ascended to the top of the Mesa over the north rim and left a description of the view from the Mesa Top in the records of the expedition.

In the early seventies, probably in 1873, Captain John Moss, in the service of Parrot Brothers, of San Francisco, made the journey through the Mancos Canon on one of his trips to or from California and observed ruins of habitations in the walls of Mancos Canon.

In 1874, photographer with the Hayden survey visited Mancos Canon to observe these ruins and to make pictures, and the next year, 1875, W. H. Holmes, also with a government survey party, discovered, in addition to the first ruins observed, a larger ruin which he photographed and called Sixteen Window House.

In 1882, Miss Virginia Doneghl, after reading reports on these ruins, visited the Canon, and in 1885, after her marriage to Gilbert McClurg, she came again, with others, and explored further up the Mesa Canons and probably saw Balcony House. This trip aroused interest and touched off a train of events and efforts that lasted for twenty years, or until the Park was finally created in 1906.

Late, in 1888, Richard Wetherill and Charles Mason, while riding after cattle, discovered Cliff Palace, and in the next two or three days, found a number of other large ruins. They came to Mancos and reported these discoveries and the news was widely publicized and the reports aroused a lot of interest on the part of some scientific groups. The ruins were rapidly explored and ransacked, one after another, and many relics and objects of the creative arts of the departed race, were taken out of the ruins. As soon as it became known that there was a market for these things a number of persons became engaged in prowling through the ruins for relics and art specimens. This aroused to action of various organizations interested in preserving the ruins and their contents and much effort was put forth to get something done to protect the ruins. The Colorado Federation of Women's Clubs was one of the most active, and Mrs. Gilbert McClurg was a tireless worker in the cause. A determined effort was made to get an area embracing the ruins created as a state park and Mrs. McClurg and some other women came to Mancos, met with Chief Ignacio and his tribal council, with O. E. Noland as interpreter, and tried to negotiate a treaty, or contract, with the Indians to get control of the ruins, and a plan was drawn up, but the plan didn't get very far. A plan for a state park was introduced in the Colorado State Assembly and a bill creating a park was twice introduced in Congress but all the first efforts failed to get results.

The women wouldn't take "no" for an answer and the effort went on. They organized the Colorado Cliff Dwellers Association and Mrs. McClurg and Mrs. Lucy Peabody continued the effort to get some kind of organized authority established on the mesa. All their efforts to establish authority and control on the Mesa failed. They worked on public sentiment, worked on the State Assembly and got a bill introduced creating a state park. They worked on Congressmen and got bills introduced in Congress, but they couldn't even get the bills reported out of the Congressional Committees. Congressman Bell and Congressman Shafroth introduced bills, but that was as far as they got. Finally the Secretary of the Interior was given authority to negotiate with the Ute Indians for an area on Mesa Verde looking toward establishing a park and a small appropriation was secured for a survey. This was an opening wedge, and centered attention on the movement. Another step was gained when interested groups prevailed on Congress to pass an "Antiquities Act" to preserve prehistoric and historic sites and objects on public lands. With this much gained, Representative Hogg and Senator Patterson introduced bills in both houses of Congress creating Mesa Verde National Park. Both the House and the Senate acted favorably on the bills and on June 29, 1906, the House Bill became a law.

Little was done in 1906 toward getting the Park established as a going concern. H. M. Randolph, a former Major in the State Guard, was appointed Park Superintendent and arrived in Mancos early in 1907 to take over park management. Office quarters in Mancos were secured in the second floor of the Bauer Bank building and an office was equipped with the necessary furniture. All the business of the park was directed from the office in Mancos until 1927.

Some funds were made available and work was started in 1907 on the first road into the Park. This first road into the park followed the old Witheril road by way of Mancos Canon. Sup't. Randolph reported an O.K. for $12,000 for Park road money for 1908. The first week in May the first work was started on Mesa Verde Park. Dr. J. Walter Fewkes of the Smithsonian Institute, came to direct the work of excavating the ruins and preserving them from further deterioration. Eleven working men and students start the work. There was no effort at restoration; only repair so they will remain as they are, and the work continued well through the summer. Also a survey of roads and trails was started and some work was done. Work on the ruins is also of a scientific nature and all specimens are carefully taken out and preserved. In all twenty-five men were at work on the ruins. Work was planned to start on the roads as soon as the appropriation became available July 1st.

Toward the end of summer work on Spruce Tree House was finished. Dr. Fewkes starts "Camp Fire Talks" and lectures twice a week on local archeology. Park headquarters, on the park, will be at Spruce Tree Camp, as the only good water that is easily available is there.

On August 1, 1908, Secretary of the Interior James R. Garifeld visits Mesa Verde, with him was F. H. Newell, Chief of the Reclamation Service; also F. A. Wadleigh, of the Rio Grande Southern, Dr. Brown and Congressman Hoggott.

Apparently the idea of a road down Mancos Canon was abandoned, as the first road to be surveyed into the park ascended the Mesa on the west side of Point Lookout and the road was constructed to the first top mesa level in 1908. The park rules no cars on the road. Road is narrow and on precipitous hillside and cars and teams are sure to have trouble.

September 1, 1909, excavating work is finished on Cliff Palace, for this season. This is the largest ruin on the park. It extends 50 feet back under the cliff, outlines remain of about 175 rooms, 100 more rooms have collapsed. Building was four stories in height and front is held by retaining wall. Twenty-three Kivas and ceremonial rooms were excavated. Also several council chambers. It is a typical ruin. Every type of architecture is shown and all different kinds of work— Kivas, round towers, square towers, living rooms, grinding rooms, and room for every purpose are found in this structure.

Work was resumed on the main entrance road and about one mile of the most difficult part of the road was constructed. $23,000 is requested for road work in 1910. A road is the most urgent need.

The park gets $20,000 for 1910. Sup't. Randolph says he will finish the road first; then continue excavation as long as funds last.

A force of 12 men start excavation on Balcony House under supervision of Jesse L. Nusbaum, who is later to become notable in this work.

On April 7, 1911, the park gets $7,500 and work was resumed on the main entrance road, beyond the Knife Edge section, where construction was much easier. All work is done by hand and by teams.

In May, 1911, the government concludes a treaty with the Ute Indians by the terms of which the government secures 12,700 acres of Ute Reservation land to become a part of Mesa Verde Park on the south. It gave the Indians 6,000 acres of government land in one tract and a second tract on Ute Mountain comprising 19,000 acres of government land in one tract. The land acquired embraces some of the most valuable ruins on the park, and the Indians were very reluctant to give up the land, knowing its value. The government had to give about two acres for one and refused to concede to the Indians other valuable concessions they wanted before they would agree to the exchange. By reason of the treaty all the important ruins on Mesa Verde are now within the park boundaries.

Reports of irregularities in the office of the Superintendent of Mesa Verde Park and a direct report to the government asking for an investigation of the affairs of the Park as they relate to the office of superintendent, resulted in the government taking prompt action and sent Mr. E. B. Linnen, one of the oldest and shrewdest men in the U. S. Secret Service, to check on the case. Mr. Randolph was suspended at once and Mr. Linnen went quietly to work on the case. The findings were a surprise, even to those who knew most about the case. Mr. Randolph promptly sent in his resignation which was promptly rejected, upon Mr. Linnen's recommendations, but the government at once notified Mr. Randolph of his suspension from the service of the United States without ceremony or apology. Mr. Randolph was given due time and opportunity to present his defense before the Department, which he did, with the result that he was dismissed from the service. He was removed from office on the following counts: General neglect of duty, serving other interests and causes for pay, during his official incumbency, misappropriating funds, use of government money for his own private purposes, any one of which would have been sufficient for his removal from the service.

Mr. Richard Wright, connected with the Attorney General's office, was called to the park to take charge until a new superintendent could be appointed.

Acting Superintendent Richard Wright was relieved as Park Superintendent and Samuel M. Schumacher takes over as Superintendent Oct. 1, 1911.

Sup't. Schumacher and Park Ranger E. C. Cline drove a car all the way to Spruce Tree Camp over the new park road July 14, 1913, the first to make the trip in a vehicle over this road. It was the first trip made to Mesa Verde from this side by this means of transportation. The park road, at this time, was not quite finished.

A party of six tourists, on July 15, made the trip to the park over the new road, the first tourists to make this trip. Horses were necessary to make the trip from Spruce Tree Camp to the ruins.

The first effort at water improvement on the park came in May, 1914, when a pump was installed at the spring near Spruce Tree House and the water was pumped up to the buildings on the higher ground for general use, but there was not enough water.

The first auto trip to the park in 1914 was May 19. Six cars and twenty-five local people made the trial trip and greatly enjoyed it. Cars are not permitted on the road for a while until there is a better, safer road, and no horses on the road.

May 15, 1915, the work of building a telephone line into the park is under way. Poles are on the ground and some are in place.

Visitors to Mesa Verde Park passed the one thousand mark for the first time in the season of 1915, the number of visitors this year being 1032. In 1916 the number of park visitors was 1408.

The park gets an appropriation of $18,000 for the fiscal year beginning July 1, 1918. They will build a new park road from the Mancos Valley side, known as the "Switchback Road." Also a small light plant is put in at Spruce Tree Camp. Navajo Indians do most of the manual labor. Thomas Rickner is now Park Superintendent.

The Switchback Road is completed June 9, 1919. It was used while the old road was being rebuilt; then abandoned.

The war over, excavation is resumed on the ruins in the park, Dr. J. Walter Fewkes again directing. Work on Square Tower House engaged the attention of the working men this season.

The Cliff Dweller ruins on the Stafford farm, in south Montezuma Valley, have been created the Yucca House National Monument and placed under the custody of the Mesa Verde Park. Ten acres of land was acquired by purchase by the government about Jan. 1, 1920.

On October 20, 1920, the season's excavation on Mesa Verde was finished. Most valuable and interesting work we have done on the Park says Dr. Fewkes who has supervised almost all the excavation and preserving work on the ruins. The greatest improvement was the building of the Inspiration Point Road to the magnificent View Point from which the road takes its name. The road is also an easy means of reaching several of the most noted ruins on the park. The ruins excavated were Painted House which name was changed to New Fire House. It is characterized by a ceremonial chamber 25x50 feet, the main building being 70x125 feet. Oak Tree House, an ordinary type ruin further down the canon, was also excavated. The new road was regarded as a very valuable improvement.

Jesse L. Nusbaum was appointed as Superintendent of Mesa Verde Park to succeed Thomas Rickner and arrives June 3, 1921. He initiated a big program of road and trail improvement, continues excavation work under the direction of Dr. Fewkes, and began the erection of some new buildings after the New Mexico Indian type. Nusbaum made a very active and energetic superintendent for the park and was able and influential. Soon after taking office he moved the superintendent's office from Mancos to Spruce Tree Camp on the park.

The park has a new road grader and crawler type tractor. Had to do some shifting of funds to get it, but the new outfits build roads in a hurry, and maintains them, and saves money. It was put into use at once.

Major General Hugh L. Scott visits the park. The first thing he said when he saw the ruins: "Ah, I see. They were pacifists."

April 7, 1922, Sup't. Nusbaum and family have spent the winter on the park, a winter of one of the heaviest snow falls in years. He was busy all winter finishing the new home for the park superintendent, the same being fashioned after the New Mexico architecture, Hopi Indian style, except that the Indians have no furniture.

The park gets an appropriation for the new fiscal year of $43,000, $21,000 for maintenance and $22,000 for improvement. $17,500 was applied on rebuilding the original park highway, later called the "Knife Edge Road." An administration building was planned after the same type architecture as the residence building.

Excavation work for the season was finished in August, 1922. The Mummy Lake Group was given attention this year: Pipe Shrine House, where a deep Kiva with shrine, and many curiously formed pipes were found; also three stone idols. Burial grounds near were explored. A complete skeleton was unearthed, left in place, covered with screen and roofed over, and a concrete wall was built about skeleton. Far View Tower, One Chamber House and Megolithic House were excavated, all very interesting and good subjects for study.

Mesa Verde Park is chiefly educational. It is the gateway to past centuries; it teaches our pre-historic history just as plainly as the printed word teaches recorded history. It is a fantastic story mutely told. Every visitor should be made to feel that the "Cliff Dwellers" are a study and that we may learn a great deal by getting a better understanding of them.

Mesa Verde Park attracted 4,587 visitors up to November 1st, 1922—students, scholars, scientists, many of them, seeking knowledge and studying nature.

Mesa Verde Park will get an appropriation of $42,000 for the fiscal year beginning July 1, 1924. This was for extensive and much needed improvement. There will be $100,000 for the road over a period of years.

On May 30, 1924, Mesa Verde Park gets a postoffice—same name as park. Mrs. Nusbaum is the postmistress. Mail scheduled for three times a week for a while.

The second deficiency appropriation bill carried $32,000 for Mesa Verde roads in addition to the regular appropriation and provides for the same amount for the same purpose for the succeeding three years.

Lack of an adequate water supply at Spruce Tree Camp has been a handicap and is getting to be more of a problem as the number of visitors increase. Week of May 15, 1925, a large metal tank is installed to store all the water available for use when it is needed later in the season. A few months back the spring under the fall was excavated and the water supply increased by 200 per cent, but the supply is still scant and inadequate.

A survey crew is busy on the park road. It is the plan to rebuild the road and gravel surface the entire length eventually.

The visit of Congressman Compton and party to Mesa Verde Park resulted in a definite decision to provide a water supply for the park—adequate for all purposes. The possibilities will be fully investigated by hydrographers at once to determine the best plan for providing this water supply.

The week of October 28, 1925, was made memorable by the ingathering of National Park Superintendents at the park to the number of 57 for a general conference and plan making for all the parks. All the National Parks were represented by high park personnel, and nearly all by the park superintendents themselves. They spent nearly a week at the park and the entire time was filled in with business and pleasure. The big items for the park were agreed upon. First is to be the gravel surfacing of the park entrance highway its entire length, and the second, an adequate water supply for the park, and that very soon. The hydrographers were at that time working on the problem to devise a plan.

The number of visitors to Mesa Verde Park for the season of 1925 climbed to 9093, a gain of nearly 2000 over the previous year.

The Hovenweep National Monument is created by the new Secretary of the Interior, Hubert Work, in the spring of 1923, out on the Colorado-Utah line. Hovenweep is an Indian word meaning "Deserted Valley." This brings the number of National Monuments in this immediate section up to four, the other three being Great Natural Bridges, west of Blanding, in Utah; the Yucca House National Monument in lower Montezuma Valley, and the Aztec National Monument near Aztec, New Mexico, the Hovenweep group containing the finest prehistoric masonry.

Late in the summer of 1913, to regress a little, the first dirt road was completed all the way into Mesa Verde Park to Spruce Tree Camp, only a dirt road, but vastly better than no road at all. It is a very scenic route, mountain high, around sheer cliffs and skirting great canons. The park has a new and enlarged camp hotel in a new location on the point overlooking Spruce Tree Canon and two other great canons, distant cliffs, table lands and far off valleys and great mountains in the far distance are visible.

In the summer of 1923 some special explorations of ruins on the west side of Mesa Verde Park by F. W. Hodges, former Chief of the Bureau of Ethnology, and Dr. A. V. Kidder, a well known ethnologist, revealed that this locality was the home of the Post Basketmakers, several hundred years before the Cliff Dwellers, proper, inhabited this region. This was an important and interesting discovery and was expected to add greatly to the attractions in the park and afford a broader field of study for those interested in America's primitive races. The Basketmakers made their homes in the caves, but of a different and more primitive type.

In the month of April, 1926, the rain gauge at Spruce Tree Camp registered a rainfall of 7.31 inches, and in May following 1.36 inches was recorded.

It had been decided to create an additional water supply for Mesa Verde by building a water catchment and two car loads of corrugated iron for the catchment were received in May, 1926.

Thirteen people, all park employees, including Sup't. Nusbaum, wintered on the park in 1926-27. The road was kept open, there was mail twice a week and a number of radios in camp, making it less lonely.

The water catchment and tanks on Mesa Verde was finished in December, 1926. The catchment covered one acre of ground, and the two tanks hold 150,000 gallons, about 23 gallons for every park visitor calculated on the number of park visitors last season. With the present water supply there will be enough water for present needs.

A new survey on the Mesa Verde main entrance highway changed the old road at Windy Point, just under Point Lookout, makes a broad switchback and ascends to top of the mesa on the Mancos side of the mesa. There is no grade on the new road over six per cent.

The government is building a new telephone line to Mesa Verde Park. The old line is inefficient and will be discontinued.

The well being drilled on Mesa Verde for a water well struck water at 3390 feet. Water was first struck at the 1800 foot level, but the water is not usable. The drilling was continued to the McElmo sand.

In June, 1931, a contract was let to gravel surface 20 miles of the Mesa Verde main entrance road at a cost of $85,000. The work was started July 20, 1931. A recent appropriation makes $128,000 available for this work and the road will be surfaced with a six inch coat of gravel all the way through to Spruce Tree Camp. The work is to be finished in 150 days.

Mesa Verde Park gets $70,000 for 1932. Of this amount $19,500 goes to park roads, $15,000 for a power line into the park, $3,000 for building construction and the balance for administrative and expenses.

The graveled road all the way into Mesa Verde Park is completed in 1932, and oiling is to come next. Oiling contract is let and the work is to start at once and be completed in 100 days.

Mesa Verde Park is becoming known as the "Gateway to Past Centuries." Mesa Verde—the Green Table, is 2000 feet above the level plain. You must climb to the top of this table land to reach the gorgeous canons where the Cliff Ruins are found.

Oiling of the park highway is completed in August, 1933.

Jesse L. Nusbaum comes back as Superintendent of Mesa Verde Park April 28, 1942, to succeed Sup't. McLaughlin who was called to the army service as a First Lieutenant in the Army Air Corps.

A pre-park note states that the first road to be built onto Mesa Verde was completed by the Witherills in July, 1899. The road followed the Mancos Canon, then up one of the Mesa Verde Canons to within three-fourths of a mile of Cliff Palace. There was transportation by vehicle to the end of the road, then on horseback. Camp headquarters are established in the Canon where a spring furnished a supply of good water. It was little more than a make-shift road at first, but was improved later. The road was never popular and was little used even before the park roads were built. The Witherills were conducting a tourist service to the Cliff ruins at this time and guests were entertained at the Alamo Ranch in connection with the trips. Shortly after this they discontinued their guide and outfitting business and when the park was created, and for some years previous, C. B. Kelly and associates were taking care of the guide and outfitting business in connection with the tourist trade to the cliff ruins.

Travel to the park has been increasing rapidly in recent years and the 1956 season registered 186,300 visitors, the greatest number in any season to date. Every season's visitors spread broader the news of the park and the interesting things one may see there. To handle this traffic the camp ground has been increased to 10 acres with parking space for 110 cars, and there are two auxiliary parks of about five additional acres that are put into use when needed. There are three permanent rangers, five extras and twelve interpretative rangers that attend parties on their visits to the ruins. There is a park museum 120x 80 feet and it is wonderfully interesting and instructive with a display of all the finest work of the arts and crafts, curios, relics and numerous articles of household and general use; remnants of bedding, clothing and foot wear. Then there is a natural history museum containing mounted specimens of all the animal, bird and reptile life on the park, and specimens of flowers and other plant growth on the park, all of which is very interesting to the visitors. There is an office building 40x60 feet, various residence buildings, tool and implement buildings, and the whole is almost completely hidden from view by a dense growth of native timber.

Ever since visitors began to come to the park in numbers, the water supply, until 1950, has been a vexing problem. The little spring under the fall was inadequate from the start. Reservoirs were built in the draw above to catch run off water. This percolated downward and increased the spring flow considerably, but not nearly enough. Then a catchment was made first covering an acre with iron roofing and the water run off caught and stored in large tanks. This catchment was enlarged to two acres, and still the need for water outgrew the supply. Then a well was drilled to 4,207 feet in depth and a supply of fair water encountered. It rose to within 1600 feet of the surface. A pump was installed and a flow of 1600 gallons every eight hours was produced, this was expensive, and the flow weakened. Finally the National Park Service got around in 1950 to putting in a pipe line to bring down a supply of water from the mountains, and this solved the water problem. While the water rises several hundred feet to the top of the mesa on the north, it is a gravity flow all the way and there is little or no care or expense in getting the water. Oil surfaced roads lead out to all the main ruins, and trails have been constructed to many other ruins accessible only on horseback.

CHAPTER XVII

MINES AND MINING

The Mancos metal mining area is located on the west slope of the La Plata Mountains and comprises the territory drained by the East, Middle, and West Mancos Rivers, and this area embraces the only metal mining enterprises of any consequence in Montezuma County. The very first permanent settlers were drawn into the area by reports of rich gold and silver deposits on the La Plata river side of the mountains, as recounted in another chapter, and a little later interest in mining became quite general locally.

The first interest, apparently, centered around placer mining. It required no effort to take a miner's pan and wash out gold colors almost anywhere along the channel of the Mancos rivers, and, in very many instances, good strings of gold were recovered from the sand and many small nuggets were found. This excited the interest of many people and a great deal of prospecting was done and attempts to do placer mining on an extensive scale were made. Capital for this work, however, was very limited, but many people invested their last dollar in food and went into the hills and prospected, or did development work, as long as their food lasted. Other prospectors were "grub staked" by people with a little money, and no inclination to do hard work, and now and then some very promising prospects were reported.

Among those who first interested themselves in mining we find the following: Jack Wade, J. M. Rush, Sr., Ed Rush, Billy Rush, Jim Rush, Jr., George Bauer, in a financial way; Curg Williams, August Streigel, Hagy Brothers, Charles Hardy, Charles Roundtree, Tim Jenkins, Bert Paquin, William Schubert, Harry Owens, Jim Miller, Freed Brittain, Jack Doyle, Jack Sparks, and many others. Many of these had mining claims they did the assessment work on year after year. The mining laws require holders of mining claims that are unpatented to do $100 worth of acceptable work on each claim every year in order to hold claim to the land. After they have done a certain amount of work per claim, they can make proof on their claim, or claims, and, if satisfactory, get a title or patent. Then they pay taxes on the property, but do no more assessment work. When interest in mining died down most of the claims were abandoned; then any one could locate the ground again. Every time a really good strike was made, or some unusual mining activity was started, that looked like a big development, the people again rushed in and staked all the mineral land; some hoping to sell for a bonus; others hoping to make a real "find" themselves. The lure of gold and the lust for mining riches is strong in the minds of many people and some of these early miners, Wm. Schubert, Tom Allard, Tim Jenkins, and some others, stayed with their prospects and continued to do work on their claims as long as they lived, and two or three died on the job.

Just as there began to be a lively interest in mining the Mancos Times was established April 28, 1893, with C. M. Danforth, editor and publisher. Mr. Danforth had another paper and other property interests in the eastern part of the state, so he sold the paper to W. H. Kelly of Ouray, and recently of the "Solid Muldoon" fame. He was better known as Muldoon Kelly. From the time Mr. Kelly took over, the Times reported sensational mining strikes and rich discoveries in almost every issue. The district was "Boosted" constantly as the richest mining area in the state. Every sample of ore brought in by the prospectors was reported with acclaim and assays were reported that indicated riches beyond the dreams of avarice. Every prospect was the certain beginning of a rich mine.

The fact that only two or three real paying mines were ever developed seems to indicate that most of these reports must be regarded as without foundation and a conclusion reached that the rich strikes weer exaggerated beyond belief, or did not exist at all. Where earnest effort was made to develop a mine, or when a real paying mine was found or developed, space will be given to them in this narrative. Almost all, perhaps all, but two or three of the companies organized to develop local mines must be regarded as stock promotion schemes in which the stockholders lost everything they put into the enterprise, and the promoters took a great many thousands of dollars which they were never compelled to account for. It is safe to say that ten times more money was put into the various mining schemes of the area than was ever taken out of the mines. The Mancos Times published some news of local people and enterprises, aside from mining, and a great deal of political slush, but it semed devoted mostly to promoting mining schemes that were either dishonest or criminally mismanaged. There was enough of this mining promotion to make volumes of reading, and some of it came on down to recent times well remembered by local people. The Mancos Times, later, the Mancos Times-Tribune, probably profited but little by all this publicity, but there is no doubt but the false promoters profited by them. We shall report some of these mining enterprises, honest or dishonest, good or bad or indifferent.

In 1894, Rush & Co. made a rich strike that developed into the Sundown Mine, and was a real paying mine. The developments will be followed.

Here are a few samples of the weekly reporting: Mr. Ashbaugh displays nugget one inch long, of pure gold, at the Times office.

Captain Jackson reports $90 per man on a 10 hour run on West Mancos property. Another trial run, on Golconda mine, $18 per man on ten hour run. Many $3 and $4 nuggets.

June 1st, 1893, an unnamed person, for an unnamed claim, got an assay of 2360 ounces per ton, Hildebrand & Carr, assayers.

130 ounces of gold and 15 ounces of silver reported by F. M. and T. C. Brittain from their East Mancos claim.

Big lead exposed on West Mancos. Two ounces of gold per ton, by Lou Davis and W. J. Lane and August Bauer. Hundreds of tons in sight. Ground just located.

In one placer operation, a yield of one ounce of gold per pan, off bedrock, is sometimes reported, Pete Richards Placer. Jackson becomes part of Golconda group.

In May, 1893, Mrs. George Bauer and Wm. Roesler sold the Bell of Mancos, a placer claim, to A. L. Raplee for $1000. This was the first bona fide sale of mining property in the district.

The end of 1896 sees a lot of mining activity in the Mancos mining area. The Prichard five stamp mill is operating on East Mancos. They prepare to install other mining machinery and do custom work. C. L. Richards buys most of North Star M. & M. Co. stock. Starts active operation June 4, 1897. The Hayden Mining and Milling stamp mill is running. The North Star gets out first mill run, gets only $10.50 per ton. Prichard and Carson buy North Star mine. Make first payment of $8,000. They have $4,000 for lumber and supplies, make second payment of $1,500 later. June 4, 1897, they are operating.

Capt. Geo. A. Jackson, who has been promoting mining in the Mancos area, transfers most of his activities to the Blue Mountains in Utah. On his way from Blue Mountains to Mancos the accidental discharge of his shotgun, in his own hands, killed him instantly. The gun was a gift from his company and his Mancos friends. Mr. Jackson was an uncle of Harry Owens.

New owners of the North Star Mine prepares to put in new mill. Late 1896.

June 11, 1897, The Hayden Mining & Milling stamp mill is running.

The Prichard mill starts on custom work. The Prichard five stamp mill is operating in East Mancos.

The Marshall-Day placer ground on East Mancos, sells to Omaha parties. Geo. E. Gibson, the buyer, comes in, takes up supplies and goes to work.

By 1898 interest in mining is manifestly on the decline. Gold production for the year was estimated at $15,000, and it all came to local people. This brought about some additional mining activity. By 1899 many men were again in the mountains and outside interests in local mining promises to revive the industry.

In 1901, James Doyle and adviser, J. P. Lonergan, head a mining syndicate and began to get control of several mining claims on East Mancos. This leads to important developments later. The Doyle syndicate finish grouping claims and the Doyle Consolidated Mines Co. is organized. R. H. Toll comes to take charge of the company as manager. A new stamp mill is being put in on the property.

Interest in mining experiences a great revival. All abandoned claims are being restaked. The Doyle movement was soon to develop into a promising mining enterprise.

During the summer of 1903, the Doyle Company makes rapid progress in installing milling and mining equipment, and in the late season the mine and mill was started to operating at full capacity, giving new hope and life to the camp. Thirty men are employed and both Mr. Doyle and Mr. Lonergan are on the ground.

Some recent mining developments are: Hydrolic placer mining tried out on East Mancos. No results that would justify continued operation.

The Prichard five-stamp mill is operating in the summer of 1898.

The Sundown, North Star, R.A.P., Tenderfoot, Timberline and Extension, ship some ore in 1898.

Prof. Arthur Lake, noted geologist, arouses much interest by declaring Mancos area next to largest oil field in the state. He locates a small field near Durango and Farmington.

Jimmie Doyle visits East Mancos property, August 15, 1905. The operations at the Doyle mine have been closed down for several months, Doyle is noncommittal as to his future plans for the property. They have 300 acres of patented ground and some work is being done, experimenting and testing for a cheaper process for handling the ore.

Meantime Mr. Doyle has been busy and has combined the Mancos Mining and Development Co. and the White Quail Copper Co., all adjacent properties in the Rush Basin section of the California Mining District, into the Doyle Consolidated Mines Co., Incorporated Oct. 27, 1907, with a capital stock of ten million shares, par value $1. Treasury stock was offered at 30c a share to raise funds for development. Three groups comprise 274 acres of mineral land and 80 acres non-mineral. Other property—a ten stamp mill and much other mining machinery and equipment, thousands of feet of tunnel work already done and there is a determined effort being made to operate in 1908. A large crew is started to work on development. Much new machinery was installed and plans made to treat the ore at the mine. It looked like a real mine and high hopes were entertained that at last the Mancos mining area was coming into its own. The ore is of a refractory nature, difficult to treat, low grade mostly, but a vast amount of it. There are some small high testing bodies. As many as fifty men were employed at the mine.

The fall of 1908, Jimmie Doyle comes over from Denver, straightens up local business matters of the company and gets some work started at the mine. There is a report that the company has a large amount of funds in the treasury and much activity is planned for next spring.

In following the developments of the Doyle Co. and its activities a number of other mining activities were passed over. Some of these will now be noticed.

The Hayden Mining and Milling Co. organized in June, 1896, is operating on West Mancos. Capt. Jackson is manager. They put in a mill, but the operation has all the appearance of being only a stock selling scheme.

During 1902, there are many mining activities. A number of companies, associations and individuals are operating, some trying to ship ore, some trying to mill ore and many doing development work. Some properties change hands with small down payments. No permanent operations come out of it all.

On July 15, 1902, the Doyle Company brings in two car loads of machinery and supplies.

Doyle mill running smooth; plan to run all winter, but terrific storm closes down the mill November 15.

MINES AND MINING BACK TO 1889

Summer of 1899 Sundown, North Star, Tenderfoot and Tammany being worked. North Star mill started to operating with very promising results. Mining is active. There is a claim that 100 men are working in the mines.

North Star mill running on Sundown ore. Retorts go out every week—$1,800 to $2,874 of very fine gold.

Owners of North Star and Sundown mine give $500 to help complete road up to their mine.

Sundown-Tenderfoot mine sold on contract to Joseph Frank of Cripple Creek for $130,000. Papers are placed in escrow. Ten local men are interested in the deal. George Bauer is the sole owner of the North Star.

August 21, 1899 Joseph Frank makes payment of $15,000 on mining deal for Sundown and Tenderfoot, and takes over the property. Cripple Creek men behind the deal.

The same day, August 21, Messrs. Horton, Brichson, Hanes and Associates of Telluride, make a cash payment to John Hurley and James and John Brown and take bond and lease on the Timberline group.

Getting back to the Doyle mine we find that the report that they had money in their treasury must have been true. James Doyle and E. R. Marden, the company's fiscal agent, arrive June 28, 1909. They go up to the mine at once and order everything put in shape for operating the mine. Confidence and hope is revived and there is widespread interest in mining. All old claims are restaked and work is resumed smaller pieces. Quite a large body of the ore returned a smelter value of one dollar a pound after all the larger nuggets had been picked out. The strike immediately became widely known and attracted many mining men and notable engineers to the scene of the strike. Many offers to purchase the property were made, but none of them looked as attractive as the mine itself. Great wealth was there in plain sight.

To help in a financial way, and with advice in developing the mine, the Starrs had associated with them George Gilmore and George Gilmore, Jr., and a company was formed and incorporated under the name The Red Arrow Gold Corporation with the five men the sole owners. They began at once producing and shipping ore, and according to a statement of one of the owners, they took out, first and last, about $300,000 worth of ore from the mine. Then two things took place: The Second World War came on and, because the mine produced only gold, the government closed it down to save the labor for other uses. Also the income tax was imposed which took most of the profits when it got up into the higher brackets. So the mine was closed and securely locked up.

Returning after the war, the owners found the mine in very bad shape, the tunnel and all the workings being badly caved. The situation called for a big outlay of cash to restore the mine to working condition, so the stockholders decided to sell the property and let more experienced people make repairs and restore the mine to working condition. All, or about all, the mine came into the possession of Don H. Peakes who still owns the property. In the fall of 1956 work was going on at the mine with a small force of men. New workings are being developed and the plan is to open the ore body from a new direction. The original owners insist that there is still a good mine there and that it will yet produce a great deal of wealth.

Meantime the Starr strike had been widely published and interest was almost nation wide. Mining men, investors, promoters, and prospectors came in numbers and in a little while the entire area, not previously taken, was staked and every kind of scheme was brought into use to make some easy money. When no more bonanzas were found interest began to wane, after a few months, and finally to die out entirely.

The Starr mine operated very successfully for about five years under the first owners, and during this time some other mining activities were taking place.

B. R. Vaughn of New York City, and B. K. Kempter, mining engineer of Denver, took a four year lease on the entire mining property of the Doyle Consolidated Mines Co.

A rich ore strike is announced on the property of Geo. W. Johnson, of Omaha, in the East Mancos area, and adjoining the Red Arrow Group of claims.

A two car lot shipment of ore was made week of July 5, 1936, one on many local holdings. The East Mancos road is put in shape for heavy hauling.

Tom Welborn and Ed Leckenby, two Mancos residents, sell Trail's End mine, on the La Plata side, for $50,000 cash in hand, after making a rich strike on the property.

At the Doyle mine, teams are on the road all the time. At the mine mechanics, carpenters, experienced mining men—all are busy. A new mess hall and shops are being built, and new machinery installed. They plan to operate all winter doing development work. $2,500 in supplies go up to mine and wagons load back with ore.

The mine works a few men all winter; in the spring the number is increased to 30, the 10 stamp mill is started to operating; also other machinery. Some of the higher grade ore being shipped and the balance milled at mine. The company announces they will put in a smelter at the mine, one unit at a time. A big volume of hauling, 8 or 10 four horse teams, to the mine is practically suspended on account of recent very heavy rains. Activities at the Doyle mine, and at other mines, bring about a lot of interest in prospecting. Recent strikes also heighten interest and the mining fever is running high.

At the Doyle mine activity continues. In the mill are rolls, crushers, screening devices, sampler, elevators, and hauling goes on. A roaster is being built and two ore bins of 100 tons each.

About Oct. 1, 1911, just as everything at the Doyle mine was ready for operation and they were making their first trial run, for some unknown reason the big brick roaster broke down and the structure fell apart on one side causing a total shutdown of the mining operations. Brick and other needed material was brought in at once to make repairs.

Repairs at the Doyle Mine were made and, some weeks later, another trial run was made. The roaster had a rotating arm arrangement in it to stir the burning ore as it passed from one bench to another just below. For some reason it was never a success, results must have been unsatisfactory, the roaster broke down again and operations were never resumed. The Doyle Co. never made another effort to operate the mine.

THE RED ARROW MINE

In the summer of 1933, one of the most sensational mining strikes in the history of the Southwest was made on Aspen Mountain, on the East Mancos. Charles Starr and sons, Howard and Raymond, made the big find. They had been prospecting all summer, found valuable float, and finally a very promising lead which began to show values at a shallow depth. Following the vein with the tunnel they encountered the rich ore body in the fall and opened a great treasure house of coarse gold in ore that was easily mined and yielded many nuggets of pure gold as large as the end of a man's thumb and great numbers of by the Red Arrow mine and one by Geo. W. Johnson from the new discovery on the Omaha Placer claim. In a few days the Omaha Placer makes another shipment of rich ore to Salt Lake City. Geo. W. Johnson and James M. Brown attended the shipment. It was said to run 118.24 ounces in gold and 31.8 ounces in silver. There was ten tons in the shipment.

In the summer of 1936 the Red Arrow mine is shipping a car load of ore a week and has 12 to 15 men on the job. There are 6 to 8 men on the Omaha Placer and many small operators and prospectors are at work.

The Red Arrow mine was a steady producer during the season of 1937. Twenty men are steadily employed and a car of high grade ore was shipped to the smelter every week or ten days.

We pause here to pay a passing tribute to a lifelong prospector, Taylor Norton. Norton is an old timer in these parts having been here since about 1885. He was born in Nevada in 1867, and that was when that whole state was an untamed frontier. He spent his entire life mining and prospecting, mostly in the Mancos vicinity, and he located and patented the first mining claims to be patented on the East Mancos. He worked for others, prospected, for others. Then prospected and worked his own claims. Some of his prospecting companions were Freed Brittain, George Carr, Ed Humiston, Bill Hagie, Sandy Rush, Jack Wade, Jim Pepper, and others. Taylor always had fat burros, one or two mules and a first class prospecting oufit.

Here is a report on the first shipment of ore made from the Red Arrow mine. There was 57 sacks of ore in this first shipment, it went to a smelter at Salt Lake and milled out a return of $6,000 after 72 ounces of coarse gold, worth $35 an ounce when refined, had been hand picked from the ore before shipment. The original 16 inch vein had widened to 30 inches as the drive on the tunnel had progressed further under the mountain.

THE HESPERUS MINING CO.

About the time of the Starr strike, another mining company was formed which the promoters called The Hesperus Mining Company, which they incorporated. They secured possession of the mining property of the Doyle Consolidated Mines Co., and began to make plans to rebuild the mill and operate the mine. The old buildings were restored to a usable condition and the mill was largely rebuilt. John A. Pratt was chief promoter and local manager, but associated with him are W. L. Kemper, M. R. Sodergren, Wes Koehler and Ralph Hartman. The following few notes indicates the plans of the company and the progress they made.

The Hesperus Mining Co. is active on the old Doyle group; also on a group of Sassor claims and they are actively on the job in January, 1934. The engineers are there to plan a new mill for the property.

The Hesperus Mining Co., in early spring of 1934 gets in car loads of machinery and mining equipment for a new mill at the old Doyle group of claims. The cars are spotted at Brayton Switch.

The Hesperus Mining Co., while making slow progress, are still on the job and their work in 1935 begins to evidence real signs of permanency. At mid season 50 men are reported to be on the job. A new bunkhouse and other buildings had been constructed, new machinery for the mill was being installed and considerable work was done on the road. The new bunkhouse is now furnished with new bedding, beds and other necessary furniture.

It is reported in Mid-December, 1935, that the mill of the Hesperus Mining Co. was almost ready for operation. Trams, snow sheds, power house and lines are completed and fuel oil for the diesel motors was going up to the mine. All necessary supplies will be on the ground in two weeks and from 30 to 40 men will be put to work. Ten thousand dollars a month has been designated for development work. This is a general picture of things at the mine of the Hesperus Mining Co. when the snow slide struck.

THE SNOW SLIDE

The greatest snow slide disaster in the history of Montezuma County occurred on February 16, 1936, when an immense mass of snow broke from its moorings on Hail Storm Ridge, near the head of East Mancos, and plunged down the mountain sweeping away the camp, mill, buildings, supplies and equipment of the Hesperus Mining Co., at the old Doyle mine site, taking six persons to their death, and injuring others. The slide struck at 1:30 Sunday afternoon, without a moment's warning and swept everything in its path to the bottom of the canon two to three hundred feet below. Those that perished in the avalanche were Parley Jensen of Mancos, age 28; Roy Guire, Mancos, 36; Clint Noble, Mancos, 32; Earl Wyman, north of Denver, 30; Charles A. Roessler, Mancos, 63; Mrs. Jane Ruse, Cortez, 45. The injured were Alvin Fink, Mancos; Neil Onsgard, Spring Grove, Minn.; George Allen, Mancos. Some others were bruised and shaken up, but escaped serious injury.

The avalanche was the result of a storm that had been raging in the mountains for a week and piling snow to an immense depth, combing over many feet deep on the lee side of the ridge. The deep snow, six feet deep at Schubert Flat, and much deeper higher up, made rescue work very difficult and dangerous, and it required much heroic effort to get aid to the injured and affect their removal down from the mountains so they could have medical care. It would be difficult to tell just how it was done. A score or more of men were engaged for many hours in the rescue effort.

As soon as the injured persons were gotten down from the scenes of the disaster the search began to recover bodies of the victims of the disaster. There was sixty feet of hard packed snow in the bottom of the gulch and the bodies taken down by the slide, were somewhere in the immense mass of snow. Finding anyone seemed a hopeless task, yet the effort was made.

The body of Mrs. Ruse was found first showing faint signs of life. She died soon after her body was recovered.

The search for the buried bodies went on. The body of Roy Guire was recovered March 2, in the crushed remains of the blacksmith shop by Foy Longwell and Linn Dean.

The body of Earl Wymann was recovered from the slide March 7, by Sheriff Jesse Robinson and party. Eight or ten men are on the job. Good weather makes work possible and the search goes on.

The body of Charles Roessler was found Sunday, March 6, in the afternoon.

The body of Clinton Noble was found Thursday afternoon, March 19, under 8 feet of snow near the place where Chas. Roessler and Earl Wymann were found.

The body of Parley Jensen, the last to be recovered, was found April 30, two and one-half months after the slide. Eight to ten men had been engaged in the search most of the time. A fund was raised by donations from all who would give, to pay those who worked.

Ben Hartley brought the first news of the disaster when he reached means of communication on snow shoes about four o'clock Monday afternoon, having left camp at break of day. He met two men on horseback, who were employees at the mine, and rode one of the horses on down to the Chas. Menefee place and reported the news by phone. There were a number of men at the Red Arrow mine, and at one or two other mines, and everyone joined in to do whatever could be done to relieve the victims of the slide.

The company estimated their loss at $75,000. The mill was never rebuilt, and no further effort has ever been made to operate the mine. A week after the slide all material and supplies that was available had been salvaged from the wreck and placed in the two or three remaining buildings left. Then a fire broke out and consumed the buildings and all the salvage materials and supplies, amounting to twelve or fifteen thousand dollars. This additional loss seems to have decided definitely and conclusively that the mill would not be rebuilt.

But Pratt was not yet through. Sensing the need of a custom mill to handle and treat the lower grade ores that were available in the district, and the ore that was being produced, he announced in September, 1936, that he and his associates would build a 100 ton capacity mill at Brayton Switch. A complete custom mill is planned. Local mining men, and many others, fell for it.

A new company was organized under the name The San Juan Milling and Refining Co. with John A. Pratt as manager. The Mancos paper, in bold headlines, states that work has started on the plant, that

187

it is to be a custom mill of 150 tons daily capacity and would cost $450,000. On October 4, 1937, thirty to forty men were set to work clearing the site, building roads, etc., and on October 10, 1937, a big celebration and dedication exercises were carried out and speeches were made promising everything. The event was advertised far and near and a big crowd was in attendance. To make a big showing lumber was put on the ground, gravel had been hauled, a water system put in, a ditch having been built to bring the water from the river, and local people were taking stock. Then the work closed down for the winter. The next we hear of Pratt he is in Washington trying to get permission to issue stock of the new company in the amount of $1,000,000. This explained the whole thing. It was just another stock scheme. Pratt finally got permission to issue stock, but if he ever sold any stock he kept the money for nothing further was ever done toward building the big custom mill.

The news was given out about four years later that John A. Pratt, who promoted the Hesperus Mining Co., and who was presently engaged promoting a plan to build a custom smelter at Brayton Switch, died after an operation about May 1, 1942. His death brought to an end all mining promotion in the Mancos area. His enterprises were never revived.

AGRICULTURE

The first settlers that came to Montezuma County came empty handed and with almost an empty purse. If they had money there was no way to spend it, there was nothing that served their personal needs that they could buy. The meager supplies of food they brought along with them were soon exhausted. There was meat for the taking. Wild game was abundant, and soon there were many cattle, but if they had bread it must be produced. So, from the very beginning of life in the new land, some land had to be cleared and started to producing something that would make food. The first crop, of necessity, was a grain crop and wheat, as always, was the bread grain. Once they produced a little grain they had no means of converting it into bread. Apparently they could think of no way to make food from grain but by grinding it into a meal. (There was no way to make it into flour.) Then make the meal into bread. For this purpose the old coffee mill was most generally brought into use, and, after a few years, a grist mill was brought in some how, from somewhere, which made a bread meal. If they ever thought of parching the grain, or boiling corn to make hominy, there is no record of it. The English have for a long time cooked wheat by boiling it and making what they call frumentia.

So wheat grain was probably the first crop the new land began to produce. It, of course, was harvested by hand and threshed with a flail or common stick, or tramped out with a horse. Vegetables, potatoes and a few eggs came very close after grain production, and some

188

milk along with these. There is no record that the settlers substituted potatoes for bread. They could have done it, and probably did. Potatoes yielded well and made more food per acre than any other crop they could grow. But their idea of bread in the diet was hard to get away from; if one didn't have bread to eat, he didn't have anything.

Coming close after human food, there must be animal food. At first there was only the native grasses for animal feed, summer and winter. The winters were often long and cold and the snowfall deep. The cattle were made to depend on the range and the horses could use their front feet and paw down through the snow and get enough feed to live on. Before overgrazing came there was always feed, even in winter. But, of necessity, there must soon be winter feed for milk cows and feed for saddle horses and draft stock. There was grass, but how to harvest it?

There is no record available as to when alfalfa was first grown in the county, but apparently the first small patches began to appear in 1884 and 1885. The grain crop was harvested with a scythe, or a cradle, and the first alfalfa was probably harvested the same way. In 1882 Joseph Sheek brought in the first harvesting machine, a "dropper," and others, no doubt, followed soon after. A dropper was an ordinary mowing machine with an attachement of a slatted platform behind the sickle bar to catch the grain as it was cut. When enough grain for a bundle was caught the platform was dropped to the ground and the bundle slid off and the platform came up again to catch the next bundle. One or two men followed the dropper and bound the bundles with a wisp of straw and the bundles were set up into shocks.

Alfalfa was peculiarly suited to local soils. It made heavy yields when the land was new, and it rapidly became the main crop. After harvesting machines, threshing machines were brought in, as is noted elsewhere in this record, and grain and hay were soon grown on every farm. For several years local sawmills made a market for hay and oats as feed for their draft animals, and after means of transportation became available hay and oats found some market in mining camps. At this point the farmers began to take the productivity out of the soil and put nothing back.

At first, every little area producing a crop and making a home was a ranch, after the Spanish-American word rancho. The term is still largely used. The new people coming in from the east, were accustomed to think of a ranch as a wide spread of land with many cattle. The local application of the word was a bit queer, but they, too, soon fell in line. Their little farm was a ranch.

From the beginning farming in Montezuma County was livestock farming. In order to make a better and more profitable use of the land, better stock were grown and they began to have better care. First it was just milk cows; then the idea of good dairy cattle took hold.

189

Potatoes became a crop, but, owing to poor markets for a long time, potatoes never developed into a major crop, although the quality and the production are both very good. Fruit became a crop, in a small way, very early, but it has been only in more recent times, after better varieties and better methods were introduced, and better transportation became available, thatt he fruit crop became important and began to make a real profit. We have traced the development of fruit growing; also the development of winter wheat and pinto bean growing in the non-irrigated area.

From here the history of agriculture in Montezuma County has been just a history of growth: more land brought into cultivation; more water brought into use. Increase in the number of acres has been largely offset by decrease in production per acre.

Non-irrigated farming is still slightly on the increase as to acres, and the dry farmers insist that the crop yields per acre have registered no decrease in production. There is a feeling that better methods will result in better crops. Commercial fertilizers are being tested out with good results, and may become a common practice when markets and market conditions justify it.

There is also a slow increase in irrigated acreage but, henceforward, increase in volume production on irrigated farms must come largely from better farming methods—better use of land and better use of water. There are strong possibilities in the increased use of commercial fertilizers, and many farmers, trying out commercial fertilizers, are getting some wonderful results. Agriculture is basic in Montezuma County. The well being of the people will always rest on agriculture; it will always be in the county's future. With present growth in wealth and population, and the promise that the future holds, it is of the greatest importance that agricultural methods be vastly improved if agriculture is to keep pace with the advancing times.

STORIES OF THE EARLY PERIOD

Hi Barber was a well known early comer into the Mancos Valley, appearing here about 1885. He had just previously been a peace officer at Animas City, where he had broken up a lawless gang and killed one of their members. One evening at a dance at the little log school house a big rowdy appeared at the door and announced to the crowd that it was time to go home and made a move to shoot out the lights. Hi Barber stepped out from behind the door, stuck his gun in the big fellow's ribs and told him when the lights go out his lights would go out too. The would be ruffian recognized Barber and greeted him in a friendly manner. The coal oil lamps continued to push back the darkness and the dance went merrily on. Hi was a little man, but unafraid. He remained in the Mancos Valley, tended his bees and produced honey to the end of his days.

At a very early time in the settlement of the Mancos Valley, and food was a scarce article with almost every one, a stranger appeared in the valley driving a four mule team hitched to a big wagon. He proposed to take his outfit and go to Alamosa, then the nearest supply point, and get a load of supplies for the people. The people turned a considerable amount of money over to him to buy supplies with. He took the money and went, but he never returned. It was a clear case of misplaced confidence.

Mrs. Menefee had a small roll of red cloth and when the Indians came around she would tear off a piece of this cloth and trade it to the Indians for wheat, which the Indians got on issue from the government. Mrs. Menefee would then take the wheat and wash it, dry it, then grind it and make bread. Once when she was away from the home for a little while the Indians came and one of the big Indian boys went into the back room and laid down on the bed. Aunt Sarah went in with a stick of firewood and brought him out on double quick time. Red Jacket, the Indian Chief, observed the proceedings, patted Aunt Sarah on the shoulder and said: "Heap good squaw," and laughs merrily.

On one occasion, when the town of Mancos consisted of two little stores and three or four other buildings on South Main St., two cowboys came riding into town at full speed yelling and discharging their guns in the air. The nearby women, thinking it an Indian raid, took their children and rushed into a place of protection on the Root place with such fright and confusion that it was a wonder that some of them were not injured or suffocated in the jam. The place was a kind of dugout that had been partly fixed up as a place of refuge in case of an Indian raid.

At Christmas time, in the winter of the big snows of 1884, the neighbors gathered in the Menefee ranch for a Christmas feast; then decided to go down to the little log school house, where the town was afterwards to be, and have a dance. The attempt was made with teams and conveyances, but the snow was four feet deep on the level and, after trying for an hour or so and getting no further than the Paquin place, they gave it up and went back home. Still undaunted the men rounded up a bunch of horses the next day, drove them over the road to break a trail and that evening they went down and had their Christmas dance. Clark Brittain and Will Willden were the fiddlers in those days.

We have related the story of Andy Menefee taking a bunch of 80 horses and going to Salt Lake City in the fall of 1877 to trade for cattle and get supplies. In this herd of horses were a number of race horses and some pretty fast ones. While at Salt Lake he matched a number of races with race horsemen of that place and took about all the money they had. He then traded his winning horse for eight yoke of oxen and two wagons, traded the other horses for 200 cattle, loaded out with supplies and headed for home. It was late autumn when they reached

191

the La Sal Mountains, out in the edge of Utah, so the cattle were left there on good grass and the ox teams came on home. In the spring of 1878, they went back and got the cattle, finding them all in good shape. This was the beginning of the Menefee herd.

On August 10, 1909, twelve Ute Indians came up from Navajo Springs with teams and wagons for what they supposed to be a car load of flour. When they found out it was barb wire instead of something to eat, they were expected to haul, they balked and no amount of persuasion could induce them to take out the wire. Surmising the use to which the wire would be put, they said they didn't want that stuff down there to pull out all the sheep's wool; that they didn't want to farm and they didn't want the country fenced up. They went home without the wire, and the next day the white man loaded the wire on his big freight wagons and took it down to the agency.

The story is related that Doug Wooley was one day sitting on a rock, for no apparent reason, partly concealed by sage brush. A prowling Indian discovered his presence and made a sneak approach to dispatch Doug with a sharp knife. Just in time Doug discovered the Indian, and being a strong, agile man, made the first charge, also with a knife. The Indian made for the fence and Doug planned to get him as he went over the fence, but, instead of going over, the Indian went under and got away. Just ahead was a set of bars taking the place of a gate and the Indian made for that. Doug planned to get him as he went over these, but again the Indian went under, and got such a start Doug couldn't come near him again, although some of the neighbors declared emphatically Doug could out run a steer.

An outstanding rider on the range was a fellow the other riders called "Old Hickory." He rode for Ben Bishop of Durango. He was handicapped by having his left hand off at the wrist, yet it was marvelous the way he could ride and rope and handle cattle, and there was not a better man on the range than he.

Back in the days when the Indians were strongly inclined to make trouble the government sought to check their depredations by giving some of their leaders a trip to Washington, a view of the whiteman's numbers and armed forces. Accordingly Chief Ouray and two of his sub-chiefs were taken on the trip. They traveled first class by train and stopped at the best hotels. They were shown the city of Washington, Congress, and met the President, and were shown a part of the army in full battle array. They demonstrated the use of the Gattling Gun, as the machine gun was called then, one of which was fired from the back of a mule. The Indians returned home and Chief Ouray made a report to the leaders of his tribe. He told them of his trip and what he saw, fast trains, great cities, the President and the army; of the big guns and of a "mule that shoots." Then he told the Indians there was no use to fight the whiteman; that there were more white men than there were leaves on all the trees up and down the creek where they were

Small part of Dr. Reddert's range herd on old Menefee ranch. Just through the winter on feed. La Plata mountains in the background. Cattle have been basic since the first white man came to the county.

A group of Mancos pioneers: No. 1, Dave Kramer; 2, Ed Noland; 3, Jim Wade; 4, Grandma Patterson; 5, Gertie Hindman; 6, Ruby Kramer; 7, Mrs. John Brown; 8, John Brown; 9, Fannie Wade; 10, Belle Humiston; 11, Ed Humiston; 12, Henry Bauer; 13, Curg Williams; 14, Emma Dodson; 15, George Dodson; 16, Mabyn Morefield (First white girl baby born in Mancos Valley and Montezuma Co.); 17, Mrs. Thomas Rickner; 18, Mr. Henry Bauer; 19, Mrs. Bill Hunter; 20, Mrs. Jim Caviness.

A building that made history. The first Mormon Church in the Webber Community and the first in the county. Original log building in the rear. Front part built on later. The original log building was built in July, 1886. The picture was probably taken some time later, and the number of people shown indicates a considerable population.

Mancos High School building, enlarged and extended at rear—not visible. Corridor and large auditorium at right not shown.

Mancos Grade School building looking south of due east. Menefee Mesa in background.

Early street scene in Mancos. East Grand Avenue looking west. The building shown partly at right foreground seems to be what was known as "Union Hall" and it stood about where the Mallet garage now stands. The hall was upstairs and entrance was gained by outside stairway. It was very popular for years and all dances, lodge meetings and other public meetings were held there. The building burned about 1896 or 1897.

Corner entrance, First National Bank of Mancos, a large two story building dismantled to make room for highway 160 through town. Children at play.

Typical grazing scenes with cattle on summer range. Cattle belonging to Mary Wallace and son, Dwight.

*One of the longest trains ever moved over the Denver & Rio Grande South-
ern railway, drawn, and pushed by four engines, at East Mancos Water Tank.
The road moved large tonnage of freight in the early years of its operation.*

*Ern Guillet and granddaughter. Mrs. Ern Guillet gave us valuable informa-
tion on early county history, and we failed to give her credit in our general
statement. This is to atone for the oversight.*

holding their pow-wǫw. Harry Lee, who had long made his home with the Indians and knew their language as well as he did his own, was present at the meeting and said Chief Ouray made a good speech.

Back in the early times, when the Town of Big Bend was yet very young, Bill Ordway and Billy May each had a small business there and at this time some Ute Indians were want to hide in the rocks above town, on the west, and pump bullets down among the inhabitants to keep up a little interest in life. Billy May and Bill Ordway decided to put an end to the sport, so they rode by a circuitous route, unobserved by the Indians, and came upon them from the read while the Indians were all unaware. With swift and accurately placed shots they dispatched the three Indians taking part in the sport and put an end to their little game. No more disturbances after that.

GEORGE BAUER

George Bauer was born at Siegen, Prussia, in East Germany, July, 1848. He immigrated to America, and the United States, in 1865. He came west at once, and we find him at Del Norte, Colorado, in 1875. It was there that he was married to Augusta E. Schultz in that year, and some time after their marriage they came to the San Juan Basin and lived for a time at Durango. George Bauer might have Scouted this area earlier, but his first recorded appearance in the Mancos Valley was in 1881, when he came in, suntanned and rough from outdoor life, riding a mule and leading three burros heavily laden with merchandise with which he started a store in a little log house on South Main St. He soon sold out his little stock of goods and went back for more. The railroad had reached Durango and a merchandise supply was available there. This was the beginning of the George Bauer Mercantile Co., which grew, in after years, into a quarter of a million dollar mercantile business. The Bauer Bank grew along with the mercantile business and served the people faithfully and well for many years.

After establishing his home in Mancos, Mr. Bauer soon gained the confidence of the people. They soon learend to trust his word and his honesty, and we feel safe in saying he never once betrayed their confidence. His business ability and rare good judgment was the foundation of a highly successful business career, and local people soon learned to trust his judgment.

From the first day he made his home in the valley, he was a loyal, public spirited citizen and he gave of his time and his money to help promote the local welfare in every way he could. He made money here and he spent it here, and three fine buildings stood for years as monuments to his faith and enterprise. The fine three-story residence building on North Main St., and the Mancos postoffice building still stand; the fine stone building that stood on the corner of Main Street and

193

Grand Avenue having been destroyed by fire some years back. Another enduring work was the building of Bauer Reservoir No. 1 and No. 2. The early home of his mercantile business on North Main St., now occupied by the laundry, still stands. During the years when there was much interest in mining he took a lively interest and put considerable money into the industry. Good fortune attended his mining enterprises, as in other things, and he made some money out of his mining interests.

When the county was formed he was appointed by Gov. Thomas on the first board of county commissioners, and his ability stood the public well in hand in getting the affairs of the new county started. When the Town of Mancos was incorporated in 1894 he was elected the first mayor and continued to be reelected as long as he lived excepting one term, when he asked to be relieved. There is no denying but that George Bauer was a great benefactor in both his community and his county. It is safe to say that no other man has to this day commanded the confidence of the people as did he, and time has borne out the fact that that confidence was fully justified. Born in a foreign land and reared to manhood there, he came to a land that was strange to him; a people strange to him in manners and customs, and with a language he did not know and had to learn. He adjusted himself to all of these, became an American citizen whose loyalty was never questioned, and a friend among many friends.

He died at a branch of the Battle Creek Sanitarium, Guadalajara, Mexico, February 1, 1905, and his body was brought back to Mancos for burial.

Oen Edgar Noland

Oen Edgar Noland hailed from Missouri, and we first find him on the western scene at Saguache, Colorado in 1873. Next he is freighting by ox team from Alamosa to Durango. He first appeared on the local scene at old Parrott City, and then a little later in Thompson Park where he had a logging contract with Frank Morgan, who ran a sawmill. The Stanley Mitchells ran the boarding house. Here he met and married Callie Mitchell about 1881. The Ute Indians had just been put on their reservation; also the Navajo Indians were put on their reservation, and Noland, while yet hauling logs, became convinced there was opportunity in running an Indian trading post. In order to raise the necessary capital and comply with the conditions of a loan he resorted to the remarkable expedient of insuring his life for $10,000 in favor of the lending firm for a like amount in cash to finance his trading business. For a man with a family to do a thing like this shows a degree of self confidence and a sureness of purpose rarely found among men of any place or time. Yet he realized his every hope and made friends and money. He made friends of the whole Ute tribe and many Navajos. This was probably the outstanding fact in his career.

The first trading post was down on the San Juan river, near the Four Corners. Here he built a stone building, with port holes and barricaded door. This was both trading post and fort. A strong log building was also built, as warehouse and storage space. A stock of merchandise was laid in and the store opened for business. The first years were not without dangers and difficulties. The trading post was in the midst of Indians, and stretching far to the west was a desolate land infested with marauding bands of Indians that had not yet submitted to the whiteman's law. Noland had a number of close brushes with the Indians, but he held on and finally convinced the Indians that he was their friend. Thereafter they call him "Bidani," an Indian term signifying both friendship and kinship.

A second trading post was established at Aneth, Utah, but was sold, after a while to Guillet Bros. Then, the Ute Indian agency having been established at Navajo Springs, he established a large trading business there and sold the post down at the Four Corners location.

The family home was maintained at Mancos, but for some weeks each summer the family lived at the trading post, after it became safe for them to be there. The first Mrs. Noland died about 1895, leaving five children, Mr. Noland was married again later to Miss Lolla Thompson and another family of four children were born to this union. A number of children survive; also the second Mrs. Noland, but only three; Edgar and Mrs. J. S. Alexander of the first family and Oen of the second family still reside in the community.

About the turn of the century Mr. Noland, in partnership with O. S. Crenshaw, bought the Bauer Mercantile business; and conducted a large and prosperous business for a number of years. He gradually closed out his trading post business, and a little later retired from business, and lived out his remaining years in Mancos in quietude among family and friends.

Mr. Noland's outstanding success was with the Indians. He learned to speak their language as well as anyone can ever learn it, and he believed in the Indians native honesty and integrity and would trust them for about anything they wanted, and the Indians were as true friends to him as he was a true friend to the Indians.

TIMBER & BRUSH IN MONTEZUMA CO.

Every part of Montezuma County grows some kind of timber or brush except a small area above timberline. The timber and brush is nearly all evergreen with some deciduous trees along the streams and in the aspen and oak belt in the mountains. The kind of timber or brush growing in different areas is determined by the altitude and there are wide variation in plant life of every kind. To start with, in the lower elevations of the county, from 4,000 feet up to about 7,500 feet, we find the sage brush, rabbit brush, pinon-pine, and juniper, commonly called cedar. In the sage brush varieties we find the big sage, often called the purple sage. Then there is the silver or white sage, low sage brush and black sage. Big sage brush grows from 3 to 7 or 8 feet tall, is found on all the deeper and better soils and its presence indicates good farm land. All the other sages are more or less dwarfed and indicate shallow, poor soil or deficient moisture. Rabbit brush is found in the entire sagebrush zone and grows on the best land.

All these brush make some feed for sheep and cattle in winter time when other feed is scarce. Sheep eat some brush all the time. Salt brush, or salt sage, grows in certain localities and is good sheep feed.

There is but one variety of pinon pine in the county. Pinon is a scrub pine and grows needles, two or three in a cluster and from one to one and one-half inches long. It produces an edible nut in a short cone that has no prickles on the cone scales. Pinons are nearly always found growing with the cedars all mixed together.

Of the cedars there are two distinct varieties found locally: white cedars and red cedars. Close observation will disclose two kinds of white cedars and three or four kinds of red cedars. All these cedars bear a one-seeded fruit called a berry. The pinon pine makes excellent fire wood and that is about all it is good for save producing a few nuts in favorable seasons. The cedars make good, clean fuel and the small trees make excellent round fence post. The large trees may be split into posts equally as good. Neither the cedars nor the pinons are classed as timber by the government and they have a low commercial value, the pinons almost none at all. For a while, however, they were sawed or hewn into railway cross ties and made very good ones.

In addition to sage brush there is grease wood, service brush, squaw brush, wild crabapple, tamarisk, willows—three or four different kind, cotton wood of the narrow leaf variety, usually classed as timber, and some other kinds. The service brush and crabapple produce a fine scented flower and, growing in cluster, fill the air with a delightful fragrance when in bloom. Squaw brush produces a berry and the crabapple a tiny apple. The wild rose grows in every zone from the lowest to the highest.

Above the low timber and brush belt comes the ponderosa pine belt, beginning at about 7,500 feet elevation. In this zone we also find the oak brush, choke cherries along the streams, and some other brushes. This zone was formerly covered by a stately forest over a vast area and was one of the finest stands in the entire state. On most of the area the timber is but a sad remnant of its former self, the commercial lumberman having harvested about all that is available.

Beginning at about 9000 feet we find the aspen belt, and the county has some of the finest stands of aspen timber found anywhere in the world. One can view some of this fine forest by driving the West Mancos road. Formerly aspen was regarded as hardly a timber at all, and of little value, but in recent years it has been found that it makes excellent match splints and very good excelsior, and great quantities are being harvested and processed into these products. There is some good pine timber in this belt, ponderosa in the lower edge and spruce in the upper rim. It is thought that spruce timber once occupied the area where aspen now is growing, fires having destroyed the spruce stands. There is a little buckbrush in this zone and some other brush. Mountain ash is prevalent in the higher altitudes above the aspen, and beginning at about 10,000 feet elevation, we come to the spruce zone which extends on up to timberline. In this zone Engleman Spruce is the commercial tree and it is being processed into vast quantities of finished lumber. There is also the Alpine fir, Douglas fir, balsam and the blue spruce. The blue spruce is an ornamental tree and is grown for its beauty in the towns of the county and on many farms. It has been chosen the state tree and is the most beautiful evergreen tree that grows in the state. The Douglas fir grows from around 7000 feet on up to regions much higher. Where there is a good stand and thrifty growth it makes very good saw timber, but there is only a small amount of this timber, in the county.

There is a vast acreage and a dense stand of young ponderosa pine that will make a vast amount of good saw timber at some future date. Most of this stand of young timber needs to be thinned and some experiments are being made by the Forest Service at trimming off the lower branches in the interest of faster trunk growth.

All timber is cut under Forest Service supervision, and one secondary purpose of the National Forests is to create vegetative coverage for wild life. Fire is the great despoiler and the great hazard in the National Forests, and man-made fires are constantly guarded against. As a protection for snow cover in the mountains, timber is not regarded as so important as it once was. It has been found by experience that solid masses of deep snow in the open provides more and later water run-off than the broken up masses in the timber where the tree reflections aid in melting the snow. About timberline, at 12,000 feet elevation, we find a stunted tree growth of willows, range pine and spruce and many gnarled and twisted old specimens stand to present a weird aspect and evidence their struggle with the elements, perhaps for centuries.

NATIVE PLANT LIFE

Colorado has more than 3,000 plant specimens that are native to the state and Montezuma County has at least 500 of these. For this reason space and time will permit us to touch on and name only a few of these. The varying altitudes in the county, from 4,000 to over 13,000 feet, makes for a very extensive variety of plant life, and many places this flowering plant life is growing in great profusion. Our native wild flowers are a great tourist attraction second only to the wonderful

197

scenery itself. We could not hope to cover the whole field without taking a great deal more time and space than is available. We will therefore touch on only a few of the more common and best known plants. We will confine ourselves to wild, or native plants, and avoid introduced garden varieties.

In the first zone, 4,000 to 7,500 feet elevation, we find many more different plants than there seems to be on casual notice. We find all these plants growing under natural conditions in the hard, dry soil with no cultivation or applied moisture, and we wonder how they do it; how such lovely flowers can grow and flourish under such adverse conditions. It shows the power of plant adaptation to its environment.

Take, for example, the Indian Pink. It grows and blooms all summer long however dry and hot the weather. The stem puts on buds and flowers. The first die and perish. The stem grows a little longer and puts on new flowers, and so it goes all summer long. Dozens of other plants, blooming only at a certain time, are just as hardy. Take the wild sweet pea, wild salsafa, canterberry bells (a beautiful flower with a bad odor), wild phlox, blue bonnets, all the wild daisies and many others, and observe how they are able to bloom and produce beauty in spite of hard conditions. Take the beautiful maraposa lilly, regarded by many as the handsomest wild flower of the state, and we wonder how such beauty can produce itself under such harsh conditions. The sego lilly is about the same flower as the maraposa lilly, except that it is yellow instead of white. It grows mostly in Utah and is the Utah state flower.

Among other local flowers we find the large evening primrose, truly a glorious flower; the prickly pear cactus and yucca plant, very beautiful and showy blooms. In addition to the above mentioned plants we find the following: wild phlox, bull thistle, rose thistle, and other kinds; the large broadleaved milk weed, and there or four others; wild hollyhocks, the bee weed, the loco plant, Colorado rubber weed, jimson weed, golden rod, iris or flags, wild onions, golden glow, Oregon grape, the first flower of spring; sneeze weed (crush it and smell it and get a spasm of sneezing—induced hay fever); yarrow, wild lettuce, wild mustard (three kinds); dodder, ground cherry, night shade, wild violets, Brigham tea (dried and used by many westerners as a tea and it's not so bad); sheep sorrel, burdock, and two or three other docks; rag weed (two or three kinds); beggar ticks and Spanish needles. There are scores of others. The writer went out to look for wild flowers and, in the course of a short walk, found a dozen or more for which we had no name and could not identify without a key.

Going into the higher altitudes, one will find many other plants most of which are not familiar to the average person. They grow under more favorable soil and moisture conditions than the flowers of the valleys. Among these we will name first the Columbine, our state flower. It is a great beauty and is well known to every one. Here we

198

find, growing in profusion, the beautiful poison larkspur; the common plantin, a beautiful blue flower; the skunk cabbage or lupin, not so attractive but very conspicuous; and the wonderful little red elephant; and the monkshood, the iris or flag growing everywhere; violets, ferns, and many, many others. You never get so high in the mountains that you can't find flowers. Right up to timberline, on many an Alpine glade, you can find a mat of wild flowering plants, two to four inches high, and many different kinds. At this altitude one finds about the same plant life you find at sea level at the Arctic Circle. That is how much altitude affects plant life.

The dandelion, a flower so common to us all, is an introduced plant, originally from France, and it is reported that the first seed was brought to Mancos, in the early history of the valley, by Mrs. George Bauer. The name is derived from the French phrase, Dent de lion, meaning the teeth of the lion, so called because the notched edges of the leaves resemble lion's teeth.

Many of our beautiful wild plants, and some not so beautiful, are poisonous to livestock. Among these are larkspur, whorled milk weed, bouncing bet, rubber plant, death camas, elder, some ferns, iris, golden rod, greasewood, water hemlock, jimson weed, sweet clover (not native), lupine yarrow and many others. Most of these are only mildly poisonous; some are a constant danger.

Our wild plants are a fascinating study, and the more one learns about them the more pleasure can be gotten from the study. Some 58 or 60 years ago, Mrs. W. S. Felker, wife of the then well-known Judge Felker, was want to come to Mancos every summer with the judge. Being a bright woman with an inquiring mind, she gathered plant specimens of every kind, growing locally, pressed, classified and mounted them and it is reported she had over 500 specimens. It was regarded as a very valuable collection and some plant museum in the east got possession of the display.

THE GRASSES

We can't pass up the grasses. Grass is the greatest and most valuable crop that grows. Nothing else that grows comes near it in its importance to mankind. Grass always has been and it always will be. The original, and the main stay, in the native grasses, is the old reliable bluestem, called western wheat grass by the college folks. This is the grass that grew everywhere in the county until it was grazed to death, or almost to death. But it had a comeback. Observe the fact on the Mancos-Cortez road west of the divide. It is coming back in many other places where it is given a chance. Then there was the grama grasses, never a great feed producer, but a persistent grower. It never gives up to dryness. Slender wheat grass is a good native grass, and there are others less important.

Timothy was the first grass to be brought in; then red top, orchard grass, the fescues, brome grass, and later came crested wheat grass, intermediate wheat grass and tall wheatgrass, and they were all very good and made for improved grazing and more and better livestock. Cheat grass, fuzzy brome in reality, just came in uninvited. It is kind of a pest, but an asset in several ways.

Kentucky bluegrass was first just a lawn grass and introduced as such. Then it just came in, or got here someway, and it came to stay. It proved to be most indigenous to our soils, it is a persistent grower everywhere it can get water, and in the elevations above 7,500 feet, it flourishes with only the natural moisture supply. Bluegrass loves our lime soils. It goes places under its own power, and it's still going. No one can tell, or estimate, how much this grass is worth to our livestock industry. It loves lots of moisture; it has to have moisture to do well, but if dry weather comes and it dries down to the roots, it never gives up. When moisture comes it is going again. We should have a deep appreciation for Old Kentucky Bluegrass. It is life and health and strength to us all.

NATIVE WILD LIFE

Montezuma County is the home of many wild animals, large and small. There are two general classes: Viz herbiverous, or those that feed on plant life and grain, and the carniverous: those that feed on flesh. Of the grazing and browsing animals we have the elk, the largest. The elk is native in the state, but not in this part of the state. A few elk were planted on the Hermosa Creek, in La Plata County, a few years ago. They have increased in numbers and spread to every part of the San Juan Basin. They have built up a considerable population and there is an open season on them every year. They range higher in the mountains than do the deer, and they browse mostly. They winter in the deep snow where their only feed is the tender twigs of brush and trees.

The deer is native. There are two kinds: the white tailed deer and the mule deer, and in recent years they have become quite plentiful; much more so than in former years. During open season each year several hundred head are killed. There still seems to be plenty of deer left and they are everywhere in the sparsely settled areas. The deer is also a browsing animal and consumes but little cattle or sheep feed.

The bear is another large game animal. He stays in the mountains and lives mostly on tender vegetation, berries and little insects or grubs he can find by turning over rocks. He also eats some flesh and sometimes kills a calf or a sheep when he gets hungry, or he will eat from a dead animal. He dearly loves honey and if he can find a bee's nest in the ground he has a feast. He doesn't mind the bees. Bears usually get very fat in the summer and fall; then, in early winter, he finds a cave, an old mine tunnel, or some other shelter, and

200

goes to sleep for the winter. Bears are not numerous and only a few are killed each year. They weigh from 200 to 400 pounds are are not considered dangerous unless they are wounded or their young are endangered.

About the only small game animal is the rabbit. The cotton tail is often eaten, but the jack rabbit is seldom used for food by the white-man.

The mountain lion is the largest of the predators. He weighs from 85 to nearly 200 pounds. He makes his home in the lower elevations, for the most part, where the terrain is very rough and rugged and few people come to disturb him. In this county he is found mostly in the region of the Mancos Canon and East Canon. His main food seems to be deer meat, but he will kill sheep or a calf if he gets hungry, and he will eat rabbits and other small animals if he can catch them. They are not numerous and the mountain lion, ordinarily, is not fierce or dangerous. In fact he is quite timid and it is said he will run from a small dog, and, if crowded a little, he will take to a tree. He will put up a fierce fight if he is cornered and can't get away and he can kill a dog very quickly in a fight. Hunting lions with hounds used to be great sport for local huntsmen, and once in a while they would capture one alive and unharmed.

The coyote is remarkable for his power of adaptation. He can live in the wild, or he can live right near the settlements. In spite of many people about, he can find a place to hide out and a way to get his living and keep up his numbers. He hunts at night and if he can get a square meal every other day he gets along. The coyote never succumbs to civilization. The fox is much the same in these respects as the coyote, and the bobcat is not far behind either of them.

Of the other flesh eaters we find the badgers, skunk, weasel, mink and a few coons. Of the small vegetable feeders, there is the jack rabbit and the cotton tail, groundhog, beaver, prairie dog, rock squirrel, the Fremont or pine squirrel—a small blue-gray squirrel which is quite a pretty animal; rats, mice, the kangaroo mouse, gophers, moles, porcupines and two kinds of chipmunks.

Of the reptiles we find the bull snake in numbers, and the rattlesnake, which is getting to be very scarce in the settlements. There are a few small brown or dark snakes of different kinds some of which are water snakes. There are a few dry land turtles, classed with the reptiles, and several kinds of small lizards.

BIRDS

The bird population of Montezuma County is building up, both in kinds and in numbers. In the early history of the county there were not many birds, but with the growing of crops, fruits and vegetables, insect life became much more abundant and there was more food for birds of every kind. Some birds also flourished on the grains of the

201

grain fields. Birds are an asset when they help to control insect life and sometimes even to destroy it.

Our birds are not all permanent residents. A great many go southward to warmer climates in the winter and return to their old habitat in the spring. Others stay with us all the year around. Also some birds live on flesh. Other on insects, worms and grain.

The flesh eaters are characterized by a sharp, hooked bill, which was given to them for tearing the flesh of animals and other birds they kill. Of these birds we find the golden eagle, the largest of these. There are only a few eagles and they catch and kill their prey. They live in the high mountains and nest among the crags or in the top of a tall tree. They are fierce in battle when defending their nest or their young. Then we have the large rabbit hawk that rarely disturbs poultry, but flies low over the ground and picks up any small animal he may find. The middle sized, swift flying hawk is the chicken hawk. He is a crafty fellow, will take his stand on a tree and wait for a chance to dive down and catch a chicken. Often he doesnt' get a chicken and must forage further afield for food, and sometimes he gets a load of shot instead of a chicken. Then there is the sparrow hawk, so swift and agile on the wing that he can catch a small bird in mid-air and kill it. Then there is the owl with his big round eyes so he can hunt by night and catch mice and other small animals that are abroad in the dark. There are two kinds of owls: the hoot owl and the screech owl. They are alike in ways of living and getting their food. Buzzards and crows, or ravens, are flesh eaters, but their food is mostly carrion. They are the scavengers of the bird family. Ducks and geese are the swimming birds and the killdeer and the crane are the waders.

Of the game birds, we have the wild turkey, grouse, pheasant and the dove, but the dove is not much sought as game. There are a few quails in the lower parts of the county. Ducks and geese only migrate through, stopping on the ponds and lakes to feed and rest. Some ducks, however, remain through the spring and early summer, nest and rear their young here.

We have many beautiful birds, but few good singers; in fact hardly any. The lark has a merry whistle, but most birds only chirp or chatter like the pinon jay. Once in a while a mocking bird appears on the local scene and makes some real bird music.

Here is a list of our common birds, or most of them: martin, oriole, western robin, swallow, ptarmigan, mountain blue bird, the chickadee in the mountains, the magpie, Rockymountain jay, campbird, meadow lark, pewee, sparrow—two or three kinds, and the snow sparrow; wren, two small woodpeckers and one large one called a flicker; the humming bird, swallow, bull bat, and the common bat, not a bird. There are a few birds the writer has not learned to recognize by name.

FISH

Fishing is our most popular outdoor sport, and, while there are a

202

great many fishermen, both local people and visitors, the streams and lakes are kept well stocked and there are always fish that may be caught. The rainbow trout, the brook trout, the lake trout and the speckled trout are in all the fishing waters, but the rainbow trout predominates heavily since this is the trout the state Game and Fish department hatches and grows out for planting. There are suckers in the lower water courses and lower still are a few catfish. The rainbow trout is far the most numerous as it is the only fish hatched and reared for planting. In 1956 eight tons of fish, 7 to 12 inches long, were dumped into the Dolores river and its tributaries, and several other streams of the county.

The fishing streams of the county are the Dolores river, the West Dolores river, the Mancos river and the East, Middle and West Mancos rivers. The largest creeks are Fish Creek, Bear Creek and Lost Canon Creek. There are a dozen or more smaller creeks, some of which have been stocked, and some mountain irrigation ditches furnish some good fishing.

Most of the lakes, or reservoirs, are stocked regularly and furnish a lot of fine fishing. The more important lakes are the Groundhog Reservoir, in Dolores County; the Narraguinep Reservoir, the Summit Reservoir, the Puett Reservoir, Joe Moore, Bauer Lake No. 1 and No. 2, and the Jackson Gulch Reservoir. There are a number of small reservoirs, privately owned, that are well stocked.

Boat racing on the rivers in flood season is getting to be a popular sport, and motor boating and water skiing on the reservoirs is also becoming popular with local people.

THE DOLORES REARING UNIT

It was a great day for the angler when in 1948, the Game and Fish Department of Colorado, decided to build and maintain rearing ponds for fish on the Dolores River. The result of this decision was the building of five rearing ponds, and the necessary buildings, on the river six miles up stream from the Town of Dolores, for the special purpose of growing fish for all San Juan Basin lakes and streams open to public fishing. Only rainbow trout are produced in this unit.

First, the fish are hatched in the hatchery at Durango and when they are an inch long they are brought by truck and dumped in the rearing ponds, which have first been emptied of all old fish and gotten ready for the new stock. Between four and five million of these little fellows are brought over every year and fed out in the ponds until they are 7 to 12 inches long. They are then taken from the ponds, by a special method, and dumped into the lakes and streams. Last year, in 1955, seven and one-half tons of fish were planted in the Dolores river and its tributaries, and a total of twenty-five tons in the lakes and streams of the San Juan Basin in Colorado.

The growing fish are fed every day, about five per cent of the estimated total weight of the fish in the ponds, and on a diet consisting of Carp fish brought in by truck loads from the big irrigation canals and lakes in northeastern Colorado, mostly. These are ground up and mixed with fish meal and rolled oats and the mixture all cooked together into a wet mash or meal. The cooking is done in large caldrons, and a number are in use. This makes a fine ration for the fish and they thrive on it. They eat it ravishingly and make a rapid growth. The food is just thrown into the water. The little fish come hurrying by the thousands, and they have a way of their own of getting the food out of the water, and they get it all. Nothing is wasted.

These are the fish local fishermen catch when they go fishing. But for this constant replenishing of the fish supply in the lakes and streams not one fisherman in a dozen would catch any fish when he goes fishing. There is much more to the rearing of fish than is related here, but these are the main points. As in everything else it takes knowledge and skill to get the best results.

As this is being written the hatcheries all over the state are short on spawn for hatching the young fish and it now seems that the State Game and Fish Department must take steps to provide at least a part of their own spawn. Hitherto the department has been depending for their spawn supply entirely on privately owned sources. Having no control over private sources there is apt to come a time and perhaps frequently, when there would be a short supply of spawn, and consequently, a shortage of the fish supply for planting in the lakes and streams.

THE SUMMIT IRRIGATION AND RESERVOIR CO.

The Summit Irrigation & Reservoir Co. was organized and incorporated in 1904 with Charley Rentz, John Withers, Hugh Rentz and Al Puett incorporators. The purpose of the organization was to combine the resources of the incorporators and construct a reservoir out on, or near, the Mancos-Dolores road, at the top of the divide, to be known as the Summit Reservoir, and to combine with it the Joe Moore reservoir and the Puett reservoir, the Turkey Creek ditch and water rights from Lost Canon, yet to be procured, and to build a ditch system to distribute the water to the land.

The first purpose of the promoters of the enterprise was to build the large reservoir and distributing system with their own labor and resources, and, after putting all their personal assets into it, they found they had gotten only well started, and that the undertaking would require much more capital than they were able to put into it. Nevertheless they tried, and they did succeed in storing enough water to irrigate a number of small farms. But it was enough to demonstrate the value and the feasibility of the project, and the work went on.

Meantime all the land covered by the proposed system had been homesteaded, land was being cleared and they would soon need much more water than the company could furnish with the storage and water rights they had. The system, now only well started, was designed to cover, and furnish water for, some eight thousand acres of virgin land of very good quality and the settlers would soon need very much more water than was then available.

So ,on April 12, 1907, a deal was closed by which David Swickheimer, of Rico, purchased a one-fourth interest in the company. By the terms of this deal the reservoir company received $12,000 in cash to be expended in completing the system and $5,500 to be paid when the system was completed, and to include one large reservoir and three small ones with a combined storage capacity of four hundred million cubic feet of water or enough to cover 9,000 acres of land with a foot of water. The terms also called for completing the ditch system.

Mr. Swickheimer was a wealthy banker and mine operator at Rico, where he had struck it rich in mining and grew "from rags to riches" in a short time. He took an active interest in the company, bought some land and cleared several hundred acres and put it into cultivation.

The Summit Company went to work at once, and the first job undertaken was the completion of the main canal, on down the ridge in the direction of Dolores to bring water to several new farms. Some small ditches were built, then the big job of raising the main reservoir dam and increasing the storage was undertaken, in 1909, and by 1911 enough of the work was completed to increase the storage capacity several fold, and there was plenty of water for all the waterusers for a while. But the settlers continued to clear more land and demand more water and, in a few years, again there was not enough water.

By 1913 the call for more water came again and the people of the district approved a bond issue of $30,000 to completely remodel the old system and put it in first class condition, and build a new ditch from Lost Canon with a carrying capacity that would fill the entire storage system in thirty days.

Apparently nothing was done at this time about improving the water system so, in 1918, a new bond issue for $90,000 was approved by the share holders and the purposes set forth were the same as under the former proposed bond issue. Under the new plan, however, the people proposed to do most of the work and take bonds in payment. They took $52,000 of the $90,000 bond issue and the new Lost Canon ditch was finished about the first of July, 1919, but too late to be of any use that season. In 1921 the ditch was put into full use and the farms under the system produced a full crop of everything. In 1956 an authoritative source gave the following figures and facts on the reservoir system:

Storage capacity, Summit Reservoir   5,000 acre feet.
Storage capacity, Joe Moore Reservoir   300 acre feet.

Storage capacity, Puett Reservoir   300 acre feet.

There is 3,000 acre feet of usable flood water in the average years.

There are 70 shareholders at this time. Shareholders owning 10 to 14 shares of water have plenty of water in normal years of precipitation, but shareholders with one to five shares of water need more water badly and there is no more water for sale until the storage capacity is increased. At present 5,000 acres of land under the system is being irrigated and water for irrigation has run, on an average, 110 days each season for the past 13 years.

The company has a water right for 100 second feet of water in the Turkey Creek ditch and 135 second feet in the Lost Canon ditch, and all water rights have been adjudicated and fully decreed. The present board is apparently doing a very good job at managing the system. In the past nine years they have paid off $45,000 in debts, paying the last of the company debt in 1955. They are now ready to make any improvement that is needed. Plans are now being considered for enlarging the storage capacity and for enlarging somewhat the Lost Canon ditch. Other plans are being considered for making better use of flood water by which additional land may be reclaimed.

The Summit ssytem is one of the best and most satisfactory small irrigating systems in the entire state, and the shareholders are very well pleased with it. Some of the best lands, and some of the best farms in the county are under this irrigating system.

CHAPTER XVIII

MANCOS CHRONOLOGY

We have traced the early history of Mancos, up to about 1892. This early history is based upon the records of the first settlers in the valley. This has come down to us from some written records that have been left behind, intact, and, in part, based upon information gotten first hand from some four or five of these first settlers themselves who have survived and come down to our own time. Most of this recorded history has been gleaned from the files of the Mancos Times and the Mancos Times-Tribune, and from these files we have also taken recorded information that applied to other parts of Montezuma County and used it in compiling events that have made history in every part of the county. We have also gleaned some facts from the files of the Dolores Star which we have made use of in this narrative.

Recorded history in the Mancos Valley, barring a few manuscripts that have come into our hands, began with the first publication of the Mancos Times on April 28, 1893, with C. M. Danford as editor and publisher. The locality is experiencing a mining boom, in a small way, and the Times was born as a result of the general interest in the mining activities of the area. The hills are alive with prospectors and there is some mining being done. There was placer mining along the streams, with some promising results, and hard rock mining on both blanket and fissure veins. The Town of Mancos is growing in population, some capital is coming in and a real boom seemed just ahead. Excitement was running high and, from the beginning, the Mancos Times was fanning the flames.

Sixteen business establishments, small and large, were then operating, the George Bauer general merchandise, the Bauer Bank, the Lemmon Hotel, the Kelly & Jarrett Livery, E. P. and E. N. Lowe, drugs, and Dr. E. P. Lowe was the Doctor. J. P. Soens had a market and grocery and there were restaurants, a shoe shop, a blacksmith shop and some other lines of business on a small scale. A Methodist Church had been organized and Rev. John Moore was the pastor.

In May, 1893, School District No. 6 had 249 children of school age. There were two country schools, Weber and Wattles, and the town school.

At about this time the Geo. Bauer store was enlarged and a big additional stock of general merchandise was laid in.

On June 2, 1893, W. H. Kelly, better known as Muldoon Kelly, took over the Mancos Times. Mr. Kelly derived the cognomen from his association with Dave Day in the publication of the Solid Muldoon at Ouray. Kelly was a veteran politician and a tireless "booster" for the local mining industry.

Mancos has a concert band led by Charles Ashbaugh.

The Montezuma County Educational Association met in Mancos Dec. 27, 28 and 29, in the eighth session. Several educators were in attendance.

Burghart & Co. open a new merchandise business in Mancos early in 1894.

The Forest Park sawmill burns in May, 1894, W. J. Blatchford, owner.

In 1894 a post office is established on West Mancos called Golconda. Cap. Jackson is promoting a big mining enterprise and is putting in a stamp mill. Wm. P. Rush opens a store at Golconda.

The Hotel Ausburn (Mancos Hotel) first section, opens for business July 8, 1894.

A Kansas City party buys 2000 head of cattle from herd of John White, Jim Frank, Mrs. Chas. Frink, Major Sheets, and Mrs. M. E. Menefee.

During the year 1891 the Denver & Rio Grande Southern railroad was built through Montezuma County, and was at once a great factor for new progress and considerable new development in every part of the county.

Capt. Geo. Jackson shot and killed A. J. Sparks, on West Mancos, Sept. 23, 1894. Jackson was acquitted.

Jess Hallar, just released from jail, went down into McElmo Canon, waylays the Carpenter family, en route to Cortez to attend Hallar's trial for killing one of the Carpenter boys, Hallar shoots one of the women through the ear, one of the Carpenters through the shoulder and kills two horses in the team, in Sept. 1894. Hallar is shot in the thigh and has leg broken below knee. He thens gets on horse somehow and rides southward for the reservation. He is soon captured and put back in jail by Sheriff Sterl Thomas. When one of the Carpenters was shot by Hallar he fell over and dropped his gun in the wagon. A boy, 12 or 13 years old, grabbed the gun and emptied it at Hallar inflicting the leg wound.

In November, 1894, the Knights of Pythias lodge was organized in Mancos.

At this time the "Kelley Cure" was getting to be very popular with many people who needed something done for them. By ones and in groups they went to Denver for treatment. There were many eligibles all over the county, especially in Mancos, where the local paper encouraged the boys to take the "cure."

W. A. Hunter rents a large frame building near the bridge and puts in a large stock of merchandise.

At this time, in 1895, the old Union Hall is the most popular place for all social events and public meetings. It stood about where the Checkerboard Hall now stands.

There is still contention as to where the town shall be. The railroad company laid out a town west of the old depot, and was trying to build the town there, using an old cow barn for a depot. Geo. Bauer has laid out the present town of Mancos and gave away town lots to anyone who would build on them. He finally won.

Jackson Day is shot by Jesse Hallar late Dec., 1894, and died at Cortez a week later. Hallar was acquitted.

The Town of Mancos was incorporated Dec. 24, 1894. The first officers were Geo. Bauer, Mayor; Trustees, C. B. Kelly, D. H. Lemmon, L. M. Armstrong, H. Caldwell and H. N. Sprague. Much horse racing on the streets and much disorder about town hasten incorporation.

The Masons organize in Mancos July 5, 1895. Ed Caviness shoots and kills Byron McGeoch in a saloon in Mancos. Trouble over cattle. Caviness is captured, tried, convicted and sentenced to 15 years in penitentiary. Ed was the youngest of the Caviness boys.

The new railway station is finished and the trains begin stopping there Feb. 14, 1896.

The removal of the county seat from Cortez to Mancos is being agitated in 1896. Creates enmity and ill feeling which goes on and on.

The railroad builds shipping pens below depot to handle growing livestock business. The old townsite is now completely abandoned.

Cap. Jackson buys a five-stamp mill for East Mancos March 6, 1896. Much mining, in a small way, is going on.

A large Mancos trade is building up from the trading posts on the lower San Juan river. Large freight outfits load out from the Bauer store, often $1,000 worth of goods in a day.

In April, 1896, the Denver & Rio Grande railroad takes over the Rio Grande Southern. Hailed as good move, locally, and better freight and passenger service is expected. Soon after large sums of money is spent on the road between Durango and Mancos. New ties and new and heavier rails are put in.

At this time teamsters are competing with the railroad in the freight haul from Durango and several outfits are hauling freight at 40c a hundred. The railroad rate was reduced.

On May 25, 1896, Newton G. Field, pioneer Mancos physician, died. He was a veteran old-time doctor, went on horseback in all weather and brought his service to the home.

As an example of the social activities of the old days, in midwinter, 1897, six bob sleds loaded with Mancos people, took off for the W. J.

Blatchford ranch (until recently the Ernest Adams place) 8 miles out on the Dolores road, two hours of hard going over unbroken snow road, to give the Blatchfords a surprise. The young folks dance to good music, old folks play cards; elegant supper at 11:30. It was a hard, long journey, but hours of supreme enjoyment paid well for the trip; no better times in the present day.

All local sawmills are closed down on account of irregularities in securing timber. The trouble was fixed up and all mills were soon going again.

In April, 1897, good cattle all over the county were selling at an average of $45 per head.

Mancos has been having a four-months school term, and is the richest district in the county, while other districts are having nine months school terms. Mancos people demand longer and better school terms. There are 243 children of school age in the district, over one-third the enrollment of the entire county. Cortez has enrollment of 38, Dolores 113, Kroeger school 30. Lincoln Fellows is county superintendent and urges more interest and better schools.

In 1897 the Wetherill boys are making a regular business of exploring remote regions of this southwest country. Expeditions are frequently organized to Chaco Canon and other localities, prehistoric habitations being the main object of their search. Relics and remains of these departed people are collected and stored at the ranch in the Mancos valley; then shipped to wherever there is a market. Apparently the enterprise has developed into quite a business. Dr. Pruden and some other scientists are also interested in these expeditions.

In 1897 Hiebler & Hamblin are operating their lumber mill on a large scale and are turning out every kind of building product for a broad market. They operated over a period of several years.

One of the first efforts at upgrading range cattle and producing a better product for the market was made in 1897 when Andy Menefee bought a $200 registered Shorthorn bull in Durango to add to his range herd. In June of this year steers and heifers were selling at $22.50 per head as against $12.50 one year earlier.

School District No. 17, Menefee, is formed July 2, 1898.

Mancos schools are crowded and old Union Hall is taken over for school use.

In January, 1898, fire destroys large building on corner of Grand Ave. and Main Street, site of present postoffice. Loss $10,000.

In 1898 Mancos trade territory is extending far westward. Loads of wool, pelts and hides come in for shipment, and wagons load back with merchandise.

In summer of 1898 Guillet Bros. build large modern flour mill in northwest part of Mancos, 75 barrel capacity. Work is rushed so mill can handle present season's crop. Mill makes trial run Nov. 15 and much wheat is turned into flour.

Mancos gets several new residences this year and has two churches—Baptist and Methodist.

Weber people complete new hall in 1897, 30x60 feet, two story, cost $3,000, all work donated. There are 60 pupils in the Weber school; 254 in District No. 6.

In 1898 T. T. Kelly erects new frame building on North Main St. for residence and business.

Taylor Bros, double size of their store, south of river on Main St.

The Jas. H. Dean & Son business building on South Main St., is completed and a stock of general merchandise laid in.

The lumber industry continues to be important locally and large quantities of lumber are shipped. Coal mining is developing and coal is being shipped both to Telluride and Rico. They like the coal.

The first attempt at feeding cattle for the market was made in winter of 1898-99. Transportation defeated the effort.

Jan. 13, 1899 Dr. Hutchins gets a set of new lock boxes for the post-office.

The summer of 1898 was very dry, no feed on winter range. Severe winter follows and there is heavy loss of stock from starving.

As a building incentive Geo. Bauer offers to give a residence lot to anyone who will build a brick or stone residence on it to cost not less than $1,000.

The year 1899 was a big sawmill year and there is much building all over the county. Lumber is low in price. Montezuma Valley is making strides of progress. In Mancos many new buildings being erected, often ten or twelve at one time.

The Bauer Mercantile Co. start work on the big stone building on corner of Main St. and Grand Ave. Hore & Snyder are building up a big general merchandise business.

The Mancos Hotel is enlarged by adding 16 rooms and a large dining room, in 1900.

The Geo. Bauer Mercantile Co. is organized to take over business. The result—a strong firm of local people.

Pete Hiebler puts in new sawmill in spring of 1900, later to become Hiebler & Hallar.

The big sporting event of a several year period was the horse races planned to take place at Mancos April 10, 11, 12 and 13, 1900. When the big day arrived the weather was so stormy that the event was put off until the 13th, and then it was still very muddy. There were baseball games and three or four races every day, but the main event was the race between Silver Dick, owned by Curg Williams of Mancos, and Big Tom owned by Milton and Whitlock, well known race horse men. This race was for 500 yards and was run in 26 furious seconds, and the side bet was $1,000, Silver Dick winning by 18 inches according to the decision of the judges. Silver Dick, in a pre-race exercise, bruised one foot badly and the race came very near being called off at the last moment, but it was decided in favor of the race and, in spite of the foot injury, Silver Dick won much to the pleasure of a great number of spectators who knew the horse. These races had been advertised far and wide and, but for the stormy weather, there would have been a vast ingathering of people to see the races. As it was 500 people, undaunted by the storms, were in attendance. A special race track was built on the Curg Williams place, just south of town, which was kept up and used for several years. The owners of Big Tom said that was the first time he was ever defeated in a race.

At the school meeting in May, 1900, School District No. 6 decided to levy a 15 mill school tax and increase the school term from 6 months to 9 months.

Silver Dick won again over Big Tom at Ouray on July 4, 1900.

The census of 1900 gave Mancos a population of 328. The Mancos Times takes strong exceptions.

Mancos has another big fire in Jan., 1901. Two story building on east Grand Avenue, belonging to O. E. Noland, and occupied by Mancos Trading Co., burns with great loss. With small fire extinguishers and water carried from river nearby other buildings were saved.

H. V. Austurn becomes associate editor, with W. H. Kelly, on Mancos Times.

Recent heavy fire losses leads to serious consideration of a plan to have a town pressure water system for fire protection, domestic use, and to lower insurance rates.

There were terribly bad roads in spring of 1901 and all heavy hauling was temporarily abandoned; crisis create road problem. Better roads much discussed, but it is realized they can't make good roads of dirt.

Mancos was always interested in good horses, especially good race horses, so on May 9, 10, and 11, 1901, a big race meet was held. There were several big purses. Races were run on the Curg Williams track and a big crowd attended.

At the annual meeting in May, 1901, the school spirit was revived. The people voted for a 9 months school and 15 mill levy to pay for it.

On May 8, 1901, work starts on the new Bauer Bank building, just north of corner store. At this time the stone store building is greatly enlarged making it one of the best and finest business blocks in the southwest.

People of Mancos began to be alarmed at the rapid disappearence of the local forests, and want something done to protect their watersheds. This was the first note sounded on the conservation movement locally. Forest Service came soon after.

New Bank building is finished in July, 1901. Workmen start work on enlarging store building. Walls are finished in August. There is a basement 50x80 feet and 9 feet deep. Main floor is 75 by 125 feet, 12 foot ceiling.

Normal Institute, District 11, hold session at Mancos July 29 to Aug. 9. Forty teachers from five counties in attendance.

Winter of 1902 Geo. Bauer digs well 12 feet in diameter and 25 feet deep for water supply for his residence. Hard digging, but no water.

April 26, 1902, Geo. Blakely of Durango establishes the Mancos Tribune.

Mancos has $18,000 fire covered by $9,825 insurance. Two large buildings burned on east Grand Avenue, opposite Bauer Store.

Odd Fellows start their big hall on South Main St.

Bauer Mercantile erects windmill and 10,000 gallon tank at their new store building for fire protection.

Summer of 1902 very dry. Mancos river ceases to flow in August. Town wells go dry. Montezuma Valley and Indian reservation very dry. Water for stock very scarce. Navajo Indians hard hit. They are leaving the reservation and begging for food.

Weber people start the work of enlarging their reservoir, on Middle Mancos. Try to finish before winter.

In winter, 1901, the hungry Indians are killing cattle. Owners appeal to the government to feed the Indians.

In April, 1902, a movement is started to have Mancos build a pressure water system.

Odd Fellows complete their building on South Main Street in Oct., 1902. Noted building for years. Dismantled in 1956.

Andy Menefee, widely known Mancos pioneer, died Nov. 9, 1902, aged 72 years.

In the fall of 1902, good two year old steers shipped to market brought around $35 a head, and the stockmen thought they were doing well.

On March 3, 1903, Mancos people voted to install a gravity water system and voted a bond issue of $25,000 to pay for it.

In the fall, winter and spring of 1902-3, George Bauer built Bauer reservoir No. 2, the larger reservoir, with 120 acre surface area, 40 feet deep in deepest part. Was partly filled in 1903, and finished and filled in 1904.

The dairy industry got a new start in 1903 when C. E. Rentz started a dairy to operating in the Mancos Valley to furnish the town with fresh milk, cream and butter, Mr. Rentz being an experienced operator. This little business was significant in that it was the beginning of one of Montezuma County's basic industries.

On January 1, 1902, Mancos has twelve places of business, large and small, and two professional men. There are six sawmills with a daily output of 80,000 board feet of lumber; a box manufacturing plant and a flour mill. There are 127 pupils in the town school and there are two country schools, Wattles and Weber. Mining is active in a small way, and the Doyle Syndicate is building a new stamp mill and installing other machinery for processing their ore. A great deal of prospecting is going on.

The telephone system in Mancos is completed in 1904 and is in complete working order. It is a very convenient service and a big improvement for the town. The movement was started in May, 1903, and a telephone line was built from Durango to Mancos providing the first telephone service to come to the county.

On November 2, 1903, the Town Board published an ordinance to grant John C. Pinyan and H. E. Herr a franchise to build and operate an electric light plant in Mancos to furnish light, power and heat from sundown to midnight.

In early 1904 the telephone lines were extended to the Weber and Thompson Park communities.

On Feb. 5, 1904, electric lights in Mancos were turned on for the first time.

On Feb. 17, 1904, the Mancos Town Board held a meeting and decided unanimously to go ahead and build the proposed water works system for the town. Water rights have been secured thought to be ample for a town of 10,000 people. The source is pure mountain water, gravity flow, and a pressure of 100 to 125 pounds per square inch will be provided. System will be built under the supervision of an experienced engineer.

Charley Kelly and Will Miller bring in two very fine draft stallions weighing over 1700 pounds each to help improve the draft stock in the county, already well known for its draft and saddle stock.

The Mancos water system is about completed and on August 20, 1904, water was turned in for the first time to test out the system before covering the pipe lines.

Cattle buyer from Montrose, in Nov., 1904, was paying $18 for yearlings, $25 to $27 for two-year-olds and $32 for three-year-olds. The Ptolemy herd of extra good three-year-olds brought $36. Cattle were shipped to Denver.

After the water system was completed, and even before it was completed, many people were putting in pipe to convey the water into their residences. Exit the old muddy ditches with water running everywhere.

The dairy industry faced a new future in the Mancos valley in 1905 when, on March 17, a movement to build a Creamery in Mancos got under way. The $5000 needed was soon subscribed and 200 cows signed up. By March 24, the Creamery was assured, a building was started and it was planned to have the Creamery ready for operation in 60 days.

On May 15, 1905, the Mancos river was the highest it had been for many years. It floods the lower streets of town and the water was within six inches of the bridge. The Dolores river was also on a rampage.

214

May 25, 1905, the Summit reservoir is located and the Summit Company organized soon after.

The Mancos schools open Sept. 4, 1905, with John A. Sexon as principal. The schools have been thoroughly reorganized up to and including the 10th grade, the course of study standardized. School adds a class in art under Geo. Carr and a class in music under Miss Petherbridge.

The new Bauer Bank building, the present postoffice building, was completed and occupied in the fall of 1905. Roessler Bros., with general merchandise, occupies the ground floor. Office rooms on second floor.

The second rural mail route is established with J. R. Freeman as carrier, for the upper valley and Thompson Park. The first rural route was established Feb. 1, 1905, for the lower valley and Weber.

By December, 1905, the new Mancos Creamery is making 2000 pounds of butter a month. There is a waiting market for the full output.

In August, 1904, E. J. Freeman and Ira S. Freeman took over the ownership and management of the Mancos Times, and on Jan. 1, 1909, I. S. Freeman became sole owner and publisher. Under the new management the paper began to give more of its space to farming and livestock, the basic industries of the county.

At the annual school meeting in May, 1906, the patrons voted to add another teacher and another grade to the high school, bringing it to include the 11th grade. Supt. Sexon proves to be wonderfully efficient as executive, organizer and disciplinarian. Two new rooms will be built onto the high school building. Prof. Sexon is again chosen principal and Miss Margaret Guillet, assistant. There are now 6 town teachers and four country schools.

The Mancos Mercantile Co. comes into being in 1906, W. J. Miller and Will and John Roessler, incorporators.

The Mancos Coal Co. is organized and incorporated by O. S. Crenshaw and E. L. Davis. They buy the old Geo. Spencer mine and build a tramway from the mine to tipple on railway spur above town. They plan to install electric cutters, supply the local demand for coal and ship coal in car load lots to points north. They have enough coal to supply all demands for a century is the statement of their engineer. Plans carried through.

The art and practice of farming without irrigation was first demonstrated in Montezuma County by L. B. Burnham, of the Mancos valley. In 1905 Mr. Burnham cleared up a few acres of sage brush land in the Webber settlement, above the ditch, and started experimenting in raising crops without irrigation. In 1906 he had about 10 acres in wheat, beans, corn and potatoes, and two or three other crops. This planting did remarkably well and demonstrated beyond a doubt that "dry farming" could be both practical and profitable.

215

Dry farming, on a larger scale, had its beginning in the Mancos area when, in August, 1906, Will Stevenson filed a homestead out on the Mancos-Cortez road near the divide, and began clearing land for a dry farm. He cleared several acres and planted winter wheat and produced a crop the following year. This land has been producing dry land crops successfully to the present, always some crop, often a good one. These first demonstrations have grown into thousands of acres producing crops without irrigation.

A Farmers' Institute, held in different places in the county in September, 1906, gave new life and impetus to better farming, better dairying and growing better livestock.

Six sawmills are operating in the Mancos area beginning of 1907, harvesting nature's crop of timber.

In 1907, 1,040,000 acres of public land was added to the Montezuma National Forest which embraced large tracts of pine forests in Northern Montezuma County, Dolores County, San Miguel Co. and San Juan Co. This was nearly all in the summer grazing area of Montezuma County cattle and sheep men and meant an end of free grazing in this area.

The range cattlemen are taking definite steps to improve their herds and raise better cattle. Many registered bulls, mostly herefords, are being put on the range.

The Rio Grande Southern railroad is replacing 30 pound rails with 52 pound rails. Increasing traffic and heavier motive power compelled the change.

At the annual school election, Dr. Clark is reelected, Prof. Sexon is retained, another year is added to the high school to complete the high school course. Vote to build a school house for the Pinewood community.

In the spring of 1907 Bauer Lake water goes out to the farms for the first time, going down to several farms in the valley for late season use.

Bauer Mercantile builds a large warehouse and elevator on railway siding in April, 1907.

In November, 1907, Mancos livestock scored a triumph when Jim Frink wins first prize on a car of two-year-old cattle at Kansas City, first on a car of yearlings and Grand Sweepstakes on the best exhibit. The entire shipment brought top market prices. The cattle were photographed and widely publicised. The county that produces the best of everything can be pretty sure of its future.

Sadie Todd, Emma Longenbaugh, Jeanie Weston and Bill Roberts, of the Mancos High School, all pass teachers' examination with high honors. All step right into teaching positions after graduation in 1908.

Just before the draft horse passes from the scene it is interesting to note the horse as a factor. Fifty head from the Montezuma mill, were brought into the Mancos Valley to winter on the Harry French ranch, worth near $500 per span. Horses furnish a market for grain and hay summer and winter. Horses furnish draft power at mines, sawmills, on the road and on farms; yet how soon are we to get along without draft horses almost altogether.

Range cattlemen are not going out of business after all. In the grazing season of 1907 there were 7000 cattle on the National Forest between the La Plata river and Lost Canon, more than ever before, owing to regulated grazing. Cattlemen are becoming reconciled to Forest management as it eliminates strife and disputes over range and gives eevry man his own territory to graze and protects him in his rights.

In 1908 W. T. Bozman drove one of his new automobiles to Mancos from Cortez in 38 minutes. That was a record time for the trip at this time.

On April 1, 1908, a full carload of fruit trees was unloaded and inspected at Mancos and another car load was expected. The county was just turning to fruit as a crop.

The Bauer lakes furnish spawn for the fish hatchery at Durango. Spawn was taken for 120,000 fish and the lake is to get 25,000 of them. 96,000 fish were planted in the upper Dolores river.

R. C. Awkerman and J. C. Spargo buy the Cheesbro place of 320 acres for $8,000. They plant 40 acres to fruit trees.

As an example of the way new business is coming to Montezuma County, 31,721 pounds of merchandise was unloaded at the Mancos station April 18, 1908. Business at the depot for March showed a gain over March of a year ago of $1,810. The first week in April was greater than for the entire month last year. Business at the Dolores station showed a like increase.

May 21, 1908, the Mancos High School held its first graduation exercises—the first in the town and the first in the county. The program and display of school work was very good. The first class consisted of Jeanie Weston, Eva Rutherford, Sadie Todd, Ruth Wattles, Belle Roberts and James Rickner.

The Mancos Creamery, the only creamery in the San Juan Basin is flourishing, turning out a high class product for an unlimited market. This was the real start of the dairy industry in Montezuma County.

The Montezuma National Forest is created west of the La Plata Co. line. Ress Philips comes to Mancos as the first Forest supervisor.

At Mancos the vote on high school bonds for $10,000 carried 47 to 21.

The years of 1906 and 1907 were years of excessive rain in Montezuma Co. The water commissioner at Mancos was not called out these two years. 1908 was a dry year and there have been others since.

The south Summit country is connected to Mancos by a new road direct to town.

217

As a matter of local history Mancos voted out the saloons by a big majority in both precincts, in 1908.

The general election was lively and hotly contested in county and state. Vote in every precinct in the county showed an increase of 30 to 70 per cent over vote of two years previous.

Early winter storms in December, 1905, blocked all railroads and passes in the San Juan Basin and snowed in all mining camps. There are many slides, but only one death.

Jim Frink wins one first and one third on car lot shipments of two year old steers, at Western Stock Show in Denver in January, 1909, repeating his winnings at Kansas City the previous year.

Bonds have been sold and contracts let for erecting the new high school building in Mancos. New building is 36x82 feet, full basement and two stories above ground. Building material is stone. Later the people vote $5,000 additional bonds to finish and furnish the building.

Mancos Community is shocked by the shooting of O. E. Noland by M. M. Baker, itinerant piano tuner, July 17, 1909. Three shots were fired in rapid succession: one entering above left side of chest and one through left side of neck. One bullet entered left eye and ranged downward. The best medical skill was called and wounds were very nearly fatal. Patient was months recovering.

Rains of early September, 1909, wiped out bridges, roads and railroads; crop damage is widespread. Never in the history of this part of the state has the country undergone such a persistent bombardment from the elements, and continuous rains and recurring floods wrought disaster to every industry. Farms, mine, mills, the railroads and highways—all have had their share of loss. Since July 18 it has frequently rained two days and nights without ceasing. All streams were higher than they had ever been known.

The Summit Reservoir Co. is raising its large reservoir dams. Will raise the main dam several feet.

Geo. D. Woods and A. J. Ames built the opera house building, 34 by 70 feet, in 1909, basement and two stories above ground.

Potatoes were an important crop in Montezuma County in 1909. Good crop and good prices.

Stock is subscribed by Mancos people to start the First National Bank of Mancos with a capital stock of $50,000 Dec., 1909.

In 1909 it looked like the day of commercial lumbering was near an end, but with the coming of the crawler tractor and heavy truck, and gravel roads, all this was changed.

W. A. Burnham drove 55 fine porkers up from Montezuma Valley and sold them in Mancos making the porkers furnish their own transportation. Many cars of hogs have gone out from the big valley to the various markets.

The new high school building is finished, received and occupied. A full high school academic course is offered; also stenography, typewriting, bookkeeping, penmanship, musical training, and a course in domestic science.

J. H. Hammond brought in 15 Holstein cattle, all pure bred but three. They are for various Webber people. They are the first of this breed to be brought in and should be valuable as foundation stock in the local dairy industry.

The Mancos Creamery club now has a membership of 50 and an active organization starting the new year 1910.

Wool growers of the county organized and incorporated the Montezuma County Woolgrowers Association with office and warehouse in Mancos. They will cooperate with the National Association.

John Sponsel, "Duke of Oats" of Thompson Park, clears up $12,000 on his ranch in 1909, from livestock and grain. The family did practically all the work.

David Swickheimer is clearing acres and acres of land under the Summit reservoir, being a one-fourth owner in the system.

R. G. Allum brought in 55 head of pure bred Shropshire sheep and 10 head of Jersey cows, 7 of them purebred, Dec. 12, 1909. The shipment was especially fine for the locality as many people came to Mr. Allum for breeding stock.

The First National Bank of Mancos opened for business March 1, 1910. Capital $50,000. They will erect a special bank building soon.

March 1, 1910, the new opera house building is completed and being occupied. A picture theater is opened and the big hall was long a favorite for its hardwood dancing floor.

The grazing capacity of the Montezuma National Forest is now 36,-000 head for horses and cattle and 25,000 head of sheep. Almost the entire grazing capacity of the Forest has been applied for.

Mancos Woolgrowers cast their lot with the Montezuma County Woolgrowers and build a warehouse by the railroad house track 44x76 feet and 12 feet walls.

The Gibson Lumber Co., operating in Mancos, opens a lumber yard in Cortez with a stock of 100,000 board feet of lumber.

Spring of 1910, forty-three carloads of young cattle, mostly black Angus, from Texas, passed through Mancos May 20 for Dolores to be put on the summer range for grass fattening. Messrs. Johnson, Dunlap and Tremble were the owners.

June 10, the telephone to lower Mancos valley is completed and 14 phones installed in ranch homes. Work starts on line to upper Valley and to Thompson Park.

P. B. McAtee, general agent for the Rio Grande Southern, made a special trip to the lower San Juan river to get the facts about the oil fields. He made a thorough investigation and reports that comparatively little development work has been done to date, mostly in one small field. Now the drilling rigs are spreading out over a larger territory and soon much more will be known. Nearly all wells are shallow and nearly all have a light flow of high grade oil. Many light rigs are on the ground.

Power machinery started coming into use in the Mancos area in 1910. Steam power is being used to operate some land clearing equipment.

The shipping pens at Mancos are being greatly enlarged in summer of 1910 to handle the increased business at this point.

Webber reservoir and the upper Bauer reservoir are being enlarged. More water needed for late irrigation.

Tom Halls, in the Webber community, harvested a crop of 60 bushels of wheat per acre.

Ern Guillet shipped in a fine jack from Missouri, first and best ever brought into the county. First cost $1,000; express $246. He goes to Guillet ranch down in the big valley. Ern plans to raise mules.

In August, 1910, the Times-Tribune editor visits East Mancos mines and prospects. Finds the Doyle mine a beehive of activity, 35 men at work; more to be put on soon. Stamp mill pounding steadily; other machinery going, a new mess hall is being built and many tons of ore being mined daily. Many thousand tons blocked out; millions of tons in evidence.

Fall of 1910 many cattle are being moved to the market, 500 to 600 head at a time, and some very high quality stuff is being shipped. Also many cars of sheep are being moved.

Racing to the front again. At the Durango Fair, Jess Hallar's Fancion won two half-mile races and one three-eighths mile. Delmar won one five-eighths mile race and one three-fourths mile race and Fancion won second place in both of them. Jennie F took third in three one-half mile races and in one three-fourths mile race.

Ten teams loaded out for Bluff week of Oct. 10, with merchandise for Bluff and the oil field.

In the fall of 1910 sports came to the front in the Mancos schools, pointing to a lively sports organization in all the county's leading schools. Sports awaken school loyalty and a lively school spirit, soon to become evident in every part of the county. Good school work goes with good, clean sports.

The new home of the First National Bank of Mancos is finished and occupied in October, 1910.

At the election in 1910 the people voted in the initiative and referendum law. Saloons were voted out in the upper Mancos precinct and in the Cortez precinct.

There was a very heavy shipment of livestock in 1910. The old winter range was passing, or no longer available and some of the stockmen were not satisfied with government regulations on grazing lands in the Forests. It was felt by some stockmen that the livestock industry was passing from the local scene. But it was only changing. Most of the old winter range was indeed gone, but good producing farms were still there with great feed producing capacity. The market for horse feed was passing and the feed must be consumed so new plans began to come into use. Trucks and tractors and cars were coming into use so the draft horse and the driving horse were soon to go, and the whole picture began to change. Gradually the old way passed but a new and better way was ushered in. No more starving of cattle and sheep through the winter. Dairy farming and livestock farming was the new order of things.

The new opera house at Mancos has a new motion picture show, the first in the county, January 1, 1911. It is popular entertainment and very good of its kind, and admittance was only 10c. The children were especially pleased.

One thing that made history in the county in 1911 was the Mancos High School basketball team, both girls and boys. The boys won the western slope championship by defeating the Mt. Lincoln team of the Grand Valley on its home floor. The Mount Lincoln team had never before been defeated. Local boys that played on the team were Bert Halls, Arthur Ogle, Ira Kelly, Charles Rash and Byron Brown. Later the boys went on a trip and played exhibition games.

The heavy cattle shipment in the fall made a shortage for the range in the spring. Sheep were bought on the outside and drove or shipped in.

In the spring of 1911—Mancos was working for a sugar factory and Cortez for a broom factory. Neither materialized.

The Crystal Creek Water Co. is organized and incorporated to bring water down from Crystal Creek for several new farms on Grand View Mesa. Some good farms resulted.

The census of 1910 gave Mancos a population of 569 and Cortez 567. The records at Cortez showed Mancos had a population of 687 and Cortez 637.

The woolgrowers of the county who stored their wool in the new warehouse at Mancos sold 190,000 pounds in late May, 1911. The price was somewhat lower than the growers expected to get.

Asback and Miller are erecting a cement building on east Grand Avenue, 1911, 75 feet front, 39 feet deep, four rooms, the west room of which became the new home of the Mancos Times-Tribune.

After a season of unprecedented rainfall, a number of minor floods and one major one, the wet season was climaxed by a general downpour on the evening and night of Oct. 6, 1911, resulting in the greatest flood in this southwest section since it has been known to the white man. The rain was a steady downpour and was general all over the San Juan Basin and in the San Luis Valley. The rivers were still on a rampage from previous rains and when the general deluge came they rose to the highest flood stage ever known, dealing destruction to public and private property. The rivers that became raging torrents were the San Miguel, the Dolores, Mancos, La Plata, Animas,

Pine, Piedra, San Juan, Navaho, Chama, and the Rio Grande. All these rivers were covering the flood plane, cutting new channels, taking bridges and washing out railroads and highways, miles and miles of them. The water swept through towns, fields and orchards, and piled debris and driftwood into every nook and corner. Every town on the above named rivers suffered some damage and had from 3 to 20 houses destroyed or damaged. In several instances families lost everything they had and barely escaped with their lives. Some six or seven deaths by drowning were reported.

The railroad had the heaviest single loss. Between Dolores and Rico fully half the track and roadbed was damaged or totally wrecked, and cost almost as much to rebuild as it cost in the first building. The town of Dolores was flooded in its lower areas by from one to five feet of water, and the flood area strewn with wreckage. Between Dolores and Durango there was not so much damage and repairs were soon made. Between Durango and Silverton it was stated that not ten miles of good track and road bed were left. Eastward from Durango one could hardly imagine the havoc wrought, especially where the railroad followed the river. It was reported that ten miles of track in one place was entirely gone. It was more than two weeks before a single train was run over this line into Durango from the east. Mail and passenger traffic was kept moving by staging over the washed out sections. Many highway and wagon road bridges were damaged or taken out entirely causing the counties and the state great expense to rebuild and repair.

From 1903 to 1911 the acreage in cultivation in Mancos Valley doubled, which shows the change taking place. There was an equal growth in every part of the county.

The last available homestead land south of the Cortez highway, toward Mesa Verde, was taken in November, 1911. These dry farmers have had some very successful years and they are very sure dry farming is a winner and is here to stay. The vast territory west and northwest of Montezuma Valley is being rapidly taken up.

The Dolores-San Juan Telephone Co. finally made connection with the Mancos switchboard Nov. 18, 1911. This gives Mancos direct telephone connection with Dolores and connection through Dolores with Lebanon, Arriola, in this county and with Monticello, Grayson and Bluff in Utah, and with a great number of ranches along the lines.

On November 18, 1911, the railroads have been repaired and cattle and sheep start moving to the market, a large shipment from Mancos moving that day, and a full train load of sheep move from Hesperus the next day. Many cattle and sheep were taken to the winter range and kept over.

On January 7, 1912, a train got through to Telluride for the first time since the big flood Oct. 5, 1911, three months and 2 days.

The Big Four-San Juan Co. has six teams at Mancos for casing in January, 1912. They will start drilling again.

John Roessler withdraws from the Mancos Mercantile Co. Jan. 1, takes over farm machinery, erects large warehouse near depot and starts a long and successful business career.

Feb. 16, 1912, John Sponsel states that last year he raised 16,000 bushels of oats on his Thompson Park farm, all harvested and threshed with his own machinery and practically all labor done by his own family. Big farm, big family, big yields.

In March, 1912, the Mancos postoffice was moved to a new and specially built building on North Main St., all new furniture and fixtures in place; all steel and mahogany finished. There are 180 combination lock boxes and 100 call boxes for the general delivery and room for rural mail carriers.

A movement gets under way at Mancos for purebred and better bred cattle for local ranch and range. Herefords are favored. The movement continued through the following years. Almost since this beginning only purebred bulls are allowed on the range.

Cord Bowen brings in from Kansas 91 head of purebred Hereford cattle, all registered, for his ranch in the Mancos valley. This is the start of a general movement to whitefaces and better cattle.

The county has a wool shipment, 1912 of 44 car loads—22 shipped from Dolores and 22 from Mancos.

Mancos has two new bridges: one, a very good one built of cement, across the river on Main St., built and paid for by the town, and one, a steel bridge, across the river on Spruce Street.

By October, 1912 cars were getting so plentiful that Mancos had to pass an ordinance regulating the use of cars on the streets.

In 1912 there was three feet of snow in the high mountains in early October. All cattle and sheep had to be brought down early and many sheep came very near being snowed in before they could be gotten out.

Mancos was incorporated in 1894 with a population of 350. By 1912 the population had grown to 700, with 150 residences. All lines of business are well represented and the town is doing a thriving business.

Cortez and Dolores are slightly behind Mancos in development, but are making steady progress and are destined to equal Mancos in every way, and Cortez, eventually, to vastly surpass either of the other two towns. The railroad is soon to be no factor at all in the growth of the various communities, and good roads, cars and trucks finally supplant it altogether and put a new phase on all local development. All aspects of pioneer life are rapidly passing, social disorders are gone and orderly progress characterizes every community in the county.

The roads froze hard in early December, 1912, and the auto owners put on their chains and skipped over the roads almost as lively as in midsummer.

On Dec. 2, 1912, a fire broke out in the roof of the new high school building in Mancos and before it could be brought under control the woodwork of the entire upper story was consumed leaving only the walls standing. The fire was caused by a defect in the air heating system. The Baptist Church was rented and classes went on as usual and repairs on the damaged school building were made at once.

The cattle industry is in a transition period and range cattlemen are selling short in the fall and go into Utah and New Mexico, buy herds of cattle and bring them in to summer on the National Forest range. Then ship again in the fall.

H. M. Davis buys the Creamery at Mancos, in late 1912, and it becomes strictly a private business. The business, as a cooperative, was never well supported and never prospered.

On March 18, 1913, Supervisor Shaw, of the San Juan Forest, received 45 head of elk, shipped in from the Jackson Hole country in Wyoming, to be turned loose on the forest. As it was early they were fed hay for a while. Then turned loose on the upper Formosa. This was the beginning of the elk population in the San Juan Basin, and all elk in the Basin are descendants from this herd. They were protected for years and now they are numbered by the thousands, and there is an open season on elk every fall. There is lots of sport in the hunting and much fine meat is taken.

Halls Bros. buy and bring in 15 head of purebred Jersey cattle, of a high producing strain, for the ranch three miles south of Mancos. The trend toward dairying is steadily gaining ground. It makes a concentrated product that can be shipped to the market even though transportation costs are high.

In the spring of 1913 Frink and Stephens bring in 15 head of purebred Hereford bulls. They have bought 800 head of cattle out in Utah and the Fred Taylor ranch of 850 acres, near Mancos; later they buy 160 acres more from Fred Armstrong, on Mesa Verde and 100 head of cattle with range rights on Mesa Verde. They also buy 300 head of cattle from Hepworth brothers. The business is being established on a firm broad basis.

In the spring of 1913, twenty-five automobile owners of the county met with the County Commissioners. They want to cooperate for good roads.

The matter of a railroad connection to the south will not down. Emil Stein makes an effort to finance a railroad to Gallup. He gets some whole-hearted support. It seems that anyone with a railroad scheme can get support. Mancos failed to come through; the movement failed.

In May, 1913, Harry French and John Stavely put in the first garage in Mancos, on North Main St., and Mr. Stavely brought in three Ford cars from Denver by way of Gunnison, Montrose and Dolores, a little over 600 miles. They made the trip in five days.

The first priest to be assigned to the Catholic Church in Mancos came down from Telluride to take charge of the work July 6, 1913. Local Catholic people had bought the old Baptist Church, fixed it up and built a rectory, with help from the church. Rev. Father Brunner was the first priest.

In July, 1913, work started on what had been designated as a state highway passing through Mancos to Cortez. The work was started at the county line on the east and was to be built through to Cortez, or as far as the $18,000 in state and county funds available would build it. A first class road was the aim, yet it was only a dirt road. Even gravel surfacing had not yet appeared on the highways.

In October, 1913, Al Puett shipped out for Kansas City 15 cars of four-year-old steers, and very fine ones at that. They believed in growing them big in those days.

In December, 1914, The Miller Hardware Co., of Mancos, shipped 10,000 pounds of oats by parcel post to Keam's Canon, Arizona. Each 50 lb. bag cost 54 cents for transport. They traveled 600 miles to get 130 miles by direct line. The shippers expect to move a lot more oats by this means of transportation.

Boys and girls clubs are organized in the schools in 1914. The boys raise potatoes, corn and livestock and the girls learn housework, cooking and sewing.

In September, 1914, the Bauer Bank and the First National Bank of Mancos consolidate, continuing the business in the name of the First National Bank.

Mr. and Mrs. Will Roessler announce their purpose to open a large stock of dry goods and shoes in the Bauer Bank Block. The Miller Hardware Co. is formed by W. J. Miller and Walter Wallace and take over the hardware department of the Mancos Mercantile Co. Mr. and Mrs. Roessler take the dry goods.

During the shipping season of 1914 Mancos shipped 160 cars of cattle, 2 or 3 cars of horses, and 140 cars of sheep, and shipped in 3 cars of cattle and 7 cars of sheep. Shipping was light this year, not nearly so large as in some former years. Herds had been reduced by heavy shipments 2 or 3 years previous. Loss of winter range caused most heavy shipments, but many stock were shipped or driven in to restock the range each year. Dolores stockmen suffered the same experience. They also shipped heavily and had to bring in cattle to restock their summer range.

A new rural mail route for the upper Mancos Valley, Thompson Park and Cherry Creek was allowed and scheduled to start June 16, 1915. The mail is to go three times a week and the route is 26.5 miles long.

C. G. Gawthrop brings in 13 head of purebred Shorthorn cattle, summer 1915. This was the beginning of a much larger herd, but just at this time rangemen were turning to Hereford cattle and Shorthorns were not so popular as they otherwise would have been.

On July 31, 1915, 470 head of purebred Hereford cattle, including 75 fine bulls were unloaded at Mancos and 140 head of the same kind of cattle were unloaded a week later. All were brought in by the government and taken down to the Ute reservation and distributed among the Indians.

When school opened in September, 1915, the Webber school was discontinued and a bus put on to bring all the children to the town schools. This was the first school bus in the county and the first experience at transporting rural children to town schools.

The winter of 1915 and 1916 was one of deep snows. In January snow was four feet deep on the level in Thompson Park and five feet on the mesa beyond Lost Canon. There were days and days of railroad blockade and all wagon roads were snowed in.

In May, 1916, the Mancos High School is accredited near the top of the list for thoroughness and high standard, merit and high standing.

Rural Free Delivery No. 3, for Mancos, was allowed and was started March 1, 1917, furnishing mail service for people northwest of town and out in the Summit reservoir country.

The Mancos Farm Loan Association was formed in the Mancos Valley in spring of 1917, and was soon doing business, and it has been doing business ever since with notable success and very little loss.

A timber survey, completed in 1917, estimates that there is 300,-000,000 board feet of mature timber in Dolores and Montezuma counties. It seems to indicate that the country is fortified against a timber shortage for a long time to come.

In 1917, some cattle and sheep were turned back on the range because no freight cars were available for making shipments. The railroads are overburdened with freight all over the country, owing to world war conditions.

The women are being called into every kind of work—farming, driving cars and trucks, everything they can do.

Shipping records at Mancos for 1916: 113 cars of cattle, 93 of sheep, 3 of hogs, 1 of horses. In 1917: 130 cars of cattle, 156 of sheep, 11 cars of hogs and 3 of horses. Stock shipments from Dolores are somewhat heavier than usual.

There seems to be plenty of money locally, with which to do business. The First National Bank of Mancos passed the half million mark in total resources. The Cortez and Dolores banks are just under the half million mark.

A report from the office of the County Assessor showed that the county had, in 1917, 156 automobiles, 4,000 horses, 205 mules, 17,746 cattle, 41,819 sheep and 4,756 swine.

G. P. Newsom, of Fort Collins, has been appointed to the position of County Agent, February, 1918, to give all his time to this county.

E. D. Smith, who has been serving in two counties is retained in La Plata County to give all his attention to the work there.

On March 22, 1917, the first crawler type of farm tractors to be brought into the county were unloaded at Mancos and taken to Cortez. They were the small type for farm use.

The war is beginning to exact its demands and a cornbread diet is coming into prominence. We must divide our wheat with our allies. We sacrificed nothing when we had to eat cornbread. America built her first colonies on cornbread, conquered the wilderness and won our freedom. Should we do less to defend it? says the Mancos Times-Tribune.

Gus Bircher of the Mancos Valley and R. E. Walker of Summit Ridge, each get a new farm tractor, the first locally. They pull two plows well down in the ground and turn six acres a day on one and one-half gallon of gas per acre. This is April 8, 1918, and the beginning of a new era in farming.

During the war pinto beans, for the first time came into general consumer use. The government bought all it could get at 8 cents a pound—twice the peace time price. They are recognized as a very valuable article of diet.

Mancos goes "over the top" in buying Liberty Bonds April 26, other parts of the county close behind, and all go over.

Note—During the war the phrase "over the top" was adapted to describe the action of the boys in the trenches when they climbed out of the trenches and over the protecting barricades to make a charge on the enemy. At home the same phrase was adopted to describe the successful culmination of any drive put on for any purpose. When any purpose was accomplished in full it was said to have "gone over the top." It had a special appeal.

Second contingent of second draft call leave April 26; 6 in number.

The quota of the county for the Bond Drive was $117,300, and was far oversubscribed.

On May 20 another contingent of boys left for training camp—fifteen in number, the county's quota. On May 27, 4 more boys leave for camp.

All young men becoming 21 years old since June 5, 1917, are ordered to register June 5, 1918.

June 24 came another call for draftees for the army and 18 men leave for training camp.

Geo. L. Jowers puts in a small flour mill at Mancos, early August, to help handle wheat crop.

An old landmark of early days passed when F. H. Wagner bought the old log building on North Main Street, in Mancos; had it torn down and moved away. Had been standing 35 years, or since 1883.

About Oct. 1st, 1918, the flu epidemic got its start in Mancos, a few cases are recorded—two of them severe. School and all public places closed temporarily.

In October war casualties for Mancos reports: Lee Halls wounded, Joseph Sponsel died in camp, Wm. Puett died of the flu, Fay Sheek died of the flu.

Sergeant A. R. Brown writes from France that the battleline is still moving forward, and it looks like the war will soon be over.

Week of November 5th, Mancos recorded seven deaths from flu.

Published statement of First National Bank of Mancos shows total assets of $544,571.96. Other banks of county made equally as good a showing.

The death rate from flu is two and one-half to four times the normal rate in cities; somewhat less in the country. Like other infectious diseases once it takes hold it must run its course. It was the worst contagion ever to hit the country. There has been a very high death rate among the Indians, especially the Navajos, their superstitious beliefs making it very hard to do anything to help them. Toward the last of December the epidemic is gradually receding. Mancos schools opened December 30, under strict medical supervision.

Week of April 25 Mancos High School is designated as one of the high schools of the state to be placed under the Smith-Hughes Act. H. M. Griffith of Fort Collins is chosen as first teacher. This is the first and only Smith-Hughes school in the county. The Smith-Hughes Act provides for vocational training in the public school, the state and government paying half and the school district paying half. The school district choses the vocation to be taught. The local board chose agriculture. The Smith-Hughes Act is now operating in Cortez.

John Roessler reports selling, in spring of 1919, over 12,000 pounds of alfalfa seed, and more orders coming. The trend is back to hay and livestock after a few years of growing grain.

Mancos gets donation of park area from Tony Boyle. Mancos accepts, and names the plot Boyle Park. There is a little over 6 acres, and title passes June 25, 1919.

On June 28, 1919, the Mancos Cattlegrowers Association vote to use only registered bulls on the range—Hereford and Shorthorn breed chosen. First organized step in this direction in the county. It took two or three years to put this into effect owing to scarcity of registered bulls and the hardship it worked on some small herd owners, but the rule was put into full force and effect and has been enforced through the years. For years nothing but high class cattle have come off the range and gone to market.

Dr. J. R. Trotter buys the old George Bauer residence on North Main Street, and converts it into a home and a hospital. Nine rooms were equipped for hospital use and trained nurses employed.

A Waterloo tractor and silage cutter come to the Mancos Valley

228

in 1919. Halls Bros. will do power farming—discing, seeding and harrowing in one operation.

In 1919 plans were gotten under way to rebuild the Durango-Mancos road, the improvements to embrace lower grades, broadening of short curves, good bridges and culverts, then gravel or crushed rock surfacing. There is available $40,000 to start the work. This will be the first real highway work to be done in the Basin. Survey work is being done late in 1919.

The agricultural class, organized in the Mancos school under the Smith-Hughes Act, was the largest west of the Mississippi river, according to L. F. Gary, superintendent of agricultural education in this state. There were 46 in the class and their teacher was Mr. Granovsky, probably the most successful teacher of agriculture that ever taught in the Mancos Schools.

The big stock of merchandise of the Bauer Mercantile Co. at Mancos has been closed out and the firm goes out of business. At the start of the sale there was a $40,000 stock. Business was started in 1881, by George Bauer and had successful career extending over about 40 years.

Jesse Bailey, of Monticello, raises 111.38 bushels of oats per acre on 5 acres and wins Farm Journal gold medal and first prize of $1,000 for the largest per acre crop of oats raised in the country without irrigation. This record was a big boost for that dry farming country where so many people are going at this time to make their homes.

In the spring of 1920 potatoes were bringing $4.15 a hundred loaded on the cars at Mancos.

The movement for real surfaced roads gets started on the Durango-Mancos road in 1920. There was $40,000 for putting the road bed in shape and getting the gravel work started.

In the fall of 1920 Mancos has a community fair. There was extensive and careful preparations and a good fair well supported. It starts with the boys Pig Club. Prof. Granovsky was the main moving spirit and C. G. Gawthrop an able assistant. Nearly 1000 entries were made. The exhibit was a surprise to all—literally a revelation to local people.

The Mid-West Oil Co., a subsidiary of Standard Oil, drills for oil in Section 23, Twp. 36 North, Range 18 West, three miles north of McElmo just out of Sand Creek. They bring in standard machinery, drill down four or five thousand feet, with many difficulties, and finally failure. They had lease of 23,000 acres.

As late as 1921 no cars went over the road between Mancos and Durango during the winter months. Usually the road was not passable until the last of April. No effort was made to grade the snow from the road, but if horse-drawn vehicles were kept on the road from day to day it was passable for teams with wagons or sleds.

Work starts on the Durango-Mancos highway April 20, 1921.

The matter of a railroad to the South keeps bobbing up to plague

229

the people, raising new hopes only to disappoint them. In 1921 the land owners of the Basin were persuaded to put up a part of their land upon which to finance a railroad, Los Angeles people directing the plan. Weeks of work and much money was put into the effort, many thousand acres of land was signed up. Then it was up to the Los Angeles people to get the money. Weeks and months passed. Very encouraging reports were made from time to time. Finally the Los Angeles people acknowledged failure, the effort was dropped and soon forgotten.

W. H. Olin, general agricultural agent for the Denver & Rio Grande R.R. is an active worker, a fine leader, and very able, and his enthusiasm is "catching." He often brings other leaders, praises the good work farmers are doing and teaches them how to improve stock and farming methods.

About 10 inches of snow fell on the La Plata peaks July 3, 1921, and near frost night of July 4 in the high valleys. It rained in the valley July 3 while it was snowing in the mountains.

The season of 1921 Summit Ridge has the best crop in its history—hay and grain. The new intake ditch, though very expensive, is paying off with abundant water for all purposes. The Crystal Creek Water Co. is also making progress. The new valve is in place in the reservoir and it is furnishing water for the present season.

The market for wool in 1921 is almost nonexistent. County Agent Clark has contacted four mills that will take wool from producers, make it up into shirts, blankets, and other garments, yarns and wool bats for comforts, etc. They will wash, scour, card and spin the wool into quality stuff that is very expensive when purchased in the usual way. A number of wool growers are taking advantage of this to get rid of some of their wool.

Mancos cattlemen finally got around to putting into complete effect their plan to allow only purebred Hereford and Shorthorn bulls on the range. All range users began at once to make arrangements to get the bulls.

The amount of the appropriation for Montezuma National Forest, for fiscal year beginning July 1, 1922, is $51,000: regular appropriation $21,000; for new road work and trails, $30,000 is made available. The main road work will be on the Dolores-Norwood road and the West Mancos river road. On the Dolores-Norwood road Montezuma County puts in $10,000, San Miguel County $3,000. Many trails and minor roads to receive attention. This is only the beginning state the Forest officials. Every part of the forest will be made accessible eventually.

The first effort to nurse young fish in ponds was tried out on the Welborn place. A pond 110 feet long, 50 feet wide and 6 feet deep, easily filled and drained, and above the high water line, is being used. The plan is to turn out two crops of 200,000 each year.

Plans for the building of an addition to the high school building in Mancos are going forward. C. B. Neeley has contract for cement foundation, P. F. Cummings for the rock work and L. Ashback for the woodwork and finishing.

Wool crop in May, 1922, sold for 23 to 30 cents indicating that the depression for Montezuma County was about over.

The old plains West repeated itself June 1, 1922, when nine prairie schooners passed through Mancos en route to the dry farming country. This is the exact way they settled the semi-dry country of western Kansas and Oklahoma.

The three county road districts start work with about 50 men on the Dolores-Norwood road June 12, 1922.

County Agent G. E. Clark resigns. No one hired to take his place. No interest on part of farmers.

Note—In the summer of 1876 came Charley Frink, Major Sheets, Pat O'Donnell, R. T. McGrew and Louis Paquin from Rio Grande County, in the San Luis Valley, with 1000 cattle and turned them loose in the Mancos Valley. It was the first of many large herds to follow.

In October, 1922, the Woody Albion community and the Oak View community put in rural telephones, privately owned lines.

Mrs. Hiram McEwen, of Mancos, early in November, 1922, had what was believed to be the first radio receiving set to come into Montezuma County. Many others were soon to follow.

In late November, 1922, there were 1,500 head of cattle (90 car loads) and several car loads of sheep and hogs waiting at Mancos for shipment. Several cars of sheep and hogs are waiting on ranches and consuming lots of feed that will be badly needed on the ranches. Some cattle from New Mexico points are being driven to Gallup. Lack of transportation at the right time this year, and in most years, occasion a great loss to the stockmen, and before they can recover from one loss they usually have to take another one.

The first gravel surfaced road in Montezuma County was a stretch on south Main Street, in Mancos, and the Webber road from town on out to the foot of Cemetery Hill. This road was gravel surfaced as an experiment and all work was donated, the county furnishing the rock crusher. The road bed was prepared in advance and the best possible job of gravel surfacing was done to see if a road could be made that would hold up the traffic under all weather conditions. This was spring of 1923.

The spring of 1923 saw considerable road work started that was of a permanent nature. Gravel surfacing had been adopted as the best and most lasting way to build permanent all-weather roads and to that end two rock crushers had been bought, the smaller one assigned to the Mancos district and the larger to the Cortez and Dolores part of the county. The road fund was larger from year to year due to revenue from car and truck licenses and there was more assistance from state and government. The Town of Mancos started graveling its streets on South Main St. The county continued the work started on the road south to the Webber community, and the contractors began in early spring to rebuild and gravel surface the five mile stretch of road west from Mancos on the Mancos-Cortez road, recently designated a state highway. The large crusher was set up on Dolores river and started crushing rock for Montezuma County roads most used and most needing this kind of improvement. Funds for this work was made available by the county commissioners at meeting April 2, 1923. The hard river rock that resists wear is recommended by state road men.

In March, 1923, a rural telephone line was built northward from Mancos into the Oak View and Pinewood communities. Private lines and there are eight new phones all in ranch homes.

Tests seem to indicate that the gravel surfaced road locally stand up under our winter condition under heaviest traffic. There was some doubt, some hesitation, until the test came. It is now felt that roads can be gravel surfaced with assurance that they will serve and last.

Another trial for oil is to be made at Mancos. Will Husbands and Nate Stein of Durango organize the Mancos Oil & Gas Syndicate, capital stock $30,000, local people to raise $10,000, to bring in rig and put down a well. Organization perfected week later, June 5, 1925.

Week of July 7, 1925, the Continental Oil Co. finished installing tanks for a bulk storage station for gas, oil and coal oil, later diesel oil, at Mancos, the first tank having a capacity of 18,000 gallons. More capacity will be added as needed. It is important as the first bulk storage station in the county, but others were soon to follow.

The first Federal Farm Loan Association in the county, was perfected for the Mancos Valley in late July, 1923. The new organization does business at once.

Editorial in the Mancos Times-Tribune: The harder the times, the more disadvantageous the conditions, the harder must one work and the better must one plan to achieve success. The same is true of the community, and the community that plays the quitter because conditions aren't just right, because there are difficulties to overcome isn't worthy of much. There is no glory in an easily won victory, no credit for success achieved under conditions that are all favorable. The glory of life is to win in the struggle, to overcome the difficulty, to succeed in spite of opposition. The hard task is the maker of men.

Another three-mile gravel surfacing contract let in the Durango-Mancos road to connect over Fort Lewis Mesa up to Hesperus, was let summer of 1923. Soon there will be a gravel surfaced road all the way through.

At the Community Health Conference, held at the Mancos School Auditorium, Oct. 2, 1923, 136 children and babies were given a thorough going over, checking all defects, by the number of doctors and nurses present for this work. The conference was a success in every way and local people were greatly pleased that so much was done for the children and their future. During the week the same kind of conferences were held at Cortez and Dolores with much interest and good results. It was felt that valuable information was obtained in the interest of the children's health and much good was done. This was but one of the many efforts being made along this line from year to year and the work was calculated to mean much toward the good health of the future citizens of the county.

During the open season for deer hunting in October, 1923, Mancos hunters killed only three deer although a number of hunters were out in the mountains to collect some game.

Joseph Edward Wheeler had a remarkable family. The two wives were sisters—Lucy A. Bigham and Harriet I. Bigham. There were 13 children by one wife and 15 by the other, and there were 13 girls and 15 boys.

An experiment at scraping the snow off the road between Mancos and Cortez after each storm, in the winter of 1923-24, proved the value of the practice. It was found that it greatly improved the road, and that the road was much better after the snow went away. Cars made the trip between Mancos and Cortez frequently and with ease and safety. This was a new experience and showed a lot of progress in ways of taking care of the roads in winter.

Two more nursery ponds for fish are selected on West Mancos, the first one proving a success. The Game & Fish department will bear half the expense.

J. O. Gill came into the community July 1, 1924, and prepares to drill for oil. He got local support, as nearly everyone does who comes with a proposition, and work on building derrick was started mid July.

There is a good grain crop in the county and dealers report much more binding twine than ever before is being used. Albert Roessler reports 60 bushels of wheat per acre. He has been on his ranch nine years, has had a better crop every year, and this year the best ever. This is real farming the local paper comments.

Two large McCormick-Deering tractors and two clover hullers were purchased locally to handle the alfalfa seed crop in the county. This is a new cash crop for the farmers. The first crop was fair to good.

The oil well was started August 30, 1924. Busy drilling out on the Bob Wilson place, 9 miles northwest of town. This is the first test for oil on the Mancos structure.

Another good farm, the W. A. Bay place, reported good yields: 98.5 bushels of oats per acre off of 8 acres, 40 lbs. per bushel; 6 acres of Marquis wheat yields 50 bushels per acre, the result of good farming for some years. Owner says he is just getting the land in shape again to produce good crops.

About March 20, 1925, the J. C. Gill interests decided to abandon Wilson Well No. 1 and gave up the hope of finding oil in this locality.

233

No definite reason was given for this action. The drill had not penetrated to any great depth and the test is considered hardly a fair one. It was planned to move rig to some point in the Farmington field where a number of wells, some very good ones, have been brought in.

Oil operations in the Mancos vicinity took a new lease on life when local people, not satisfied to give up the oil test, rallied new support for the enterprise and decided to get an oil geologist's report on the locality and, if favorable, make a new drill test. John A. Viles was brought up from Farmington; he went over the ground very carefully and his verdict was that the oil was there. The oil deposit according to Viles, lies east and north of the old well and a drill site was selected three-fourths of a mile northeast of the first well. Six hundred feet would find the oil the geologist estimated. Mr. Viles had a very good record as an oil geologist. He has made 46 locations for oil with only 5 dry holes to his credit, and 41 producing wells. For that reason the undertaking received strong local support.

W. Fairbanks and Waldo Kidder were in the county in late June making demonstration plantings of grass pastures, using the Morton mixture. Four pastures were planted in the Mancos area and a number in the Montezuma Valley. This is the first supervised planting of grass for pasture in the county. The Forest Service is also planting grass on range to determine best varieties and mixtures to use in building up the range on the forests.

A permanent county road was laid out in 1925 from the upper Mancos Valley up to and across Exon Mesa and the county road crew began work at once. The road is laid out on a maximum of seven and one-half per cent grade.

May 1st, 1925, the Mancos Interests in the Wilson oil well, joining with the Gill interests, began moving the drilling rig from the old site to the new site about a mile and a half east. J. W. Doak, the new driller from Farmington, was on hand to supervise the work.

In the years 1922 to 1925 predatory animals were so destructive to range stock, especially to sheep, in the county, that the stockmen organized to cooperate with the biological work of the state, in destroying mountain lions, wolves, coyotes and bobcats, and assessed a small amount per head on cattle and sheep owned by the stockmen to help defray the expenses of the work. Four state hunters and trappers were put on the job in the county.

1925, two work trains are busy on the railroad, one operating a power ditcher and the other distributing ties along the road to be put in by section men.

Friday, May 15, 1925, the oil refinery at Farmington began delivering their gas to customers in Montezuma County. A home product for home use. By eliminating the freight on long haul the price of gasoline to consumers was reduced four cents a gallon, with promise of further reduction. The gas is being made from the highest grade crude and the quality is very good.

New oil well spudded on May 8 and drill running steadily.

On May 18, nine cars of wool were loaded at Mancos and six cars at Dolores for the Philadelphia market. The two shipments brought above $60,000 into the county.

Week of June 12, 1925, the work of gravel surfacing seven miles of the Mancos-Durango highway from Grand Avenue, in Mancos, eastward was completed, and the work of preparing the road bed, beyond the gravel, is going on. The work of improving and gravel surfacing the road west from Mancos for five miles, is to start in 30 days. Wood and Morgan are finishing gravel surfacing the stretch of road between Hesperus and the Thompson Park.

G. T. Cline and George Cline sell their interest in the First National Bank of Dolores to J. J. Harris & Co. Bankers. The two banks at Dolores consolidate later.

The first elk to make their appearance on the Mancos side of the La Plata Mountains were seen in late July, 1925, up near the Hogback where two fine specimens of the species were seen. If there were two, there were doubtless others that had not been seen as, in recent years, elk have become quite numerous in this territory and many carcasses have been brought down every hunting season by hunters in other localities. The first planting elk in this part of the state was made several years ago when a few head were brought over from Wyoming and turned loose on the Hermosa where they thrived from the very start.

Some very good improvements were being made on the Mancos telephone system in August, 1925. The office is being moved from the Bauer Block to the Noland residence building on East Grand Avenue and a new up-to-date switchboard, with much larger capacity, is being installed. The wires on all the heavy laden poles were put into cables and the service improved in many other ways. A new copper line to Cortez is soon to replace the old steel circuit.

Mancos oil interests and outside associates resumed drilling October 22, 1925.

Early in October, 1925, a crisis in the coal industry developed when the coal producers of the county were notified that every mine had to put in a ventilating system with power driven fans to ventilate the mine up to a certain standard. Also every mine employing over three persons had to have a specially qualified foreman at what seemed like a very high salary of $200 a month. The first thought was that all the coal mines would have to close down and quit producing, but most producers decided to comply and add the extra expense to the price of coal.

An outstanding character in the pioneer history of Mancos came to an end Oct. 2, 1925, with the passing of Thomas Rickner of Mancos.

Mr. Rickner was among the earliest residents of the Mancos Valley, was married here, to Miss Lillian Honaker, scion of another pioneer family, and reared a large family, every member of which was a credit to the community. Although he had only the fundamentals of an education, he made his life useful, supported the community in its every step of progress, and became well and favorably known throughout the entire county. His only public service was as Superintendent of the Mesa Verde National Park from 1913 to 1921, and one term as mayor of the town of Mancos.

During the shipping season of 1925, 250 cars of cattle, sheep and hogs were loaded at Mancos for the market and between 50 and 60 cars were shipped by Mancos owners from other points. A full season's shipment of livestock was also made from Dolores. The price was good average.

Oil drilling is suspended. Mancos interests and associates cease drilling at about 700 feet. The drill passed through three well defined oil sands. Approaching the last sand it looked like an oil well was certain and drilling was stopped until casing and other material could be gotten on hand to control the oil flow should it be encountered, but when the well was drilled into the sand it was dry. The next oil formation is the Pennsylvania Sand and it is deeper than the backers of the enterprise feel justified in going.

Fall, 1925, the agricultural evening school, that has been going on for some days, resulted in the organization of a dairymen's association. It was resolved to adopt the Holstein breed and use only bulls with recorded high production, and eliminate low producing cows as fast as possible. Three bulls are to be bought at once. The school was conducted from Nov. 30 to Dec. 11, 1925, and by a vote of the members, dairying was chosen as the industry most suited to this locality and the one to concentrate on.

After two years down in New Mexico, George Menefee comes back to his ranch in the upper valley, bag and baggage, and all his cattle, Nov., 1925. Jim Frink also comes back, poorer in purse, but much wiser, than when he moved away.

In May 16, 1926, William Roessler, premier business veteran of the Mancos area, passed suddenly away with a heart attack.

Five miles of gravel surfaced road Mancos towards Cortez, was finished in July, 1926. Two and one-half miles of road from Stevenson's corner on over divide to beyond half way mark to be built this year. Bids called for, contract is let for two more miles on toward Cortez as gravel surfacing goes on.

In 1923 the Mancos Times-Tribune started a strong campaign to develop the dairy industry in the county. It took effect in every part of the county and did much to establish the dairy industry on a firm basis and the results are still in evidence in the county. The college people helped and meetings were held in every part of the county, and Mancos had a regular dairy school.

On March 21, 1926, saw the passing of Wm. J. Miller, a veteran business man of Mancos, who had been a strong stay in local affairs for years and leading public spirited citizen of ability and influence.

The radio fever is taking hold, a very good radio receiving set has come onto the market at a price the people can afford and they are going into many homes. The radio set is no longer a luxury.

Alfalfa seed growers made a little history in November, 1926, when they shipped 100,000 pounds of alfalfa seed—two full car loads—from Mancos. The seed brought 14 cents a pound or $14,000 for the shipment. Thomas Coppinger and Talcott and Carpenter were the main producers, with many small producers. In some cases the seed grown on an acre of land was worth nearly as much as the land was worth.

On Dec. 7, 1926, there died at his home in Mancos F. M. Hamblet, aged 91 yearms. He was survived by his wife to whom he had been married over 70 years. He had lived nearly all his life in the west.

July 14, four truck loads of oil drilling machinery moved in. Will drill on Bert Halls place two miles south of Mancos.

Apple industry growing. Estimated 100 car loads of apples shipped in season of 1927.

Second big storm period hits Nov. 19, 1927, last for one week. Railroad and highway bridges washed out again, much damage on farms and great loss.

The Detroit Oil Association, drilling a well on Louis Halls ranch, Nov. 1, 1927, struck small flow of oil 3 to 5 barrels. Drilling continued.

In spite of great increase in rolling stock and tractive power the Rio Grande Southern is swamped with freight it cannot move. Embargo placed on lumber from McPhee mill until livestock and other perishable freight can be moved.

One man, Bill Lyons, produced a car load of honey from his colonies in the lower Mancos Valley.

Late fall of 1927, it looks as if prosperity was coming back to the cattle industry. Roy Caviness shipped twelve narrow gauge cars of cattle to Denver market. They brought the very top of the season's market, weighed an average of 887 pounds and brought an average of $106.50 a head. Some of the large steers brought $130, at 12c a pound on foot. This was a history making event in the local cattle industry.

F. C. Hallar, drilling for oil out on the divide eight miles west of town, strikes good flow of gas. Applies for gas franchise for Mancos, Cortez and Dolores, with a view of drilling more wells to get gas supply for all towns.

F. C. Hallar gets another and stronger gas well out on divide, at depth of 725 feet.

During the summer of 1931 a five mile link of gravel surfacing on the Durango-Mancos road was completed thus making a gravel surface road all way between two towns.

Another gas well brought in by Hallar out on divide, July 4, 1931. Best well yet.

Mancos puts on a real good livestock show and fair, on Oct. 22, 23 and 24, 1931. Very good showing made.

Mancos has an airport, the first in the county, and was dedicated and used first July 4, 1932. Two planes make first use of the air strip, taking many passengers on trips during the day.

The plan to finish graveling the Mancos-Cortez road finally approved, early Sept., 1932. $120,000 was appropriated under the National Relief Act, emergency relief act. Work to be done by employing common labor for every part of work where such labor can be used.

Effort was made for the first time, 1932-33, to keep the Mancos-Durango road open all winter. Truck and car competition with the railroad forces discontinuance of passenger train. Motor bus, "the Galloping Goose" starts operating. Livestock and most heavy freight still moving by rail, 1932.

Big snow storm in Dec. 10, 1932, leaves 1 ft. of snow. All road work suspended on Park road oiling, and graveling on Mancos-Cortez road.

After two days of intermittent rain and snow, on Feb. 14, 1933, the temperature dropped at Mancos to 40 degrees below zero, official record, the lowest temperature ever recorded here before or since. The lowest previous record was in January, 1905, when 27 degrees below zero was recorded. On two other occasions the temperature dropped, once to 23 below and once 22 below. Ordinarily the lowest temperature recorded is 10 to 12 below, only occasionally. Low temperatures are always attended by a breathless stillness in the air. The very low temperature noted above was attended by gusty wind and blowing snow squalls in the afternoon, and a display of thunder and lightning. It was followed by a full week of very cold weather.

Well being drilled out near Hallar's Auto Camp strikes some oil. Drilling resumed early in March.

Grazing heavily the year round was what knocked out the fine stands of native grasses that covered this entire county, and gave the brush a chance to take over, and the brush did.

In 1933-34 the winter snows closed all highways as usual, remain closed until May.

Artesian water reported struck out on Mark Willden place April 20, 1933, at depth of 120 feet. Smells strongly of sulphur. Hallar found it drilling for oil.

The First National Bank of Mancos closed for keeps Oct. 6, 1933. Also the Montezuma National Bank at Cortez has been closed. Chas. B. Reid appointed receiver for Mancos Bank. This leaves the county with only one bank—J. J. Harris & Co., at Dolores.

When Mancos was incorporated in 1894, George Bauer was first mayor, Lewis Armstrong, Mayor pro-tem, Board Trustees, Henry Cadwell, Harry N. Sprague, Harry V. Ausburn, C. B. Kelly, Geo. Carr, Clerk and Jerome DeJarrel, Marshall.

In May, 1934, the First National Bank of Mancos paid dividend checks in the sum of $40,000 to its creditors.

On Friday, June 1, 1934, the first sound pictures were put on at the Mancos Theater, the first "Talkie Pictures" to appear in the county.

On Feb. 15, 1935, a movement was started by the American Legion to import from Oklahoma 100 wild turkeys to stock the Mancos locality. The turkeys arrived later and were turned loose on the range. They have increased to several hundred head.

Mrs. Keturah Exon died at the age of 94 years. She had been a resident of the Mancos Valley for 52 years.

In March, 1935, the roads got so deep in mud that grades one to six of the Mancos schools were dismissed until road conditions improve so the buses could go. Also the railroad bed got so soft no attempt was made for a time to run trains on schedule. Heavy snows held up nearly all traffic for a few days.

The long drouth of 1934, affecting the entire county, was effectively broken in the winter of 1934-35. Although the soil was dry to a great depth the fall of rain and snow was sufficient to restore moisture all the way down.

Mancos Valley people vote to form a Water Conservancy District to build a reservoir to store water for use of the Mancos Valley farmers, last of August, 1935.

It is announced in late December, 1935, that Highway No. 160 will be oil paved in 1936, beginning at Pagosa Springs and working westward. An effort will be made to do the entire road in the year if at all possible, starting in early spring. Large crushers and oil mixing machinery already on hand.

We pause here to pay a passing tribute to the life of another citizen and pioneer. Samuel Warner Carpenter was born in Cincinnati, Ohio, August 20, 1854, and died at Mancos, Colorado, March 20, 1936, in his 81st year. He graduated from Cornell University, specializing in law and civil engineering. He came west early and was first employed as an engineer on the Mexican Central railroad. He came to Colorado in 1880, practiced law in Denver for a time. Mr. Carpenter came to the Montezuma Valley in 1886 as superintendent of the Montezuma Valley Irrigation District and at once identified himself with the future of the county by filing a homestead which he made final proof on and held for years. In 1892 he opened a law office in Cortez and, until the time of his death, was one of the leading attorneys in this part of the state. In 1895 he was married to Jennie B. Smith, daughter of H. M. Smith, one of the first settlers in the Mancos Valley. To their union four children were born two of which survive together with his wife.

His record shows 50 years of unbroken service to the people of Montezuma county in many, many ways. As an attorney he served the county and the Montezuma Valley Irrigation District through many trying times. He guided their destiny with wisdom and understanding, and it was through his unending effort, along with the work of other men, that brought success out of failure and victory out of defeat when, at times, it seemed that all was lost. As an office lawyer Att. Carpenter was very thorough and efficient and his ability commanded the confidence of a large clientele.

After months of planning and figuring on the route of Highway 160 through the Town of Mancos, it was definitely concluded in June, 1936, to wreck the First National Bank building in Mancos and build the highway straight through to Grand Avenue from the east.

Early in September, 1936, work of rebuilding and oil surfacing Highway 160 was started with 20 men on the work, to be increased to 40 later.

W. H. Jackson visits Mancos August 1, 1936. He helped to start Parrott City, and was in Mancos Valley 62 years previous to present visit and was official photographer with U. S. Geological Survey, went down Mancos Canon and photographed Cliff Ruins 14 years before they were discovered on the park.

In September, 1936, the First National Bank building is being torn down to clear the right-of-way for the highway. A three mile stretch through Mancos will be built first.

The final dividend to creditors of the First National Bank of Mancos was made March 21, 1937, and amounted to 49 per cent. This brings the total dividends paid to creditors up to 70 per cent. $68,000 in round numbers was the total paid in the final dividend.

The snowfall for the winter of 1936-37 on Mesa Verde National Park was the greatest on record according to the report made public in April, 1937. The total snowfall, according to the record, as reported by Paul R. Frank, Acting Superintendent, was 145.5 inches. It was a winter of deep snows all over the San Juan Basin and deep mud the following spring. For six weeks the roads of Montezuma County, and especially in the Mancos Valley, were all but impassable and the schools were closed down at Mancos three weeks in one stretch as it was impossible to get the country children in to school.

On July 1, 1937, Highway No. 160 was being oil surfaced through the town of Mancos.

The first combine in the Mancos section was brought in by Grady Clampitt, a Case combine, 10 feet cut, in August, 1937.

In the summer of 1937, twenty-two miles of Highway 160, between Durango and Pagosa Springs, and 5.7 miles between Pagosa Springs and Wolf Creek Pass was graveled and oil surfaced.

240

In the summer of 1936, 100 turkeys were trapped on the game preserve in the Wichita Mountains in Oklahoma and turned loose on the Montezuma National Forest, near Mancos. They survived and there seems to be a few hundred turkeys in the entire locality.

The record of the Mancos School, for 1881, shows that the school started in February and lasted 6 months. This locality was still in La Plata County. There were 27 boys and 22 girls, and a very satisfactory school in the old log building.

In 1938, petitions were circulated and public meetings were held with the result that action was taken at once and the Mancos Water Conservancy District was formed. The engineers then went over the prospective reservoir sites and the work of taking subscriptions for water was started. The land owners granted rights of ways for ditches and area for reservoir and a movement was started to get some WPA labor allocated to the job of doing preliminary work on the reservoir. After considering available sites Jackson Gulch was decided to be the best site—most feasible and most practicable, and a large volume of water could be stored.

Mr. and Mrs. C. B. Stone, of Durango, for years of Montezuma Co. as pioneers, celebrated their 65th wedding anniversary at the home of their daughter, Mrs. W. H. French, Oct. 2, 1938, in Mancos. The Stones were very early in the big valley, homesteading in the Beulah neighborhood in about 1888, and were neighbors of the George Lonenbaughs.

In 1938 the construction of the Mancos sewer system is under way. The government will expand, through the WPA $40,572, or 80 per cent of the cost and the town will furnish the balance, or about $11,000. In the summer of 1938 trenching and laying sewer pipe is being done and manholes, septic tanks, filter beds, etc., are being built. This is a very vital improvement in the growth of the town and very good in the interest of the public health.

Grady Clampitt set a record as a wheat grower in Montezuma Co. when, in January, 1939, he shipped from the Mancos station at one time, 13 cars of fine milling wheat—high protein test, all grown on his Mancos Valley dry farm out by Mesa Verde. All went to Graden mill in Durango.

The Mesa Verde Silver Fox Farm, owned and built up and operated by Byron Brown, makes a record almost every year with silver fox fur, producing tops in quality and bringing tops in price. Brown goes on the New York market and his pelts outclass those produced by the largest and best producers in the industry.

The Jackson Gulch reservoir plan has finally been approved by President Roosevelt. $1,600,000 will be made available for construction of the dam. $680,000 will be allocated out of the general fund of the U. S. Treasury and $920,000 appropriated out of the C.C.C. and

241

the W.P.A. fund, October 25, 1940. Water Conservancy district next move in order.

The Mancos sewage system is completed in November, 1940. The WPA then starts work on new reservoir for the town.

An open meeting was held in Mancos August 23 on the matter of forming a water conservancy district and there was a good attendance, although it rained. Irrigation experts spoke and answered questions form land owners, and funds were raised at once to pay costs in forming the district. Attorney Chas. Reese was employed, petitions were drawn for signing. The petitions were promptly circulated and the necessary number of land owners signed in favor of the reservoir movement. Notice of hearing was published and, no organized opposition materializing, the hearing was held on January 6, 1940, in the District Court Room at Cortez, and the Mancos Valley Water Conservancy District was formed. $22,000 in WPA Funds were allotted and $200,-000 in reclamation funds was granted. The reclamation engineers have spent $12,000 surveying and digging and drilling test holes about the dam site so that actual construction can begin as soon as arrangements can be completed. The movement is not to create a boom; it's just to supply a need.

The Mancos Home Demonstration Club was organized in December, 1940, second meeting in January. Demonstration Clubs are open to all home builders in town and country and are free to everyone. No dues or expenses. Through the club and the county agent help is received from the extension work of Home Economics at Fort Collins. Special help in home work, home planning and home economics, in clothing, is furnished. They promote young girls' clubs and furnish leadership in many lines of home and club work. The work has gone on constantly since it was organized. Home Demonstration units, like the one in Mancos, are operating in every part of the county.

The first Board of Supervisors, or Directors, for the Water Conservancy District were appointed by Judge O'Rourke. The first board selected were: District No. 1, R. Y. Gibbs; District No. 2, J. Lewis Halls; District No. 3, A. W. Schwartz; District No. 4, H. V. Carr; District No. 5, Ira E. Kelly.

Kelly Hill will have to be graveled one and one-third miles to handle the heavy hauling incident to the construction of Jackson Dam.

The first work on the reservoir was clearing the timber and brush from the site and other surface work. 54 WPA workers were put on the job January 25, 1942.

The milk producers of the Mancos area contacted Senator Clark, milk distributor of Gallup, and arranged for a cooling plant and receiving station at Mancos in November, 1941. The arrangement proved to be satisfactory for all concerned and opened a market for whole milk that has continued and expanded to this day. The station also furnishes a market for sweet cream.

The first call of the Selective Service draft was made in October, 1941, to report at Denver November 6, for induction into the armed forces. The call for 8 men took the following: Robert R. Miller, Cortez; Bob A. Schwartz, Mancos; Glen E. White, Pleasant View; Harlen W. Mikes, Cortez; Martin W. Hunter, Dolores; Jack D. Reed, Yellow Jacket; George Edmonson, Cortez; James A. Bauer, Mancos.

The Future Farmers of America organized in the county. Object: Build up agricultural leadership; improve community by developing sound farming practices; to develop character and train for useful citizenship. It was organized in Mancos and at several other points in the county in October, 1941.

The first airplane to be located in the county was brought in by Joe Piccone and is kept in a special hangar at the airport. It was made available for charter trips and local flying service.

Work of graveling the road to Jackson Dam is started, first a coat of river rock—then gravel surface. Reclamation drag line is loading trucks.

The cold storage plant in Mancos opens for business Oct. 11, 1941, just in time for the deer season. This is the first up-to-date locker plant in the county. Butchering, chilling, cutting, wrapping, grinding, sharp freezing and storage of all meats. Smoking, pickling, rendering. Store meat in any style. This is a new service that is just coming to the people of the county.

All mines operating for the more precious metals are being closed down to make the labor available for more important work. Mines providing the basic metals along with gold and silver and have to have the income from the more precious metals to operate profitably, are allowed to continue operation. The Red Arrow and other producing mines in the Mancos Area were closed down.

The county planning committee and the U. S. Department of Agriculture War Board began organizing their forces into various subcommittees in March, 1942. The aim is to direct all local industries to reenforce the war effort and produce according to the needs of the nation.

First Aid classes are organized to learn wnat to do and how to do it in any emergency.

Jackson Gulch gets an appropriation of $36,393 to keep the CCC's and the WPA's at work on the dam, or doing preparatory work.

The water users of the Mancos Water Conservancy District ratified the contract between the government and the conservation district by a vote of 116 in favor and 23 opposed, the election being held June 20. This cleared the way for building the reservoir.

Nine Veterans of the Spanish American War, living in the county, attended a reunion and picnic at the Yeoman ranch July 26, 1942.

Early in May, 1944, development operations, under the Case-Wheeler Act, got under way in the Mancos Water Conservancy District. Many pieces of heavy machinery were moved in from San Luis Valley. They do land clearing, leveling, plowing, deep chiseling, build and rebuild ditches and ditch systems, and a great amount of good work was done on the farms. Most of the machinery was busy all the time for several months and much new land was cleared and put into cultivation along with much other work. The object seemed to have been to put the farms in shape to use Jackson Gulch water when it should become available.

Preparatory excavation going on at Jackson Gulch, excavation for dam foundations, placing of concrete in cutoff trench, setting of forms for concrete outlet works. First actual construction the last of May, 1944.

John Derrick Halls, of Mancos, killed in action in France, June 6, 1944, first day of the great invasion onto French territory. Halls was in the paratrooper division.

In midsummer the W.C.U. unit working in the Mancos Valley receive additional heavy equipment. Survey and plans for improving land is furnished free. The personnel recommends the kind of work that should be done and directs the work. Land is also drained and new ditches and ditch systems laid out. All work is done on a per hour basis.

August 15. In spite of the stress of war life goes on and 280 pioneers attend the reunion at Mancos.

In late September the P. G. A. gets additional heavy equipment for doing renovating work on farms in Mancos area.

Dr. L. H. Clark, veteran physician at Mancos, dies at his home Oct. 14, 1944, aged 82 years.

The Water Utilization & Conservation program is doing much work in Mancos Valley getting land and farms ready to use Jackson Gulch water.

Herbert M. Roberts killed in hit-and-run accident at Ada, Okla., Dec. 25, 1944. At home on leave from army.

Sgt. Tom Weaver killed in action in Belgium, Dec. 20, 1945.

Private James Starr dies of wounds in France early in March, 1945.

On January 6, 1946, Mrs. Fred Armstrong dies. Before her marriage she was Miss Mabyn Morefield, the first white girl born in the Mancos Valley, and therefore the first in Montezuma Co. She was born June 22, 1878.

In January the company that is building the match factory at Mancos buys 5,000,000 board feet of aspen timber.

The contract for building Jackson Gulch Dam is awarded to the Vinnell Co. of California, also for outlet and inlet canals, the bid for the work being $1,925,904.50.

The Montezuma National Forest is merged with the San Juan National Forest with office in Durango. The Norwood ranger district goes to the Uncompahgre National Forest. The combined acreage of the San Juan forest is now 2,101,249 acres.

A County Planning Board has been created in the county and is very active in promoting beneficial activities in the county. Tours are sponsored each year to view meritorious enterprises in every part of the county—farming, livestock, fruitgrowing, good roads, new industries—and every kind of enterprise is promoted and encouraged.

By the terms of a new contract with the government the users of Jackson Gulch water agree to pay $900,000 on the costs of the Jackson Gulch reservoir instead of $600,000 as first agreed on, increase is due to the much higher cost of construction. The time for payment is extended from 40 years to 60 years so that the annual payments will be the same.

The effort at upgrading of range cattle by using only registered bulls on the range is showing good results since the practice was started 10 years ago. The whole county has been cooperating and the cattlemen say that great improvement in the quality of cattle being produced has been made.

The planning board recommended that the County Agent be given more help for 4-H Club work and as a result an assistant agent has been employed to have charge of 4-H Club work which is getting to be a very important work in the county. Livestock judging has been added to the work.

County Agent Morteson is building up a lot of interest in agriculture and related industries. At a meeting July 12, 1946, 60 men from the Planning Board were in attendance and committees were appointed on roads, weeds, livestock, dairy, crops, poultry, gardens, education, 4-H Club work, potatoes, transportation and the county fair.

The Empire Electric Association is rushing work all over county, setting poles, stringing wire and a new substation at Mancos is nearing completion.

Aug. 10, 1948, election on formation of the Mancos Soil Conservation District, carries by vote of 20 for and 5 against.

Jackson Gulch finished 1949 and dedication exercises July 3, 1949. Reservoir full of water. Valves are opened for first time.

BACK TO 1946

The Brest-Forster-Dixfield application to build a match factory at Mancos approved by Civilian Production Administration. The plant to cost $155,000. Construction starts at once.

1952

Dr. J. R. Trotter, veteran physician of Mancos, died February 27, 1953, after a long illness. He had been practicing medicine in Mancos 50 years, and had made a place among Mancos people that will be hard to fill.

Mancos moves in April, 1954, to provide more high school room and a modern combined auditorium and gymnasium. On May 17, the voters approve a bond issue in the sum of $125,000 to put their plans into effect.

Lieut. Raymond Starr, of Mancos, dies April 24, 1954, in a plane crash near Montrose, Ark. He was an instructor for jet pilots.

CHAPTER XIX

CORTEZ CHRONOLOGY

Cortez was born a county seat town, coexistent with the county itself. While yet in swaddling clothes it was called upon to be host to court personnel and wait upon a demanding public that was coming its way. Creating something out of nothing was not an easy matter in those pioneer times and, for quite some time, the struggle for existence was both real and earnest. Sitting in the midst of great potential wealth the blood of commerce was slow in giving it life and strength. It endured with patience and bided its time with fortitude. It was as if greatness was there, but always just out of reach. The time was long in coming, to those who had to wait; too long for many heroic souls who failed to last out the waiting period. They worked while they waited. They knew they were building for a great future, but no one could divine or imagine how soon, or how late, it would come. It was theirs to toil in faith and patience hoping for a reward that never came. We take up here to trace its history as best we may. All the early files of the Montezuma Journal have been destroyed or they never existed, and much that was history has been lost. We have already related the story of the early settlement period, in another chapter. We take up here the consecutive events as they came to pass from year to year.

On May 25, 1893, there was a session of the District Court at Cortez and several cases were on the docket; also a Grand Jury was called into session that lasted for several days. This was the first Grand Jury session held in the county and it returned fourteen indictments, and fourteen cases were entered by District Attorney Miller upon information. This seemed to have been a kind of clearing of accumulated offenses and apparently it was their plan to wipe the slate clean.

There was an Indian uprising down on the San Juan, below Guillet Brothers' trading post and Sheriff Adam Lewy received from the state armory, on request, 100 guns and 2000 rounds of ammunition.

The first Teachers' Institute to be held in the county, was held at Cortez in August, 1893. D. M. Longenbaugh was the conductor.

John R. Curry came down from Telluride in late 1888 and started publication of the Montezuma Journal. It was born to a life of early hardships and a hectic career.

Sterl Thomas was directing the fortunes of the paper in 1889.

Hotel Clifton was built and opened its doors to the public in May, 1893.

Cortez had a big celebration July 4, 1893, and almost everyone in the county attended. A water supply had finally come to the town and things were "looking up" for the village.

The Cortez Land and Security Co. pays $4,390 in delinquent taxes June 1, 1894. It is now out of debt and ready to do business on a firmer basis.

The 1894 political campaign was a hot one in Colorado from constable to governor and Montezuma had three or four full tickets in the field. In 1893 Congress ceased to buy silver for coinage thus completely demonetizing silver and the silver market went into a tailspin. This closed all silver mines, and some gold mines, threw thousands of miners out of work and distress ensued in all the local mining camps, and the agricultural town suffered with the mining town. Bimetallism and the free coinage of silver in a ratio of 16 to 1 was the burning issue. Our silver camp at Rico was almost completely closed down and Telluride, Ouray and Silverton were hard hit. The Populist party was going strong and was the leading party in Montezuma Co. drawing recruits from all the other parties. The Populist carried the county by a strong majority. Six organized voting precincts voted. They were Upper and Lower Mancos, Cortez, McElmo, Dolores and Arriola.

The season of 1894 was one of water shortage all over the county and there is much talk of doing something about it.

James Carpenter sinks a well for artesian water three miles east of Cortez in the winter of 1895.

The Montezuma Journal is again resurrected with Charles Day as publisher, April 12, 1895, after being suspended for some weeks. Day is a pretty good newspaper man and does a good job, but has poor support from the town. The people were nearly all poor people and money was scarce and everyone had to care for his own and do the best he could.

The Journal was again suspended in 1895, but was going again in 1896 with Chas. Day again in charge.

The state appropriates $3,000 for an artesian well, and the Coppinger well is abandoned. State engineer Summers selects a new site four miles south of Cortez in what was called the Mud Basin.

A Mr. Schaff builds a flour mill at Cortez early in 1896. Journal wants the people to organize and build another mill. Not enough grain for one.

A case in the 1896 term of the District Court was the trial of Jimmie Hatch, an Indian, for the murder of an Indian man and a boy at their tepee camp on Chicken Creek, and, later, the murder of the Indian's wife (squaw). He was convicted of murder in the first degree and sentenced to be hanged. The Indians had already tried Hatch in their

Tribal Council, condemned him and would have put him to death if the white man's law had failed to convict.

Robert Wilson had his hand torn badly by a rope when he roped a steer. He was taken to Durango for treatment, but the wound was so severe the hand had to be taken off.

In the fall of 1896 the allotment of land to the Ute Indians was ratified and the agency headquarters is established at Navajo Springs. Work starts at once on the site and soon a number of buildings were under construction.

The season of 1896 was another very dry season. Grain crop is short and there is only one crop of hay. This set the people to thinking about a reserve water supply.

Fall of 1896 the new flour mill at Cortez is operating. The Bauer Mercantile, at Mancos, sends down several thousand bushels of wheat to be ground into flour. Then hauled back and distributed from Mancos. Later, Scott and Myers, of Durango, buy the mill. It was expected the new owners would make a better flour and a better market for wheat, and reduce the amount of flour shipped in.

The election of 1896 was a red hot campaign. Bryan and McKinley were running for president and the silver issue was paramount. Adams is elected governor and J. J. Harris state senator. All the following tickets were on the state ballot: Straight Republican, Silver Republicans, Straight Democrats, Peoples' Party, National Peoples', Silver Populist Party, National Silver Party and the Socialist Party, Labor Party, National Party and the Prohibition Party. McKinley wins in the nation. Adams in the state.

The $3,000 appropriated by the state for drilling for water four miles south of Cortez, and the $1,000 raised by the people of Cortez, is all spent and the well is down 756 feet. Senator Harris introduces bill for $4,000 additional funds to continue drilling.

In April, 1897, good cattle were selling in Montezuma County at $45 a head on the average.

In 1896, O. E. Noland has sold his trading post down at the Four Corners and is building large and substantial business quarters at Navajo Springs, in early summer, a big stock of general merchandise is laid in immediately for both Indian and white population. Also several government buildings for the new agency are being built.

In the fall of 1897 an effort was made to make a new market for McElmo Canon fruit. J. D. Hall and J. T. Giles build a cannery building and brought in some machinery for canning peaches and some other fruits. D. Mayer, of Mancos, contracted to make the cans. Considerable fruit was canned and it appeared on the market in many stores of this section. They turned out a very acceptable product, but for some reason the enterprise failed to survive for long.

Guillet Bros. buy flour mill from J. E. Shutt, who, now, seems to be the owner, and proceed to make a market for grain and flour. The

249

mill burns down a few months later. The mill had just resumed operation. 400,000 pounds of wheat was destroyed; also 75,000 pounds of flour. Total loss was $12,000 with only $6,000 insurance. This was in February, 1898. The fire was believed to be of incendiary origin.

Indian Agent Smith reports that there are about 600 Ute Indians registered at the Navajo Springs Agency. All are receiving rations regularly.

In March, 1898, a fire starts in Hotel Blackmer and spreads to a hardware store and three other business houses, opposite the stone block. Loss estimated at $15,000.

On April 8, 1898, the Montezuma Valley Canal Co. applied to the county commissioners for permit to raise water rate charges. This raised a storm of protest from the irrigation water users. The farmers never have enough water and can't pay more, unless they get more water. Farmers willing to pay more if plenty of water was furnished.

In April, 1898, Charles Donaldson was shot and killed by George Eaton, in Arriola community. It was the result of a feud of long standing. John Eaton, also party to the row, was struck by Donaldson with a shovel after he fired a shot. Eaton was knocked unconscious and died later. Mrs. Donaldson, who was grubbing sage brush near by, while Donaldson was working ditch on the Eaton place, witnessed the whole affair. George Eaton was tried, convicted and sentenced to 18 years in penitentiary.

In the fall of 1897 McElmo Canon fruit wins many awards and much distinction at the Festival of Mountains and Plains in Denver. The largest apple in the state was on exhibit. It was over 16 inches in circumference and weighed 25 ounces. A large display of fruit was put on.

In 1898 Cortez begins to experience considerable new growth. The Woodmen are building a large new hall, the Methodist Church is moved from its old location to its present site and much improved; several new buildings are being built. Growth hitherto had been very slow. In 1897 the school enrollment was only 38 pupils according to a statement by Co. Superintendent of Schools.

The Ute Indians are issued live beef animals each month at the agency. On these occasions the Indians reenact many lively scenes of their aboriginal life in these parts.

The Montezuma Journal suspends publication again in fall of 1898. Charles Day goes to Silverton to edit the Silverton Herald.

In 1898 the Spanish American War was on and the patriotic feeling was running high. The fourth of July was celebrated with much patriotic feeling and loud acclaim.

Articles of Incorporation of the McElmo Water Supply Co. were filed November 26, 1898. The new corporation proposes to take over the Colorado Water Supply Co., the Montezuma Valley Irrigation Company, and the Dolores No. 2 Land & Canal Co. Has capital stock of $500,000. The new company has vast plans and great expectations. Three Colorado men, three of New York and one of Connecticut are behind the new company.

Sterling Price Thomas resurrects the Montezuma Journal for the fourth or fifth time and gets it going again. Still going in 1899.

In 1897 Cortez has a new opera house, the only one in the county in the new W.O.W. Hall.

The new Clifton Hotel in Cortez becomes the leading and most popular hotel in the county seat, in 1899. It stood just west of the stone block.

In 1899 brome grass began to be planted in the county as a pasture grass, on dry and irrigated land, a very significant incident.

On August 18, 1899, 19 teams of horses and mules pass through Mancos and Cortez to the lower San Juan country loaded with new and shiny placer mining machinery. The region was boomed for years, lots of money was spent, but none of the enterprises ever made good. They were mostly stock schemes.

In September, 1899, a movement was begun to refund $30,000 in county bonds, issued to pay the old La Plata Co. debt, mostly.

Fall of 1899 Jasper Halls appears at the Festival of Mountains and Plains with large exhibit of fruit and, in a statewide contest, won a number of 1st, 2nd and 3rd prizes. Noah Barnes took first on Melons.

J. E. Schutt signs a contract for the erection of a 72 barrel capacity flour mill in Cortez, work to begin in the spring of 1900.

Back in 1898 fire had taken the Cortez flour mill for the second time, and a fire wiped out block in the center of town. Hoer & Snyder, the losers, erects a new building on the old site which was one of best business buildings in town.

In January, 1901, Will Springer takes over as editor and publisher of the Montezuma Journal.

Cortez is building a new flour mill in 1901. Modern and 50 barrel capacity.

The market price for hay, all over the county, is $7 per ton, fall of 1901.

When Cortez finally got their new water system—a ditch system at first, to working it was supplied with water from the irrigating system by means of a long flume that brought water in from the northeast. This flume was quite a land mark. It was 40 feet high in the highest place, and several hundred feet long. In July, 1901, 50 feet of this flume, toward the north end, was blown down and the town's water supply was shut off. Carpenters were set to work at once to make repairs. Supt. Blake had the water going again in a few days.

In August, 1901, a crusade against the "gun toter" was started. Carrying a revolver was a universal practice in early settlement days. In late years the practice has been largely abandoned, and the man with a gun seemed out of place. Some, too many perhaps, still thought they needed a gun.

In January, 1902, Springer Brothers sell the Montezuma Journal to D. M. Longenbaugh. Mr. Longenbaugh resigns his school in Mancos and takes over the paper.

Frank Mowry of Delta buys foundation of old mill at Cortez and began, soon after, the erection of a new flour mill.

The Cortez town board has a well drilled for artesian water for a town water supply. They drill to 594 ft., 8 in., but get no water. The board pays the bill and quits.

The Montezuma County Horticultural Society was organized April 5, 1902. Object is to grade fruit to the highest quality and market only the best.

Cortez is still having water trouble. They arrange with the ditch company for water, and plan to build a ditch to a high point near the old Court house. Here a pumping plant will be built to pump water to a tank in the highest part of town and water will be distributed by pressure by a system of pipes. This was in the spring of 1902.

The effort is continued to settle the irrigation water troubles. T. C. Henry submits a new proposition to the water users, but water users reject it, in May, 1902. Some leading citizens think Mr. Henry has offered a fair solution of the water problem.

The dry season brought about a movement in Cortez to incorporate the town so they can bond and build a water system as the only solution of the water problem. Sentiment is divided. The town is small and valuation low for such an undertaking.

The Montezuma Valley, with the turn of the century, began to make some real strides of progress. Much new land was cleared and put into cultivation and the old land was producing good crops. Many new citizens began coming in bringing a little new capital and creating some employment. Several Mormon families came in at this time bringing new energy, thrift and enterprise. This is in 1902 and 1903.

In 1903 the old flume that supplied the town of Cortez with water, failed completely to give service and the town installed two large windmills to pump water to a reservoir in the highest part of town, through a three inch pipe, a distance of 300 yards. They planned to build a standpipe for water pressure at a later date. This was in March, 1903. Also a ditch to bring water as near as possible to the town is proposed.

In June of 1903, the people of Montezuma Valley vote to form an irrigation district the purpose being to take over the old irrigation system. This was the beginning of a long struggle for survival that was to last nearly twenty years. The directors elected were John T. Duncan, Chas. Matson and Henry Kroeger.

In 1897 R. R. Smith opened a general merchandise store in the building just vacated by E. R. Lamb.

Also back in 1897 Dave Hafferty opens a store in Cortez and M. A.

252

Blackmer opens a hotel, also, and Johnson & Waldron open a new dry goods store.

In April, 1901, a Knights of Pythias lodge is organized in Cortez with 34 charter members.

On April 8, 1904, a concerted movement is started in every part of the county to promote the potato growing industry in the county. A campaign was put on and agreements were signed by farmers to grow 455 acres of potatoes in the Mancos and Montezuma Valley. A special railroad shipping rate of 50c per 100 pounds to Missouri River points and 67 cents to Mississippi River points was secured and plans were made to have some qualified man on the ground to show the farmers how to grow potatoes.

Winter of 1903-1904 was very dry and there was almost no snow, even on the mountains. Some farmers planted no crops in the spring because they figured there would be no water. Most farmers planted their land and raised pretty good crops. It was cold and ice accumulated in the mountains, melted and made lots of water for a time. There were some good summer showers.

In late 1903 Montezuma Valley people have perfected the formation of their irrigation district, but don't know where they are going from there. Water is not their only problem. There are other difficulties such as markets and transportation. They need markets so the farmers can make some real money, which has been their main difficulty all along.

The windmills provide insufficient power to furnish water for Cortez. A steam pumping plant was decided on and a cement reservoir will be built.

Springer Brothers step down and out on the Montezuma Journal and the Beall Brothers take over in Aug., 1904. The new owners are inexperienced in the paper business.

In November, 1904, a big potato crop is being harvested and the market is so low there is no profit in them, and late shipments face freezing in transit. Most growers plan to hold potatoes until spring for a better price. An earnest effort was made to find a market since the business men were instrumental in getting the farmers to grow potatoes.

The controversy over the ditch and water situation in Montezuma Valley grows in intensity. General discussions in the newspapers of the county, while it led to some feeling, was effective in clarifying many matters and led to a broader understanding of the whole affair. In the end it helped in working out a solution to the problems. The people of the district voted for the bonds, by a large majority, which strengthened their position in their efforts to deal with the irrigation company. But the conditions still impose an impossible situation under which the district could act only in cooperation with the ditch company.

As a result of the dry winter and spring of 1904 the springs at Navajo Springs, always freely flowing, all but went dry. Plans were made to move the agency if the water failed entirely.

At the St. Louis World's Fair, in 1904, Colorado won on her exhibit 16 grand prizes, 150 gold medals and 348 silver medals, making a total of 514 prizes and medals. Montezuma County was well represented and received her full share of the awards.

On May 1st, 1905, active construction work on telephone line from Mancos to Cortez is under way. Poles are being hauled and set.

In the very year Montezuma County farmers were persuaded to plant potatoes a tremendous crop was produced and harvested all over the state. Result: Lowest market price for potatoes ever known. Many growers are disgusted and quit, but potato growing held on. The people had learned they could grow good potatoes and produce a good yield, and potato growing has continued to this day.

Settlement of the water question in the big valley seems near at hand. The district contracts to take over old irrigating system, June, 1905.

In the summer of 1905 the town of Cortez narrowly escaped being taken over by the bond holders. The town had defaulted on payment of bonds and interest and a plan was on foot to sell the town at Auction to satisfy the bondholders. A restraining order preventing sale was effected by a temporary court injunction. The town got the money and satisfied the bondholders claims.

The telephone line from Mancos to Cortez was opened for business Aug. 20, 1905. It was built by the Montezuma Telephone Co., an association of local people, mostly of Cortez.

The deal between the Montezuma Valley Land & Water Co. and the newly organized district has fallen through, fall of 1905. The survey that is being made to determine irrigatable acreage in the district is still incomplete. The proposed deal met with strong opposition on the part of the people, causing failure to ratify.

The people of the county are beginning to give some attention to dry farming. Also steps are being taken to induce farmers to grow certified seed grains with some success.

Good roads, and the necessity for them, is being discussed in every part of the county. Up to this time good dirt roads are the only kind being thought of and that always means poor roads in wet times. Gravel surfaced, or all weather roads, are not even deemed a possibility.

Season of 1906 the county has 1900 acres planted to fruit that is bearing and 1240 acres that has not reached the bearing stage. Apples predominate.

C. A. Frederick, of Paonia, takes over the Montezuma Journal from D. M. Longenbaugh, buying the business, August 1, 1906. Mr. Frederick improved the paper, builds up the business and is a power for good in the community. He was a tireless worker and "booster."

J. M. Mitchell was in the county in November, 1906, and started a movement to get a sugar factory. This was the beginning of a long and continued effort to get a sugar factory that never was built.

A movement for better dairy cattle gets under way in 1906. Eugene Grubb of Carbondale talks to the people and persuades them that milking Shorthorns is the cow they need. They ship in 10 head, mostly bulls.

In 1906 the county produced the largest grain crop in its history up to that time.

Early in 1907 terms were finally agreed upon and the irrigation district took over the entire irrigating system in Montezuma Valley, details of which are given in another chapter. As a result a county wide "Booster's Club" was organized. The situation calls strongly for more people and more capital. Some good results were obtained.

Settlement of the irrigating question brings in many new people, Cortez is growing and the schools are overcrowded. A movement is started to erect another school building.

Real estate is moving in the valley. Week of July 6, 1907, $42,000 of value in real estate exchange was recorded in one week. In McElmo Canon $15,000 was paid for the Galloway ranch consisting of 187 acres, $81 per acre. There are 55 acres of orchard on the place in solid bearing fruit.

The County Commissioners settled tax matters with the old water company, compromising on $12,500 to be paid to the county on back taxes. It seemed to be the best possible deal.

Fall of 1907 sees influx of new citizens into the county with money to buy, build or create something. Land in the big valley is at last becoming to be worth something. The new wealth and new people are needed to help bear the new burdens assumed by the people.

A. P. Culley of Loup City, Neb., W. F. Mason, F. B. Paist, W. T. Chase and L. Hansen, in the fall of 1907, organize and open The First National Bank of Cortez, capital stock $25,000. This makes the fourth bank in the county.

The town of Cortez starts, in 1907, the work of putting in a pressure pipeline to bring a water supply to the town. Seems to be a private enterprise. It will supply a long felt want.

Bank deposits are growing and the volume of business transacted shows a vast increase all over the county—more people, more business. The county goes through the brief panic of 1907 without a ripple on the financial surface. Not a bank check written but was honored.

On November 20, 1907, the Cortez National Bank received its charter to do business. Incorporators are P. T. Guillet, H. M. Guillet, E. R. Lamb, J. O. Brown, P. H. Rudy and R. Lilley, who is President of the Hammond State Bank of Hammond, La., and interested in the new bank. The bank opened for business Jan. 1, 1908, with a capital stock of $50,000. The officers are H. M. Guillet, President; Ed Lamb, Vice Pres., C. H. Rudy, Cashier; C. L. Coston, Assistant Cashier.

Year 1907 closed with high per cent of growth for year in business, in building and in population all over the county.

The mild panic of 1907 closed the State Bank at Rico, the Colorado State Bank and the Smelter City Bank at Durango and the Pagosa Springs State Bank at Pagosa Springs. The examiner said that the cause of closures was that the banks were not well managed. Panic didn't touch Montezuma Co. where business is built on solid assets and products that are staple in the markets of the world.

Contractor Crawford dropped out of the ditch building job in the big valley, but assures the people that the big job of building the ditch system and the reservoirs will be completed on time.

In March, 1908, the first automobile came to the county. The real estate firm of Blatchford and Bozman bring in two for use in their business, and Hi McEwen, the liveryman, gets one.

The Cortez Herald comes onto the scene in Cortez early in 1908, George Hutt of Rico is the owner and publisher.

On May 6, 1908, a peculiar thing happened. A stampede of cattle, below Navajo Springs, ran into a deep arroyo and 28 head were killed and many crippled. Frank Hepworth of Mancos lost 14, and several others lost a few. The stampede was at night and the men were making their spring roundup.

C. A. Frederick sells the Montezuma Journal to Mrs. Lillian Hartman Johnson and Frank Hartman is the new editor. In May, 1908.

Headquarters for the Montezuma National Forest is moved to Mancos. It occupies three rooms in the Bauer Bank Block.

The growth of the Town of Cortez brings up the water question again as the water supply is rapidly becoming inadequate. $50,000 is needed to build a gravity water system. A movement is also started for a cooperative telephone system for the entire county.

Work on the Montezuma Valley water system is progressing rapidly. Narraguinep dam is completed. The entire construction force goes to Groundhog.

About July 1st, 1908, a 160 foot section of East Lateral, near the tunnel, went out and many farmers were out of water for 10 days. Also Hartman dam went out, but not many were affected. New construction causes these troubles as the new dirt has not settled.

Chas. Clark sells Cortez Herald to Hubert Halls and daughter. They are inexperienced in newspaper work.

The people of the county are convinced they have a fruit country. Many large orders are placed for trees and hundreds of acres are set to orchards. Planting wrong varieties was their undoing.

On August 13, 1908, the most terrific downpour of rain in the known

Operating a rotary snow plow with two engines between Rico and Vance Junction.

Four engines on rotary snow plow boring its way through Nigger Baby Slide, above Rico. Railroading, in winter time, was difficult and perilous work.

Mr. and Mrs. Norman Halls, 1887. Jasper Hall and Norman Hall were the fruit wizards and McElmo Canon pioneers.

Mr. and Mrs. William Coppinger. Early in lower Montezuma Valley and granger king and cattleman.

This is the type of engine used to draw the trains, said to have been the most efficient railway engine ever built. Almost the entire weight of the engine was on the eight drive wheels. As many as four engines were used to move a single train on the heavy grades.

Apple orchard scene, Tom Cox fruit farm, fifteen 50-pound boxes on tree ready for harvest. Filled boxes under tree in background.

Early street scene, Cortez, Colo.

The elderly gentleman, standing at the rear center, with the heavy mustache, is Grandfather Henry Walters, and the group is descendants and relatives. For particulars see chapter on settlement of lower Montezuma Valley.

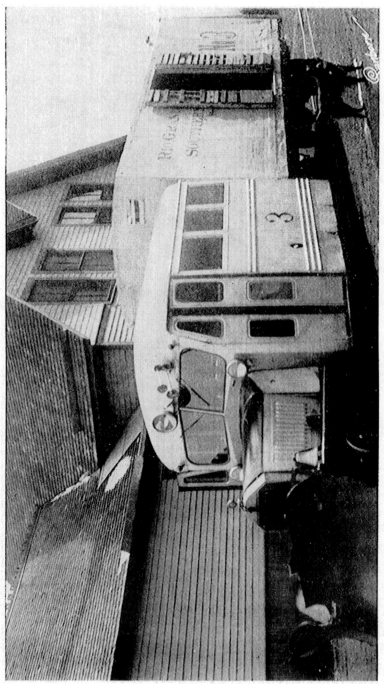

The "Galloping Goose" on the Denver & Rio Grande Southern. In a last effort to keep the road alive, the company installed these little motor driven outfits to take the place of trains. But car and truck competition was too strong and the little railroad had to give up the struggle. The town of Dolores has one of these in its City Park.

Denver & Rio Grande Western train of the old days, still operating between Alamosa and Durango and between Durango and Silverton, one of the very few narrow gauge railroads still operating in the U.S.A. Note the snowplow, always prepared for the worst.

An early County Fair — perhaps the first. The town of Cortez was then only a village and the fair grounds were what is now the southwest part of town and within the present city limits.

Mr. and Mrs. A. W. Duncan, very early settlers in McElmo Canon.

Victor N. (Rick) Ashbaugh, Mrs. and Mr. "Sandy Tozer, and Walter Brown, among the first settlers in McElmo Canon.

George W. Menefee came to the Mancos Valley with his parents in 1877 at the age of five years. Eighty-six years old May 30, 1958, he still lives on a small portion of the old home place and rides after cattle almost daily during the grazing season. His mind is still clear on early history and we are indebted to him for much help in preparing this book.

history of the county fell in Montezuma Valley, mostly in the north portion. There was much damage to the irrigating system.

County Assessor Brittain attended the state meeting of County Assessors in 1908, and in making comparisons found that Montezuma County had the lowest tax levy in the state; also showed largest per cent of taxes paid in any county in the state. The total tax valuation of the county was $2,100,000, an increase of $300,000 over previous year. Increase was mostly on improvements on non-commuted land indicating extent of new settlements that have been made.

There were big crop yields in 1908. Wheat made from 25 to 50 bushels per acre, oats 40 to 80 bushels threshermen report. There was also a good hay crop. Range cattle got very fat and an unusual amount of good cattle were shipped.

The Montezuma Telephone Co., at a stockholder's meeting, voted to sell the entire property holdings of the company, consisting of line from Mancos to Cortez and the Cortez system, to the Montezuma County Telephone Co. This is a new company formed for the purpose of taking over the old company, putting in an exchange at Cortez and extending lines to every part of the county, and to the Dolores exchange and also to make long distance connections with the Colorado Telephone Co. Fifty phones were signed for in Cortez, 1000 spruce poles contracted for early delivery and new switchboards at Dolores and Cortez are in the plans. Stock is sold only to home people and only as the money is needed. President of the new company is P. T. Guillet, Secy. H. Brigham, Jr., Attorney S. W. Carpenter of Mancos. There is a rush to get outside work done before winter.

The State Fair in 1908 was the largest and best in its history and Montezuma County had a big exhibit there. County wins fourth place and prize of $25 for the best general fruit display. Besides these general prizes, individual prizes were won as follows: 36 first prizes, 10 second prizes, 11 third prizes, 6 fourth prizes. W. T. Bozman alone won 27 firsts, 9 seconds, 2 thirds and 3 fourths. He also won first place over all competition for the best and largest collection of perfect apples.

The National Forest employees do some very constructive work by gathering 150 bushels of pine cones to reseed burned off areas on the Forest.

The big poles and net of new telephone wire in Cortez and Dolores are giving the towns quite a dignified look from a business standpoint.

A YEAR OF PROGRESS

The year of 1909 probably shows the greatest progress and the highest level of prosperity that had ever come to the county up to this time. Every part of the county shared in this prosperity wave. Many new business establishments came into existence and scores of new homes were built in every part of the county. Also there was more rain than in any year in recent history, and there was a big crop of everything grown on the farms: a big fruit and potato crop, good grain and hay crops, thousands of fat cattle and sheep were marketed, and the market for every product was the best in recent years. The mining industry is reviving and many thousands of dollars were being spent in developing the industry. At the time it looked as if some real and successful mining was being done. The agricultural industry of the county, and the stock raising industry, now began to cast a shadow before and to indicate definitely the future of the industries. Fruit, especially apples, and peaches, have clearly come to stay. Fruit was to endure vicissitudes and disappointments, but it was clear that quality products and good management would win. Potatoes was a good crop as long as there was a market; quality and yields were fully established. Grain, hay and livestock must always be basic. Good prices had brought these industries to the front and they can, and will, stand through good and bad years. Almost every individual was better off financially at the end of this year than he had ever been before, and the growth of bank deposits was proof that the people were getting "out of the woods" in a financial way.

The long standing water trouble in Montezuma Valley has been settled at least for the present, but their troubles were not over as the years and subsequent developments show. The present wave of prosperity was built on, first, the one-third million dollars that was being spent for the rebuilding and enlarging of the ditch system in Montezuma Valley and the building of the Groundhog and the Narraguinep reservoirs; second, many new people came in bringing new energy and new capital, and, third, there were good crop and good prices. Not one of these phases of local prosperity was destined to last. The ditch work was finished and the money spent; immigration dropped off, then almost ceased; crops were not so good and markets were lower too very much lower. The mining activity passed in a few months and ceased to be a factor. But the great burden of debt and of maturing obligations went on, production costs were high for the times, and the people were soon facing obligations they could not meet. From 1910 or 1911 to 1920, there were distressing times for people who struggled to save themselves and meet obligations that others could not meet, or did not try to meet. The district defaulted in meeting its obligations and there was little or no funds to keep up maintenance of the irrigation system. The struggle continued through the years, but was never given up. Many fell by the wayside, but the heroic souls held on. Victory was ahead, but few there were who could say how long it would take to achieve that victory. The day of new hope and confidence came in 1920, when the finances of the irrigation district were reorganized on a new basis.

H. H. Smith is elected Chairman of the irrigation district board to take the place of Charles Matson who has served long and most acceptably on the board. He deserves a well earned rest.

Cooper and Collier, Mancos lumber producers, open a lumber yard and there is much building going on in the county seat; also in Dolores and Mancos and many elegant new homes are coming into being.

S. G. Todd is opening up a vein of fine coal on Mesa Verde to supply the Cortez area with coal.

The work of enlarging and rebuilding the Montezuma Valley water system is making rapid progress. A contract has been let to build flume to irrigate the Redlands.

In 1909 we find the county still building its hopes for the future on railway transportation to the south. It seems to be the only relief the people can think of.

The County Commissioners will spend $1000 on the McElmo Canon road to Utah state line, in 1909. The volume of freight and travel to the San Juan oil fields and placer grounds demand a better road.

Three country schools and 45 new settlers are the results to 1909, of the building of the Summit reservoir. This in 4 years of time.

In spite of the disappointing results, previously, of potato raising a new effort was made in 1909 to get people to raise potatoes. A special train, bearing college people to lecture on potato growing visited the county. Large crowds met the trains and practical potato growers discussed every phase of potato growing and marketing. The visitors were pleased with the large crowds and the interest shown. They are just trying to help, they state.

The State Assembly approves $2,000 for the East Mancos road and $3,850 for prospecting for artesian water in Montezuma Valley.

R. R. Smith shipped 30 cars of potatoes to the market from Dolores at $1.25 per 100 pounds on board cars. Potatoes will bring from $12,000 to $15,000 into the big valley.

Hubert Halls sells Cortez Herald to Geo. Hutt and Clarence Howard. Halls was inexperienced and was glad to get out.

Successful farmers' institutes in the county indicates interest and progress all over the county.

A potato and fruit grower's association was organized at Arriola in August in 1909, for Arriola and Lebanon communities.

A heavy hail storm September 6, 1909, nearly wiped out the fruit crop in McElmo Canon, especially the peach crop which was just being harvested. The loss ran into thousands of dollars.

W. T. Bozman, of McElmo, markets three car loads of apples in Denver, the first of the shipment, and fiteen cars yet to go, all to one firm. They sold for the highest prices paid on the Denver market, fall of 1909.

The Montezuma Valley Fair Association is incorporated. J. W. Bozman, Guy Harrison, G. H. Rudy, W. F. Mowry, R. R. Smith, H. Brigham, Jr., and George Reeder are the incorporators.

Joseph Sparks Sheek died Nov. 8, 1909, aged 82 years, 11 mo. 16 days. Mancos' Grand old man and grim warrior in many of life's battles on the frontier. He came to Parrott City in 1876 and engaged in business and mining. He came to Montezuma Valley and takes up what was later the Geo. Taylor place and in 1879 he settles on a ranch in the Mancos Valley where he lived, for the most part, until the time of his death.

The Coppingers are the grain kings of Montezuma Valley. Bill Coppinger has 6,491 bushels of grain and sells oats on ranch at $2 per 100 pounds, and puts 50 fat hogs on the market. Tom Coppinger had 6,100 bushels, Charley Coppinger $2000 in grain and a herd of hogs, fall of 1909. Hay is going to the mining camps by the car load, $14 for alfalfa hay and $16 for timothy, and many cars were sold.

The Masons organize at Cortez Nov. 21, 1909. A large Mancos delegation is in attendance.

The County Fair Association has a capital stock of $10,000 which will be sold to raise money to buy a site for a county fair and put up the necessary buildings.

There is much activity in oil below Bluff. Four new rigs are just on the ground and others are coming. The Arcola Oil Co. has two good wells and starts to marketing their product.

Jean Powell, well known Bluff freighter, made 25 trips last year and 23 for this present year of 1909. There are others, which indicates volume of freight being moved.

The county is being connected to Monticello by telephone line. Work was completed in December, 1909.

Cortez finally gets a pressure water system. The fire plugs were installed in December, 1909, and the town has real fire protection for the first time.

A real estate deal of historic importance was consummated Dec. 10, 1909, when Bert Campbell, of Iowa, bought 1400 acres of land in Montezuma Valley paying $40,000. He bought the land for farmers who are coming in from Iowa.

Telephone connection is made between Cortez and Bluff. Phones are hooked up along the line. The new water works system in Cortez was accepted from the contractors by the Town Board December 25, 1909. The town now has an abundant supply of water and a gravity water system with pressure sufficient to insure good fire protection.

On February 29, 1910, the new Methodist Church at Cortez is dedicated, Presiding Elder Lee and Chancellor Buchtel conducting the ceremonies.

Early in 1910 work was started on the Bluff City road, hitherto a very poor road. The volume of traffic is demanding a better road.

C. H. Rudy brought in five fine horses from Indiana. Two of the stallions were especially fine, one a Belgian weighing 2,200 pounds, and the other a Percheron weighing 2,400 pounds. When they attempted to change these horses to narrow gauge cars at Alamosa they found that the big fellows wouldn't go into the small stock cars so they were compelled to provide a baggage coach and put one in each end.

P. B. Gates receives a $50 prize on his exhibit of the best 10 boxes of fancy picked apples at the International Apple Exposition, held in Denver in fall of 1909. They were Rome Beauty Apples and were exhibited in competition with the best growers of the best fruit in the entire United States. This kind of success makes history for fruit growing in Montezuma County.

The year 1910 opens with a very active season in real estate in Montezuma Valley; the price and volume of business best yet experienced.

The election in the Montezuma Valley irrigation district, held April 9, 1910, on the question of issuing $125,000 in bonds carried with only one dissenting vote. The funds so derived are to be used in paying obligations already incurred, completing the Groundhog reservoir and putting the finishing work on various parts of the valley irrigating system.

About April 10, 1910, water for irrigating was turned into the new Montezuma Valley irrigating system, all but one lateral where construction work was not yet completed. This is the first head of water for the rebuilt and enlarged system.

The County Commissioners buy a spraying outfit to spray fruit trees to be hired to the fruit growers at a cost to them of $5 per day. Anyone who needs to spray his trees, on the report of the County Horticulturolist, and does not do the job, the county commissioners will order it done and the expense charged to the owner.

June 10, 1910, W. H. Blake, for years manager of the Montezuma Valley irrigating system, resigned his position. He is regarded as having done an excellent job for the district.

The Fort Lewis Indian School is closed. All School equipment and supplies will be moved to Navajo Springs, hereafter agency headquarters. Navajo Springs is being renovated and rebuilt and the water supply improved.

The Montezuma Oil & Development Co. is organized by Cortez people. They secure oil leases and plan to bring in a standard rig and test for oil to the 5,000 foot level.

In 1910 Montezuma County farmers are harvesting a bountiful grain crop, 60 bushels of wheat and 80 to 90 bushels of oats per acre is not an uncommon yield.

The grain and fruit exhibit taken to the state fair at Pueblo in 1910 made history for Montezuma County, A. W .Dillon, B. P. Porter, W. G. Clucas and W. T. Bozman took the exhibit and the winnings on grain were as follows, partial list of awards: 1st, 2nd, and 3rd on winter wheat, 1st on redtop grass, 1st on orchard grass, 1st on Russian Millet,

2nd on German Millet, 1st, 2nd, and 3rd on field corn, 2nd on wild grass, 2nd on alfalfa, 2nd on white oats, 2nd on timothy, 1st on largest watermelon, 1st on largest pumpkin, and every one won a prize. The fruit exhibit was equally successful, under W. T. Bozman and they took down premiums by the score: 1st for the largest apple, 1st for the largest 5 apples, and many others. The Montezuma showing attracted a lot of attention and whole crowds were amazed at the exhibit shown.

The County Assessor report shows a property valuation of $1,937,-372 assessed at less than half the valuation, and shows the largest gain in one year on record.

W. T. Bozman is doing a flourishing real estate business, closing up to $10,000 in deals every week. He is advertising constantly by putting on displays of county products at fairs all over the country. He brings in new people and new wealth.

Thomas Tully, of the State Highway Commission, came to confer with County Commissioners Halls, Byers and Myler in regard to the proposed state road east and west through the county. No information was given out, but the Mancos paper got some facts. The proposed road is to be a part of a national highway from Kansas City clear through to Mesa Verde Park, and on west into Utah without a single break. This was the beginning of U. S. Highway 160 from Kansas City through Colorado, and Montezuma County, all the way to Salt Lake City.

Real value is coming to land in Montezuma Co., land is changing hands regularly and sales up to $100 an acre are not uncommon. Land is getting to be worth paying taxes on, the delinquent tax list being the shortest this year it has been in several years.

The census of 1910 shows Montezuma Co. had a population of 5,029 as against 3,058 in 1900.

The directors of the Montezuma Valley irrigation district, in December, 1910, succeeded in placing the $125,000 bond issue, voted sometime previous, got an initial payment of $15,000 with balance to come when needed. This money is supposed to complete the water system in full and pay up all past due obligations.

About April 7, 1911, Cortez gets its first motion picture show to be housed in the new building erected by Geo. McEwen. Harry Freeman is putting in the picture machine.

C. H. Rudy, Cashier of the First National Bank of Cortez, purchases and takes over the Cortez Herald, leaving George Hutt out in the cold. Difficulty over town affairs caused the action. In the town election every available vote was gotten out and 204 votes were cast. The issues were more imaginary than real, and the town survived in fine shape and went marching on to success and triumph.

The daily mail service between Cortez and Bluff was discontinued and a weekly service substituted. It causes a great congestion of mail in Cortez. Bluff is an important point on account of the oil activities.

Land values are still going up in Montezuma Valley, in spring of 1911. There was one sale at $125 an acre, one at $140 and one at $150.

A new, and much needed, concrete bridge is being built across Mc-Elmo Creek below Cortez two miles.

Cortez cleans up old school grounds, summer 1911, preparatory to erecting a new school building.

W. G. Swigart has 60 men at work on the Montezuma Valley irrigating system, cleaning and enlarging ditches and canals. The system has never given as good service as it should and this work is designed to remedy all defects and weaknesses.

A bid for the purchase of the Cortez Herald was rejected, so, on April 5, 1911, the First National Bank is still in the newspaper business.

The oil drilling rig of the Big Four-San Juan Oil and Development Co. is brought in from Pagosa Springs and unloaded at Mancos. The company will drill first in McElmo canon near Battlerock.

Between Jan. 1, 1911, and April 25, 20,000 acres of land was filed on in Montezuma Co. as oil land. The number of claims filed was 130.

The Montezuma Valley Produce Co. was organized and incorporated at Cortez with a capital stock of $50,000. Will support and promote interests of the producers. One of the first things they will try for is a broom factory.

As of May 12, 1911, the vast stretch of rolling country out around Yellow Jacket and beyond is beginning a transformation. Scores of homesteads have been taken and these pioneers of progress are clearing hundreds of acres of land, using every means at their command, and many new farms are coming into existence.

The postoffice at Navajo Springs was established about April 1st, 1911.

D. M. Longenbaugh purchases the Cortez Herald and takes over, April, 1911.

Cortez is establishing grade lines on all streets preparatory to putting in cement walks.

The Mesa Verde Oil & Gas Co. starts, in June, 1911, to drill a test well four miles south of Cortez.

The first oil to be found in Montezuma Co. was encountered by the Big Four-San Juan Co. in the well being drilled at Battlerock in McElmo Canon. The time was Wednesday evening, July 12, 1911, and the depth was 150 feet. The spark of hope that nestled in every breast was soon kindled into wild enthusiasm as the news became known. Tidings were passed from lip to lip as the magnificent possibilities of the country loomed up before excited imaginations. In a little while the wires were busy in every direction and the message was sent to Denver and other outside points. The oil was found in what is known in the San Juan field as the "Baby Sand." There was only a light flow of oil and, on account of the water that also came into the well, the exact amount of the flow could not be determined. The satisfying fact was that oil had been found and was proof that the San Juan oil field extends well into this area. The strike proved to be only a light flow of high grade oil and no other flow was encountered in the well.

A rain historic in intensity and in its disastrous consequences fell the week of July 10, 1911, in Montezuma Valley, and well over the county. A number of important flumes, in the irrigating system, were washed out and some that were expensive. The big laterals were broken in a dozen or more places, and it was reported that McElmo Creek was the highest it had ever before been known. The floor worked havoc and the repair work was a big expense to the district, already burdened with financial difficulties. The rain was also heavy in the mountains and all streams were on a rampage and much damage was done to roads, bridges and crops.

A new postoffice called Lewis was established in July, 1911. Growth in local population called for the new office.

Recent big floods make a canon in a canon down in McElmo Canon. One ranch residence is gone and parts of several orchards and 40 acres of fine wheat on one farm were washed away. Some damage to other farms.

The Colorado Land & Development Co. takes bankruptcy. They own the Lebanon townsite and other property. S. H. Phleger masterminded the enterprise.

The Mesa Verde Oil & Gas Co. drills a well for artesian water 635 feet deep. They find a pretty good flow of water, but not a flowing well. Some gas is reported. The state accepts and pays for well.

The total assessed valuation of the county climbed to $2,288,269 in 1911, a gain of $380,582 in one year.

The State Land Board decides to sell 8,000 acres of land in the Montezuma Valley Irrigation District in small tracts to farmers to get as many new settlers as possible in the district. Cortez plans a big county fair and asks the land board to hold the sale during the fair.

The well of the Big Four Co., being drilled for oil, was down 500 feet in October, 1911, and struck water which rose 400 feet in the well. This made an expensive job of casing out the water.

The movement for a state highway from one end of the county to the other, is revived. The county is to put up $5,000 and the state $5,000. They decided to try to get 100 convict laborers for the job.

The Mesa Verde Oil & Gas Co. starts works on a new well on their own lease the last week in Sept., 1911.

C. A. Frederick again takes charge of the Montezuma Journal, after a few years in California in the interest of his health.

The county fair, October 4 to 7, which had been advertised far and wide and for which extensive preparations had been made, was greatly handicapped by the heavy rains that prevailed. The exhibit of orchard, field and range products was the largest and finest ever shown in the county, but attendance, especially outside attendance, was light. The sale of 1500 acres of state land was arranged to take place during the fair and the State Land Board was on hand, but buyers were scarce.

The sale of state land started, as scheduled, Oct. 6, and 246 pieces of land were offered for sale and, of this number, only 40 pieces were bid in, almost all at the appraised price. About half of the buyers were local people taking land adjoining their own holdings, and half outside buyers. Only a few pieces sold above the appraised price. The land board was greatly disappointed, as was every one else, and the sale was adjourned to Denver to be continued there.

The floods washed out the big wooden bridge in McElmo Canon and did so much other damage to the road that the County Commissioners abandoned it and built an entirely new road from the Hallar-Cox place on down the south side of the Canon to a point even with the big orchards, where the new bridge was built.

The Arriola school house, the best and finest rural school in the county, burned to the ground the week of Oct. 27, 1911.

The Dolores-San Juan Telephone Co. is extending telephone lines and connecting many Summit Ridge farm homes into their telephone system.

The year 1911, with its abundance of rain, produced good crops and many record yields of wheat, oats, barley and hay were reported from every part of the county. There was an unusually good crop of corn in McElmo, and in other localities where corn is grown. There are reports of yields of 100 bushels of oats per acre, 75 of barley, 40 to 60 bushels of wheat and corn up to 100 bushels per acre.

The work of putting Montezuma Valley irrigating system back in condition after two heavy flood damages, was a tremendous task, but Supt. Henry put all the help he could get on the job and repairs were pretty well finished before winter came on. The closest race was on the Mesa Verde Lateral that takes water to the farthest part of the district on the south side.

Livery men of Cortez made regular trips to Placerville with passengers until railway transportation was restored.

There was a good crop of apples in the fruit belt of the county in 1911 and the flood damage to the railroad was a serious matter for a while. Many growers had cellars and stored their apples until they could ship them. Cattle men had the same trouble and some drove their cattle and sheep to points beyond the washouts and loaded them. Others held their flocks and herds on grass or in the fields until transportation by rail became available. As an example of the apple crop Tim Irvin, of Lake View, picked 526 boxes of apples from 32 trees. Other high yields were reported from the fruit belt.

All of the 126 suits brought by B. N. Freeman against the water users, and former water users, of Montezuma Valley were dismissed from the district docket week of Nov. 10, 1911, in session at Durango.

C. C. Halbrook of Alamosa took the action, he sitting in Judgment on the case. The cases involved cases against the water users for water used, in past years for irrigation, the water users claiming that, in justice, they owed nothing. This ended for all time the controversy that had been so long pending.

W. C. Miller won prizes amounting to $325 at the Denver apple show. Most of the prizes were won on Delicious apples.

The Interstate Bank of Denver, in late 1911, bought several thousand dollars in Irrigation District warrants. This greatly relieved financial conditions in the district and was evidence of the faith this noted Denver firm has in the ability of the big valley to make good.

J. E. Brown takes over the Cortez Herald in January, 1912.

The Gibson Lumber Co., of Cortez, announces plans for building storage facilities at Cortez to handle potatoes, onions, beans, grain, apples, etc. They plan to operate large motor trucks between Mancos and Cortez, the first time this class of transportation is mentioned.

The automobile is beginning to make history in Montezuma County. Cars and trucks are calling for better roads. The trend continues through the years—fine cars, fine roads.

In 1912 the county fair was a great success. The showing of poultry and livestock was the best ever. Almost every kind of grain, vegetables, grass—wild and domestic, and every kind of fruit grown in this latitude, and alfalfa and all clovers were on display. It was truly an amazing exhibit.

On Feb. 9, 1913, there was an oil strike in the Meadows, fifteen miles below Farmington, at 1700 feet. Oil rose in the well to within 400 feet of the surface. Farmington is wild with excitement and it quickens the oil fever here.

In the spring of 1913 many people still are settling out in the dry farming country, and much improvement is going on. The greater future of the country is coming into view.

One of the remarkable things about the people of Montezuma County is their unfaltering faith in the greater future of the country. They made the unvariable mistake of thinking this greater future laid just ahead—in the immediate future. They lived and died in the faith. Greatness was on the way, but no one realized how long it would take, or how much capital and labor it would take to bring about the new conditions. They could not realize how much time and patience, how much toil and endeavor, how much capital and faith it takes to develop a new country; that a community must grow into greatness rather than achieve it in a day. Every new country must work out its own salvation and Montezuma County is still working on hers.

Twenty-five motorists meet with the County Commissioners. They want to cooperate for good roads. Automobiles were a factor for good roads from the start, and are yet.

In the spring of 1913 the county reaches the road dragging stage of

266

its road maintenance program. Men and teams are hired on standby basis and go over the roads with a steel drag just as they are drying up in the spring or after rainy periods. Does much good in lieu of nothing better.

Summer of 1913 crop land in Montezuma Valley has grown to 15,-000 acres. This acreage is actually producing crops.

The summer of 1913 began to witness the passing of the horse and buggy days. Everyone who needed new transportation bought a car.

The last of August, 1913, the new six cylinder cars began to appear in the towns of the county—self-starters, electric lights, 35 horsepower —some car for the time.

The County Fair association is incorporated. Plans are for the association to own their own grounds and buildings. Will erect exhibit building 48x72 feet.

The summer of 1913 very dry. No winter range in the lower country. Some cattlemen bought hay. Others shipped, and shipping was heavy. Plan to restock in the spring.

Frank and Mike Knight are very successful farmers of Montezuma Valley and valuable citizens, as an example to others as to how to get good results farming and get things done.

The Big Four Co. abandons well. The reamer stuck in the bottom when casing was raised so they could never get it out, the well caved and the hole was abandoned. They will sink a new well.

In 1913, ranchers began to complain that their land was not producing as well as it once did. This was the first indication of soil depletion and that the land was being mined of its fertility and nothing was being done to restore it.

The Stein scheme petered out. Now it is the Albuquerque, Cortez & Salt Lake R. R. that has surveyors in the field. The people are still grabbing at straws.

County fair in 1913 splendid success; fine program and wonderful exhibit of farm products, livestock and school work. Almost paid expenses. Will try for bigger and better fair next year.

In 1913 the Delicious Apple began to be recognized as the apple best suited in every way for the commercial apple of this county. The altitude, soil, sunshine, and other climatic conditions make it a leader in flavor, food value, texture and color finish, and favored over all others as an eating apple.

In Nov., 1913, the County Commissioners bought the old W. B. Wilson place of 160 acres for a poor farm, in the interest of economy. It proved to be a mistake.

For a few years, beginning about 1912, hog raising became a main farming industry in Montezuma Co.; first, fat hogs for the market, then stock hogs for San Luis Valley to be fattened in their pea fields. Hundreds of car loads were produced and shipped, then it was all over, or nearly all over.

In December, 1914, the County Commissiners, at the insistence of Prof. Snyder of the Fort Lewis school, agreed to hire a County Agent for La Plata and Montezuma Counties, the government putting up $1,000, La Plata Co. $1,000 and Montezuma Co. $500. This was the first step in Extension work in Montezuma Co. although some club work among the boys and girls was being done.

After coming up through great tribulations, the Montezuma Valley Irrigation District, was able, on June 1, 1914, to come forward with a good healthy statement, and money to pay its semi-annual interest promptly and on time. The district seems to have never passed up an interest payment entirely, but there has been little money for maintenance and other costs.

Early in June, 1914, T. C. Henry, Supt. of the Montezuma Valley Irrigation District, announced, under his own signature, that the District, for the first time in its history, could give a full head of water to every water user, and have water to spare at the end of every ditch. Three years ago, he recites, there were 22,000 acres under cultivation in the valley. Now there are 26,000 acres. At the present time our water supply would irrigate 100,000 acres. In 1911 it cost $77,804.21 to operate the system. In 1912 the cost was $32,203.40. In 1914 the cost was $24,160.84. He predicts that next year, if everyone pays their taxes, the water rate can be cut down one-half what it is now. There is a big crop and he thinks everyone is contented and happy.

Tractor farming was just getting under way out in the dry farming country in 1914. J. F. and M. A. Barton put into service on their farm a big gasoline tractor and implements to go with it. They had 300 acres of wheat which was so good they wished they had 3,000 acres. Hitherto steam tractors had furnished all the power for power farming.

Auditing the books of the County Treasurer in August, 1914, caused quite a furor of discussion. Chas. Reid was County Treasurer. The checkup revealed that Reid had a good set of books and little fault could be found with the finances. It showed further, that the affairs of the county were, in 1913, conducted at $15,000 less cost than in 1912, which caused a better feeling among the taxpayers.

A postoffice is established at Lake View, Feb., 1914. The name is changed to Lake Vista.

The people of Redlands Mesa finally got their flume completed in 1914, and ready for water. Cost was $16,000 and it is to be taken into the irrigation district. It was a metal inverted cyphon and didn't last long.

In 1914 a car load of field peas were shipped in to be planted to produce hog feed, after the practice of the people in San Luis Valley. It didn't last.

The Moqui postoffice in McElmo Canon is discontinued, April, 1914, Star Route will serve the postal needs of the people.

Ike Stevens buys the Big Four Oil rig. Moves it to Disappointment country and will test for oil in the "Saucer Basin."

On Oct. 1, 1914, 23 cars of very fine cattle were loaded out at the Lost Canon loading pens. It was the largest single train shipment of cattle ever to go out over the Southern.

In the fall of 1914 many new cars came into use in the county and cars became quite common on the road. Nearly all local trips were being made in cars.

Oct. 31, 1914, passed away Mrs. Wm. Roessler, formerly Mrs. Geo. Bauer. She came to Mancos with her first husband in 1881. She was married to Geo. Bauer at Del Norte in 1872.

In January, 1915, a movement is started for a better overland road from Cortez to Gallup.

A furor of resentment and much carping criticism was stirred up in January, 1915, when a movement was started at Mancos for the formation of a new county out of the east end of Montezuma Co., to be called Mancos County. The movement came about when Mancos people became dissatisfied with the way county matters were being handled and with the weakness and indifference of the county government and the large amount of delinquent taxes that had not been collected. The effort was blocked in the legislature and failed, but the people were awakened to the real situation. They resolved that conditions could be improved, and they were improved, and, after a time, the matter was dropped and was no longer an issue.

About March 1, 1915, E. D. Smith, of Cedaredge, was appointed to the position of County Agent to serve both Montezuma and La Plata Counties, the government to pay $1,000, La Plata County $1,000 and Montezuma Co. $500. This was the beginning of agricultural extension work in this county. Mr. Smith proved to be a very able and efficient man for the work, but the farmers didn't know what it was all about and took little interest in what Mr. Smith was trying to do. A good start was made, however, dozens of boys' and girls' clubs were organized, and many older people came to a keen realization of the importance of the work. After a year Mr. Smith was called to higher duties in Extension work, but he did some very good work while he was here. He was always anxious and willing to help. First Boy's Agricultural Clubs are organized.

On March 10, 1915, the first Parent-Teachers Association was organized in District No. 6, with 40 charter members. Has been active all through subsequent years.

The sale of state land in the Montezuma Valley Irrigation District was nearly a complete failure although it was widely advertised. The finances of the District seemed to have been the main trouble. The Board levies an assessment of 80 cents an acre foot for maintenance under condition that one-half must be paid before water is turned in.

County Agent E. D. Smith is on the job and doing good work, May 10, 1915. Farmers, for the most part, are pleased with his help.

The Montezuma National Bank and the First National Bank of Cortez consolidate their business effective June 1, 1915. The Montezuma Valley National Bank continues the business at the same place with the same officers in charge.

Holders of Montezuma Valley Irrigation District bonds file a suit in the Federal District Court at Denver for $6,015 due on interest Coupons the first of last January. It is a test case to determine if the land of those who have paid taxes can be held for the taxes others have failed to pay.

The first meeting of the County Farm Bureau Federation was held June 9, at Cortez, 1916. The Bureau goes in for improved livestock, crop improvement, silos and boys' and girls' clubs. E. D. Smith was hired as County Agent for another year. More than ten thousand dollars worth of livestock and other property change hands through the Exchange Bulletin during the previous three months. The Bureau plans to cooperate with and help the County Agent. Committees were appointed and a lot of work planned. Farmers and leaders from every part of the county are interested in the work.

On August 16, 1916, the people of the San Juan celebrate at the top of the Continental Divide, now called Wolf Creek Pass, the opening of the new state highway, now known as the Navajo Trail. It was a very important event in the history of the San Juan Country, and a very important highway. Highways were still only dirt roads.

On July 1, 1916, there were 103 automobiles registered in Montezuma County, and several new ones not yet registered.

The "Indian Highway" across the reservation from Cortez to Gallup gets a Federal appropriation of $15,000, through the efforts of Edward T. Taylor. The aim, ultimately, is for a good highway.

Settlers are still going into the dry farming country in numbers. Just when it is thought that all the good land is taken, it is revealed that there is still room for more people on the dry land.

On July 17, 1916, Dick Kermode received at Mancos the first motor truck ever to be put into use in Montezuma County. The new vehicle of transportation was put into service at once taking a load of freight to Cortez. It wasn't long until motor trucks were plentiful and, like the cars, calling for better roads.

The county fair, last of September, 1916, was largest and best ever held. Drew the largest crowd the last day ever assembled at one place and at one time in the history of Montezuma County.

At the International Soils Products Exposition held at El Paso, Texas, in October, 1916, Montezuma County won second place in the all county competition and was close contestant for first place, on general display of farm and orchard products.

There is an additional appropriation of $15,000 for the Indian Highway from Cortez to Gallup.

After three years of bloody war and unending struggle in Europe, on April 2, 1917, the war comes home to us, calling for maximum production from every farm, calling for the service of every person able to do any kind of work or render any kind of service; calling for our young men to bear arms and join in the conflict that was not of their making, but calling for the defense of a cause that was as dear to us as life itself. The people of Montezuma County responded with their strength and their lives.

The first volunteers for army service came forward May 5, 1917. They were Wilkes Bozman, Sam Longenbaugh, Cop Ellard, Merle Ellis, Delbert Guillet, Horace Kermode and Hugh Kelly. Roy Freeman goes to Navy, Lee Halls to Coast Artillery; David Halls, Harlan Beaber, Dilworth Halls, David Carr and Roger Owen volunteer into army the last of May. Rodney Sheek goes to Navy.

Tuesday, June 5, first registration day. About 400 in the county register subject to call to service in the armed forces. People all over county hold public meetings and organize to do everything they can to support the nation's war effort.

The women organize for service. They will support the war effort with all they have in strength, mind, and skill.

Early after the declaration of war the call came to all farmers to bend their efforts toward top production of every farm product, and Montezuma County farmers responded with a will. Not an acre of land was left idle, and to take the place of the workers drawn into the army car loads of farm machinery, labor saving machinery, was put into use. There were no slackers in the army of the soil. In addition to producing more the farmers were asked to save more—to save food —something unheard of in this country before. It was hard to realize that the country was really at war. There was nothing to disturb the quiet day or night, and nothing to disturb the mind. There was that tenseness of feeling however; a foreboding of sorrowful days to come.

July 20, Ed Lewis and George Sherwin, having volunteered, were called into the service, and Horace Stevenson volunteers, passes muster and goes at once into the armed service.

The Farm Bureau is well organized all over the county, and through it, the farmers are discussing their problems, planning together how to meet their difficulties and cooperate for best results. County Agent Smith is on the job night and day.

The year 1917 brought a dry summer. There are good crops, but feed on the winter range is very poor and many more cattle must be fed through the winter than usual.

Montezuma County women are working through the Mesa Verde Chapter of the National League of Women's Service. They organize various branches for war work, and have local working units. Operation headquarters are at Cortez.

The first call for army service came Aug. 6, 1917. The call is for 24 men, but many of the boys fail to pass muster requirements, so several more of this number had to be called.

The third contingent of Montezuma County boys leave for induction center Sept. 27, 1917.

Week of Dec. 10, 1917, eight more boys were called to the army, being the fourth call. There were four volunteers.

Homesteading new land goes on without ceasing. The Durango land office had 77 land filings in the month of December, 1917.

The United States Circuit Court of Appeals has reversed the decision of the United States District Court in the suit between the bond holders of the Montezuma Valley Irrigation District and the District; the Court of Appeals holding in substance that the payment of the district tax by a landowner did not release his land from further assessment to make good the deficiency caused by the failure of others to pay their taxes. This made a new and more hopeless situation in the valley, and the people were almost unanimous in their determination to pay no more taxes until matters are straightened out on a more equitable basis.

War Savings Stamps and Thrift Stamp go over with a big sale, old and young buying all they can.

Last contingent of the first draft went out Mar. 4, four in number. As usual there was a big demonstration when the draftees entrained.

G. P. Newsom is accepted and employed by the County Commissioners as County Agent, Mar. 4, 1918.

The first Liberty Loan drive failed to go over by a broad margin. Only one out of 93 bought bonds and the bonds bought amounted to only $3 per capita. The second drive last of March and first of April, organized for results. There was a determination that it must go over the top big and strong. The effort is organized all over the county. In the first drive there was no organization and no effort. Sentiment: Let the rich buy the bonds.

April 6, 1918, was the first anniversary of the war and was observed by appropriate ceremonies. The Third Liberty Loan drive was started.

The drive for big crop production is also on. There is more need; we must feed our allies as well as ourselves; food will win the war.

The women are all working and they resort to everything to raise money. 60% goes to Red Cross; 40% to local organizations to buy material to make things—pajamas, socks, sweaters, gauze, bandages, compresses, etc.

First contingent of second draft called March 28. Only 2 in first call.

County Council of Defense holds meeting at Cortez. Committees at work in every part of the county, and they are getting down to real work.

County Agent Newsom is directing the war work among the farmers and organizing for results. The work is being directed through the Farm Bureau.

All wheat in hands of farmers or dealers is ordered to be turned over to the government at local mill or elevator by May 1st, to be paid for by the government. It is ordered also that all persons having more than 30 days supply of flour on hand report to the government or nearest county food administrator. Our allies are getting short on food.

The county was canvassed for old clothing of every kind by the Mountain division of the Red Cross, for Belgium, and 300 tons was gotten together in the Division.

The Red Cross work is supported locally by membership donations, monthly. Considerable sums came in and Red Cross Chapters all over the county are busy making everything the army can use, especially hospital supplies.

The Junior Red Cross is organized in the schools and put on campaigns to raise funds and they get it.

June 25, another contingent of boys off to training camp—16 in number.

On June 21 and June 23 the county had two good rains, the second assuming flood proportions. Very unusual rains for June, but they were welcome as the previous winter and spring had been dry.

The nation calls for 300,000 men and Montezuma County is to furnish 40 to be taken in three calls. Aug. 5, 10 are called; Aug. second call, 19 are called; Aug. 15, 10 are called.

On July 18, nine men were called and departed for the training camp.

On July 24, 8 boys entrain at Mancos for camp; two from other points in county.

Cars on the road more plentiful than ever. County licenses 331 cars up to Aug. 9, 1918. 256 previous year.

Another call comes for young men to register for military service. All who had become 21 years of age since June 5, 1917, must register Aug. 24, 1918.

Another contingent of boys left for training camp August 12, 10 in number.

On September 12, 1918, all men between 18 and 36 were called to register, that were not already registered.

The Fourth Liberty Loan, asking the county to buy $139,250 in bonds came first days of October. Everything was made ready for a quick campaign to be finished by Oct. 12, 1918.

Oct. 15, seven more soldier boys left for training camp.

The flu epidemic is getting serious in every part of the county and deaths are being reported. Closing ban on schools and all public places still effective.

The county "goes over the top" in the liberty loan drive for $139,-250, with a few thousand to spare, making up for early failures. The women were a large factor in putting over this loan. There were 838 buyers and a total subscription of $154,350.

County has furnished its quota of Student Nurse Reserve; some counties are behind quota; call for surplus.

The War Work Campaign quota is $7,360, all for benefit of soldiers at the front.

Wardell Allis, northwest part of county, dies of flu. Kipling Wade, of Mancos, dies at Leavenworth, Kansas, after days of illness.

Up to noon, Nov. 1st, Silverton had had 128 deaths from flu, largest death rate of any town in the state.

The Montezuma Valley Irrigation District was denied a new hearing in the Federal Court, of the case of the bondholders of the district against the district, which means that the recent decision of the Court must stand. This is to the effect that all property in the district is security for the payment of the bonds, and the payment of taxes exempts no property from the bond mortgage. It was apparent now that a new bargain must be driven, or the affairs of the district be reorganized on a different plan. Some change must be made, and that very soon.

Armistice is signed on the terms demanded by the allies, November 11, 1918, and warfare at the front ceases. The terms of the treaty, in detail, are yet to be worked out. The news of the signing of the Armistice was hailed with great rejoicing by the people of the county, state and nation.

In late 1918 we continue to make history in the county as motor trucks come into more general use. By their use towns are brought closer together, distant ranches are brought nearer to town, real estate values enhanced in almost every place.

December 27, the old year is going out with much sorrow and great rejoicing. No year in history has witnessed so much sorrow and suffering; so much tragedy, and crime committed in the name of war. With the dawn of peace what a burden of anxiety and moral fear is lifted from the heart and mind.

At the county tax sale 1919, 246 sales were made against 110 the previous year.

When an Indian dies, by the Indian rule of inheritance, the dead man's brother gets his property. The government has considerable trouble getting the Indians to change this.

The boys are coming home from the army one, two and three at a time mostly from camps in the United States.

A movement is under way down in the big valley to put all irrigation indebtedness on an individual mortgage basis, in April, 1919.

The county authorities have purchased a book designed for the special purpose of recording the discharge papers of all Montezuma County boys that served in any way in the armed forces of their country. Should be a valuable service to the boys.

Although the war is over Montezuma County puts over another Liberty Loan drive, some thousand over the amount called for.

The old Episcopal Church, a fine church building and one of the oldest buildings in Cortez, burned in April, 1919.

The Farm Bureau is reorganized. Prominent farmers from every part of the county take an active interest. Plan to do some real good for the farming industry. June 16, 1919.

During 1919 County Agent G. P. Newsom makes strong effort to be useful, and dozens of girls and boys clubs are organized, but it is hard to get the interest of the farmers. Indifference is the main fault.

Along with the use of more cars come better cars. As an example the new Fords came equipped with self-starter, electric lights, storage battery, demountable tires and other improvements.

F. A. Morgan is putting in a small, Marvel type flour mill at Lewis to help take care of the rapidly growing grain crop of that locality.

In September, 1919, Montezuma County has 3.41 persons to the square mile, the assessed valuation is $931.36 per person and the bank deposits are $204.97 per person. These figures explain why tax levies were high, roads were poor, and why we are of so small commercial importance. A big county for a few people and small capital.

Cortez has added another hook and ladder wagon and another hose cart to her fire fighting equipment. Calculated to lower chances of fire destruction and encourage building new and better homes.

The county fair in fall of 1919 was a success, especially in point of attendance. A good agricultural and fruit exhibit, the usual sports events and an airplane exhibit, the first many of the people had ever seen.

The work of reorganizing the Montezuma Valley irrigation district is just about completed under the able direction of Ex-Governor Carlson and they are about ready to dissolve the old district. Under the new plan individual mortgages will be executed and every person will pay for his own water. The aggregate of all these mortgages will be the basis for a new loan to pay off the old bonds.

In October, 1919, Montezuma County had 25 school districts and school was being conducted in every one of them. Sixty-three teachers are employed. The Mancos district has 16 teachers, Dolores 11, Cortez 6, Arriola 3. A few others employ 2 teachers and the rest only one.

The vote on the proposition of reorganizing the Montezuma Valley Irrigation District resulted in 209 for and 20 against. The near unanimous vote will be a big asset to the new order of things. All the bonds must now be called in, the necessary steps taken to dissolve the old district and individual trust deeds made out for all the land owners.

275

Under the new plan land can be sold for taxes and title passed. Every one knows the exact sum he is liable for. Under the new plan land can be sold or exchanged and clear titles given. Taxes and interest must be paid and if anyone feels the burden too heavy he can sell a part of his holdings, or all of it if he so desires, and relieve himself. The new plan soon improved the finances of the county and was a great benefit to every interest.

One year after Armistice Day finds nearly all the Montezuma County boys back home. The first anniversary was celebrated in every part of the county, by the boys, and everybody joined in.

Mrs. A. W. Dillon died Jan. 16, 1920. She was an early pioneer in the county, first at Lone Dome, then at Big Bend, lastly, near Arriola in the big valley. She was always a leader in social and cultural affairs, and beloved by many, many friends. Survived by one son, Ralph Dillon, and four daughters: Mrs. Walter Longenbaugh, Mrs. Ed Winborn, Mrs. Frank Royce and Miss Florence Dillon.

In the fall of 1920 automobiles and trucks put the McElmo Canon fruit crop on the market, moved the producer nearer the consumer. Most of the fruit sold at the orchards.

The action of Judge W. N. Searcy rendering a decision dissolving the old irrigation district in Montezuma Valley and all the liabilities of the old district being taken care of by the individual liability method, the old district became a thing of the past. A new district was now formed that was free from debt and set up to administer the new order of things. The blanket mortgage, which imposed a repressive weight on the people for almost twenty years, has been lifted and land can be exchanged freely and at full value. Water can be paid for in full and good, sound titles can be given. The decision dissolving the old district took effect September 20, 1920.

The population of the county by the 1920 census was 6,260. Ten years ago it was 5,029, twenty years ago it was 3,058 and 30 years ago, or in 1890, it was 1,529, one year after the county was formed. The last 10 years showed the smallest growth in the population of the county of any decade in its history, the increase being only 1,135 for the entire 10 years. During this time the Irrigation District was defaulting on its interest and bond payments, taxes were not being paid, few people came in to make their home and there was dissatisfaction and discontent.

Populations of the towns of Montezuma County for the past three decades, census figures:

	1920	1910	1900
Cortez	541	565	125
Dolores	465	320	108
Mancos	682	567	383

The new ditch association for the big valley organized and started to operate about Nov. 1, 1920. E. H. Kittell, Pres., W. I. Myler, Vice

Pres., John Wesch, Secy-Treas. Wesch was also assistant to the Supt. E. W. Henry, who was retained.

On November 18, 1920, the County Farm Bureau reorganizes and prepares to do a lot of good work; Committees were appointed on various phases of farm work, and boys' and girls' clubs are especially stressed.

A depression came on in 1921 and seemed to grow in intensity as the year advanced. The prices of livestock and grain went down. Labor, lumber and merchandise remained rather high. There was no panic. The people quietly rode out the depression.

S. W. Morgan comes to be the new County Agent. Ill health causes him to resign.

Wm. Glenn comes back to manage the Montezuma Valley water system. He has had years of experience and does his best to make the water system work and win.

To replace Morgan, recently chosen as County Agent, Glenn C. Clark is employed. Clark comes highly recommended by E. D. Smith, former County Agent, who is now higher up in the state work.

Assessor Clark Hickman reported in July, 1921, that the county's total valuation was about the same, or a little higher, than last year in spite of the depression and the very low value placed on livestock. There are more stock in numbers, some newly patented land that is taxable. The depression has been very effective in reducing prices on livestock and farm products but living costs and wages remain relatively high, causing much dissatisfaction and discontent among producers.

Road building out in the dry land section is active. With many new people there comes a need for many new roads. Roads are needed so badly that the people take it upon themselves to build the road, the county laying them out.

The meeting of the County Commissioners in June, 1921, was noteworthy on account of the fact that the last $1,000 on the original Montezuma County bonded indebtedness was paid. When the county was organized in 1889, it was bonded for $30,000 to pay its share of the La Plata County debt, this county being formerly part of La Plata County, to provide funds for transcribing that part of the La Plata County records that applied to Montezuma County, and to pay a part of the expenses of the new county for the first year or two. This debt had drug along through the years and the last of it was paid in June. The county's share of the La Plata County debt alone was over $20,-000. All, or practically all, of this money was spent in La Plata County, and Montezuma had little to show for the money.

L. M. Alexander starts the Inland Empire at Dove Creek, September, 1921. Another public servant working for the good of all.

After weeks of operation with a standard rig the Mid-West Oil Co. suspended operations just before Christmas, capped the well and sealed it over with cement. They had gotten through the Red Beds, in which they had been drilling for a month before suspending and there was a lot of speculation as to what results were obtained, if any. For weeks the people in the west end of the county had been on the tip toe of expectation, and, to them, every act of the oil company inspired confidence and hope. They were, naturally, greatly disappointed in the results of the drilling, but were still hoping that results were obtained which the company did not make public. There was a feeling that drilling would be resumed in the spring, but in May, 1922, the casing was drawn and the rig dismantled.

The County Commissioners, in January, 1922, reported all the different funds of the county in good condition with some surplus in every fund. The county road fund, only two years back, badly in debt, had a cash balance of $15,000.

Cortez is building a new gym to be finished in January, 1922. The bonds for building an addition to the high school is approved by the voters. An addition to the rear of the high school building, 44x80 feet is proposed. A large auditorium that may be used for indoor basketball, and a number of class rooms is planned. The rough plans have been passed on to an architect for complete plans and specifications.

The McElmo well, being drilled by the Mid-West Oil Co., week of March 25th, struck a heavy flow of gas at a depth estimated at 4,200 feet. The showing of oil in the gas was thought to be from the oil sand above in the well. The gas sand was barely peentrated. They continued with the drilling.

E. C. Cooper is given full charge of all road work in the district and is to make daily reports. There is $13,500 of county money for road building and $6,500 of state money for maintenance.

A series of meetings on the care and pruning of fruit trees was held in the county on week of March 26, 1922, by H. D. Lochlin, Deputy State Horticulturalist, assisted by County Agent Clark. There was a lot of inteerst and the fruit industry of the county was greatly benefited. Mr. Lochlin in one of his talks said: "I can see as great an opportunity for fruit growing in this county as in any other county in the state."

The county gets its first crawler tractor, for road work, a Holtz, supplied by the state. Was used first on the Cortez-Dolores road, then under construction, June, 1922.

A new voting precinct was created at Sylvan, a new community out westward from Pleasant View, near Utah line. New, but well populated and vigorous and progressive.

The big railroad campaign failed after so much effort, time and expense. One big mistake the railroad campaigners made was in telling the people that the proposed railroad was our only hope for the future; that without it our future is forever hopeless. The failure of the railroad movement and subsequent developments that have since come to pass proves that the wisest of them were entirely wrong. It would probably have been better if the attempt to build the road had never been made.

At harvest time, 1922, potatoes are 50c a hundred on the market, and sacks cost from 15 to 25 cents. Many potatoes are not harvested. People who could do their own harvesting, dug their potatoes and sold them for whatever they could get, or couldn't sell them at all.

The first real oil well drilled in the San Juan Basin, came in late in October, 1922, at a depth of 1000 feet and with a daily production of 500 barrels. Location—15 miles west of Farmington.

After months and months of effort the undertaking to finance the building of a railroad from Gallup into the San Juan Basin, on land subscribed by the landowners, the matter was given up as a failure in January, 1923, and all the land contracts were released. 1382 contracts, embracing 191,931 acres valued at $5,833,270. The people put in their poorest land and there was a heavy indebtedness, and this seems to have been the ultimate cause of failure. The syndicate organized to finance the undertaking were unable to swing a deal. It was a relief to the people. It had been such a long drawn out affair, always uncertain in its outcome, and they were glad to get it off their minds and get to other business.

In 1923 Montezuma County had 557 cars and 60 trucks and the license fees amounted to $3,726.95 and it all goes into the road fund.

Power farming getting started in early spring of 1923, a number of Fordsons and some other tractors, being put into service in every part of the county.

At its session in the winter of 1923, the State Assembly passed a law levying a tax of 2 cents a gallon on gasoline, the first of its kind, but not the last. The money goes into the road fund and everyone approved. The first new tax that ever met a welcome.

A new era in the history of the Montezuma Valley irrigating system was ushered in in 1922 by the purchase of a new Koehring Ditcher for cleaning and enlarging its canals and big ditches and building new ones. Ever since the canal system was first built cleaning the canals and laterals has been an almost impossible job, always expensive and never done well. The new machine lifts the accumulated mud out of the big ditches two to three cubic yards per minute and does as much work for a dollar of cost as men and teams can do at a five dollar cost, and does it better.

Following this innovation, in the spring of 1923 the system management set in to make a lot of improvement that would be permanent. Weak and rotten headgates, flumes and other wooden structures were replaced with cement structures that would apparently last for all time. The big tunnel, through the divide from the Dolores river, was given a thorough cleaning, the east portal was concreted in and the wooden headgates at the west portal replaced with concrete. Canal

279

No. 2, that runs down the river from point of diversion was thoroughly cleaned and enlarged where enlargement was needed. This is a heavy duty canal and carries water to irrigate a large portion of the west side of the valley and fills the Narraguinep reservoir. Experience had taught them that flumes made of Oregon fir and creosoted were cheaper and much more lasting than either native lumber construction or steel and thenceforward flumes of matched fir staves only are constructed.

By the beginning of 1923 the county had far enough recovered from the depression as to show new signs of life and growth. In both Cortez and Dolores new cement sidewalks by the block had recently been laid and much more walk was being laid. Many new homes were being built and many new business concerns came into existence. There were new merchandise businesses and new lines of merchandise were coming into use. Garages and filling stations had already put in their appearance, and more came into existence as more cars, trucks and tractors came into use.

An era of change began to take place and was hastened forward by the building of gravel surfaced roads. When the county began to get out of the mud the entire county began to improve in every way and to make progress.

The first active work to improve and make permanent the Gallup to Shiprock road was started August 27, 1923, when the government put two surveyors from the Federal Bureau of Public Roads to work surveying for a permanent highway. The road is to be built at government expense as 90 per cent is on Indian reservations.

The Cortez Light and Power Co., late in September, 1923, gets its new system of electric lights and limited power in working order, in part, in time for the county fair and the bright, new lights along Main Street lent a spirit of levity and good cheer to the local population and visitors alike. This was the feeble beginning of a system for power and light that was to grow into vastly greater things in the few years just ahead.

Congress set aside $800,000 for the building of the Gallup-Durango highway, spring and summer of 1924, announced by J. A. Clay, Feb. 18, 1924.

The total shipment of hogs from Montezuma County in 1923 was about 23,000 head, mostly stock hogs. Hogs are getting to be a major industry in the county.

In 1924 the number of taxpayers in Montezuma County had grown to 2,300.

School District No. 1, Cortez, votes an $8,000 bond to build an addition onto the high school. Growing population, growing school needs.

One good sign of the times is the action of the people of the Montezuma Valley irrigation district in voting a heavy tax to put the system in first class conditions, increasing the assessment from $1.00 to $1.50 per acre. There are 200 miles of main lateral, 100 flumes aggregating more than 2.5 miles, 18 big headgates and many sets of spillways and numerous drops, and all need repair or rebuilding . "Bill" Glenn, superintendent, had a complete report ready on the needs of the irrigating system. The proposition of $1.00, $1.25 and $1.50 assessment was put before the people and they voted the highest assessment.

A new step in road building was taken in 1924 when the County Commissioners decided to try out Fordson tractors for draft purposes on the roads. The experiment was entirely satisfactory and road building and maintenance by tractor had its beginning on Montezuma County roads.

A movement is started by the Peppard Seed Co. to have Montezuma Co. farmers grow alfalfa seed. Some 5,000 acres were asked to be signed up so the seed company can keep a man here to show the farmers how to grow the seed. Needing a cash crop, many farmers signed up to grow seed and the conditions were fully met.

C. E. Krater, of Lewis, continues to show the way to successful dry farming. His display of dry farm products at the county fair in 1924, was a sensation—his second triumph. It was a most significant display and showed what anyone can do with proper methods and good farm practices.

The contractor finished the addition to the Cortez high school Nov. 11, 1924. It was the plan of the district to put up the walls, put on the roof and close the outside openings and leave it that way as they didn't have the funds to complete the work. At this juncture the people awoke with a new interest and public spirit, and started a subscription list for loans and gifts and raised all the necessary funds to finish the building, furnish it, enlarge the heating plant and wire for lights. It was a magnificent response to the public urge to get the work done so the much needed school room could be occupied. The addition was 30x50 feet with basement and two floors above and embraces a large assembly room and a number of class rooms, providing for present needs and future growth.

Two miles of road, gravel surfaced, out of Cortez eastward on Cortez-Dolores road, was completed last of December, 1924.

There will be a large program of road building and surfacing on state highways in the county in 1925. $30,000 is designated for the Mancos-Cortez road with other funds to be added to that. The gravel surfacing on the Durango-Mancos road will be finished.

Montezuma County ends the year 1924 and starts the year 1925 with new hope. The hope pinned to new railroads and railroad transportations has at last been buried and there is a tendency to place our hopes in new things: new and better roads, and highways, new methods and modes of transportation is adding confidence to hope and giving a new birth to enterprise and industry. There is evidence that the county is on the road to progress toward better things and a more abundant life, with new cars increasing in number and trucks in almost every business and on many of the better farms. In 1925 Montezuma County, for the first time in its history, began to take itself out of the mud. In short, Montezuma County has ceased to be the graveyard of hopes.

The new Indian Agency at Towaoc is near enough to completion to begin work in all departments. T. E. Reed, the new agent at Towaoc, reported 160 Indian children in school from 1st grade up to the 8th grade, when any pupils are advanced to that point. In addition there are something over 400 older Indians on the reservation, and these are under supervisors who are trying to teach them farming, stock raising and such subjects. The new plant seems destined to do a good and valuable work.

H. A. Garwood and Charles Milton, and associates, organized to put down a test well for oil at Ackmen. They have many thousand acres under lease.

Traffic from Gallup is pouring over the desert sand, even before the road is built. Commerce and trade will have its way. There is no barrier where there is profit at the end of the trail.

The Montezuma County Fair marked its 20th anniversary with the finest and largest exhibit in its history. Everybody and everything was represented: livestock, farm products, fruits, vegetables, the schools in their every department, fancy work and embroideries, and the dry farm folks were on hand with an exhibit that was complete and very fine, and proved beyond a doubt that dry farming in this county is an unqualified success, and has a great future. The sports events were many and very good and the parade was fully as good as anything ever before attempted. The fair, as a whole, indicated a rebirth of interest in the county's basic industry. E. C. Krater, the veteran winner with dry farm products—grains, grasses and alfalfa seed, was still in the winning.

The first highways in this part of the state to be called "State Highways" were designated and posted in the fall of 1925. They were the highway from Walsenburg to Alamosa, the road from Durango to Mancos to Cortez and on northwestward to the Utah state line, and the road from Cortez southward to the New Mexico state line; thence on to Shiprock and Gallup.

Some very good yields of alfalfa seed were reported in the 1925 seasn, but many low and unprofitable yields were obtained. It is beginning to look as if the growing of alfalfa seed was not to become a new industry in the county.

A history making session of the Cortez Commercial Club was held October 26, 1925, to take positive action on the efforts being made to bring about the building of the Cortez-Gallup highway. Forces were set to work to bring about the desired result, a committee was appointed to go over the route to ascertain the most pressing needs and $550 was raised in cash at once to start the work. A gravel surfaced road, and, ultimately a hard surfaced road, was the immediate aim.

The passing of the homestead domain was signalized November, 1925, when the land office at Durango was closed and all the business of the office transferred to the land office at Pueblo.

Two hundred men and teams are at work on the Gallup road in the spring of 1926. A good road bed is being thrown up, bridges built, culverts put in. A first class dirt road is being built.

A. W. Wark and son, W. C. Wark, bought the flour mill at Marvel and moved it to Cortez.

The effort at growing alfalfa seed is still being made and the total shipment of seed was approximately 100,000 pounds. It was a rainy season and the growers estimate that 50 per cent of the seed was lost in harvesting. The total shipped in 1924 was 30,000 pounds. The industry trebled in 1925 and an estimated 800 acres of seed crop was handled. A. W. Kermode received the highest price of any of the growers, getting 15½ cents per pound and his yield was 230 pounds per acre. Tom Coppinger got 430 pounds per acre after taking off a hay crop. Julius Bailey took 15,000 pounds from 60 acres, B. Day living just north of Monticello, harvested about 600 pounds per acre.

In these years of the mid-twenties, prices on farm products held steadily low to lower and farm machinery, and practically everything the farmer must buy advanced in price year after year. Cities and all industrial centers were "rolling in wealth" and the farm population grew poorer or barely held their own. One can see now that the great depression that broke in 1929 was then in the making.

From the foregoing figures it can be seen that the alfalfa seed growers were not doing so well, but vastly better than the growers of other farm products. There was a lot of fruit produced and shipped, and one grower reported that he made $5 on a carload of apples shipped to the market. The farms had been farmed out until production was low on all field crops. While some good farmers were producing 4 to 5 tons of alfalfa per acre the vast majority were getting two tons or less, and alfalfa hay was worth only $5 per ton when it could be sold at all. It was much the same with grain crops. Good wheat often sold at less than $1.00 per hundred pounds and rarely for more than that amount. Under these conditions it was natural the farmers should turn to any new crop, such as seed growing, and it can be safely assumed that the farmer who did a poor job of farming made a failure at that.

Through the 1920's the automobile was coming into general use very rapidly. Every young man, and many older ones, never thought of saving to have a home, a start on a farm or a small business. They saved only, if they saved at all, to buy a car. This was one reason, at least, why farm values and home values were very low with almost no market. It was a condition that had to work itself out. Progress of the real kind had to await the time in our economy when the average person could buy a car and also buy the other things he needed or wanted. A generation has passed and we are still not over this phase of our economy. A desire for a good car is still strong and often rules out any other consideration.

In May of 1926 a pressing effort was made to get the San Juan Country to raise 10,000 stock hogs for the San Luis Valley market to be fattened out on field peas in that valley. Montezuma County had already produced a lot of stock hogs—hundreds of car loads in all—but the price dropped to 13 cents and that was the end of raising stock hogs. The new effort was to revive the industry.

Mr. Billingsly, pioneer of Montezuma Valley, reported that in the fall of 1926 Montezuma County shipped five car loads of comb honey and three car loads extracted honey, all of very fine quality.

The apple crop of 1926 went largely for pig feed—fine Rome Beauties and Grines Golden for pig feed. Hogs live better here than people do in many places.

The Sugar beet crop of 1926 make only a fair yield, some 400 or 450 car loads being produced. The Holly factory at Delta paid the farmers $6 a ton, one dollar more than contract price, in order to compensate, in part, for the light yield, and to encourage the growers to try again.

January, 1927, survey work starts on road from Cortez to Shiprock, that part across the Ute Indian reservation, welcome news to all the county. Road wil be built and gravel surfaced as soon as survey is completed and approved. Road from Cortez to reservation line also in the making.

Heavy rains of flood proportions, struck the county last days of June. Washed out roads, railroad and bridges, two railroad bridges on Dolores river above town and badly damaged one below town. This rain was notable in that it was the heaviest rain ever known to fall in this county in the month of June, uniformly a dry month with almost no rain. Rain does a lot of damage to the Montezuma Valley Irrigating system, breaking ditches, taking out fiumes, making considerable expense for repairs. Train service north restored July 25; service to Silverton Aug. 1st.

Oil fever going again. Move to drill for oil in Glade country, North of Dolores. July 1st, some machinery on ground.

Cortez goes on a building spree. Town hits stride in growth that put it far ahead of other towns of county in 1927.

The Denver and Rio Grande Southern, through the D&RG, pays several years of delinquent taxes, on Dec. 20, '27, by the terms of the compromise Montezuma county gets $24,445.28.

The Highland Utilities Co. buys power plants at Mancos, Cortez and Dolores, early 1930.

G. H. Talcott and associates start oil well on Talcott ranch five miles southwest of Cortez. They strike water at 60 feet.

In March, 1931, the movement for a co-operative creamery for Cortez finally goes over, a building 40x56 feet is erected and full equipment of up-to-date machinery installed. P. T. Kuhre is chosen manager and Walter Carpenter plant operator. Creamery opened for business Sept. 7, 1931.

A. F. Hoffman is employed as County Agent 1931, after the county has been for some years without an agent.

The dry farming area about Dove Creek has record crop of grain and potatoes 1931. Also of other farm products. The acreage planted to crops is being greatly enlarged.

The Cooperative Creamery is starting off with a good patronage and early in October shipped by truck, 5½ tons of butter to Los Angeles. Creamery has good patronage from all over county. Product soon becomes widely and favorably known.

James H. Totten, born in Canada, came to Montezuma County in 1890, homesteading northeast of Cortez. He and Judge G. A. Morton built the dam that created Totten Lake, now part of the irrigating system. D. H. Saylor was neighbor and close friend of both settlers.

The newly hired county agent is dismissed in the interest of economy. Record shows very good work done. Some cut in wage and salaries for all county employees, Dec., 1931. Depression is on in earnest.

ROAD NEWS OF INTEREST

The first move for oil surfaced highways came in Dec., 1931, when the County Chamber of Commerce appealed to the government to oil surface road south of Cortez across Ute Indian reservation.

About Feb. 1, 1932, Gov. W. H. Adams signs highway budget carrying $60,000 for construction work on highway 160 between Mancos and Cortez, work to start early and to be done by local labor to give idle workers employment.

On March 1st, 1932, Mancos gets $2,360 gas tax money to use on construction and gravel surfacing work through town, on highway.

The grading and graveling of the Mancos-Cortez road to its completion will cost $70,000, including the necessary bridges.

CHRONOLOGY RESUMED

In July, 1932, the depression is on in earnest, and the government began rationing out flour and some prepared feed for stock and poultry. A car load of flour is brought in, and a lot of feed grain, to be distributed to those most in need—60,000 pounds of flour and 120,000 pounds of cracked wheat distributed in two months, all under Red

Cross supervision. Many people in this great land of plenty were glad to get it.

A slight sign of depression relief began to be noticed in 1932. In June butter fat went up from 11 cents to 13 cents. It had reached the bottom; it could only go up.

Large consignment of relief clothing and cloth received by Red Cross Oct. 20, 1932, and cotton for making comforts and mattresses. The women folks in every part of the county, under expert guidance, made a great many mattresses and bed comforts.

The Montezuma County Creamery is now, in Oct. 20, 1932, furnishing a market for 251 cream producers. Total assets at end of first year $4,775.26.

During the depression hair cuts went down to 35 cents in Montezuma Co. Shaves to 25 cents and shave and haircut 50 cents.

Franklin D. Roosevelt took office March 4, 1933. His first act was to close all banks, declaring a bank holiday. Plans and purposes are unknown, but all banks closed for the week's moritorium to await results and orders. Before the time was up, the moritorium was extended indefinitely. State banks also observed moritorium. Banks were closed mainly to head off heavy runs on banks in the east and stop the hoarding of gold. Banks open soon on restricted basis.

Conservators are appointed for all banks in the county and restrictions mostly removed.

Spring of 1933 period of big egg production. Price dropped to an all time low of 6 cents per dozen.

The First National Bank at Mancos and the Montezuma Valley National Bank still on restricted basis. J. J. Harris and Co. on full operation basis. Deposits received by banks on unrestricted basis. Some funds released in part.

Eggs go up to 15 cents a dozen in April, 1933. Wheat 65 cents a bushel—wheat went up from 35c to 60c in 30 days; corn came up to 33c, oats 20 to 21 cents.

The Cortez-Mancos road gravel surface completed early June, 1933, gravel all the way and two new bridges.

E. W. Barr, new county agent, gets busy at once with corn-hog program, early April, 1934. He reports laer that 98 corn-hog programs have been signed by young folks in the county.

Spring of 1934 a large quantity of relief supplies received in the county, just plain food for the needy—in the midst of a gold mining boom.

A record drouth struck Montezuma County in 1934 and was probably the driest year the county has experienced since its occupancy by the white man. With a very light winter snowfall, almost no spring storms and very scant summer rains, crop production was at the lowest level the county has ever known and distressing condittions were bound to ensue. These conditions being generally prevalent in the southwest, the government took measures to relieve the situation. Funds were made available for buying cattle off the rancher thus reducing the number to what could be taken care of. Buyers came to every ranch and bought cattle paying $12.50 a head for average grown cattle of every kind and young stock in proportion. The best of these were shipped into southern areas where cattle were less plentiful and there was plenty of feed. Hundreds of head of the poorest stuff in the county were simply driven off to some isolated spot and shot. In cases where stock were mortgaged half of the proceeds were given to the mortgage holder and half to the owners. There was no flood water from snow and little water in the reservoirs. A Thompson Park reporter said they had the only drouth the Park had ever experienced.

County Agent E. W. Barr gets work started on organizing 4-H Boys' and Girls' Clubs throughout the county.

Grasshoppers, prairie dogs, bean beetles, potato psyllids added to the dry weather calamities in Montezuma County. The government furnished tons of grasshopper poison and prairie dog poison and bean growers and potato growers fought with sprays, and, with the constant help and advice of County Agent Barr, any great calamity from these plagues was averted.

Rain fell during week of July 20, 1934, some rain in every part of the county and a good rain in the vicinity of Ackmen and Yellow Jacket. Beans and corn had survived the dry weather and the rain brought on a fair crop in many places in the dry farming area. It was something to have a good crop in 1934.

George Bowen, of near Cortez, has fine herd of registered Jersey cattle, and is proving a real benefactor to the dairy industry in the county. In addition to producing lots of cream he is furnishing breeding stock to other dairymen and is a real factor in the building up of the dairy industry of the county.

During the 6 months prior to Aug. 31, 1934, Montezuma Co. farmers made 48 Land Bank loans amounting to $64,400. These loans were to take up outstanding indebtedness and gives the farmers long time and low interest rates. The loans do not increase the borrowers indebtedness.

Cattle buying by the government closed Nov. 6, 1934. A total of 3,941 cattle were bought from 402 owners and brought a total of $28,864, an average of $12.50 per head. 611 were condemned as unfit for use. A total of 6,030 sheep were bought in Montezuma Co. and 300 in Dolores Co. Total paid was $12,660. An additional allotment of $6,000 was made for buying sheep in Montezuma County.

A heavy flow of gas, estimated at 250,000 cubic feet, was struck in the McElmo well being drilled by Teague & Coon, at a depth of 3,131 feet. The well is 12 miles west of Cortez on the Jesse West place and the operators have been engaged in the drilling task for nearly two years, local Cortez people financing the well largely. They have had many difficulties to overcome. There was a showing of oil in the well April 3, 1935.

A determination to gravel surface all rural mail routes in the county, and all school bus routes was one result of the extremely bad roads in March and April, 1935. The County Commissioners decided in favor of this action and preparations were made to make an early start on the work, the survey work coming first.

The use of pure seed for planting crop received fresh impetus in 1935. Thirty-five county farmers planted pure seed of potatoes, alfalfa, wheat, barley and oats. A lot of seed was donated by growers of pure seed grain and potatoes in the county.

A tragic episode in the county's history took place on July 15, 1935, when County Sheriff W. W. Dunlap was shot to death by McDaniels Brothers four miles below Placerville, in San Miguel County. The sheriff and his deputy, Len Duncan, were bringing the McDaniels to Cortez. They had been arrested at Glenwood Springs for the murder of James Westfall of Lewis some time previous. The sheriff stopped the car to investigate a car wreck, leaving his gun in the glove compartment of the car. While the deputy was looking out the car window, one of the handcuffed men seized the gun, forced the deputy from the car, shot the sheriff twice and drove off in the car. They hid hid the car further down the road and took to the mountains on foot. The County Commissioners posted $500 reward for their capture, dead or alive. Jesse H. Robinson was appointed by the County Commissioners to fill the office made vacant by Mr. Dunlap's death. Otis McDaniels and Herbert McDaniels were captured at Guffey Park, 4 miles northwest of Canon City, and confessed their identity. Later the McDaniels were convicted in the District Court at Durango for killing James Westfall. They were given life sentences.

The dry year of 1934 was followed by one of plenty of water and good crops were reported from every part of the county. Thirty to forty bushels of wheat per acre, 60 to 90 bushels of oats, 40 to 70 bushels of barley were common yields where a good job of farming was done. Considerable certified pure seed was used this year and plots planted with this seed invariably out-yielded crops from other seed. This indicated a turn to better farming and that County Agent Barr was furnishing able leadership. Almost all seed grain and potatoes planted this year were treated before planting to ward off disease and grain smut.

Allotment of grain acreage to limit production started with wheat and cotton as far back as 1933. The same plan is still in use, and applies in the county. Aim is to avoid overproduction and stabilize prices at parity—or a higher level.

Week of Oct. 18, 1935, the McDaniels trial at Telluride for the murder of Sheriff Dunlap, resulted in conviction of Otis McDaniel for first degree murder and life imprisonment for Herbert McDaniels, the younger of the two.

Costs of schooling in Colorado, and in Montezuma Co., reached a climax in 1935. Average cost per pupil per year in Montezuma Co. was: Class three district $52.26 per pupil; Class two district $53.36 per pupil. School District No. 1, Cortez, had an average daily attendance of 409 pupils at a cost of $45.10 per pupil. School District 4, Dolores, average daily attendance of 262, had a cost per pupil of $57.10. School District No. 6, Mancos, had an average daily attendance of 327 with a cost of $57.40 per pupil.

Mid November saw the beginning of gravel surfacing on the Cortez-Dolores road.

Fall of 1935 new addition to the Cortez High School is being built. Stone quarried and hauled by W.P.A. help. Reduces cost considerably.

With the return of better farm prices comes higher taxes. New taxes are appearing and no old taxes are being overlooked. Business can pass taxes along to consumer, but the working man and the farmer can pass his taxes along to no one. He can only shoulder the burden as best he can.

County Agent Barr closed an active year and reports that during year there has been 3,659 office calls, 529 telephone calls, 557 different farms and homes visited, 71 circular letters written, 618 individual letters written, 48 meetings held, 340 news stories published. Agent spent 164.5 days in the field, and 140 days in the office. He has enjoyed the year's work very much. The people of Montezuma Co. are kind, generous and friendly and, above all, it is a nice place to live.

The end of 1935 found Montezuma Co. in the best condition, financially, it has been in for 12 or 15 years. A total of around $90,000 in taxes has been paid in and all county liabilities were paid off excepting registered warrants against the road fund, evidence of better prices, better conditions and that the long depression is over.

County Agent Barr, John H. McConnell and W. V. Alin took an exhibit of 61 samples to the Pure Seed Show, in Colorado Springs, in Feb., 1936, won 22 placings on premium list and a silver plaque. C. E. Krater, the veteran dry farmer of Yellow Jacket, came through with three winnings: pinto beans, second; Brunker oats, 2nd; Minnesota 13 corn, 6th.

BEGINNING MAY 1, 1936

The first oil surfacing of highways got under way at Cortez May 1st, 1936, when the State Highway Department started work on highway No. 160, at Cortez, building toward Mancos.

The Citizens' State Bank was opened for business at Cortez, June 1st, 1936, with a capital stock of $25,000 and forty stockholders. The first set of directors were J. W. Bozman, N. E. Carpenter, P. P. Schifferer, C. S. Warren, W. C. Wark, N. R. Usher, Cashier. The new bank occupied the building vacated by the Montezuma Valley National Bank. All deposits are insured.

A fire destroyed the flour mill at Cortez May 22, 1936. It was owned by Mrs. Maude Bryce and Keene McGalliard. Loss reported as $40,-000, partly covered by insurance.

The agricultural conservation program initiated by the Roosevelt Administration, got under full headway in Montezuma Co. the season of 1936-37. The practice of improving the soil and checking erosion is being encouraged by paying the farmers, in past, for many kinds of work. There is a long list of practices where a part of the cost is paid. Started as a temporary measure, it is still going and promises to become permanent. Some very good work is being done.

In addition to the $28,000 or $30,000 in the building fund, the county has secured approval of W.P.A. project fund amounting to $29,250 and plans are being rapidly completed for the erection of a new and much needed County Court House, July 31, 1936. The work will start at once.

Monday, September 21, the contract was let for the building of the new County Court House. Work is to start by October 15, 1936.

Call is made for bids to gravel surface 11.4 miles of the Cortez-Dove Creek highway, beginning in October, 1936, at Cortez.

The county has employed a new County Agent in the person of C. L. Reiser, Nov., 1943.

Hog cholera made its appearance in Montezuma County for the first time in November, 1936, on two farms. Introduced by hogs brought in by truck from outside the state. Strict quarantine imposed to prevent spreading and to stamp out the disease.

The D. V. Burrell Seed Co. of Rocky Ford is growing a portion of their seed supply in Montezuma County, and is giving the county some valuable publicity in their seed catalog.

Final dividend payment to the creditors of the Montezuma Valley National Bank were made March 27 at Cortez. 600 checks were ready for distribution and the total payment was around $50,000. The bank will pay a total of 95.51 per cent on its liabilities, which seems to indicate that there was no real reason for closing down the bank.

A powerful Coleman 5 ton truck, equipped with drag line and snow plow, used alternately, was purchased by the County Commissioners at a cost of $10,395, 1937 session. The machine is to handle the work too heavy for ordinary road equipment.

Alfalfa weevil made its appearance for the first time in Montezuma Co., season of 1937, in northwest Montezuma Valley. A quarantine on the movement of hay, straw and potatoes into New Mexico was imposed. Infestation was not bad the first year, but precautions were taken to prevent the spreading of the pest locally.

The County Commissioners approved the memorial plan for W. W.

Dunlap and a suitable plaque will be designed and placed in the main hall of the new County Court House.

The year 1937 opened an era of new and better roads in Montezuma County. South of Cortez a 27 mile stretch of Highway 666, gravel surfaced and oil paved, was completed. Later in the season the oiling equipment was moved to Mancos and the work of oil surfacing a three-mile stretch will be completed. The connecting highway between Dolores westward to the Cortez-Dove Creek road, was oil paved. Work on Highway 160, northwest from Cortez was under way. Bids will be called for soon on 20 miles of highway 160 east and west from Dove Creek, in two projects, to cost about $500,000.

The close of the building season we find a fine stretch of oil surfaced highway between Mancos and Cortez. A stretch east of Mancos, but not quite so good. There is a good road from Dolores to Cortez, by way of Lewis, or near Lewis, and a road from Dolores to Cortez by the Y, but not so good. Weber has a graveled road from Mancos, but it is not holding up well under heavy winter storms.

At the meeting of the State Highway Advisory Board in Denver, attended by County Commissioners from every part of the state, including McCabe and Martin of this county, over forty miles of road in Montezuma County was designated as a part of the State highway system. This means that the road, or roads, so designated, will be built and maintained by the state highway department, and it means more surfaced roads for the county.

On April 3, 1936, a new bridge spanning the San Juan river at Shiprock, was dedicated, with a big crowd and appropriate ceremonies. The bridge is 1005 feet long, 6 steel spans, a truck load limit of 15 tons, width 24 ft., vertical 14 feet, sidewalk 5 feet. The bridge means a lot to the future of Montezuma County as the county grows in commercial importance.

The Public Health Service began to be an active factor in Montezuma County in 1938.

C. L. Reiser, County Agent, resigns to take a job in California. He has been a busy man on the job and it was considered he did a valuable work with the ranchers and with the boys' and girls' clubs.

Montezuma County gets two road improvements designated to be done by W.P.A. labor. The first project is for 5.5 miles of road from the Dolores Cemetery, on the Mancos road to the corner of the Morrison place; thence two miles south to the Green place. The second project is the Mancos school bus route in the lower Mancos Valley, over 5 miles. The first project cost $11,716 and the second $11,718, total $23,434. These were gravel surfacing projects.

The county bought a small rock crusher in 1927 and it proved a valuable investment, and since then many short pieces of road have been improved in the county. The Dolores-Lebanon road was one of the roads so improved with a gravel surface. The plan is to keep the crusher busy and surface other roads as fast as funds are available, mostly from gas tax and car and truck licenses.

Something unusual in business took place in September, 1938, when the Highlands Utilities Co. voluntarily made a reduction on town lights to Cortez, Dolores and Mancos amounting to 28 per cent.

The Public Health Service is busy and 1941 the county nurse is active with tuberculosis clinics, crippled children clinic, eye and ear testing, and the work is still going on. There are many different phases of the work and the women organizations are cooperating in every part of the county, and much good work in the interest of the better health of the school children must have been done. Miss Anneke Kolloewen, as county nurse, is very capable and efficient.

K. G. Parker is appointed the new County Agent in 1939. He takes over the work at once.

Work scheduled to start on Groundhog reservoir June 1, 1939. The lowest bidder for the work is Gerald Knuts, of Kansas City, bid being $238,629. The W.P.A. will be doing a large part of the work.

The office of Supervisor of the Montezuma National Forest was moved from Mancos to Cortez October 1, 1940.

In January, 1941, the County Commissioners decided to continue school nursing service in county. Health education, a most important service, applies not only to school students and school personnel, but also extends into the homes and to parents. The child practices at home what he learns in school. Plan to conduct adult classes in home nursing, first aid, baby care, etc., classes to last from 10 to 20 weeks and may be organized in any community. Another service is home visiting by the nurse. Her service is not just to school children, but also to the baby and grandmother as well. One special service is to instruct a member of the family to take care of a patient in the home, trained to follow doctor's orders. The nurse organizes clinics in the county such as immunization clinics, crippled children's clinics, tuberculosis clinics, etc., and organizes local people to help with work.

Miss Anneke Kolloewen gives lectures to the Boy Scouts on First Aid treatment and is planning a campaign to immunize against Small Pox and diphtheria.

In December, 1941, events seem to draw us nearer and nearer to a war crisis. For months the administration grew more and more apprehensive of the immediate future and the possibility of being drawn into the European conflict now raging with the utmost fury. Enlistment volunteers fort he army, navy and air force were being encouraged and a great many boys, and some young women, were offering their services.

The Red Cross was working in full force to relieve European suffering and destitution and civilian defense units began to be organized. War bonds were being urged upon the people and war preparations were going on apace. It looked like the entire country was being put on a war basis and the people of Montezuma County were responding to every appeal with wholehearted support. These were stirring times and the government at Washington sought to prepare the nation for any eventuality. A selective service law had been enacted.

The climax came December 7, 1941, when the Japanese Air Force, without a moment's warning and before any war declaration had reached this country, made a sudden and death dealing attack on Pearl Harbor, Hawaiian Islands, with results that are now history. Congress, being in session, declared that a state of war with Japan existed, the vote being 82 to 0 in the Senate and 388 to one in the House. President Roosevelt signed the declaration at once. The war was now on in dead earnest. It was either victory or defeat, and our country had no notion of accepting defeat.

The tense situation was now relieved by action. Regular calls were made upon our young manpower and every call was met promptly and in full. The civilian population girded itself for the fray, for the war must be fought by every one. This was the third time in the short life of the county that war had doffed his noble plume and called upon our people to give their all.

Pruning demonstrations have been held in the fruit areas of the county for three years and was continued with the year 1942. As a result great improvements were made in the kind and quality of fruit produced in the county and many orchards with the more desirable varieties are getting on a profitable producing basis.

Oct. 15, 1941, the farmers met to plan war defense program. They reached the conception early that food will win the war and write the peace, so each and every farmer was asked to make an all out effort to produce food, and more food.

Congressman Edward T. Taylor died in Denver April 3, 1941, ending a career of 40 years in Congress as representative from the 4th Congressional District of Colorado. His was a long, very successful and valuable career.

A second telephone line is installed between Durango and Cortez to accommodate the increasing long distance service.

A drive is started to collect discarded aluminum. The Boy and Girl Scouts were designated to collect from door to door. Receptacles were placed at convenient places to receive any articles from any place.

They began issuing food stamps April 15, 1942. These stamps were issued to people with low incomes to pay part of the cost of living.

The third registration for army service took place Feb. 16, 1942. Something over 500 men in Montezuma County registered at this time.

The fourth registration for war duty for the county numbered 891 men. Registration was Monday, April 27, 1942, under the selective service law.

A crew of about 30 men re-oiled the road south from Cortez, and northwest toward Dove Creek, several miles each way, and re-oiled a large section of the highway each way from Mancos, in May, 1942.

Dr. E. E. Johnson passed away of a heart attack at Santa Monica, Calif., Feb. 15, 1943. Dr. Johnson was a practicing physician and surgeon in Cortez for thirty-five years and made history in the county by establishing and operating the first hospital in the county seat. Although it was not a grandiose institution, this little hospital, but it was a boon to the people of the county and served mercifully in many ways and for many years. Dr. Johnson did a world of good while passing this way. He was born in Sweden and came to this country when about fourteen years old.

The Lions Club, of Cortez, erects a Memorial Board, on the Court House ground, 50 feet long, to record and commemorate the names of the men and women of Montezuma County who served in the armed forces, or auxiliary forces, during the Second World War.

The largest call for Sale of War Bonds came in April, 1943. The quota for the county was $125,000. The Bond Sales organization was ready for action and put the drive over the top in short order. Sales exceeds quota by about 12 per cent, or $143,590.25 in total sales.

When the war got well under way there was an organization for every purpose and service. Here are a few of the more active ones: Red Cross, War Labor Board, Victory Gardens Clubs, Rationing Board, 4-H Boys and Girls, Boy Scouts, Bond Sales Organization, War Savings Bond and War Savings Stamp Campaigns, Extension Agent work in Food Production, Food for War Prisoners drive, Food and Clothing for European relief, and some others.

The Red Cross is called upon to collect donations of blood, one pint from each donor, for use in saving lives of the wounded on the battle front.

Sale of War Bonds and Stamps through the postoffice goes strong in county. First fifteen days in May sales total $52,200, 345 per cent of quota.

Organized to produce food and to save food, canning campaigns now get under way.

Then comes gasoline rationing along with food rationing. Tire inspection order enforced to save rubber.

Names of the soldier boys are going onto the Memorial Board on Court House grounds. An effort is being made to get all names, and on July 13, 1943, the Memorial Board was dedicated with appropriate exercises.

June 23, the largest contingent to date was called to army service, a total of 41 being called. This is the first call to include 18 year olds.

And now, with so much war work going on comes a teachers' shortage. 42 teachers are need in the rural schools of the county fall of 1943, there are 27 vacancies. Many old teachers who had retired, go back to work.

Gasoline has been rationed for some weeks at three gallons per week per car for cars in ordinary family use. This was increased to 4 gallons per week, July, 1943. Coffee, clothing, shoes, meats, processed foods, coupons for all are required.

Early in July, 1943, the first married men were called for army service; men without children were first to be called.

On July 27, 1943, of the 53 enrollees called for service only 22 passed the test. This was an alarming situation for the army people. They began to think they had set the physical requirement standards too high.

The largest quota for War Bond drive to date came Oct. 1, 1943, call was for $277,990, but it was subscribed in full with a few thousand to spare.

The United War Chest makes a drive for $3,100 for seventeen relief agencies. This call is filled by donations, but is made in full.

Herbert DeVries came in as new County Agent October, 1943.

Montezuma County get "A" award for outstanding performance of food and fiber in 1943, awarded to only one county in each state. There was a special program of acceptance Jan. 8, 1944, many notables attending.

Largest contingent yet was called for examination in January, 1944, 73 men. Previous largest was for 70 men, 36 of whom passed muster.

The fourth war loan drive for sale of bonds sold $260,789.50. Quota for county was $214,000, 121 per cent of quota. January, 1944.

Beginning 1944 farmers plan for record production: fertilizing, growing cover crops, harvesting legumes and grass seed, carrying out erosion control, water conservation practices, land leveling, etc.

The boys and girls 4-H Clubs get into war production with full strength and much determination. They are well organized and have big membership.

Gas ration for autos is cut to 2 gallons a week. The aim is to make more gas available for farm power use.

March 29, 1944, 85 enrollees for military service were called to take pre-induction tests. Many 18 year old enrollees were taken in this call.

Registrants called to Denver for pre-induction examination was 201, the largest call to date, April 20, 1944. This call shows the extent the manpower of the county is being drawn upon.

June 15, 35 men take their pre-induction physicals in Denver.

June 1, 50 men were called for pre-induction examination in Denver, and on the same day 31 men were inducted into the service.

July 17, 1944, 27 men were called to take their physical examination. Four who had previously passed examination were inducted.

The Stanolind Co. strikes gas in their well in McElmo Canon, depth 4,762 feet. There was a tremendous rush of gas and a showing of oil, and blew mud over everything. Plan to resume drilling when the gas can be brought under control.

Induction goes on, but smaller numbers are being called as the county is drained of its young manpower. Seven men go to Denver for their physicals Sept. 18, and on Oct. 3, 26 men, already qualified are taken into the armed services.

The sixth war loan drive started Nov. 20, 1944. Fourteen billion is called for and the county allotment is $196,000. It was subscribed in full.

The Stanolind Co. decides to abandon its McElmo Canon flow of gas and a showing of oil. They plug the well after spending one-fourth million dollars on the test.

Small contingent called for military duty Jan., 1945. County is now well drained of its young manpower.

A movement is started by Cass M. Harrington as receiver for the Denver & Rio Grande Southern, to abandon the 170 miles of railroad from Durango to Ridgeway. Prompt action was taken to forestall abandonment. War needs saved the road for a time.

May 28, 1944, 50 boys left to take pre-induction tests, and 31 men are inducted into armed services.

Wm. G. Bainbridge of Mancos is killed in plane crash June 20, 1944, on training flight.

June 18, 35 men are taken for their pre-induction test.

Word is received that John Derrick Halls is killed in action June 6, first day of French invasion. He was a paratrooper.

Herbert DeVries, as County Agent, is doing a good job getting production on farms.

July 4, 8 men go for induction into armed service, and on July 13, 27 men go for examination.

Sept. 10, 10 men are inducted into armed services.

Early in January, 1945, 14 men taken for examination, and 6 men go Jan. 25, and 11 men leave for induction Feb. 5.

Mar. 14, 22 men called for examination, Mar. 21, 6 men go for induction, 11 for examination. 4 go for induction, 11 transferred for pre-induction examination.

On April 12, 1945, President Roosevelt dies of cerebral hemorrhage at Warm Springs, Ga. Vice President Truman was sworn in at once as president.

April 20, 1945, word is expected momentarily of German surrender.

April 23, Germans sign surrender terms and the war in Europe is over.

The war with Japan goes on, and the call for soldiers goes on, but for brevity's sake we will discontinue notations of calls for army service.

All public services supporting the war effort go on and there is no lessening of the activity in any line of endeavor.

Germany out of the war, it was known that Japan could not continue the conflict, so, on August 14, 1945, Japan signs peace terms.

The army is now rapidly disbanded and the government plans to discharge 150,000 soldiers per month, mostly those in training. Inductions drop from 80,000 per month to 50,000. Large army of occupation must be kept in Europe and in Japan. From this time no persons over 26 years old were called into military service.

The whole county joins the nation in celebrating. Gas, oil and foods removed from ration list.

The Mobile X-ray outfit is in county in August, 1945, and several hundred people take X-ray test.

At this time a movement is started by the Lions Club of Cortez to build a memorial hospital at Cortez, and a drive to get free gifts for the building fund is started.

The government still has need of great sums of money and a Victory Loan drive is started to sell $159,000 in bonds in the county.

During September and October, 1945, discharged soldiers began to arrive home from the army, mostly from the training camps. From this time on scores of men were discharged every month and go back into civilian life. At the same time the call goes on for men for the armed services to take the place, in part, of the men discharged. The armies of occupation must still be maintained at nearly full strength.

Joe V. Whiteman comes in as new County Extension Agent.

Enough funds are in sight to insure building of the hospital at Cortez, a site is selected on road southwest of town. J. W. Ertel gives 3 acres for site.

In 1946 the government is still calling for maximum production on farms and Montezuma County responds with action. Although the war is over, there are millions of hungry people.

In 1946, the W.C.L.—S.C.S. farm program gets going in a big way in the Mancos Valley getting farms ready for Jackson Gulch water.

A County High School is voted by Cortez and west end of county, 544 for 4 against. Dolores rejects the high school plan by 203 against and 3 for. Mancos votes 352 against and 15 for plan.

June 15, 1946, Cortez purchases five second feet of water in the Dolores River, of a low priority, for City water supply. Figure enough water for 10,000 people. They vote a new bond for $25,000 for water works improvement extension of mains in City and to hospital site.

An open house is held at McPhee Saturday, July 20, 1946, mill will operate, workers will donate work for the day, the government will donate stumpage and the company will donate entire output of mill for the day to the Southwest Memorial Hospital. In all 104 people are employed at the lumber mill.

The whole county joins in celebrating anniversary of close of war, Aug. 14, 1946.

On Aug. 3, 1946, all that part of the county voting for the County High School vote for bonds to carry out their plans.

In September all schools of the county are delayed in opening for one week on account of threat of polio epidemic. No polio in county, but widespread in state and nation.

H. H. Norton of Pleasant View wins Master Seedman award for all Colorado.

The State Highway Department did a notable work on stabilization and reconditioning on Highway 160 and improving Highway 666 south of Cortez to the New Mexico line. The improvement includes stabilization, reconditioning and seal coating 48 miles between Durango and Cortez and improving the road south from Cortez and approximately $200,000 was expended on this work. In addition $56,955 was spent on gravel surfacing Highway 145 between Dolores and Rico.

The county continues to show signs of growth. The tax valuation of the county showed an increase of $300,000 for 1947 over the valuation of 1946. Most of the increase was on improvements on real estate.

The practice of applying phosphate fertilizer to farm land got under way with increased emphasis in 1947. Six car loads, 240 tons, were received and applied by farmers in October and November and another six cars was received and allocated earlier int he year making 12 cars in all. The farmers are reporting excellent results and the practice of applying commercial fertilizers promises to be permanent.

The San Juan Basin Health Unit is organized in 1947, under the laws of the State of Colorado, and Montezuma County is one of the five counties joining to form the unit.

Mesa Verde Park has 52,225 visitors during the summer tourist season of 1947.

Fire again destroys the big lumber mill at McPhee, Jan. 17, 1948. Loss $100,000.

The Montezuma County Planning Board makes land-use survey Feb., 1948, survey on crop programs, conservation programs, fruit production, weed control and water conservation. Aim at more and better roads; also Federal Aid to future development, production and marketing.

Ernest Adams is first to sign an agreement with the Mancos Soil Conservation District December, 1948. Object: Improving ranch for more grazing. Sheep and purebred cattle.

Memorial Hospital dedicated March 29, 1948.

July 16, 1949, four governors meet at Four Corners. Governor Lee Knous, of Colorado; J. Braken Lee of Utah; Thomas J. Mobry of New Mexico; Don Garvey of Arizona, making a historic event. The four governors clasp hands each standing in his own state. Judge Noland was the speaker.

Dedication Ceremonies Aug. 14, 1949, of the Montezuma County Airport. Large crowd and barbecue feast.

Aug. 15, 1949, the Planning Committee stages its third agricultural and inspection tour. There were 150 on tour and much interest shown.

Travel to Mesa Verde in August, 1949, was 27,497, 218 cars a day and 772 people.

Tax valuation of county in 1949 showed a half million dollar increase over previous years.

H. H. Norton of Pleasant View wins title of Master Seedman for all Colorado.

The Montezuma County Planning Board is reorganized and called the Montezuma County Planning Association. Is organized by 40 nonpolitical groups from all parts of county.

Six San Juan Basin Counties sign contract to pay the Water Resource Development Corporation $50,000, and $10,000 Administration costs for 12 months operation, the Water Corporation, for and in consideration of this sum, guarantees to double the amount of the annual precipitation in these counties. Montezuma County's share is $16,194. The silver iodide crystals method is to be used.

One very good accomplishment this year is the work of the Soil Conservation Service, taken over from the Case-Wheeler organization. Much good work is being done for the farmers on the farms.

After some years of high prices for farm products and livestock all market prices began a steady decline in 1953. It worked a hardship on many people who had made their plans on the basis of high prices.

Only 65 per cent of normal snow fall was recorded in the winter of 1953-54, and a shortage of irrigation water ensued.

On June 1, 1954, the Federal Power Commission authorized the Pacific Northwest Pipeline Co. to commence construction of a 1500 mile pipeline from southwest Colorado to the Pacific Northwest to cost $160,000,000. The pipe line was constructed at once, and passed diagonally through Montezuma Co. adding many thousands of dollars to tax valuation and to county and school district revenue. The towns of the county all plan to have a natural gas distributing system.

A contract is awarded for building 3.9 miles of highway from the west La Plata Co. line westward, at a cost of $397,701. A very fine piece of highway was the result.

The County Commissioners vote to withdraw from the San Juan Health Unit. Later a health unit was formed consisting of Montezuma County alone, and it still stands.

Cortez is selected for the site of a $11,000,000 power plant for the Colorado-Ute Power Co. Dissention arises, the decision is reversed, and Nucla is selected as the site. The big plant is being built. It is to furnish power for the Rural Electric Associations in southwest Colorado.

OUR HONORED DEAD

The war over we pause to count our honored dead. A careful checking of the records reveals that the following named persons lost their lives while serving in the armed forces, either in action or otherwise while in the line of duty, in what has been designated the Second World War:

MONTEZUMA COUNTY

Adelbert C. Armstrong
William Bainbridge
Lloyd A. Brixey
William H. Butler
Dean K. Carver
Carl A. Divine
Ben Fitzgerald
Raymond J. Francisco
F. E. Gray
Ronald A. Hackett
John D. Halls
Dave O. Hays
Roscoe Hill
Lewis R. Hucke
Walter M. Jewell
Reamor J. Leavell
William J. McDaniels
O'Neal Morrison
Donald A. McGill
John R. McGregor
Donald Neal
Allan Pratt
Jack Rippetoe
Herbert M. Roberts
Berson Rose
Robert J. Simmons
Roy Slavens
James Starr
Virgil Stevens
Donald Swift
Billy M. Toadvine
Frank G. Ward
Clyde T. Weaver
Glen E. White
Robert R. Williford
Richard S. Winbourn

DOLORES COUNTY

Clarence Bartlett
Dick McCabe
Troy Young

Note: The writer has made every possible contact he could make to get the names of all the death casualties in World War I, and the Korean War, and failed. We feel this information is available somewhere, but we failed to find it.

COUNTY EXTENSION WORK,
COUNTY NURSE AND HOME DEMONSTRATION

County Nurse and Home Demonstration

Some time prior to 1913 Congress passed a law authorizing Land Grant Colleges to offer extension work to the farm population of the states, and early in 1913 the State Assembly of Colorado passed a law, under this act of Congress, enabling the counties of the State to hire County Extension Agents, or advisors, the government paying part of the expense.

In December, 1914, the County Commissioners of Montezuma County, at the instance of Prof. Snyder of the Fort Lewis school, agreed to hire a county extension agent for La Plata and Montezuma Counties. The government put up $1,000, La Plata County $1,000 and Montezuma Co. $500. This was the first step in extension work in Montezuma County, although some club work among the boys and girls was being done through the schools.

About April 15, 1915, O. D. Smith, of Cedaredge, was appointed County Agent to serve both La Plata and Montezuma Counties. This is the beginning of extension work in the county. It is called extension work because the work of the State Agricultural College, in teaching and in practice, is extended to the farming population of every county that will hire an agent or advisor to teach the farmers and furnish leadership. Mr. Smith proved to be an able and efficient man in this work and got a lot of good work started.

On March 4, 1918, G. P. Newsome, having been hired as County Agent, came to take charge of the work in Montezuma Co., and Mr. Smith was employed as County Agent in La Plata Co.

On March 10, 1915, the first Parent-Teacher Association in the county was organized at Mancos. It was soon organized in every part of the county and has been doing good, constructive work ever since, and is still functioning.

On April 2, 1917, the United States became an active participant in the First World War. The call came at once for maximum food production. County Agent Smith organized the farmers and dozens of boys' and girls' clubs, appointed club leaders and everyone worked to produce food, for it was realized at once that food would be a strong factor in winning the war.

G. P. Newsom takes charge of County Agent work March 4, 1918. The Farm Bureau is organized all over the county and the County Agent is working through the Bureau to step up farm production. At first the farmers didn't know what the County Agent work was all about, but by the end of the war a much better understanding had been arrived at, and many farmers were cooperating in the work and doing much good for themselves.

S. W. Morgan followed Newsom as County Agent, but soon resigned on account of ill health. Glenn E. Clark came as agent in 1921. Clark resigned June 1, 1922, and no agent was hired to take his place. Not enough interest on the part of the farmers the County Commissioners say.

A new agent was hired later and the work was kept going, but with more or less indifferent success. Many farmers took an active interest and made an earnest effort to improve their condition and do a better job at farming. A great many others took little or no interest.

The County Fair in 1925 marked the 20th anniversary of its organization and was one of the finest and best ever held. The work of the County Agent showed splendid results and the boys' and girls' clubs made creditable showings. For a time after this we lose sight of County Agent work, but it comes back strong when C. L. Riser comes in as county extension agent in 1936. The long depression intervened and took most of the incentive out of the work. K. G. Parker was appointed in 1939 and Herbert DeVries came in 1943, and did a lot of earnest, hard work during the Second World War.

The Public Health Service began to be an active factor in Montezuma County in 1938. A county nurse had been appointed and is active with tuberculosis clinics, crippled children's clinics, eye and ear testing, and the work is still going on. There are many different phases of the work and the women's organizations are cooperating in every part of the county, and much good work was done especially among the school children. Miss Anneke Kolowign, as county nurse, was very capable and efficient, and a tireless worker. This was in 1941 and Miss Kolowign was the first county nurse. The County Commissioners decided in favor of a county nurse in January, 1941.

This proved to be an important service in health education. The service applied not only to school students and school personnel, but extends also into the homes and to the parents. The children are trained to practice at home what they learn in school. A Plan is started to conduct adult classes in home nursing, first aid, baby care, etc., classes to last from 10 to 20 weeks, and may be organized in every community. Another service is home visiting by the nurse. Her service is also to the baby and to the grandmother in the home. One special service is to train some member of the home to carry out the doctor's directives and do simple nursing. Miss Kollowign gives lectures to boy scouts on first aid treatments, and starts the work of immunizing against smallpox and dyphtheria.

About this time Home Demonstration Work among the women was started in connection with County Extension Work. The work was soon organized in every part of the county and clubs were organized among the young people and leaders appointed. The women and the young folks took to the work with avidity and the interest is being kept up to this present day. There is no doubt but that the movement is doing a splendid work in the homes. Theres is a specially trained leader in charge of the work.

In 1946, in response to the recommendations of the Planning Board, the County Commissioners hired an assistant County Agent to have special charge of the boys and girls clubs and direct the various projects on the farm. The boys' and girls' clubs have been doing some splendid work right along and in district and state competitions they have won fully as many honors and meritorious placings as the leading counties in the state, and have brought to Montezuma County some real distinction in several fields of farm endeavor.

County Agent work is such a broad field and has so many ramifications that it is impossible to go into details. Among the adult farmers, we have to admit that the work, generally, has not attained notable results, but with a great many individuals there has been many cases of outstanding success, and here, again, we haven't time and space to recite details. When there are more and better price incentives no doubt much better and more noteworthy work will come to the farms.

CHAPTER XX

THE TOWN OF DOLORES

The Town of Dolores had its beginning with the building of the Denver & Rio Grande Southern railroad, as related in another Chapter. By 1893 the town had absorbed all the business and buildings that was Big Bend and that budding community was no more. By this time Harris Bros. had gotten well established in the new townsite in a large brick building 40 by 90 feet with a large stock of general merchandise; also hardware and farm implements. Montezuma Valley was settling and demanding many things for home and farm use. The newly settled lands along the Dolores river were turning into hay farms and lfvestock farms, and there was resource foundation for a village or a small town. Accordingly Wm. Ordway moved his grocery stock and the postoffice, up from Big Bend, and a saloon, a livery barn, a blacksmith shop, stage headquarters were added to the small collection of houses. Several new residence buildings, some very good ones, had been built as the town now had every indication of permanency.

Rico is growing into a flourishing mining camp, was demanding the products of the ranch and farm and an effort was made to get some kind of a road from Dolores to Rico, although they had the railroad. Accordingly they advertised for bids and the offer of J. A. McIntyre & Co. to build the road according to specifications, if there were any specifications, for $9,753 was accepted. The road followed the river and the distance was 40 miles, so it can be seen that little in the way of a road could be built for this sum. This was the first real effort at building a road between the two towns, and it was to be many years before anything like a good road was built.

Early in 1896 the little town had its first newspaper when Fred Holt started the Dolores Herald, a very small sheet, and ran it for a few months.

In November of the same year the Knights of Pythias was organized in the village with 28 members.

The flour mill was finished in the fall of 1898 and began making wheat into flour, which they named "The Pride of Dolores." It found a ready sale. The whole county had a good wheat crop on a comparatively small acreage, and flour made from it could only be sold locally.

The price paid for wheat was the very low figure of 70 to 75 cents a hundred pounds. A new mill was also built at Mancos the following year of 1898 and began producing flour. This was a larger mill and modern in every way.

In these years little history is made that is outstanding. Most of the land that could be irrigated had been taken, hardly any one was yet making money, but progress was made in a small way and many herds of cattle had been started by local ranchmen. The railroad had made shipping facilities available locally and this was giving fresh impetus to the livestock industry. Soon some real wealth was being produced.

In 1900 the trouble between the cattlemen and the sheepmen flared up again, not serious, but a trouble. Cattlemen pretend to think that the cattle and horse industry was endangered and that sheep ruined the grazing for other animals. Cattle was held to be far more important than sheep.

In July, 1897, Dolores claimed a population of 200.

Charles Hoppe established a lumber yard in Dolores late in 1897.

The elevation of the Dolores River valley, in this county is from 6500 feet at its lower part to 8000 feet in the highest place in the county.

In the fall of 1897 steps were taken to improve the road to Mancos, a road much used at the time. It was then little more than a trail.

In 1897 Dr. Hoeffeli locates at Dolores as physician and surgeon, the first doctor on record at Dolores.

The Silver Star, a small weekly newspaper, made its first appearance April 8, 1897, with R. B. Hawkins as editor and publisher. Apparently the Dolores Herald had ceased publication and Hawkins took over the plant. In the first issue of the Star we find the following advertisements:

J. J. Harris & Co., General Merchandise; Dolores Meat Market, Exon & Rush, Props.; Southern Hotel, E. L. Wilbur, Prop.; W. H. Ordway, Grocery Store; The Spot Cash Store, Charles Johnson, Prop.; H. E. Brumley, liquor; Frank Glacier, Stage Line to Cortez; Saddle Rock Restaurant; Fred Hubert, Prop.; The Rio Grande Southern railroad advertisement. A school had been started in a good building and with two teachers.

In addition Dolores had the following stage lines operating: Dolores to Monticello, Utah, three times a week; Stage to Cortez daily, except Sunday; Stage to Lone Dome and Formby, some miles down the river, arrives at Dolores Saturdays and returns Sundays following; Stage from Dolores to Arriola, in Montezuma Valley, round trip Tuesdays and Saturdays.

The Dolores area has three summer schools as follows: D. M. Longenbaugh at Johnson School; Miss Lou Pyle at Moore School; Miss Rae Provis, at Pomeroy School.

There is a new Town Hall for public meetings of every kind, dances and entertainments, and that old "institution" of every frontier community, a "literary society" or club, was organized to make a get-together occasion and entertainment. The local spirit runs high—feasts and dances, visit and go places. There is no form of public amusement and entertainment, so the people must make their own.

About this time the name of the local paper was changed from The Silver Star to the Dolores Star.

Dolores gets elegant new Catholic Church, 1902.

Chas. Bear takes over Dolores Star in 1901.

J. J. Harris & Co. build new addition to their store, more than doubling floor space.

August Kuhlman has large ranch 10 miles below Dolores Town, and J. C. Ormiston, father of W. C. Ormiston is also a resident of same locality.

Exon & Rush complete their new mercantile building, with large meat room at rear, in 1906. New Southern Hotel built 1st year of new century.

In 1900 the railroad finally gets around to build a new, modern depot building, after 9 years of makeshift quarters.

Chas. Johnson & Wm. Mays start movement to build flour mill. Project completed later.

In fall of 1908 Dolores schools opened with 66 pupils; 38 in higher grades, 28 in lower grades.

Passing of O. D. Pyle in 1907 removes a landmark in early history.

On April 8, 1908, the Montezuma & Dolores Stock Association was organized in Dolores. It lasted for years and was a factor for good.

Dolores is connected, through Cortez, to the outside world by telephone on Dec. 23, 1908. Miss Nellie Monsanto, trained at Mancos, is in charge of the Cortez exchange. The Dolores exchange is temporarily in the Southern Hotel. All towns in county are now connected by telephone and the phone is proving to be a great convenience and a valuable business asset, and a factor for progress in every line.

In late 1904 the building of the Summit Reservoir was started. This was destined to add a large and rich area to Dolores' trade territory. Soon after some settlements on Granath Mesa were started.

JANUARY 1899-1900

The town of Dolores was incorporated July, 1900, First Mayor, Charles Johnson. Board of Trustees, W. F. Ordway, H. B. Wallace, C. M. Smith, H. V. Pyle, E. L. Short, J. M. Rush, Jr. First session Tuesday evening, July 31, 1900.

In March, 1926, the Harris Brothers Mercantile Co., John J. Harris and Andrew Harris, owners, of Dolores, started closing out their entire stock of general merchandise. At this time this was the oldest Mercantile business in the county, and the largest. The action was due to the ill health of one member of the firm and the desire of both to retire. Harris Brothers pioneered in the County and there is a great deal in the history of the county connected with their name.

Just at this time work was started on a new building in Dolores, 25 by 60 feet, which is to be the new home of the J. J. Harris & Co. Bank. The entire building is to be occupied by the bank, with a business destined in a few years to outgrow even these new quarters.

Another effort was made in the spring of 1926, to get a sugar factory for the San Juan Basin. The Holly Sugar Co. was behind the movement. The farmers weer asked to sign for 1000 acres and as much more as they would. Campaign was carried on all over basin and two car loads of seed were shipped into Durango.

Shipment of cattle and sheep was large, fall 1926, the prices were fair to good and pushed bank deposits in every bank in the county up to a record high.

During 1926 the Denver & Rio Grande supplemented their rolling stock by adding several hundred cars and a few dozen engines to their equipment. Result: greatly improved transportation service, most cattle and sheep moving on schedule. But hundreds of cars of sugar beets and other hundred of cars of apples piled up freight beyond their capacity to move it. The beets were finally all moved, but fully half the apples in the county were never gathered or gathered in roughly and fed to hogs.

Season of 1926 county produced and shipped $11,000 worth of turkeys, start of a new industry. Two truck loads of these turkeys were taken to Los Angeles, the first shipment of this kind ever made. The trucks loaded back with grapefruit and sugar.

Apple crop brings growers $40,000. Bee keepers ship 6½ cars of comb honey 1½ cars extracted honey in 1926.

Many cars of wheat are sold, $1.50 to $1.55 per hundred weight.

Potatoes are low—80c to $1, in San Luis valley; one car load of apples shipped from Mancos brought $1.50 a box for Delicious; $1.00 for other varieties.

In fall of 1927 witnessed early shipment of cattle to Denver. Tops bring $10.50; lower quality brings $9.50.

In the fall of 1927 beans definitely came into the county's farming industry as a main crop. Many yields of 800 pounds per acre reported and the contract price to the growers was $5 per hundred. Many fields of 60 to 120 acres were planted to beans. Highest yields were reported from the dry farming territory near Lewis. Beans were shipped by the car load and many cars were shipped.

The Ackmen section of the dry lands has more wheat than can be harvested. Wheat growing is a growing industry.

Messrs. Bower and Willford bring in two new 18-30 Case tractors and two wheatland one-way discs, near Lewis. They plan to clear sage brush at wholesale rates, converting raw land into producing farms;

plan also for large scale wheat farming. This is an advanced unit of power farming shortly to become common practice, Nov. 1, 1927.

Along with the growth of wheat growing industry beans are also coming along fast as a major crop. A conservative estimate placed the volume of the bean crop in 1927 at $100,000. The turkey crop is also growing, the estimated volume of the turkeys marketed this year being between $25,000 and $30,000. The values of the apple crop marketed was estimated at $75,000.

In summer of 1931, the passenger train between Dolores and Telluride was discontinued, the passenger train from Durango turning back at Dolores. Motor service was put on from Dolores to Telluride.

The S. H. Phleger warehouse at Dolores is doing real business. Truckers bring in truck loads of bean sacks to handle the bean crop and take out loads of peaches and pears.

A published statement of the J. J. Harris & Co. bank at Dolores, June 30, 1934, showed resources totaling $363,654.87, toward the end of the depression.

Summer of 1934, water situation on the cattle range getting serious and may force the sale of many cattle that would otherwise be held in the herd.

Cattle buying by government starts week of August 6th in every part of the county. Purchasing quota is 300 cattle a week.

Up to Aug. 28, 95 farms and ranches had been visited by the appraisers and the ranchmen sold a total 923 head to the government. The first 583 head brought $12.43 a head, calves brought $4 to $5 per head. Quota increased to 450 per week, 3,800 listed to sell; 2,700 yet to be bought. A week later purchases had reached the 1400 mark.

Sheep buying campaign started week of Sept. 24, 1934. 1000 head bought the first week. Price $2 per head for ewes and wethers.

The shipping season of 1935 opened with a good market, comparatively, which seemed to indicate the long depression was drawing to a close. There had been five to six years of it, and the depression was universally declared to be the worst and the most disastrous to business and property interests the country had ever experienced in all its history.

1909-1914

The Colorado Land and Improvement Co. of Lebanon sends large exhibit of fruit and produce to State Fair.

Fruit crop in Montezuma Valley begins to pay dividends this year in a way, and promises a bright future for the industry. Apples $1.00 per box, 250 to 500 boxes per acre. Area about Lebanon, Lewis and Arriola is producing most the fruit. McElmo Canon produces some apples of high quality. Bozman ship full car load, win $1,000 prize.

The Montezuma Valley Fruit and Potato growers sell all their apples to a Kansas City firm for $1.50 a box all varieties. Company receives and pays for fruit as it is loaded on cars at Dolores. Fifteen cars of choice grade sold.

The town of Dolores begins figuring on a water system, Dec. 15, 1909, and calls for an election to be held April 4 to vote on a $40,000 bond issue to construct a gravity water system.

The San Juan and Dolores Telephone Co. is busy stringing wire and connecting points in the upper Montezuma Valley. Plan is to connect Dolores, Lebanon, Arriola, Monticello, Grayson and Bluff and the oil fields in Utah.

W. E. Miller of Pueblo, formerly general agent for the D&RG railroad, resigned his position and was elected president and manager of the Colorado Land and Improvement Co. The Company owns the Lebanon townsite and extensive holdings in the valley. Mr. Miller will move his family to Lebanon at once.

A full train load of immigrants and their families detrained at Dolores February 7, 1910, fifty in all. They were mostly working people.

Feb. 7, 1910, work starts on the new steel bridge that spanned the river two miles west of Dolores town, excavating for abutments being first work. This is the first steel bridge to be erected in the county. It was thought to be strong enough for any load and would serve for all time. It had to be replaced in 1954 with a wider and stronger bridge to handle the heavy traffic.

Early in 1910 the San Juan-Dolores Telephone Co. is erecting building in Dolores for their telephone exchange and office.

Eight carloads of household goods, stock and farm implements unloaded at Dolores in one day week of Mar. 10, 1910.

Sunday, May 8, a picnic was held at the new steel bridge across Dolores River, celebrating the opening of the bridge. People from every part of the county attended.

Ten thousand fruit trees were set out in the Lebanon community week of April 15, 1910.

The Dolores State Bank opened for business April 25, 1910. This makes six banks doing business in the county.

W. I. Myler builds a twelve room residence on his ranch on the Dolores-Cortez road. It stood for years as a kind of land mark as a ranch residence.

June 6, 1910, Dolores voted a $50,000 bond to put in a gravity water system for the town. The vote was 26 for and 10 against.

On July 4, 1910, the community of Lebanon put on a big celebration for all the county, and others as far as Durango and Rico. The program was extensive and carried out in full and visitors seemed pleased. The largest crowd ever assembled at one time and in one place in the county was on hand. Lebanon was at this time, only a townsite just laid out in the north end of Montezuma Valley, and was the work and enterprise of the Colorado Land and Development

Co. Buildings at the time consisted of a small hotel and an office building and a two story building about 24x40 under construction to be used for general merchandise, some two or three residences and a school building near by. Many new people have come in, acquired land and set to work to convert raw land into producing farms and orchards. Subsequent development have proved that they were right about the orchards. Their hopes for a flourishing town, however, were doomed to disappointment. The day was long and hot and dusty and dry.

By the school census of 1910 Montezuma County had 1,207 children of school age.

A car load of Jersey cattle from Kansas City was unloaded at Dolores in July, 1910, for foundation stock to build local dairy herds.

In November, 1910, Dolores people organize and incorporates a Board of Trade to look after community interests and promote the public welfare.

In spring of 1911, five car loads of fruit trees were unloaded at Dolores in one day and at one time. P. B. McAtee, who observes everything, suggested that the people get some pictures of the sight, and they did. This was only a part, probably the smaller part, of the spring shipment, about April 1, 1907.

The Town of Dolores, after voting bonds to build a water works system for the town, closes a deal with H. Sutherlin of Denver by which Sutherlin agrees to construct a water works system, according to plan and specifications already drawn, and take $42,000 in bonds in payment and to pay $3,000 in cash into the Town Treasury in exchange for $3,000 in bonds, water system to be completed by June 11, 1911.

Dolores is experiencing a lively growth activity since the new water system was put in. New people, new capital, and new enterprises are coming to town. There are new business houses and many new homes. The people have money and they are spending it for what they want.

The Lebanon townsite has been laid out and surveyed into streets, blocks and lots. A South Dakota company buys 200 acres adjoining land and 60 town lots. The 200 acres will be laid out in 10 acre tracts, set in fruit trees and sold.

The Montezuma Fruit and Produce Co. is organized and incorporated at Dolores with a capital stock of $25,000. They erect a large warehouse to handle their business and will handle fruit on a commission basis as a specialty.

Montezuma Fruit and Produce Co. is erecting building 30x150 feet to handle the big Montezuma Co. fruit crop.

Saucer Oil Co. is organized in Dolores. It will operate over in the Dissappointment country.

A new school house, 28x48, is being built at Stoner. Indicates population growth in the Dolores Valley.

Telephone lines are being stretched to the town of Dolores and a switchboard will be installed at once.

New automobile added to equipment at Kelly & Moore livery. First car for the town, Aug. 18, 1911.

In October, 1911, the Town Board of Dolores orders a survey to establish grade lines all over town and ordered that the plot of the town be finished. Preparing for the progress in growth that is just ahead.

Lebanon is building a new school house. The town promoters are broke, but the best interests of the town go on.

The Dolores water works system reached the construction stage in September, 1911. They will try to have it completed before the rigors of winter come on.

Fred Taylor, Jesse Robinson and Bill Silvey drove 5700 head of sheep from Rico to Lizard Head the first days of November, 1911. They were 11 days on the road and had every kind of bad weather for the trip. They shipped from Lizard Head.

The first week in November, 1911, there were 18,000 boxes of apples stored in Dolores awaiting shipment. After the trains started moving November 18, 80 car loads of fruit were moved out of Dolores and other local storage.

The telephone exchange at Dolores is in working order, Nov. 1, 1911, and doing business. Miss Celia Squires is the operator.

The Montezuma Fruit & Produce Co. shipped 53 cars of fruit, 21,-672 boxes, for season of 1911. The Gold Medal orchard in McElmo Canon sold 2,000 boxes of apples which netted $2 a box.

The Methodist Church at Dolores was erected in 1910, mostly on credit; paid out in full in 1912.

On March 22, 1912, Dolores gets busy with its water works construction again, which was interrupted by the winter's cold.

The San Juan-Dolores Telephone Co. is pulling out of its financial difficulties. It appears that soon it will reach a firm financial basis.

As an example of how the county is gaining in population, on March 1st, 1912, 14 cars of implements and household goods, belonging to nine families, arrived at Dolores. All located in some part of Montezuma Valley.

March 11, as spring flood time approaches, Dolores people are taking steps to mend river channel to protect the town from floods. Work continues through the years until town is well and substantially protected and there is no longer any fear from floods.

After two or three years of heavy shipment, livestock, especially range stock are coming back to the range. There are applications in this spring of 1912 for practically all the available grazing in the National Forest.

The very heavy winter storms and consequent deep snow in the mountains caused high spring floods and the railroad between Dolores and Rico was again damaged and a number of bridges damaged or taken out. It was days before repairs could even be started on account of the high water. The road bed was weak from last year's floods.

In 1912 the automobile began to be a noticeable means of transportation when the roads were dry and smooth enough. Car travel began, in a small way, to replace railway travel and the horse and buggy.

June 20, 1912, The Dolores Lumber and Supply Co. is building a large grain elevator at Dolores.

A new voting precinct, No. 12, was established for the Summit Ridge community, July 1, 1912.

The Colorado Land & Improvement Co. took bankruptcy, Aug. 21, 1911, and their entire property holdings were sold to satisfy creditors. The company was not a success financially, but it really did a lot of good for the county and especially the locality about Lebanon. Many new people and much new capital was brought into that locality.

Water was turned into the Dolores water system July 20, 1912, for the first time after months of delay. The pressure registers 70 pounds in the upper edge of town and 76 in the lower edge, enough for fire protection and provide pure running water for the homes and all other uses.

The first picture show comes to Dolores about Nov. 1, 1912. Le Roy Parker of Mancos put in the show equipment.

Thirteen cars of household goods and implements were unloaded at Dolores March 11, 1913, many of the immigrants going out to the dry farming country. With more population will soon come more wealth.

In late March, 1913, Dolores people plot their new cemetery, one and one-half miles out of town on the south, on lower Summit Ridge. There is a five acre tract laid out into 400 lots 20x20—some 20x25 feet, with convenient driveways. It is being irrigated with water from Summit system.

On March 15, 1913, 9 cars more of immigrant stock and household goods were unloaded at Dolores—three cars containing 31 head of horses and cattle, besides pigs, chickens, etc. Some go to the big valley; others out into the new dry farming area.

On May 9, 1913, three full train loads of cattle were shipped through from Santa Fe to Dolores. They were brought in by Dolores stockmen to replenish the herds they graze on the Montezuma National Forest.

Dolores had a fire experience July 6, 1913, that proved the value of their water system as a protection from disastrous fires. The people were at once convinced they need not hesitate to build good homes. From that date good homes have been the rule in Dolores and many of the finest homes in the county have been built in the town.

The Summit Reservoir Co. vote to bond for $30,000 the purpose of which is to thoroughly renovate the old system and put it in first class condition, fix up the old intake ditch and build an entirely new ditch from Lost Canon large enough to carry a stream of water that will fill the entire reservoir system in 30 days.

Shipment of apples from Dolores amounted to approximately 100 cars in 1913. For once there was a good demand and a steady market.

In January, 1913, a new road was started up the Dolores River toward Rico. The old road along the river was completely abandoned and a new road will be less expensive to build in that there will be no expensive bridges, where as the old road crossed the river several times and made several bridgese necessary—bridges that were often washed out or damaged with every recurring flood. The south hill slope makes for a better and drier road.

J. J. Harris & Co. is incorporated into a new firm under the name The Harris Brothers Mercantile Co. The Harrises retain an interest, but new stockholders are taken in. This was in January, 1913.

During the fruit season of 1914, 90 cars of apples were shipped from Dolores. Returns estimated at $28,000, and $5,000 more for other fruits.

In late 1914 a rural telephone line was constructed several miles up the river from Dolores and a number of the dwellers along the river were given telephone service.

Back in the halcyon days of 1912 to 1914 cattle, sheep and hogs were shipped by the car load and the train load—scores of them. Prosperity was riding in on the crest of the wave.

Dolores is moving for street lights at last. In January, 1915, the poles are on the ground and there will be light in the streets before many moons.

The fruit business, especially apples, is very poor business with almost no market. War in Europe cut off market there making a great surplus.

The Dolores State Bank changes its name to the First National Bank of Dolores. Capital remains at $25,000 and there is a surplus of $2,000.

Stock business seems reduced more and more to an annual turnover —buy stock, range them, then ship to market. Many small flocks of sheep are coming to the farms. Prices are fair and the aggregate bank deposits is the largest in the history of the county.

A movement is initiated by Dolores people to move the county seat to Dolores. Not a very warm response anywhere. The people of Cortez and the big valley have enough trouble of their own. In August, 1916.

One hundred cars of hogs were shipped from Dolores in 1916, almost all from Montezuma Valley.

A Federal Farm Loan Association was organized at Dolores in February, 1917. Starts business with a substantial number of members.

A movement is started at Dolores to take in outlying districts and consolidate in the interest of better schools. Later they do consolidate and vote in bond $19,300 to build a High School.

In 1916 the Mancos Cattlemen's Association and the Dolores Cattlemen's Association united to form the Dolores-Montezuma Cattlemen's Association. In 1917 the Association had a membership of 98 and still others are coming in. At their meeting the officers elected were: Pres. J. L. Morrison; Vice Pres. Jas. A. Frink; Secy-Treas. Harry Pyle; Advisory Board, Chas. W. Johnson, John R. Tremble, John M. Johnson, W. W. Belmear and Mr. Clifton. The association is doing much good work for the cattlemen.

New land is opened for settlement near Dove Creek and many new settlers are coming in and homesteading.

The Summit Reservoir people vote a bond of $90,000 to make improvements. They plan a new, and additional intake canal 4 miles long, new headgate in reservoir and enlarging distributing system. The people buy their own bonds, do most of the work themselves, taking $52,000 of the $90,000 issue.

In February, 1919, a daily mail service was established between Dolores and Monticello.

New intake canal for the Summit Reservoir completed and water turned in June 10, 1920. It is a valuable improvement, but too late to be of much value the present season.

Dolores lays claim to being the wealthiest town, per capita, of any town in the state. Cattle and sheep are the foundation for most of their wealth.

The spring floods of 1920 were the most destructive in several years. The railroad along the Dolores river was washed out in a dozen places, and there was heavy damage along several other stretches of the road in the Basin. Water was so high no repairs could even be started for days. It was weeks before through service could be resumed.

During the summer of 1920, $40,000 was expended on the Cortez-Dolores road straightening bends, reducing grades and widening road bed, preparing for the gravel surface to follow. Of this sum the government furnishes $20,000, the state $10,000 and the county $10,000. There is also $30,00 for the Cortez-Dove Creek road.

February 25, 1921, the Town of Dolores grants A. A. Rust a franchise to build and operate an electric light and power plant in Dolores.

Range herd and flock owners were pleased to see the market on cattle and lambs getting back to a pretty good price in January, 1922. Good prices for livestock helps everyone, and makes for renewed progress.

Week of October 9, 1922, 28 cars of hogs were shipped from Dolores and Mancos. The county has never since produced so many hogs.

Fifteen cars of stock hogs were loaded out week of Dec. 20. One party stated that there was still 2,500 stock hogs in Montezuma County awaiting shipment, and they were cleaning up much needed feed.

Dolores rural people get their first mail route, August 1, 1918. Serves Summit Ridge community.

Work starts on new Summit canal, Aug. 1, men and many teams at work first day. A number of Navajo Indians help solve the labor problem. The Indians are good workers.

The shipping situation gets worse. On Dec. 16, 1922, there are 215 cars of cattle awaiting shipment at Dolores, 87 cars at Mancos and up to the first week 90 cars of hogs are awaiting shipment in the Mancos vicinity, a few cars of sheep, and many more loads in Montezuma Valley.

The New Mexico Lumber Co. is putting in a big sawmill on the Dolores river some five miles below the town of Dolores. The mill was moved from Lumberton and scores of carloads of machinery and equipment is being moved in by rail. The McPhee-McGinnity Lumber Co. are behind the enterprise. They will build a railroad connection, a small town at the sawmill site and a railroad several miles out into the timber to bring in the logs. Early in 1924.

The McPhee and McGinity Lumber Co. was the successful bidder for 70,000,000 board feet of timber in the north part of this county and in Dolores Co. The company is expected to buy the entire unit of timber consisting of 253,000,000 board feet.

Escalante, after the early Spanish explorer of this region, was suggested for the name of the sawmill town, but the name McPhee was finally selected.

Dolores had a $100,000 fire May 19, 1943. The property destroyed was the Montezuma Fruit and Produce Co. office and warehouse, J. M. Kinsley, owner; Odenbaugh Bros. garage, Andy Miller's garage, building, warehouse and 75,000 pounds of wool belonging to woolgrowers, with 20 per cent insurance.

J. M. Kinsley is taking steps to rebuild his warehouse at Dolores, which was destroyed by fire a few days ago. It is the Montezuma Fruit and Produce warehouse; it served a very useful purpose and the community can't get along without it. The new building will be 30x50 feet.

The first effort to get Montezuma County out of the mud was started in the summer of 1924. The Durango-Mancos road was graveled in part and a good start was made on the Cortez-Dolores road. Cars and trucks demand better roads and they are helping to pay for them. There is strong indication that every main road in the county will eventually be gravel surfaced as the funds are made available. It is distinctly a new thing in rural road building, and it has come to stay. No one will ever want to go back to the mud. Building of the Gallup-Shiprock road by the government is also getting under way.

"The Birth of the West," a motion picture show, is being filmed in the vicinity of Disappointment Creek. It is the first motion picture to be made in the county. On Aug. 15, 1924, they were about ready to start shooting. Ute Indians and local cowboys are taking part.

Having no county agent, E. D. Smith, former county agent, and now in general charge of club work in the state, comes into the county to get the club work going again. He covers the whole state and can come to any county only once in a while.

The Colorado Picture Corporation begins filming "Birth of the West," at the Morrison Ranch on the Dolores river, August 18, 1924.

The cement sidewalk movement has struck Dolores and many blocks of new cement sidewalks were put in last of 1924. The good work was continued in 1925.

The county's honey crop was shipped out of Dolores last October '24, five thousand cases of fancy comb honey, 24 one pound sections to the case and it brought $4 for first class honey and $3.70 a case for No. 2. J. M. Smithson was the only Mancos producer represented in the shipment. Most Mancos producers ship extracted honey and some producers from other parts of the county. There was a good crop and a good year for the beekeepers. Dry season enabled bees to work nearly every day. The honey crop is a clear gain—so much wealth garnered and saved.

A real town comes into existence at McPhee in one short year. A town has been laid out in streets, blocks and lots, and a water system has been put in to furnish water pressure to every part of town. Fifty small houses have been built in the rough for the working men, and about 25 larger houses, better finished, for managers and skilled workers. A school building nears completion, and a very large frame building for a general store, which, in itself, is a large, modern business. In the same building is a picture show and a pool room. An immense building 3 stories high, houses the sawmill plant, with corrugated iron outside finish. The mill and finishing machinery are mostly on the second floor and the logs are drawn up the logway from the log pond by an endless chain belt. The power house is built of stone; also the fuel house near it. There is a large shop building, storage warehouse, shed, loading platform and other buildings. The mill itself consists of an immense lot of massive machinery for making and finishing lumber. The log pond covered three acres and was already filled with logs. The log railroad was operating and everything has the appearance of permanency. The plant is expected to start operating Nov. 15, 1924. The output of the mill will be 2.5 million feet a month.

May 1, 1925, all the departments of the big sawmill at McPhee are operating and all products being finished in the mill. They are turning out 120,000 feet of lumber every day.

Early in May, 1925, Forest Service engineers started to surveying a new Forest road up the West Dolores River to Dunton. Some funds were available for construction and the work was started as soon as the route was laid out. Four miles were built that year beginning at the Dolores-Rico road and working northward.

315

Fred Bradshaw, recently of Ignacio, buys and takes over the Dolores Star, Sept. 1, 1925. Editor Bear, who has published the paper since 1902, moved to Oregon to make his home.

Much rains damage the alfalfa seed crop. A high yielding grain crop is being harvested.

Montezuma County produced, in 1925, what was probably the largest apple crop ever produced in the county up to that time. For about two weeks six cars were loaded with apples every day at Dolores. The growers realized a very low net profit, and some orchards were not gathered at all. Some producers sold to any one who would come and pick the apples, at 35c a box, choice fruit. There was a fair potato crop and the growers realized well on this product at $1.40 a hundred pounds.

Nov. 1, 1925, finds the New Mexico Lumber Co. mill at McPhee running full capacity. The logging railroad is extended beyond Rock Creek, and still being extended to reach a winter log supply.

BEGINNING MAY, 1936

Late December, 1936, the bean movement made history when a train load of fourteen cars of beans left Dolores for the market. Each car carried 30,000 pounds of beans and the price paid for them was $4.40 a hundred pounds. It was the largest single shipment of beans ever made from the county, but it was only a small part of the total crop.

Collection of taxes in 1936 was the best in years. Some delinquent paid up two and three years of taxes in one transaction.

March 19, 1937, the big lumber mill at McPhee practically closed down putting a small army of men out of work in the county.

The Montezuma National Forest was created by a proclamation of Pres. Theodore Roosevelt June 15, 1905. The forests of the area had already been cut into, heavily in places, when the Forest was created and some of the finest stands of timber fell to the lumberman, but there was still hundreds of millions of board feet of ponderosa pine, red and blue spruce and Douglas fir left, which has been protected and the cutting of timber carefully regulated. Millions of board feet are being cut each year with a sustained yield yet beyond the volume cut. Only a part of the Forest is in Montezuma County. The Montezuma National Forest was recently combined with and joined to the San Juan National Forest, with supervisor's office at Durango and in the enlarged Forest is an estimated 200,000 feet, board measure, of ponderosa pine, still stands. Besides this there is many million feet Engleman Spruce and Douglas fir standing in the higher altitudes. Grazing is regulated and many thousands of cattle and sheep graze on the Forest in the county, a continuous source of wealth for all future time.

Montezuma County, in the better years, has 3,500 colonies of bees with a present investment of about $70,000. In the average season the honey production is about 350,000 pounds, which commands the highest market price. Eight car loads were shipped to the market at one time a few years ago, and large shipments are common, in recent years going by truck. Honey production, in recent years, is mostly in the hands of the large producers who understand the work, know how to care for the bees and produce a high class product.

The Montezuma National Forest grazes, on the average, 28,000 cattle and 65,000 sheep most of which are owned by residents of Montezuma County. All the irrigation water originates on the Forest, which makes it another source of wealth which, if properly protected, will never grow less as far as we can see into the future.

Some of the oldtimers at the picnic, in Priest Gulch, June 12, 1936, were Mrs. N. S. Black, Mr. Dennison, Sill Kaufmann, Harry Brown, Hank Snyder, Mrs. William Ordway, Al Nunn, Jesse Robinson, Sr., Jesse Robinson, Jr., and others.

June 30, 1941, the big lumber mill at McPhee was completely burned by fire. The kiln, planer and box factory was saved. Loss $25,000. The mill had been operating since 1924 at a capacity of 125,000 feet daily, and 400 men were employed.

The bridge across the Dolores river, 20 miles below Dolores, that was washed out last summer, is being replaced with a concrete and steel structure. The bridge is badly needed by the stockmen and the Forest Service.

As a matter of market history we record that, on March 19, 1942, the government bought 12,300 bags of beans at Dolores for a total purchase price of $52,185. The price paid for No. 1 beans was $4.35 and for No. 2 $4.20 per 100 pounds, F.O.B. Dolores.

The lumber mill at McPhee has been rebuilt in part and resumed operation in June, 1942.

The big saw milling plant at McPhee is being dismantled, March 1, 1944. Liquidation of town and plant at McPhee is the present plan, and plant is being sold. A small mill in the Glades country and a box factory at Dolores seems to be in the present plans.

Up to April 20, 1944, 85,000 fruit trees were received at the Dolores station for setting in the new orchards of the county. D. V. Burrell is setting out a large orchard west of Arriola.

May 2, 1945 word is received of the death of Allen Pratt, of Dolores, who was killed in action in Philippine Islands.

Some very good flood water control work was done at Dolores in spring of 1952, under the direction of the army engineers. $10,000 in government funds was spent on the project with very good results.

The high school gym and the Reo theater at Dolores were destroyed by fire Oct. 13, 1954. Loss about $10,000.

PAGEANT OF PROGRESS

Now we are here. The time of which our poets sang, for which our people yearned, and of which our sages told in years of your, has come. Quietly, unobtrusively the old has passed and the new has been born. We look back to struggles and hardships, to defeats and triumphs, to causes lost in the conflict and to victories won. The way is lighter now. The past is a great beacon light that beams us on our way; that lights our pathway; that strengthens our hopes. Peace and plenty is here, but there are still tasks for our toil, conflicts in the struggle for the right, victories to be won. To hold fast to what we have gained, to improve constantly on what the past has produced, and to plan a future that will be safe and sane and secure: that is the task ahead. It is no small thing to do. The work before us will still be arduous. There will be dangers in the days that are to come: toil for our hands, suffering for our fortitude, disappointments for our hopes. In the past you have had but few around you, and there was an abundance for all. But, in the future, people will become your problem, and how to manage, how to provide, how to control may disturb your serenity and pose new problems the like of which you have never known. With this view before us how urgently it behooves us to plan wisely and well. The time to overcome difficulties, of course, is when we come to them, but if we can see their approach, if we can surmise ahead and anticipate somewhat the future, it would be a great present help in solving problems when they come.

The past is but the place where we have been, and the future the place to which we are going. We are ever on a new frontier. We are ever treading ground we have never trod before. The man of yesterday is bewildered with the wonders of today and the man of today will be mystified by the things of tomorrow. The only thing in time we have is the present. We build the future upon the past, but all our building must be in the present, and the fortunes of the future depend on how wisely and well we build in this present time.

We look back and say we have made great progress; that the things that are, are vastly better than the things that were. But are they better in intrinsic value; better in real worth? Is there more genuins happiness, more pure pleasure; more of the things that make for true friendship; more of the things in our life that make life really worth while? We can have all these things in our new life if we will to have them. We can have everything in the new life that they had in the old life, and comforts and pleasures and conveniences as well. The only real progress is the progress we make toward a better life and a better way of doing things. We still use and waste and consume just as our forefathers did. All that we have today is what we have saved out of the past, and what we have created in the present. What we waste and destroy and consume never builds anything for the future. All that counts for anything is what is saved out of the wreck and ruin of the past and is perpetuated into the future. Be not deceived. There is an end to everything that does not constantly renew itself.

Now let's get back to basic things. What is the real foundation upon which our future will be built? It is that one resource we have that constantly renews itself—the soil. The soil may be weakened by misuse, and its power to grow things depleted, but the good soil is still there. Its richness and producing power can be restored. It can again be made to respond to good tillage and produce in great abundance. We can have a real Soil Bank upon which we can draw for all our wants and still have more left in the bank than we had before. We can use it and use it, and still have it. We can draw upon it for happiness and pleasures and comforts, and even luxuries, and still not diminish the source of these things. No bounties from an all bountiful government, no gift from man, no other things that we can acquire or possess, can give a greater feeling of security than a home on a good farm that we can call our own. We will always be rich as long as our soil is rich. Oil wells and gas wells and rich mines may bring great wealth, but there just isn't anything in life that is so vitally important to human welfare and human happiness as the good earth under our feet. This thought should bring a feeling of importance to every owner of a good farm. The farmer is the one indispensable man.

There may be overproduction and low prices; the spread between the buying and the selling price may be too great; the national economy may be running counter to the farmer's welfare, but the farmer can always build up his own fortune by putting something into his Soil Bank. There isn't any safer investment; nor one, in the final analysis, that pays greater dividends. The very fact that your county seat is growing, and increasing in wealth and commercial importance makes it doubly certain that greater values are coming to every Montezuma County farm. The county has always needed at least one good town of real commercial importance, and this new growth is but the fulfilling of this need.

Better times are ahead. Poor neighbors and poor towns are no asset to anyone, but wealth in any place, wealth possessed by any individual or group of individuals, is sure to add something to the wealth of all. Don't think that all the wealth is going to the cities and towns. It is just as surely coming to the farm, and a good farm is just as surely going to be a more valuable farm. The time is here and now when the more you put into your farming operations the more you will get out of it. It is time we were putting some new life and purpose into the farming effort.

Now for a retrospective view of the past to see from whence we came and where we are going. The experiences of the past are our guide for the future. We waste too much sympathy on the past; deplore too much the privations and hardships of the pioneer. The pioneer was a pioneer by his own choice. He loved the life. His was a gift from creation. In this untamed wilderness he found what he was looking for—a land filled with natural wealth ready for the taking. Upon the mountains and high mesas stood a noble forest of virgin pine and spruce and hemlock, the work of nature for a thousand years, and all was his. The grasses on the landscape grew and bloomed and ripened, then perished and grew again. For centuries they had grown yearly, and perished back into the earth building a richness that awaited only the coming of man to turn it into wealth and human happiness. The pioneer had only to harvest the grass with his flocks and his herds. Deep in the bowels of the earth were hidden treasures that were his for the taking. There was energy in the coal strata to light and warm a million homes. Wild life was abundant in all the land. All this was the heritage of the pioneer. Did not he have abundance? Were not all the things about him to arouse his cupidity and fill his heart with joy? The pioneer asked for no more. He could ask for no more. He had everything. It was his only to reap what nature had sown. Life presented some hardships; dangers sometimes beset his path, but he gloried in the life. The new earth under his feet; fresh, pure air all about him to give new life and strength, the great sea of blue above and swift flowing streams of purest water to give new life to the land. The pioneer never realized that his rich inheritance imposed a fearful responsibility. To him all this natural wealth was his only to exploit, to use, and often to waste and destroy.

Nature gave to the pioneer an environment that was self sustaining. There was an equilibrium that balanced out production against consumption, with the balance, if any, on the side of a build-up for a better, safer condition in nature. Man's first act was to disturb this equilibrium. He began by destroying the forest and doing nothing to recreate the forest anew. He overgrazed the grasses and made a barren, eroding landscape and a brushy plain. He took the plant food from the rich earth, and did nothing to sustain its fertility. It was all right, they reasoned. The earth would never exhaust itself. The way to get wealth out of the grass was to use it to the very limit of its ability to produce. Timber grew to be used and was good for nothing else. The wealth of the mine was there to be taken and squandered in wreckless living. The pioneer figured that he owed nothing to posterity. Those who should come after him could take care of themselves just as he had done. He never thought that he might make it impossible for the coming man to take care of himself; that he might impose a hardship on his children and his children's children that would be hard for them to overcome. This had been the way of pioneer life for all past time. We could hardly expect our own pioneers to make a change. The example was before them and they knew no better than to follow it. The result was that the following generations have inherited a soil largely exhausted of its fertility elements; they inherited a grass land that is nearly bare—a land that was being damaged by sheet erosion and gashed and scarred by deep wide gullies and grown up to an almost useless and worthless plant life.

The soil is in our county's future. It will always be. A soil more or less depleted of its fertility, a brush covered plain to take the place of the grass; stump land and brush and vacancy to take the place of a noble forest: This is the heritage of our coming generations. And now comes the task of building back, of replacing what the pioneer took away; of restoring richness and productivity in the soil. The work of destruction quickly comes to an end, but the task of restoring and rebuilding must go on and on. In the interest of safety it can never end. We must adopt farming methods that will always leave more productivity in the soil than there was before we took the crop away. We must destroy the worthless growth on hill and plain and re-clothe them with grass and valuable trees; we must protect and conserve our water supply that none may be wasted. All the highest and best production in nature is going to be needed in the generations ahead. So far as we can see now we must always live by the land. How serious then is the task before us!

We are building now, apart from the soil. We rejoice now, most of us, in the riches that are coming our way, and we can't envisage an end. Yet every natural resource is exhaustible. There may be, and probably is, some unknown power or substance or element to take the place of natural gas, the oil in the ground, the uranium deposits in the hidden places of the earth, but present conditions do not justify needless waste. There is no doubt but that we are wasting our natural resources just as our forefathers did. Wealth that can be grown from the soil can be augmented or replaced, but valuable, active substances the Creator placed in the earth, when once exhausted, can never be replaced. We may find another something to take their place, but it too, may be exhausted. Can this thing go on forever? Is there also an infinity in the supply and use of things? Or is there an eventual consummation of all things? All these things were in the mind of the Creator from the beginning, but no one can tell what wealth, what riches are still in stock in the great storehouse provided for man from the foundation of the world.

But the past teaches us one certain thing, if nothing else, and that is that waste is never justified. "Willful waste makes willful want" is a trite old apothegm that is always and forever true. "Waste not, want not" is saying the same thing in reverse, and it is equally true.

As we conclude this article waste goes on—waste of water, waste of soil, waste of material things. In Montezuma County we have the Soil Conservation Service, the Agricultural Stabilization and Conservation Service, the Agricultural Extension Service, and one or two other agencies perhaps, all working hard for better farm practices and better farm methods; all trying to stop or check erosion, deterioration and misuse of the land. Much very good work is being done and some substantial gains are being made in some parts of the county, but in other large areas these agencies are failing to win; there is still more destructive loss than there is constructive gain. Many farms are producing at less than half their potential capacity, and production is still on the wane. We are gaining in one way. We are replacing the old grasses by new and better grasses. We are gaining in grass farming and livestock farming, holding the soil in place and building back fertility on many farms. For years we have been gaining in acreage in the irrigated areas, but losing in production. Is it not time we were doing something about it?

Here are some things we can do if we will: Realine ditches and rebuild the ditch system on many, many farms; land leveling to give even water penetration; to save water and labor in irrigating, and to save washing of the soil; rotate faithfully from year to year—alfalfa or clover, grain, grass; fertilize—natural fertilizers and commercial fertilizers; add organic matter in any form to make humus, for soil without humus is dead soil; drain swamp lands and seep lands. The best lands in the county are, in many instances, producing only swamp grass, sedges and cattails; drain and filter out alkali lands, and lastly, fill and even over all gullies and arroyos and tie the soil down with a good stand of grass. These are things every landowner can do.

Montezuma County has hundreds of the finest farms in this state, and many of these finest farms are the least productive, or vastly under productive.

Many farmers are in a rut, using archaic methods, poor soil management or none at all, and are making no effort to get out of the rut. New methods, new advances in cultivation and soil management, the many new things in soil improvement and soil research, have no appeal to them. As long as any farmer is satisfied to stay in the old rut, and has no desire to improve or do things in a better way, there just isn't anything that can be done for him or his farm. They would like to be a better and a more successful farmer perhaps, but they don't want to pay the price. It seems, in many cases, the only way to get a change in methods is to get a change in management.

The non-irrigating farmers are doing better. They are taking care of their land, protecting it from wind and water erosion, improving their farm methods, grassing in their water ways, putting all crop residue back into the soil, using better farming methods and many are beginning the use of commercial fertilizers. Grass, to some extent is coming back to the land, and a few livestock are making their appearance here and there. The dry land farmer is doing his work pretty well.

Now, this is the end. We have recorded all the history on which we could get information. We have traced developments, described the customs and manners of the past, criticised the present and pointed the way to a better future. It is not that we are not doing well; it is that we should do better. We inherit the future, whatever it may bring, and bequeath the past to the past. Only the present is ours. Our fortunes and our failures depend altogether on how we use the present time.

A GLANCE INTO THE FUTURE

The first thing impressive we see in the future is a teeming population—more people, more work, more wealth. As we analyze the present we can see that agriculture is basic; that uranium mining and oil from the earth are bringing great wealth into our borders and the future of these industries is very bright. We can't begin to see the point of exhaustion. Only growth and expansion can be discerned in the immediate future. In the industries named above we find food and raw materials. So long as there is plenty of food, and an abundance of raw materials that can be marketed, or better still, processed and marketed, our future is secure. As a rule only labor creates new wealth, and every worker that furnishes a valuable service is a factor in producing more wealth and more jobs. In the same way business makes more business. Given the basic things in abundance, great population means great wealth.

At this time another great source of local wealth is appearing in our future. Our fine climate is an enduring asset, and people, in increasing numbers are coming this way to sojourn for a time to escape the oppressive heat of other lands. There is not the shadow of a doubt but that ours is a great vacation land, a summer home land of the immediate future. We have a climate that is air conditioned by nature; where extremes of temperature are seldom experienced; where not too warm days and wonderfully cool nights are conducive to perfect relaxation and blissful sleep. Here the vacationers can find contentment and the weary can find rest.

In fact there is nothing on this old planet quite like life in Southwestern Colorado. The more you've had of it the more you want of it. Not too warm in midsummer. Not too cold in midwinter; there is just that element in the mountain climate to give tone to the body and zest to life. Verdant spring, bright summer, glorious autumn and old winter with his cold and his snow, each furnishes its variety and adds spice to life and joy to living. Every season has its charms to make it welcome. There is no monotony; no continuing sameness. Neither are there those extremes of temperature experienced elsewhere to make the heat of summer and the cold of winter things we dread. Montezuma County, Colorado, is rich in climate and rich in other things. It has a colorful past and an inviting future. It is a land of homes; a place for happiness and contentment. Verily, it is a privilege to live in Montezuma County, Colorado; land of promise and fulfillment.

323